1936

1936

Sean Alexander League

Cover and book design: Brief Candle Press.
Editing: Heather Bungard-Janney.
Cover image: NASA/Goddard/John Sonntag.
Map: Sean League.
Character portraits: League family collection, Henryk Mościcki, Jan Cynarski.
Fonts: Doves Type, England Hand and Niagra Solid.

First Brief Candle Press edition published 2017.
www.briefcandlepress.com

ISBN: 978-1-942319-25-2

For my wife,
Qiong

I would also like to thank those who helped to edit, correct, and give suggestions along the way:

Greg Gittings
George and Sandra League
Henry Gessler
Zheng Zi Ling (Lynn)

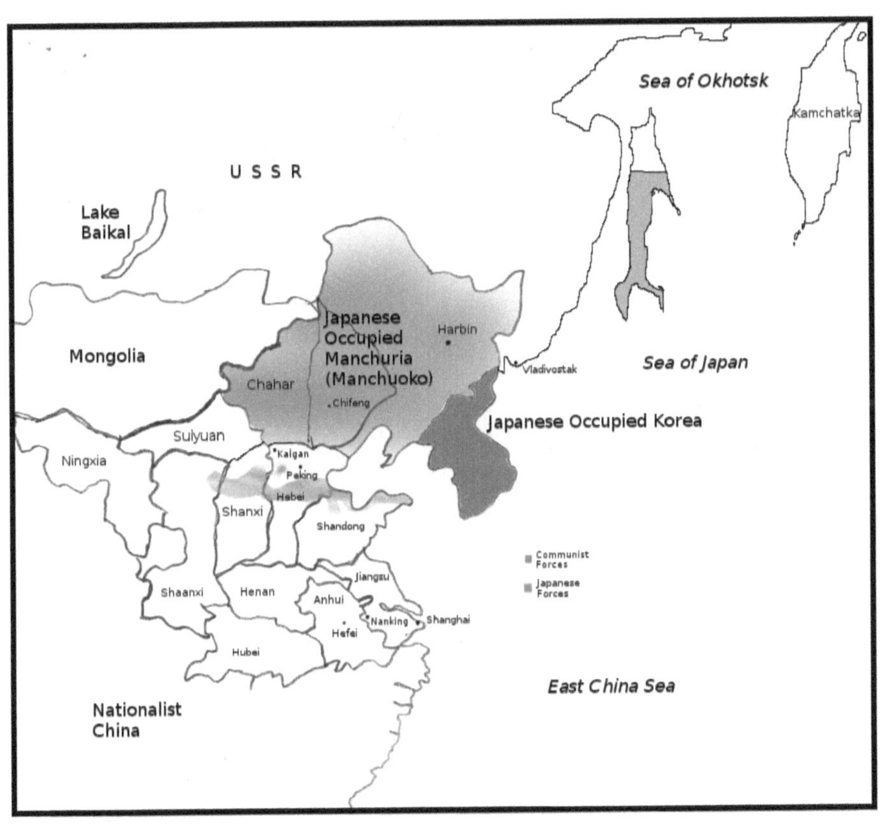

Northeast China and surrounding territory in 1936

Chapter 1

Returning Home

Henry Elliot watched the rows of lush Iowa corn flash by as he drove. Feeling the touch of Maria's hand on his, he looked over at her. Her long black hair was whipping in the wind from behind her white Garbo-style hat, but she wasn't looking back at him. Henry followed her gaze forward through the partially opened windshield; he could see their farm in the distance, and a smile grew on his face as he sped up. The Model A fishtailed a bit as he slid into their driveway, and he glanced at Maria to gauge her reaction. She was smiling back at him, but then she slammed her hand against the dash with a scream.

"Henry!"

Henry looked forward to see a large tree limb lying in the driveway. He jammed on the brakes, but it was too late; part of the branch smacked the front windshield shut with a bang, as the front wheels hit the main trunk. The front of the car bounced high into the air, its center crashing back down onto the main trunk of the branch, bringing them lurching to a halt. The abrupt stop made the car stall, and it suddenly became quiet.

Henry reached up to his throbbing forehead and looked at his hand. "No blood." He looked over at Maria, who was shaking her head and massaging her wrist. She looked back at him with her right eyebrow raised, as if to scold him for being an idiot, but she couldn't maintain the look. A smile erupted and quickly became laughter.

Henry tried to open his door, but it was blocked by part of the branch, so he pointed wordlessly at Maria's door and they both scooted out her side. Maria watched as he walked around the car inspecting the damage. He bent down, looking under the car, and then walked around to the front. Finally, Henry stood on the limb, leaned on the radiator, and looked at her while he rubbed his forehead. "Well, it actually doesn't look too bad. Bumper's bent, a bit of a scratch here where the black and red paint meet and the bent running boards, but," he pointed at the windshield, "it didn't even break the glass . . . and hell, she's already eight years old anyway." Henry stepped off the tree and walked around to Maria, and put his hands on the front of her hat to straighten it. "Looks like you bent it a bit."

She slapped him in the stomach, causing him to flinch. "No. It was you who bent it!"

He just smiled and put his arm around her. "It's good to be home! Come on. I'll take care of this later."

They began walking together up the dirt and gravel driveway to their two-story house with its wraparound porch. She looked back at the car. "My poor baby."

Henry changed the subject as he nudged her along. "Look, you can hardly see the driveway from all the grass that has grown. As they stepped up the three stairs that led from the driveway onto the front porch, Henry stopped and threw a branch that was blocking the door before kicking a pile of sand aside. "Must have had a hell of windstorm while we were gone."

Henry pulled the screen door open before opening the front door, and with the sound of its familiar creak, they stepped inside.

Maria immediately walked over to her piano, as Henry took a deep breath of the cherry-wood smell that permeated the house. Maria grabbed a cloth and wiped the thick dust off the keyboard cover, and then opened it. The floor creaked quietly as Henry walked into the kitchen. He looked around, before leaning on the sink and whispering to himself. "Just like we left it." He turned to see The refrigerator door still open and he spoke up as he briskly wiped his hands together. "Hon, we'll have to go to town tomorrow and get some food."

Maria didn't respond, but instead "You Made Me Love You" began coming from the grossly out-of-tune piano. Henry walked back into the front room, and his wife looked up at him and smiled as he leaned on the piano. He sat down next to her on the little bench, pushing her white dress aside. Maria pecked him on the cheek and kept playing, but he returned it with a passionate kiss. Her right hand lifted from the piano and wrapped around his neck. She continued trying to play with only her left, until Henry put his arm around her and pulled her toward him. The music stopped, and then a stream of ascending notes played as she dragged her hand across the piano to meet his face. She began a sigh of pleasure, when the slamming of the screen door against the wall made them both jump. A large cloud of dust whirled across the room as the curtains lifted in the sudden gust.

They both looked over, then Henry said, "Well, it looks like we are going to have to do some serious cleanup work around here." He looked back at her, but noticed the long shadows forming outside the window behind her. "I'd better get the car off that log and bring in the luggage before dark."

Maria pecked him on the lips. "Come on. I'll help."

Henry grabbed his old hat off the rack by the door as they walked out. "I missed this thing. My new one just isn't the same."

Maria looked up at his hat. "It's got at least three holes in it. It's shot, dear."

Henry stepped out onto the porch and looked over at the barn. A slight smile appeared on his face. "Well, at least I can still wear it at home." He shook the hat and a cloud of filth came off it, which made Henry pause to look around again. He tilted his head in puzzlement. "This dust is just ridiculous!"

Maria looked too, as momentary curiosity came over her face. "I don't know."

They walked out to the large barn and, pulling the key out of his pocket, Henry unlocked the oversized padlock. The heavy wooden barn door rumbled as he slid it aside to reveal a huge, dirty, dark green tarp. Henry stopped and stared. Maria put her arm on his shoulder. "Take a look. You haven't seen your baby in almost two years."

He glanced at her and smiled, and then like a child at Christmas, grabbed the tarp and pulled it off, releasing a huge cloud of fine dust. As the tarp slid away and the dust cleared, the unveiled bright yellow Stearman biplane scintillated in the sinking sun. Henry stood for a second, then ran his hand down the front of the wing as he walked around her, feeling her leading edge as though he were caressing a woman.

Maria let him have a minute with his plane, and then grabbed his hat. "Hey! You're making me jealous!"

Henry grabbed for the hat back. "Well, she is beautiful."

"And I'm not?" She dodged and took off with the hat in

hand.

He ran after, feeling a grin stretch across his face. "Yes, but you're a pain in the ass." They chased each other around the plane twice, until Maria tripped over a chock and fell against the fuselage.

Henry pressed up against her and pushed her arms outward. "Gotcha!"

Her gray eyes softened and she looked at his lips as a drop of sweat ran down to meet them. Henry watched her smile fade as he saw her desire appear, but when he kissed her, she suddenly snapped out of the trance and ducked away. "It's getting dark. You have work to do!"

Henry stood there, still leaning against the plane with both hands. Maria popped up from in front of the wing with his hat still in hand and laughed. "Here's your hat." She threw it through the wings, and Henry caught it with a quick jerk of his left hand. He gave her a look as if he intended to chase her some more, but she turned coy and pointed to the tractor. "Work." Henry glanced over at the tractor and nodded.

She watched him from a distance as he fiddled with the tractor. After a few tries, he got it started, and blue and white smoke poured out, followed by black as he revved the engine. He put it in gear and looked up to see the sun setting behind Maria. The orange-red light was shining right through her dress, and he could see every outline of her. She saw him staring and cocked her head in puzzlement. Henry reached back over and shut off the tractor; he stepped off, put his hat on the cowling, and walked up to her.

His hands embraced Maria's waist, running around to her back and then down, before he lifted her lips to his and kissed her.

Maria didn't say a word, but Henry could feel the passion in her kiss. She wrapped her arms around Henry's neck and shoulder and pulled him in tight. They stumbled further back into the barn, locked together. Henry pulled her towards his plane and lifted her onto the wing. Maria pushed his suspenders to the side and let them drop. His hands receded from her soft rear, down her dress, and back up again. Still locked in their kiss, he pulled her panties down her legs, while she unbuttoned his trousers.

They stopped for a second and took a breath. Henry stared into her eyes until the glowing edges of Maria's silky black hair, silhouetted by the deep orange sun, drew his attention. Maria yanked his attention back as she put her arms around his back and pulled him to her. Then she reached down and pulled him into her.

The biplane's wheels squeaked against the chocks as their passion poured forth. They both moaned as the outpouring of their love ended with a release of all their tension and stress, and the relief of being home . . . together.

They finally collapsed onto the dirty tarp that had been draped over the plane. Henry watched Maria's soft, gently smiling face turn to a red hue as the sun set. She pulled him next to her and his arm over her breast. They lay there and fell asleep to the sound of lonely frogs and crickets. An hour or two later, Henry awoke to see Maria lying on her back, looking at the Milky Way stretching across the night sky. He scooted close to her and she glanced over at him. "Henry, do you want to have a child?"

Henry hesitated, not knowing what to say. "Well, yes . . . someday."

Maria rolled onto her side and put her left hand on his chest. "We've been on plenty of adventures, and we have enough money now. Why don't we settle down and have one?"

Henry pulled away and sat up, feeling uncomfortable from the conversation. "Well, we don't have enough money yet. You know how this 'Depression' has hit everyone. We are so lucky to get the jobs we do, but the future is so uncertain, and we have to earn more."

She sat up and clasped her hands between her legs. "But we are doing very well." She waved her hand at the plane and into the darkness where the car and house were. "The future will always be uncertain."

Henry looked down with a grimace and tilted his head off to the side. "I—I'm just not ready. We're not ready yet. We have to—"

Maria interrupted and tried to comfort him. "But we are. We would make wonderful parents, and we would love every minute of it."

Henry stood up while pulling his suspenders back on.

She looked up at him. "Henry?"

He didn't return the look. "No. I . . . I—" He grabbed his hat and walked off into the darkness toward the house.

Maria sat staring into the dark, hoping he would return, but her hope faded when she heard the slam of the house's screen door. A tear ran down her cheek.

With a deep breath, she wiped it away, stood up, and composed herself, then looked down at the ground to find her missing shoe and panties. The starlight was just bright enough to see the white of the panties, but she couldn't find her black flat shoe. Maria searched, feeling the ground for it, but she was very worried about Henry. She felt anxiety come over her face as she tried in vain to find the missing shoe. Finally, not wanting Henry to stew in his anger, she limped across the yard with her remaining shoe. The pain of sharp rocks made walking slow, but the thought of her husband's anger made her walk faster.

⋏⋏⋏

Henry heard a yell from the front yard. He turned and ran down the stairs, "Now, what?". The screen door banged the outside wall as he flew through it. "Maria! Are you all right?"

He jumped a little when she responded from only a few feet away. "Yes, thanks to you, I just stepped on something."

Seeing her outline, he jogged down the front porch steps and put his arm around her; they took a step, but she cried out again. Henry put his other arm under her legs, picked her up, and carried her through the open screen door to the couch. He reached over to the lamp and turned it on, making them both squint and look away. As his eyes adjusted, he could see her bare foot. "Where is your shoe?"

Maria pointed over her shoulder back toward the barn. "I don't know."

Henry lifted her foot. "Ooh, looks like you stepped on a spiny seed. It's still in there. Hold on." He sat down cross-legged on the floor and pulled her foot toward the lamp, then grabbed the seed and pulled it out. "Well, it looks like there is still a small piece in there."

He reached into his trousers and retrieved his pocket knife.

Maria pulled her leg back instinctively, but Henry held tight to her foot. "Hold still." With the tip of his bone-handled knife, he tried to jab the small sliver and slide it out. After two unsuccessful

8

tries, he carefully pushed the tip of the blade into the seed and slid it out. "Got it."

Henry folded his knife and kissed her foot. Finally, he looked up at her and gave a slight smile. "Good as new!"

He let her foot down and stood up, offering her his hand. "Let's go to bed. Shall we?"

Maria reached up to meet his hand and smiled as he pulled her off the couch. She leaned on him as they walked up the stairs together.

Chapter 2

The Telegram

The sound of a car's horn brought Henry to consciousness. His eyes came to focus on the sunlit white curtains, whose small floral patterns were swaying to the morning breeze coming in through the window. Upon hearing the car horn a second time, he sat up with a start and searched for his pants. He looked over to find Maria gone, but then heard her call, "Henry, someone's here!"

He could smell eggs cooking as he ran down the stairs, still putting his suspenders on. Henry looked back at the kitchen as he put on his shoes, and went out the front door with his stomach grumbling. As he walked out onto the front porch, he could see the Western Union man standing next to the Model A, which was still stuck on the tree. The man raised the usual yellow envelope in the air, and Henry quickly made his way down the driveway to meet him.

As he got close, the man walked around the tree to meet him. "Henry Elliot?" He pointed to the stranded car. "Bit of a pickle, eh?"

Henry chuckled. "Yeah, didn't see it when we were coming into the driveway last night." Henry signed a form and the Western Union man handed him the envelope. "Thank you."

"Thank you, Mr. Elliot—and good luck with the car."

Henry smiled and nodded as the man climbed back into his

truck and drove off. He flipped over the envelope, finger working under the flap, but the thought of food sent him back to the house.

Maria was just sliding some eggs and bacon onto his plate as he came into the kitchen. Steam was rising from them, and Henry's eyes got big. "Where did you get these?"

With her spatula still in hand, Maria pointed east. "Mr. Weaver, next door. I saw him this morning. I was telling him that we had just gotten back from Antarctica and that we had a lot of work to do to fix the place back up, first of which was to go to town and get food. Then when I thanked him for keeping an eye on the place, he offered me some of his eggs and bacon."

Henry devoured his food while he nodded. With his mouth half full, he said, "We will have to do something nice for them, they have been good neighbors. Wait . . . what were you doing up so early? What time is it?"

Maria sat down, smiling. "It's after eleven, dear. I got up around eight, but didn't want to wake you, so I went for a walk. So, what's in the telegram?"

Henry looked at the yellow envelope, still clutched behind the handle of his fork. "Oh." He put the fork down and opened it.

"It's from Chicago." He looked up for a second and then read. "Henry. Have new job for Manchuria. You back from Antarctica now. Meet Chicago 7 pm Saturday, Palmer House. Bring wife. Your uncle, Jimbo Mata."

"That's tomorrow!" said Henry in surprise, but his excitement faded instantly as he saw Maria's disappointment. His hand, holding the telegram, sank until it touched the table. "What's wrong?"

Maria reached out and put her hands around his, partially

crushing the telegram. "I thought we were going to stay home for a while. I thought . . . I thought we could finally have a family."

Henry closed his eyes and took a deep breath. "If I know my uncle, this is a good paying job. We aren't free yet, and we need this."

"Henry, we have this place, we are hidden and no one knows about it; well, no one except your uncle. How could they find us?"

Henry opened his eyes and stared at her in disbelief. He stood up and walked to the sink, looking out the window at the empty yard. "You know those people. If we don't pay them back, in full, by the end of the year . . . they'll find us." He turned, looked at her, and raised his finger. "And we are not having a child until this whole mess is cleared up! The discussion is over!" He threw the crumpled telegram on the table and stormed out of the room.

⅄⅄⅄

Maria heard him slam the front door open against the wall as he yelled, "God damn it!" She looked down at her own plate of food, but her appetite had vanished. Maria sat there for a few minutes, staring out the window; eventually, she whispered, "Shit," and got up.

She heard the tractor start up as she got to the front door, and squinted from the reflected sunlight off the car's windshield as she watched Henry hook up the tractor. He pulled the car off the tree limb, and then angrily attached the tractor to the fallen timber, dragging it out of the driveway. Maria slowly walked down the driveway to make amends.

Once Henry had pulled the branch clear, she watched as he stopped the tractor and tried to unhook from the timber. Maria was getting close, and jumped when he hit his fist on the tractor's cowling. He was about to get into a fight with the branch, when he turned and saw her approaching. His shoulders sank and he threw his right hand up in a halfhearted wave. Upon seeing the gesture, Maria ran the rest of the way to him. He wrapped his arms around her and held her close, burying his nose in her hair.

"I am sorry. I am so sorry I got us into this mess. I worry so much about you, and I just couldn't stand to worry about you and a baby, too." Henry pulled his head back and looked at her, sad but determined. "And I couldn't live if something were to happen to you."

Maria put her hand on his lips. "No, it's my fault. I know what we have to do, and—and I don't know why I pressure you so much. I know that you love me and just want to protect us. It's just, I want the dream so much. And when I am here, on the farm, it gets the better of me." She took a step back and looked up at his eyes. "Let's go meet your uncle, get the money we need, and end this."

Henry nodded, grabbed her and pulled her back in tight to his chest with his large hand around her head. "I love you!"

Chapter 3

Chicago

The next morning, Maria awoke to the sound of birds coming from the open window. She looked over; Henry was not in bed with her, but his side was made. She heard the sound of banging metal outside, smiled, and got up.

Looking through the front door screen, she saw that Henry had pulled the biplane out of the barn into the driveway, and was getting it ready for their flight to Chicago.

She opened the screen door and yelled, "Good morning!" Henry pulled his head out from the yellow engine access door and waved at her with a screwdriver in his hand. She yelled again, "I'll make us some breakfast and pack a lunch."

Henry nodded and watched her go back into the house. He thought for a second, grinned, and went back to checking the fuel system. Thirty minutes later, Maria, in a cheerful mood, handed a plate up to him in the rear seat. Henry leaned back, took a deep breath, and stretched, his arm shaking the plate as he did so. Maria hopped up on the wing and looked in on him. "I made your favorite!"

He took a huge bite of the fried egg sandwich and nodded, "Mm-mm!" and smiled while trying to keep his mouth politely closed. When he had nearly finished his first bite, he leaned forward and pecked her on the cheek. "Thank you, dear! I am almost ready.

Already went to town to get fresh oil and fuel. We should probably pack a bag for a few days' stay."

Maria reached in and wiped a spot of mayonnaise off his face. "Already did. Do you want me to bring it out now?"

Henry shook his head and swallowed. "Nah, Nature's calling me anyway, so I'll grab it. I should also call ahead about the weather, assuming the phone's working, and we should plot our flight plan." He handed Maria the empty plate and waited for her to climb down before he stepped out onto the wing.

Fifteen minutes later, they were both sitting at the kitchen table with a Chicago-area chart laid out. Henry pointed to the map. "Looks like we will be going to Ravenswood Airport. I gave them a call and the weather looks good for the day. So, you ready?"

Maria nodded and stood up, wearing her khaki flight pants and beige button-down shirt, and grabbed her leather flight jacket, goggles, and leather hat. She walked to the door and looked back to see Henry still sitting at the table. "Well? You comin'?"

Startled, he whipped his head around and looked over at her. "Uh . . . oh, yeah. Just a sec." He stood up and quickly folded the map, then grabbed his flight jacket and leather cap. He was looking around impatiently, when Maria, with her hand out, said in amusement, "Here they are."

Henry turned to see his goggles in her hand. As he took them, Maria grabbed his dark pants and tucked in a loose piece of his green shirttail along the side. Henry eyed her with a expression of contentment and excitement. He kissed her quickly. "Let's go."

He grabbed the plaid bag sitting by the door and they both stepped outside. Henry turned to lock the door. "Do we have everything? Did you call the neighbors again?"

Maria nodded. "Yes, yes. Everything is ready," she said, and pulled the door shut.

When they got out to the plane, Henry threw his coat and hat into the cockpit and grabbed the pre-flight checklist. He opened the baggage compartment door, checked the oil level, and then put the bag inside. Maria hopped up into the front cockpit as Henry performed his walk-around inspection. When he got to the propeller, he turned it, listening and feeling for any problems. After finishing the rest of his inspection, he put the screwdriver and tools into the luggage compartment and made sure it was securely fastened.

Henry climbed up into the rear cockpit, opened the fuel valve, set the mixture to "rich", and began stroking the primer. Even though no one else was in the vicinity, he still looked all around the outside of the plane, and yelled, "Clear prop!" before pushing the starter and engaging the magneto switches. The propeller went around two cycles and a loud "pop" sounded as the first cylinder fired; then another, "pop, pop-pop," as the rest joined in. As the oil pressure climbed, Henry listened to make sure all nine cylinders were firing and set the throttle at 1000 rpm. He took in a deep breath and could smell the fresh 100-octane fuel. "Yeah!" The old girl hadn't flown in a couple of years, but she hadn't suffered a bit.

Maria looked back at him and shouted, "The field. We never had time to mow it!"

Henry smiled and pointed off to their right. "I'll just use the road!"

She looked out at the road and back at him, nodding in agreement.

Henry released the left brake as he throttled up. Exhaust and dust flew up in a huge billow behind them as the Stearman taxied down the driveway.

As they approached the road, Henry looked both ways, checking for dust clouds in the distance, the telltale sign of a car.

Not seeing any traffic, Henry turned onto the road and into the wind. He reached up and tapped Maria on the shoulder; when she responded with a thumbs up, he ran the throttle up. Henry took in a deep breath and then let it go with a satisfied grin. As they picked up speed down the road, he saw Maria waving to someone. Off to the left, the neighbors had come out to watch the show. As they reached seventy miles an hour, Henry let the Stearman rotate into the sky, then banked east.

Henry watched the green fields of corn below and was amazed by the contrast of the deep blue sky above. The warmth of the air and bright colors were a huge contrast to the solid freezing white of Antarctica. It was a fantastic day for flying, and he was thrilled to be back in his own plane.

When Henry looked forward, he found Maria looking back at the farm with longing on her face. Upon seeing his gaze, she quickly feigned a smile. Henry nodded in understanding before turning back to his instruments.

Twenty minutes into the flight, as they flew past some small, isolated clouds, Henry saw a note being pushed through the side of his instrument panel. He reached forward and grabbed it; inside was a not-so-well-drawn picture of a biplane and two happy faces. At the bottom it said, "I love you!"

Henry leaned forward and reached for Maria's shoulder. She squeezed his hand, before he withdrew it and put it back on the stick.

At about noon, Henry yelled, "Chicago!" Maria put her thumb up as she made out the buildings in the distance. Henry made a slight correction to the north and began to look for Willow Creek, and the single hangar that made up Ravenswood. He could see the Curtiss-Reynolds Field to the north, with its huge hangar with "CURTISS" written across the roof, so he knew he was close. It took him a minute, but Henry finally recognized the forty-acre sod grass field, and brought her in.

After touching down softly on the green sod, Henry taxied over to the hangar, found a suitable place to park, and cut the engine.

A middle-aged man with overalls and wool cap came out and approached the plane. "Afternoon! You need a hangar space? We have one left."

Henry thought for a second. "Nah, I think we are just going to be here overnight, we'll just tie her down. Can I call you later, if things change?"

The man nodded. "Sure. It's twenty-five cents for the night and I will get you my phone number. Do you want me to fill her up?"

Henry got down from the plane and walked over to him, handing him a quarter. "No, thank you. Do you have a car, or someone that can take us downtown?"

"Sure, my brother can take you. Where are you heading?"

Maria interjected, "The Palmer House—but do you mind if we use your restroom, so we can get a little cleaned up?" The man nodded and pointed to the building behind the hangar.

Henry and Maria were fixing their hair when they heard

a truck pull up and toot its horn. Henry grabbed his jacket and walked out to meet the man, who said, "This is my brother, Art. He can take you where you need."

Henry reached out and shook his hand. "Name's Henry. My wife, Maria, will be out in a second. I'll go grab our bag from the plane."

When Henry walked back over, Art was already showing Maria to the truck, where she climbed up in and slid to the middle of the seat. Henry threw the bag into the back and hopped into the front, while Art cranked the truck over, and it started up with a cloud of black smoke.

Henry, trying to make small talk, inquired, "This an AA?"

Art waved to his brother as the trucked lurched forward. "Yep—well, the closed-cab version, anyway, an 82-A. She's been a good truck . . . So, what brings you folks to town?"

Maria said, "His uncle has some work for us, maybe in the Far East. We are supposed to meet him at the Palmer House."

"Well, it shouldn't take us too long to get there."

As they entered Chicago, Maria was leaning forward watching out the front window with wonder in her eyes. "I love visiting the city! Do you think we'll have time to see a play, Henry?"

Henry, who had been enjoying watching her face, said, "Maybe, we'll just have to see what Uncle Jimbo has planned."

Without taking her eyes off the view, she put her hand on his leg.

As they rounded the corner, the twenty-five-story Palmer House came into view. Art stopped at the front entrance, and a doorman rushed out to open Henry's door. Henry helped Maria out and then asked Art, "How much we owe you?"

Art put up two fingers, and Henry handed him a two-dollar bill. "Thanks! Really appreciate the ride!"

As they walked up the stairs into the lobby, Maria looked up at the ornate ceiling. To her, it looked like something out of an ancient European cathedral, with pillars of marble that expanded out to hold the ceiling's grandeur forty feet above. She was lost in the beauty of its painted goddesses until she felt Henry's touch. She looked down to see Henry pointing at the lobby bar. "There he is!"

Maria looked over to see a older fellow with a pronounced mustache sitting at the bar, almost facing them. He wore a white cabana hat with a black band, thin, round-rimmed glasses, and a pinstriped suit with a double-breasted vest. As they walked over, she could see gold watch chains hanging ornately across the vest.

The man pulled a dark pipe out of his mouth as he recognized Henry, then stood up and swaggered the few steps to greet them. "How are you, Henry?" Before Henry could even respond, he continued, "Oh, and this must be your wife, Maria. How lovely you are!" With that, he took her hand and kissed it gently. Maria pulled back ever so slightly in response to this unexpected gesture, smiling with a rare moment of shyness.

Henry interjected. "Maria, this is my uncle James Mata. He was—"

Henry's uncle interrupted without taking his eyes off Maria. "Please, call me Jimbo. Or 'Uncle' will do." He motioned to some lounge chairs and a table. "Let's have a seat. We have a lot to talk about." As they walked over, he signaled one of the staff. "Henry, Maria, would you like something?"

Henry nodded. "Sure. A ginger ale would be great."

The waiter appeared almost instantly and Maria said, "A White Russian, please."

Henry looked at her with a smirk while Jimbo ordered. "Ginger ale for the gentleman, and a Forty-Three on the rocks for me."

The waiter nodded and pulled out a set of matches. "For your pipe, sir."

Jimbo waved him off. "That's okay. Don't smoke."

The waiter, looking a little puzzled, stood up straight, said, "Very well," and headed back to the bar.

Maria and Henry tried to talk at the same time, but Henry stopped mid-sentence and his open mouth turned to a slight smile. He sat back silent, while she continued. "Don't smoke? Then why do you have a pipe?"

Jimbo laughed. "It gives me charm, and something to fiddle with while I'm thinking."

Maria smiled widely. "Guess it's better than chewing on a pencil or something."

Jimbo leaned back in his chair, putting the pipe in his mouth. "Exactly! So, you two just got back from Antarctica, I hear. What is it that you were doing down there?"

Henry sat forward again and responded, "We were working for the Graham Land Expedition. They needed aerial surveys done, but we also moved supplies and whatever needed to be done. We were flying a De Havilland Fox Moth."

Jimbo's eyes lit up and he pulled the pipe from his mouth. "Where did you land it? Did it have skis on it or something?"

Henry leaned forward excitedly. "On the ice mainly, but we could land in the water, too. It could be fitted with skis or floats. The Fox Moth is really a versatile little plane. Actually, I was most amazed by how well it operated in the cold."

The waiter appeared and Henry relaxed as he placed the drinks on the table. "White Russian, ginger ale, and your Forty-Three. Do you need anything else, sir?"

Jimbo shook his head. "Not at the moment. Thank you."

Henry pointed to Jimbo's drink. "What is that?"

Jimbo pulled the pipe from his mouth and took a sip. "It's called 'Licor Forty-Three', because it's supposed to have forty-three different ingredients in it. It's from Cartagena, Spain. Thought I'd have some before I can't get it anymore. You heard about the civil war?"

Henry shook his head, puzzled. "No; civil war? We haven't heard much of anything. I mean, you know we've been a bit removed from society for the last couple of years."

Jimbo nodded and handed him the glass. "Try a little. It's good! Well, the Spanish Fascists and the Republicans are openly fighting in the streets, after an attempted coup last week. From what I'm hearing, it's going to be a long fight. So, I figure it's going to be hard to get any of this for a while."

Henry took a sip, savoring the combination of vanilla, tangy fruit, and spices. "Thick . . . you're right, it is good."

"I'll get you a glass."

Jimbo smiled in satisfaction and moved to signal the waiter, but Henry put up his hand to stop him.

"No, that's okay. I don't drink."

His uncle looked at him with a mix of amusement and consternation. "Whyever not? It's legal now, after all."

Maria was watching them, being thoroughly entertained by the exchange. Henry glanced at her and smiled himself. "Well, I can't stand the feeling—" Maria interrupted, "He's always thinking, and if he can't think, he feels vulnerable." Henry rolled his eyes with a bit of embarrassment.

Jimbo saw his expression. "Hey. Nothing wrong with that. I mean, here I am, a nonsmoker with a pipe. We all have our quirks." They all chuckled and became more at ease.

After a short silence, Jimbo spoke. "Okay, let's get down to business, shall we? Now, let me tell you what I've got planned."

Henry stayed in his relaxed state, sitting back with his ginger ale as Jimbo continued. "Let me give you a little background first. In 1919, I was sent to Russia to help the Whites defeat the Reds during the Russian Civil War. Specifically, I was assigned to Admiral Kolchak, who gave me to General Anatoly Pepelyayev."

Maria interrupted. "Assigned? By whom? For what?"

Jimbo smiled at her enthusiastic curiosity. "By the US government, to supply arms and support. We even sent in troops, but I was just an adviser, and I supplied arms," he lowered his voice and glanced around, "legally and illegally. We actually won a few battles. The machineguns we provided really made a difference, but the Whites weren't united and it was soon clear that it was a lost cause. When General Pepelyayev fell ill with typhus, he fled to Manchuria for treatment, and I decided to go with him. He recovered in the summer of '22, but by then the Reds had won. But, Pepelyayev wasn't satisfied, so he gathered up five hundred volunteers for a suicide mission to take back the East, specifically Yakutsk. I advised him not to go. Told him we could make a fortune and live well on all the contacts and trade we had set up."

Jimbo sighed and adjusted himself in his chair. "But he was a stubborn, patriotic man, and was determined to get his home back, no matter what the cost. So I supplied him and his band with what weapons I could get, and they went north. They actually did better than I thought they would, but it didn't last."

Maria leaned forward. "What happened?"

Jimbo looked at her sadly. "They were slaughtered, and the general was captured. They were going to execute him for being a traitor, even though he was one of the most loyal men I have ever known. Then something strange happened. The head of the new Soviet Union, Mikhail Kalinin, gave him a partial pardon and just sentenced him to jail. In fact, I heard he just got released. Anyway, the point is that I ended up in Manchuria with a lot of connections, and I've been conducting an import/export business there ever since."

Henry asked curiously. "What do you need us for?"

Jimbo took another sip of his Forty-Three. "As you probably know, part of the Japanese army, without permission from its government, invaded Manchuria in '31. Well, the Chinese nationals—they're called the Kuomintang, led by Chiang Kai-shek—made a deal with the Japanese and set up a 'neutral zone' where neither party should cross. I don't think it will last, but we will see. In any case, there is a resistance movement in Manchuria itself. I am supplying them . . ." he leaned forward, whispering, "actually, I am supplying both sides."

Henry's right eyebrow went up, and he glanced at Maria,

but said nothing. She put her hand on his in acknowledgment, and he knew she was just as unhappy as he felt.

Jimbo continued. "Well, it turns out that most of the resistance is made up of Communists, under a fellow named Mao Zedong; or at least, that's what Chiang Kai-shek believes, so he's cut off all supplies to the north. No trains, no trucks, no nothing. So, now I have a dilemma. A huge demand, with no way to get goods in. That's where you two come in."

Maria inquired harshly in a loud whisper, "So, you want us to fly goods in? From where? What's the legality of this?" Henry nodded, in agreement with her questions.

Jimbo took in a deep breath. "Well, it depends where we fly and who we encounter as to whether it's legal." He smiled defensively. "We will be flying out of Mongolia, but staying out of mainland China—that's where the greatest risk is. Since we supply both the Japanese—well, the underground, criminal element of the Japanese, anyway—and the anti-Japanese forces, both of them should permit us to fly freely, assuming we can keep it secret that we are supplying both. So far, I have managed to do that fairly well."

Henry, with concern in his voice, said, "This sounds pretty dangerous . . . and supplying the Japanese? I thought we were helping the locals."

Jimbo shook his head and his hand moved in a silencing manner. "I said I was supplying the criminal element of the Japanese. I will admit, at first I was supplying everyone, but some of the things that the Japanese have done—I just couldn't—But, listen my boy, supplying the bad element in their ranks creates more chaos and actually hurts them, while still giving us the advantage of free movement."

Henry rubbed his face and glanced at Maria again to judge her reaction, before thoughts of their situation came flooding back. "What's the pay like?" he asked reluctantly.

Jimbo laughed. "Ah, straight to the point. I'll give you two twenty-five percent, which should be on the order of $2000 or more a month."

Henry tried not to choke on his drink at the amount. Two thousand dollars was an incredible amount of money . . . And then Maria piped up, "Thirty-five percent," and Henry nearly choked again.

Jimbo and Henry looked over in surprise. Jimbo's teeth showed wide. "Thirty."

Henry held up his hands frantically. "Whoa, whoa . . . let's get more details here!"

Maria leaned over and whispered seriously into Henry's ear. "You said yourself we need this. Do you have an alternative?"

Henry turned slowly to her, and he shook his head almost imperceptibly.

Maria turned back to Jimbo and said in an enthusiastic voice, "Yeah. What are we flying?"

Jimbo put his pipe back in his mouth and grabbed a brochure out of his pocket. "It's the Douglas Corporation's newest plane, the DC-3. After I heard about its performance, I made a deal and bought one. It's perfect for what we need."

Henry looked at the brochure and his eyes lit up. "You *bought* one?"

He looked up, expecting a response, but saw Jimbo looking at Maria, and Maria looking across the room with a pale face. She grabbed his arm. "It's one of Rocco's goons!"

Henry followed her glance over to the bar to see a familiar face looking back at him. "Shit, I think you're right. Jimbo, let's get out of here."

Jimbo nodded and got up. "You'll have to tell me exactly what you are into this guy for."

Henry responded in a loud rushed whisper, "Fine, fine, let's just get out of here first."

As he and Maria turned to get up, a man in a black suit and fedora stepped in front of him, pulled a .38 pistol, and pointed it at his stomach. "Sit right back down. Rocco wants to have a word with you two." Henry turned and began to sit down, when from behind Jimbo two more men came up with nickel-plated .45's drawn. The gangster put up his hands.

Henry looked at the two newcomers with puzzlement, while Jimbo yelled at them, "The bar!" One of the newcomers turned to look, but the goon from the bar already had his gun on him.

Henry sat down. "What the hell is going on?!"

Jimbo gestured to Henry. "Don't worry, these are my men."

Then another voice said, "And these are *my* men." Henry turned in his seat to see two more guys in gray suits, guns drawn, with Rocco standing between them. Under his breath, Henry whispered, "Shit."

Rocco looked at Henry with narrow eyes and a forced grin. "What? You not happy to see your old boss?"

Henry mumbled, "Not particularly."

Rocco looked over at Maria, who was still standing, looking

at him with disdain. "Hey, Maria, you hot thing. Sit your little tush down." She obeyed slowly, her bitter eyes locked on him.

The gray goons and Jimbo's men stood there staring at each other, each side waiting to see what the other would do, but then the goon from the bar muttered under his breath, "Cops!"

They all looked at the entrance stairs to see two policemen walking in. Everyone slowly put their guns away.

As the situation calmed a bit, Rocco looked at them appraisingly and then pulled a chair over. "Look, I just want to talk. So we will have a little conversation, and then you can be on your way."

Maria started to stand up in anger. "What the hell do you want with us?! We pay your damn $500 every month. A few more months and we're even!"

One of Rocco's gray-suited thugs pushed her back down in her seat, but this made Henry get up in protest. Rocco pointed to both of them. "Whoa! Sit the fuck down!"

Everyone became quiet as the two cops walked by, eyeing them. Jimbo said, "Afternoon, officers." One of them tipped his hat in response and their look of suspicion turned to disregard.

When the cops were out of hearing range, Rocco spoke up. "Yes, you have been good about the payments . . . but they will end when I say they do!"

Henry leaned toward Rocco. "The hell they will. We had a deal, and we have fulfilled our end!"

Rocco's face turned red as he clenched his fists, "You're the one who got my nephew killed, and that wasn't part of any deal. You're just lucky I let you two live."

Henry's voice got louder. "And I've told you before, I

don't know what the hell happened that night. The Feds were waiting for us. Someone tipped them off! Probably someone in your organization! You have never—"

Maria stood up in a rage. "If you think we are going to pay you a dime more than we bargained for, then you've got another think coming!" Both Henry and Rocco were shocked at her outburst. "You bother us after we're paid off and you'll regret it! I will kill you mys—"

Henry, never seeing this kind of anger out of Maria before, grabbed her and spun her towards himself to stop her from continuing. Rocco laughed, "That's right! Keep your woman under control!"

Henry turned and took a step towards Rocco in defiance, when one of the policemen asked, "Is there a problem here?"

Henry caught a glimpse of startled apprehension on Rocco's face before he looked over at the officers. Jimbo stood up and feigned a smile. "Everything is fine, we were just about to leave." He put his arm out for Maria and she took it.

Henry gave Rocco a defiant smile while waving his fingers at him. "Bye, now." he said and walked off. Jimbo's guards followed while the cops watched, again with suspicion.

Jimbo rang for the elevator. When they had all piled in and the doors closed, there was a collective sigh of relief. Jimbo asked, "What is with you two and that thug?"

Henry replied, "Let's get to your room and I'll tell you."

Maria's voice was still hot as she sneered, "Did you see his fear of the police? He has lost all of his power! Prohibition is over, and now so is he. And he knows it!"

Henry nodded. "Yeah, I bet that's why he needs our money

so badly. I wonder how many others he has paying him a monthly 'stipend'?"

They reached the 23rd floor, and one of the guards stepped into the hallway ahead of them. The others waited in the elevator until he said, "It's safe, boss," then they all proceeded to Jimbo's room.

The two guards stayed outside the door;

Jimbo and Henry sat down in chairs, while Maria flopped on the bed. "Wow, that was intense!"

Henry chuckled a bit. "Yeah! I can't believe how you went off on him! I thought we were going to have a shootout!"

Jimbo asked in a level voice, "So, what's the story?"

Henry started to explain, while Maria turned to lie on her stomach so she could watch them. "Back in '29, we were broke and there weren't any jobs. We ended up working for Rocco flying in booze from Canada. We did it for years and made a good life. Never had a problem, until one night we landed on this small strip in Wisconsin. Rocco's nephew, Jimmy, and a few other guys got out to start unloading the cargo. Maria got a little frisky in the cockpit, so we stayed up there . . ." Henry winked at Maria, but she averted her eyes. He continued, "It wasn't our job to load and unload, anyway. Then, without warning, the place lit up like daylight. We heard shots, and Rocco's nephew yelled to start the plane, so we did. Just as I got the second engine started, bullets raked the fuselage and Jimmy started firing his Tommy gun out the side door."

Henry gestured with hands out. "There was gunfire coming from everywhere, so we hit max throttle . . . and as we were gaining speed, Jimmy got hit. We managed to get airborne and got away, but Jimmy was dead. We were lucky, because one of Rocco's guys survived and vouched for us, so he didn't shoot us outright. But we had to make a deal with Rocco, to pay back the price of the shipment and what he thought was a fair price for Jimmy. It worked out to $500 a month, until the end of this year. We used up most of our savings paying it, and we've been taking risky jobs, like this one you're proposing."

Jimbo rubbed his chin for a few seconds. "I think you and Maria are right, about him needing your money now. And I think he will keep harassing you or worse unless we do something about it. But we can worry about that later. Once we leave for the Far East, he won't be a problem. I assume you are in on the deal? I really need good pilots I can trust, and that's you two."

Maria pushed herself up to kneel on the bed. "Count me in!"

Henry looked at her affectionately. "Well, I certainly can't let her go alone, she might hurt someone. When do we leave?"

Jimbo grinned. "Tomorrow. We will take a train to LA, and pick up the DC-3 at the Douglas factory."

Maria's eyes widened. "Tomorrow? We don't have enough clothes, or supplies or—"

"Don't worry," interrupted Jimbo, "everything will be provided. I had already arranged a room for you two here, just in case, and I have had the things you need sent up."

Henry asked, "What about our Stearman? I can call Ravenswood to have them put it in the hangar, but someone will have to pay them while we are gone."

Jimbo nodded. "Not a problem, I will have one of my people take care of it. Okay?" He reached into his vest and pulled out a key. "You two have the room next door. My guards will keep watch outside our doors. We can discuss this more on the train, which leaves at 7:15 tomorrow evening."

Henry took that as their cue to leave, and stood up. "Goodnight, Uncle!"

Maria got up in response to Henry. "Thank you for the hospitality . . . good night."

Jimbo saw them to the door, looked at one of the guards, and nodded. He then pointed to their room and said, "Good night, you two, and sweet dreams."

When they had entered their room and shut the door behind them, they both leaned against the door and looked at each other. "Wow, now that was an interesting day!"

Maria looked over at the armoire. "Do you really think there are clothes in there for us?" She ran over and opened it to find two dresses, a suit, and casual wear. "Henry! Look at this!" She pulled out a long black silk dress with pleats and held it up in front of herself. Then she reached up and pulled down a matching hat. "Wow! This is going to be great—even if it is a bit scary."

Henry watched her marvel at the clothes. "Yes, I agree." Then he looked down at his pocket watch. "It's only five o'clock! Why are we going to bed? Why is Uncle Jimbo going to bed?"

Maria looked back at him. "Probably from him traveling. He's not adjusted to the time. As for us, we can go to bed, but we don't have to sleep." She winked and giggled, hung the dress back up, ran to the bed, and jumped on it. "Order some room service!"

Henry's mouth fell open. "Ah . . . okay. What would you like?"

She thought for a second. "Pizza, shrimp, some macaroons, and a Coke!"

Henry shook his head fondly and picked up the phone. "Ah, yes, room service please . . ."

Chapter 4

LA and the Douglas Corporation

The next afternoon they all met in the lobby. Maria was wearing her new black dress and she could see the look of approval from Jimbo.

Jimbo signaled the concierge, and two boys came to retrieve their luggage. A polished black Lincoln, a brand-new Model K Series 300, pulled up; the bellhop opened the door, but no one moved. It took a second for Maria to realize that the car was for them; then she finally got in, with Henry climbing in beside her and Jimbo sitting in the front. As Maria watched, Jimbo's guards got into a car behind them, which followed as they pulled away into the street.

"Union Station, please," said Jimbo. He looked back at Henry and Maria. "I'll tell you, that dress looks better on you than I could have imagined."

Maria blushed a little. "Thank you, and thank you for the dress."

Henry, apparently detecting a little too much movement on his girl, blurted, "Hey, hey there!"

Both Jimbo and Maria laughed out loud in response.

As they were about to turn onto Canal Street, a car pulled up beside them. Maria felt the sudden squeeze of Henry's hand, causing her to look at the other car, only to see a man looking right back at them.

"It's Rocco's men!"

The man gestured as if he were holding a gun and shooting it, before the mobsters drove off through the red light.

Jimbo waved out the window furiously, and his bodyguards pulled their car up alongside. "Hey! What the hell was that?! You guys need to keep alert! Make sure we aren't bothered till we get on the damn train."

Jimbo's men nodded and drove the remaining hundred feet ahead to the curb at the terminal. With hands on the guns under their coats, the two men proceeded to check surrounding cars and people. After thirty seconds, one of them waved Jimbo's car to the curb while still keeping a watchful eye on the surroundings. As they pulled up, one guard opened the door, letting Henry and Maria out before quickly escorting them to the terminal doors. The second guard helped Jimbo out of the car while watching passing vehicles, his right hand still inside his jacket.

Both Henry and Maria stopped when they stepped inside the newly constructed Great Hall. The bodyguard pushed them lightly to move on, but they were staring at the skylight, 110 feet above them.

Jimbo, now moving quickly with his guard, stopped and turned around to see them still staring up. He pushed out a hurried laugh and said, "Come on. We don't want to miss the train."

Maria hurried to catch up, with Henry right behind. "What train are we taking?"

Jimbo handed her a ticket. "The *City of Los Angeles*. It's a new diesel electric, and the train has the best accommodations available." He handed Henry his ticket. "According to the schedule, it will take us thirty-nine hours and forty-five minutes to get there."

They wove through the crowd of travelers until they reached the platform, one of the guards going ahead to check out their car and accommodations, while the other looked suspiciously at boarding passengers. Henry was looking at the train itself. Its sleek, rounded frontal grill looked odd to him, but the yellow and gray coloring was actually quite beautiful.

Maria grabbed his hand. "Come on, Henry, they're telling us to board."

One of the guards led them to their Pullman sleeper before Maria turned to him. "Thank you. What's your name? I never caught it."

The guard looked at her and gave the slightest smile. "It's Seamus. George or I will be outside your cabin if you need us."

She smiled at him, "Thank you, Seamus," and gently closed the door.

⋏⋏⋏

The next day, all five of them met for lunch in the dining car. Henry wiped his face with a cloth napkin. "So, how are we going to get the plane to Mongolia?"

Jimbo took a second to finish chewing his steak. "Well, I had them put in extra fuel tanks to extend its range from 1600 to 3600 miles. That should get us to Hawaii, but from there I was going to let you choose the route. We can't land in China, Japan, or the Soviet Union, so that's going to make it tricky."

Henry looked out the window at the snow-covered Rocky Mountains. "Okay, we'll just have to plot it when we get to LA."

Maria looked at Seamus. "Are you coming with us?"

Jimbo answered. "Nah, they just work for me here in the States. They will escort us until we take off."

Maria replied quietly, "Oh. That's a shame."

Seamus smiled at her.

The next morning, they arrived in Los Angeles. Jimbo had a car pick them up at the station and take them out to Santa Monica, where the Douglas Corporation was located.

Henry was looking out the window, watching the oil wells go by, when Maria put her hand on his leg. "Are you excited to see the new plane?"

Henry swallowed and gave a forced smile. "Yes. Very much so." Then he leaned to whisper into her ear. "But I am a little nervous about flying a new plane across the Pacific."

She nodded. "Me too, but together we can do it." His smile turned genuine and he put his hand on hers.

Jimbo turned from the front seat. "We're here!" The guard at the front gate pointed them toward a hangar. As the car pulled up to the hangar, a gentleman approached and they came to a stop.

Jimbo got out and shook his hand as Henry held the door for Maria. "This is my nephew, Henry Elliot, and his wife, Maria. Henry, meet Donald Douglas."

Henry gasped and shook his hand. "How do you do, sir?!"

Maria stepped forward, eyes wide, and Mr. Douglas shook her hand as well. "Well, would you like to see your new aircraft?" He whistled, and the hangar door began to open. As the door slid to the side, the sun reflected brilliantly off silver metal. The plane was almost entirely made of reflective metal, with only the engine cowlings and wing flaps painted reddish orange.

Henry's jaw dropped as he walked toward the plane. "Wow—it's beautiful! And big!" Henry ran his hand down the prop and moved onto the wing.

Maria came up behind him. "It really is gorgeous!"

Henry and Maria walked around the wing to see two men at the back of the plane, painting over an American eagle logo. Henry looked at Jimbo. "What's with that?"

Jimbo chuckled and walked over. "Well, American Airlines was going to get thirty of these; now they're only getting twenty-nine."

Henry looked over at Mr. Douglas, who was watching them, and then back at Jimbo. "What kind of deal did you make?"

Jimbo waved his hand. "Never mind that. Get in, get in! Check out the cockpit."

They walked around to the door and ascended the five steps until they were inside. Henry looked back at Jimbo. "What's with all the beds?"

Jimbo replied, "Don't worry, most of those will be gone later today, when they finish putting in the extra tanks."

Henry walked up to the cockpit while admiring the partially installed amenities. He sat in the left pilot's seat, and Maria came up and sat in the right as he looked over the instruments. "A direction finder, that should be useful; radio . . . anti-icing . . ." He looked over to see Maria just smiling at him.

"You're in love again, aren't you?"

From the outside of the plane, they heard Jimbo call, "So, what do you think?"

Maria turned to her right and opened the sliding glass

window, leaned out, and said, "It's fantastic! When can we take her up?"

Jimbo walked to the rear of the right wing. "Patience."

Mr. Douglas, now standing in front of the plane, cleared his throat. "We will have it all ready by this evening."

Maria turned to face him, her hair spilling out the window and swinging in the light breeze. "This is a hell of a plane you've built here! My husband is in love—makes me jealous!"

Mr. Douglas laughed with appreciation on his face. "I will take you up tomorrow myself, and show you how she flies."

Henry opened his own window and leaned out. "That would be great! We can't wait!"

Jimbo walked around the wing to the front, and waved at them to come down. "Come on. We have cargo to pick up. We'll come back tomorrow, and you can take her up to give her a good shakedown."

As they got back in the car, Henry asked, "Do we have time to see Griffith Observatory?"

Jimbo turned to him. "Sorry, we don't have much time today. We have to drive down to Torrance to pick up a truck and the cargo."

An hour later, they pulled up to a garage, and Jimbo got out to talk with a scruffy-looking man waiting in the garage doorway, before signaling to Henry.

Henry came over to him. "What's the scoop?"

Jimbo pointed to a box truck and handed him the keys. "Follow us."

Maria got out of the car. "I'm going with Henry."

Henry stepped up into the truck and watched Jimbo, who

had the driver transfer their luggage to the car with his guards before climbing in with them. The car that had been driving them pulled away.

Maria looked at Henry with puzzlement. "I wonder why he did that."

Henry watched and replied without looking at her. "He doesn't want any outside witnesses to get a look at the cargo."

Maria looked forward again. "Oh."

Henry started the truck as Jimbo's guards pulled out. He followed them for about fifteen minutes until they pulled into a warehouse. As soon as Henry's truck was inside, two tough-looking men closed the doors.

Henry shut off the engine and watched as the two went over to the car and talked to Jimbo for a few minutes. Then Jimbo and his bodyguards made their way over to a large tarp, before waving for Henry and Maria to join them.

Henry looked at Maria and shrugged before hopping down out of the truck. The two men pulled off the tarp and handed a crowbar to Jimbo, who rammed it underneath the lid and opened the first crate. Henry looked at everyone, not knowing what he should be doing, but then peered into the opened crate. "Tommy guns?!"

Jimbo looked at him with a smile and grabbed one of the submachine guns. "Here, feel that!"

Henry took the Thompson. "Snazzy, a Chicago Typewriter. This what we're selling to those in need?"

Jimbo smiled. "Well, it's some of what they need. This run alone will pretty much pay for the plane."

Maria watched Henry with interest, as he held the

Thompson. Then she gestured toward the crates. "What's in those big ones?"

Jimbo walked over to the first one. "These? These are for us." He cracked open the lid and dropped it onto the floor. "A water-cooled 1917 Browning .30-caliber machine gun," he leaned over and opened another, "and in this crate, a Browning M2 .50-caliber belt-fed." He pointed to some more crates. "Those longer ones are BARs."

Maria's face lit up. "Like Bonnie and Clyde!"

Jimbo paused. "Well . . . yeah."

Henry bit his lip in concern. "For us? Are we going to need these?"

Jimbo started sealing the crates back up. "Don't worry, my boy. They're just a precautionary measure. Bring the truck on over here, and let's get this stuff loaded."

They stayed in a motel that night, with one of the guards sleeping in the truck. The next morning, Henry awoke to sunlight shining in his eye through a small hole in the dark green curtains. He rolled over to see Maria still sleeping, so he got up and walked toward the bathroom as quietly as he could. As he reached the door, the phone began to ring with a rattling clamor. Startled, Henry turned and rushed to get it before it awoke Maria, kicked the bedpost, and fell with a heavy thud. "Son of a—"

Maria, naturally, awoke not at the sound of the phone but at the impact of his foot against the bed. "Holy cow! Are you okay?"

The phone kept ringing and Henry started to crawl to it, but Maria just rolled over. "Don't worry, Henry, I've got it." As she reached for the phone, Henry just let himself fall to the floor.

She picked up the heavy black receiver. "Hello? . . . Right. We are, but it will take Henry a few minutes to be ready. . . . Yeah, we'll be down. . . . Okay. Umm, French toast, scrambled eggs, a Hershey bar, and a Coke. Yeah. What's wrong with it? . . . Sure, he'll take the same. Okay, bye." She looked at Henry laying on the floor. "Oh, dear. Are you okay?" She bent down and helped him up onto the bed, and dropped a little kiss onto his lips. "What did you do?"

Henry pointed to his right foot. "Kicked the damn bed when I turned around."

She bent down and kissed the top of his foot. "Aww . . . there, is that better?"

He smiled affectionately and nodded. "Did you just order me one of your wacky meals?" She innocently nodded in the affirmative. "Oh, come here." Henry pounced, rolling the two of them back into bed and throwing the sheets over their heads as he dove in for a kiss, and then several more.

After a few minutes enjoying the darkness under the blankets, Maria pulled away and asked, "Shouldn't we get ready? We do have to fly a plane across the Pacific today."

He chuckled. "Yeah, we do! Let's go, then."

Jimbo and George were already eating when Henry and Maria walked in with their hair still wet. "Mornin', fellas." Henry sat down, looking ruefully at his now-cold eggs and French toast. A Hershey bar sat on the edge of his plate. He looked up at Maria, who was already beginning to eat. She stopped chewing and grinned at him. He looked back down at his plate, whispered, "What the hell," and grabbed the Hershey bar.

Jimbo watched him eat the chocolate with disapproval on

his face. "Good morning, you two. We will be heading straight over to the Douglas Corporation, and you two can get some time in the DC-3. While you two lovebirds are flying around, the rest of us have some other errands to run, including getting better charts of our course."

After breakfast, Henry got in the truck with Maria, while the other three led the way in the car. After a few minutes on the road, Maria reached over and turned on the radio. "Let's listen to some tunes." She tuned through a morning show and some ads, until she got to "Pennies From Heaven".

"Oh, I love Bing Crosby," she exclaimed, and smiled at Henry, who returned the smile fondly.

She was staring out the window when she heard, "Earhart." She reached over and turned the radio up. Both Henry and Maria listened intently as the radio reporter spoke, " . . . and after her recent solo flights from LA to Mexico City, and from Mexico City to New York, she announced that she wanted a real challenge. To circumnavigate the world, possibly next year. The Lockheed Company has provided her with a specially built Electra, right here in Burbank, Califor—"

To Maria's surprise, Henry turned off the radio suddenly, and when Maria looked over at him to ask why, he was gripping the steering wheel tightly. The expression on his face filled her with anxiety. "What? What is it?"

Henry replied, "Cops."

Maria looked in her mirror and could see the flashing lights approaching fast. "What should we do, Henry?"

He kept his eye on the mirror. "I guess, we just pull over . . ." The siren began to blare and Henry nervously started bringing the truck to the shoulder, but the police car just raced by. Henry had been holding his breath, but let it out and got back on the road.

"Holy crap," Maria said as she put her hand on his arm, "that was close." She looked back at the crates of machine guns. "I thought we were busted for sure."

A few minutes later, as their anxiety subsided, they pulled into the Douglas Corporation's lot and then into the hangar.

Donald Douglas walked up as they were parking inside, and introduced a new man. "Jimbo, Henry, Maria, this is Carl Cover. He is my test pilot. He'll be taking you up and showing you the ins and outs."

Henry shook Carl's hand. "Glad to meet you. She's a gorgeous plane, and, I have heard, a good one too."

Carl nodded and looked at the DC-3. "You bet. This is one of the finest aircraft ever produced. With the Wright R-1820 Cyclone 9s, she will fly on one engine, even during takeoff. The structure is tough as nails, yet flexible. She has the latest instrumentation on her—"

Mr. Douglas interrupted while smiling. "Yes. Yes, what he says is all true, but unfortunately, I have to go. Have a meeting with United. It was a pleasure to meet all of you, and I really appreciate your efforts in purchasing one of my planes."

As he walked off, Jimbo remarked, "Great guy. Well, we are going to get some things done. You three have fun. See you in a few hours." He half-saluted and got into the car.

Carl looked at Henry and Maria. "Shall we?" Both of them nodded excitedly, and made their way to the cockpit.

Henry was getting into the right-hand seat when Carl said, "Take the left. You're flying; I am just advising."

Henry looked at him and paused in surprise. He let out a smile. "Okay, great."

Carl handed him the pre-flight checklist. "I already did the exterior pre-flight."

Henry nodded and looked down the list, still smiling, "I'll just have to trust you."

They buckled in while Maria stood behind, leaning on their seat backs.

Henry started to go down the list. "Landing gear pins?"

Carl pointed. "Here."

Henry continued. "Circuit breakers, check. Hydraulic quantity, check. Pressure?"

Carl replied, "840 psi."

They continued down the list, while Carl explained anything new.

Henry looked out at the right engine. "Ready to start?" Carl nodded, and Henry looked over his shoulder. "Maria, strap in." He heard her moving about as she found the jump seat behind the cockpit and got settled.

Henry looked down at the list. "Fire guard?"

"Posted."

"Right engine clear?"

"Clear."

Henry opened his sliding window and shouted the standard warning, "Clear prop!" before pulling his head back inside. "Battery master, on; right booster pump, on . . ." He pressed the right starter, and the whine of the starter motor made him smile. Henry looked over to see Carl studying him and knew that his excitement was showing. He stiffened up and set the mixture to auto, engaged the magnetos, and advanced the throttle. The engine came to life, and the plane shook as black smoke billowed back.

Carl reached over. "Don't forget to disengage the starter once she catches."

Henry nodded. "Oil pressure looks good. Right boost pump, off; primer, off. Fuel pressure, looks good . . ."

Within a few minutes, Henry had both engines idling at one thousand RPM. He looked back at Maria. "Ready?"

She couldn't stop smiling. "Yes!"

Henry looked out towards the runway. "Brakes, check. Flap handle, up; flap indicator is . . . zero. Setting flap handle to neutral." He checked the instruments and throttled up for taxi, and the plane wheeled majestically out of the hangar. Waves of air rushed across the grass as Henry began to taxi down the runway. Henry watched out all the windows for traffic and kept his hand steady on the throttle.

When they reached the end of the runway, Henry pressed hard on the brakes and ran both black-balled throttles forward to perform his run-up test. The gauge read 1700 RPM, and the roar of the engines shook his chest while the plane bobbed, wanting to lurch forward. With the test complete, he returned the throttle to idle before setting the props forward and the pitot tube heater to "on", checking the warning lights, and making sure the flaps and trim were zeroed out.

Henry, a little nervous, throttled up both engines while swinging the plane around. "Set the cowl flaps to trail, and tail wheel is . . . locked. Okay, we're ready. Check for traffic."

Carl looked out his window. "Clear."

Henry, once again, pushed the black throttles all the way

forward until the thrust pushed him back in his seat. Even with the roar of the engines, Henry heard Maria let out a yelp of excitement from her seat. He chuckled to himself; then, when the air speed indicator read "100", Henry rotated the plane and she jumped into the sky. "Wow," he said to Carl. "This thing is a beast, but she feels solid."

Over the next hour, Carl took him through stalls, and the plane's general capabilities. Carl then signaled for Maria to take over. Henry relinquished the controls and made his way to the navigator's seat, where Maria had been sitting.

Once there was room, Maria nervously stepped past Henry and made her way to the pilot's seat. She put on the headset and smiled at Carl, who nodded in return. Feeling the yoke for the first time in flight, she moved it from side to side and felt the lag time in the plane's response. "Big puppy!"

By the time they landed, with Maria still flying, Jimbo and his men were back with food, supplies, and charts. Carl took Maria through the shutdown checklist, while Henry came down to greet them. Jimbo walked up and slapped him on the shoulder. Henry grinned in acknowledgment and beamed, "That was marvelous!"

Henry looked up at Maria, still in the cockpit, and back at Jimbo with an unending grin. "Bloody fantastic! Great plane!" He then pointed to the paper rolls in Jimbo's arms. "I assume you have the charts? We have a small problem."

Jimbo looked down at all the charts in his hands. "Yeah, I've got every chart I could get of the Pacific and China. What do you mean by problem?"

Henry pointed to the truck. "All that cargo of yours must

weigh at least a ton. That's going to limit us to a range of twenty-five hundred miles or so, even with the extra fuel."

Jimbo stared at the truck. "Oh, hell . . ."

Henry responded, "Exactly. We can't make it to Hawaii. We will have to plan a different route, because I assume you don't want to leave the cargo behind."

Jimbo played with his mustache. "Right, right."

Maria abruptly skipped over with an excited grin on her face. "Did you tell him about the range issue?"

Jimbo and Henry nodded. Henry looked over at Carl, who was coming from the plane. "Carl, is there any place with a big table where we can plan out our flight?"

Carl pointed to a room adjacent the hangar. "In there. You're trying to get to Mongolia, right?"

"Yeah, that's right."

Carl continued. "Well, we have all the distances between airports that we know of already plotted out. He's right that you won't be able to make it to Hawaii with any cargo, but you can make it to Alaska. From Alaska you can reach Midway and go from there. Let me go grab the numbers and meet you in there."

Jimbo touched him on the shoulder as he passed by with a quick "Thank you", before they all proceeded to the room with the large table. Henry put down a large map of the Pacific, looked around, and grabbed a yardstick. "Okay, so we know Hawaii is out. That means Seattle, then Anchorage . . ." He measured the map's scale. "Hmm . . . that's too far to Midway. Maybe there is an airport in the Aleutian Islands. Is there a map of the Aleutians in here?"

Jimbo thought for a second. "I don't believe so. Just one of

Alaska."

A minute later, Carl popped in with his own charts. "Okay, here are the charts we used to plot potential flight plans for the DC-3. We were researching them last year at the request of Pan-Am." He laid a chart of the Aleutian Islands over the Pacific map. "Okay." Carl looked over the chart, remembering the potential routes. "Yes—here, Naknek. There is an airport there," he looked at a chart the Douglas Corporation had made, "and it's about twenty-three hundred miles to Midway. From there you hit Wake Island and Guam. From Guam, you have your pick of stops before Mongolia."

Henry looked at Jimbo and back at the chart. "Well, we have a bit of a situation. We can't land in China, Japan, or the Soviet Union."

Carl moved the topmost chart to reveal the map of the Pacific again. "Well, what about Hong Kong?"

Henry looked at Jimbo again. Jimbo was chewing on his pipe and squinting thoughtfully at the table. "Hmm . . . that might do. I'll need to make some phone calls." He stepped to the side and gestured for Henry to come closer. "I am worried about Hong Kong customs," he whispered. "Since they are British, they will be hard to pay off. Is there any way we can make it direct?"

Henry looked back at the chart, found Guam, and used the yardstick to measure the distance to Mongolia. "Well, if we just enter the eastern part of Mongolia, it should be in range, but we won't have fuel to spare." Carl watched what he was doing and then looked at the truck. "What exactly are you guys carrying? Oh, wait. Never mind, I don't want to know."

Maria raised her hand. "Well, we could wait for favorable

winds."

Henry smiled at her. "That's true, but that may be a bit of waiting."

Jimbo smiled. "Then we can go play on the beach until it does—as long as it's not too long."

They spent a few hours working out the final plan, including getting weather reports, while Jimbo's guards loaded the plane.

Henry and Maria started rolling up the chart. Henry looked up at the clock. "Two o'clock. We better get going. We want to get to Seattle before dark." Everyone reflexively looked at the clock and started to hurry.

Twenty minutes later, Henry, Maria, and Jimbo each shook Carl's hand. "Thanks, Carl, for all the help."

Carl responded, "It was my pleasure. Have a safe flight!"

Jimbo walked over to his guards and shook their hands in turn. "Farewell, George. See you soon, Seamus. You two keep an eye on things, and we will be in touch."

Henry stepped over and shook their hands. "I really appreciate you keeping us safe, and my—"

Maria interrupted with a shout out the cockpit window, "Bye, Seamus. Bye, George. Thanks!" Both guards looked at her hanging out the window, and waved back with a smile.

With that, Henry and Jimbo boarded and sealed the rear door.

A few minutes later, they were in the air and turning north. As they reached cruising altitude, Henry stared out over the ocean, watching the sunlight sparkle off the waves.

By seven o'clock they had reached Portland. It was a very clear day, and Maria commented, "Look how green it is!"

Henry leaned forward. "Yeah. And there is the Columbia River, so that must be Mount Hood, and the pointy one across the river is St. Helens."

Maria looked at the chart. "That one must be Adams, and the distant one in front of us is . . . Rainier, I think. We're getting close."

Henry looked over at her smiling. "Yep, about forty-five minutes."

Henry took off his headset and rubbed his ears, only to hear snoring. He looked back and saw Jimbo lying in one of the few bunks they had left on board. He tapped Maria and pointed back. Maria laughed at the sight; she looked again, a calculating look on her face, and then at Henry. She crooked her finger to beckon him closer. Henry leaned over, and she pecked him on the cheek. He pulled his head back in puzzlement. "That's it?

Maria laughed playfully. "It's enough. You're flying, remember?"

Henry rolled his eyes and looked back out the front window, before letting a smile take over his face.

Thirty minutes later, Henry reached for the PA button. "Attention, passengers! We will be landing at Seattle shortly, so wake up and buckle in!"

Both of them looked back, Henry grinning and Maria sympathetic, to see a groggy Jimbo trying to sit up. "All right, all right. I hear you."

Maria gave Henry a look and mouthed, "Mean."

Henry just stuck his tongue out at her and laughed.

Chapter 5

Naknek

Henry awoke to the sound of a Boeing 247 starting up near them. Sunlight was shining into the cockpit and Jimbo was sitting in the right seat, reading a book. Henry got up and stretched as he moved into the cockpit. "Whatcha reading?"

Jimbo lifted the book, revealing the cover. "*From the Earth to the Moon*, by Jules Verne."

Henry looked at the cover. "I didn't know you liked Jules Verne . . . I love his work, and so does Maria."

Jimbo smiled. "What's not to like? Adventure, new frontiers. I mean here we are, flying halfway around the world. Who's to say the stars aren't next?"

Maria, suddenly appearing from the rear, asked, "Do you really think we will go into outer space someday?"

Henry answered as he moved his headset to sit down. "I'll bet that one day our grandkids will live out there."

Maria tilted her head. "But that would mean we would have to have kids."

Henry looked sidelong at her over his shoulder. "Yes. Yes, it would."

Maria just smiled, not wanting to push the issue. When she glanced at Jimbo, his eyes immediately went back to the book.

She grabbed a sweater off her bunk. "Let's go get some breakfast!"

After getting some directions, they walked to a small coffee shop and sat down. Maria pointed to a pay phone sign and Henry turned towards it. "Excuse me for a minute while I call ahead for the weather."

Maria nodded and looked at the menu until a waitress came by.

"Morning. You two want coffee?"

Maria shook her head, but Jimbo said, "Yes please, black."

Maria looked up at her. "I'll take a hot chocolate, some oatmeal with strawberries, and a piece of apple pie . . . with ice cream."

The waitress paused, but wrote it down, then looked at Jimbo. "Toast is fine for me." Jimbo glanced at Maria. "What about Henry?"

Maria, who had been looking back at the menu, looked up again. "Oh, uh . . . the same for him."

As the waitress left, Jimbo asked, "So, what is with you two and having a baby?"

Maria was a bit shocked at the question. "Well, I want one, and I think Henry does too, but he says not before we pay off Rocco. He says he doesn't want to have to worry about keeping a baby safe along with the two of us."

Jimbo pulled out his pipe and started chewing on it. "Well, I guess that makes some sense, but I think you two would make great parents."

Maria smiled. "Why thank you, Uncle. What about you? You ever been married?"

Jimbo looked right at her and stopped fiddling with his pipe. He pulled his pipe out of his mouth and looked down at the table. "Well, there was a girl, Zhanna . . . Zhanna Korenyiko. She was from Irkutsk. Tough girl, always had a wit about her, even in the direst circumstances. We met while I was working with General Pepelyayev. I was out one evening with a guard and there was shooting in the street. Don't know who they were, but when they shot at us, my guard fired back. Soon, we had several people firing at us that we couldn't see, so we broke into a store to hide. Well, when we got to the back of the store, a door opened and a woman, Zhanna, saw us hiding behind the counter. She invited us in and let us stay the night. Between Zhanna's broken English and my broken Russian, we managed to talk all night in the dark. We talked about everything, from politics to exploration and the meaning of life. I had never met a woman like her and I fell head over heels. I used every excuse to visit her from then on. We were soon engaged to be married."

Maria looked at his tortured face. "What happened?"

"When Irkutsk fell, we retreated east across frozen Lake Baikal, at the same time that Admiral Kolchak was executed by the Bolsheviks. Then General Pepelyayev came down with typhus, and he was to be sent to Manchuria, so I decided we should go with him. By then, the war was going very badly and I didn't see any sense in staying. Zhanna didn't want to leave her home, but I convinced her to go."

The waitress set down their plates to silence and walked away.

Maria quietly prompted him, "Then what?"

Jimbo's eyes were tearing up and he cleared his throat. "She never made it off that godforsaken lake."

Maria put her hand on his. "I am sorry . . . and if there—"

Henry abruptly sat down, jarring both of them from the moment. "Well, the weather looks—" He looked at them both. "What's wrong?"

Jimbo sat up. "Ah, it's nothing. Let's eat."

Henry looked at Maria for a clue, but she said nothing, so he finally went to eat his breakfast. "What's this? Apple pie? Ice cream?"

Maria looked up at him, as if wondering what was wrong with it. "It's good!"

After seeing their faces, he didn't feel like protesting and just ate without further complaint. "Well, the weather in Naknek is overcast and raining, but visibility under five thousand feet is good. Just hope it stays that way."

Maria put some of her ice cream into her mug of hot chocolate and drank it. "So, what time do we have to be there by, to avoid darkness?"

Henry was grinning. "That's the good part. It only gets dark for a couple of hours or so each day this time of year, so as long as we don't show up during them, we will be fine."

Henry could see the wakes of ships coming and going in the Puget Sound below as they climbed to altitude. "We have enough fuel, so I think it would be best to stay in sight of the coastline as we work our way up."

Maria nodded in agreement as she watched out her window.

For the next six hours they watched the deep blue of the ocean, and in the distance, the green forests of British Columbia, glide by. There was no discernible difference when they crossed into the Territory of Alaska.

Henry heard Jimbo snoring in the back and glanced at Maria to see her equally amused by it. The plane jerked suddenly, and Henry heard a moan and indiscernible swearing coming from Jimbo. The plane shuddered further as they entered a weather front.

Henry pulled back on the throttle a bit. "Damn, it's getting thick. I am going to try to take us above it." He throttled back up to climb. "Put your oxygen on." At 17,000 feet, after he had applied full throttle, he looked over at Maria. "I can't get any more out of her."

She took a good look out the window at the wing. "Ice!"

Henry sat straight up and scanned the cockpit for the deicing control. "Okay, I turned on the pneumatics. Any change?"

Maria watched out the window until chunks of ice started breaking off the leading edge of the wing. "Yes! It's working."

Henry pulled back on the yoke. "Okay, she's climbing again."

Jimbo had come to the front and was watching while trying to hold on tight, but the bumps were coming harder and more often, and he looked a little pale. "Are we going to be able to get over this?" he asked, his voice thready.

Henry gave him a quick glance. "Sit down and buckle in! I hope so . . . we are at 22,000 now." He looked back again, but didn't see Jimbo. Checking over his shoulder a third time, Henry saw Jimbo falling against a bulkhead while grasping the air for something to hold onto. "Where's your oxygen? Use the navigator station's . . . put your oxygen on!"

Jimbo was trying to sit when they hit a large air pocket,

slamming him to the floor. He yelled and started to slide.

Henry whipped his head around in response. "Shit. Maria! Take over! Keep us climbing." He unbuckled, undid his mask, and moved back down the aisle to help his uncle up. "You okay? Come on . . . let's get you in the seat and hooked up." As he tried to lift Jimbo, a bag fell on Henry's head. Henry's heart was pumping hard now and he was starting to get light-headed. Gasping for breath, he pulled and dragged until Jimbo partially got to his feet. Henry turned him and sat him down in the navigator's position. When he saw Maria looking back at them, he panted, "Never mind us. Fly!" She nodded and looked straight ahead. Henry got a first strap buckled and the oxygen mask on Jimbo.

Maria yelled from the cockpit. "It's clearing, we're almost over it!"

Henry looked forward and then at Jimbo. His uncle gave a thumbs-up, and Henry patted him on the chest. He kicked the bag out of the way and stepped back into the cockpit. As he buckled in and put his oxygen back on, Maria looked over at him anxiously. "You okay?"

He put up his hand. "Yeah . . . just give me a minute."

The sun began to shine into the cockpit as they cleared the tops of the clouds. Maria began leveling out and took in a deep breath. "Okay, looks like we're clear."

Henry shook his head and squinted out at the bright white clouds. He felt for the sunglasses that he had packed, but they weren't where he had left them. "Damn."

Maria looked over at him, already wearing hers. "Damn what?"

"I can't find my glasses. They must have slid somewhere

during the climb." There was a tap on his shoulder, and he glanced back to see Jimbo holding them out to him.

Henry studied Jimbo's face, trying to get a read on his condition, while simultaneously taking the glasses. "Thanks."

Jimbo nodded. "Thanks for helping my ass up."

Henry smiled and nodded, before he put his glasses on and scanned the sky. "Well, we're going to have to fly in using the directional. Maria, can you operate the RDF? You should be able to lock onto a radio station in Anchorage."

She unbuckled and waved for Jimbo to come forward. "Okay. Excuse me, Uncle, I need to use that station."

They traded places, and Maria tuned the radio for a few minutes. "Okay, I've got Anchorage on 750 kilocycles and Juneau on 800 kilocycles. Give me a minute to figure our position."

Henry looked over at Jimbo, still concerned about his condition, and smiled encouragingly.

A few minutes later, Maria handed Henry a piece of paper. "Here is where we are. We need to maintain a heading of 310 degrees."

Henry studied the sheet. "Great. Want to pump one of those stations through?"

"Benny Goodman or Billie Holiday?"

"Goodman." She flipped a switch and they listened to "Stompin' at the Savoy" as they flew over the cloud tops.

Two hours later, they were still above the dense cloud layer. Henry turned to Maria. "Our position?"

She responded, "We should be about fifty miles out."

Henry thought for a second. "Can you see if you can reach

the airfield, and ask for the current cloud ceiling?"

Maria looked on the chart, found the airport's frequency, and started to transmit. A minute later she tapped on Henry's shoulder. "The say they have twenty-mile visibility and a cloud ceiling of six thousand feet."

Henry pointed to the chart. "Any mountains we need to avoid over six thousand?"

She looked carefully. "No, nothing that high. We should be fine."

Henry glanced at Jimbo to see how he was doing. "Okay, radio them that we are inbound. Then I need you back up here. Jimbo, go back and take over talking to them."

Jimbo nodded and unhooked himself, but then paused. "But, what do I say?".

Henry responded. "Just talk normal and relay what is said." He cleared his throat. " "Everyone ready?" and let off the throttle. They began to sink through the clouds, and Henry watched the wings flex as they flew through the turbulence once again. There was rattling throughout the cabin, but everyone was strapped in this time.

At 5,500 feet, the clouds cleared and Henry pointed. "Look, I think that's the Naknek River."

Maria was watching too. "Wow . . . lot of lakes." She grabbed the chart. "Yes, I think you're right. The airport should be near the end of the river as it flows into Kvichak Bay."

Henry banked the plane slightly west. "Okay. I am going to take her down to three thousand and see if we can find the runway."

Finally Maria pointed. "There it is! At one o'clock."

Henry leaned forward in his seat. "Oh, yeah, I see it."

They flew in over the river and landed softly on the dirt strip. When they reached the end, Henry turned the plane around and taxied back to the nearest building before shutting her down. "Whew. That was a bit hairy, but not too bad!"

Jimbo's eyes got wide and he looked at Maria for her reaction, which wasn't there. "Am I the only one who was scared out of my wits?"

Maria and Henry eyed him with matching smirks. "Oh, come on. It wasn't that bad. Just a little turbulence . . . we lived, didn't we?"

Jimbo nodded skeptically, headed for the back of the plane, opened the door, and got out before bending over and holding his chest.

Maria looked at Henry. "What's he going to think when we really get into a hairy situation?"

Henry grunted in agreement. "It'll be fine. Let's go find some dinner!"

As they stepped out of the plane, they were surprised to see people gathering. A man approached them, wide-eyed. "Wow. Never seen an airplane like that before. What is it? What are you doing here? Where are you going?"

Henry glanced at Maria and back at the gentleman, as others gathered around. "Ah . . . This is a Douglas DC-3. Most of the new planes are all metal like this." He smiled as he presented the plane like it was his. "We are just here to get fuel and food . . . and we are heading to Mongolia."

Someone in the crowd asked, "Where's that? Up north?"

An older woman came up to them with her husband. "We

don't really have a restaurant here, but we would like to invite you to our house for supper."

Maria peered up at Henry with an "oh please" expression. Henry said, "Well . . . sure. We would be delighted!"

Henry closed the door on the plane and locked it. "Lead the way," he said with a smile. As they began walking down the street, a crowd followed, but soon started to thin.

The older gentleman said, "I'm Fred, and this is my wife Esther."

Jimbo spoke up first. "Call me Jimbo. These are Henry and Maria. Glad to make your acquaintance, Fred! So, what do you two do up in these parts?"

Fred glanced back at Jimbo. "Well, we're just retired. After the war, I just wanted someplace quiet and far away." Fred caught his toe on a rock and stumbled, but Henry caught him. "Whoa, I guess I should be looking where I'm going! Thank you, young ma—uh, Henry."

Henry nodded. "No problem at all. Thank you for inviting us."

They finally came to a small cabin with a well-manicured yard, an apple tree in the center and the edges full of rosebushes. Pink and white petals were strewn around the perimeter of the yard. Fred opened the small gate and motioned for everyone to come in, carefully closing and latching it behind them as they stepped onto the wooden front porch.

Esther opened the front door for them. "Please, do come in."

Maria closed her eyes as the smell of baking bread filled her senses. "Oh, that smells so good!"

Esther smiled "Oh, yes. It will be ready soon. Please, have a seat," she pointed to the living room, "while I make dinner for us."

Henry thanked her again, and they stepped through into the living room. A white couch with wooden trim, covered with two afghans, sat against the wall. A stone fireplace with a cooking rack inside was the centerpiece; above it, a picture of a young man in military uniform. There were two matching chairs against the window, and a small table with a lace cloth and an amber glass lamp on top.

Henry and Maria sat down on the couch while Jimbo walked over to the fireplace. As a grandfather clock chimed in the corner, he pulled out his pipe to chew on, and examined the photo. "This you, Fred?"

Fred, just coming through the door, looked over. "Ah, yep. That's me. Or was me, back when I was handsome!" He chuckled.

Maria studied him, with his dark brown trousers, beige shirt, and dark gray vest. A silver chain ran from his mid button into his watch pocket. He wore round, wire-rimmed glasses, and had a slight five o'clock shadow on his face. "You're handsome now!"

He nodded in appreciation and walked into the living room. Jimbo pulled down the picture. "So, you were in the 27th Regiment?"

Fred cocked his head a bit. "Yeah, the AEF. Why? Were you in the war?"

Jimbo set the picture back on the mantel and turned to Fred, while forcefully chewing on his pipe. "Yes, I was there under

General Pepelyayev. I assume you were with Kolchak?"

Fred stopped, almost stunned. He sat down, took off his glasses, and set them on the table. "Well, I was under Colonel Styer and William Graves, but Kolchak was certainly trying to help us, even though Graves disliked him. You were under Pepelyayev? Which one? Viktor or Anatoly?"

Jimbo smiled. "Anatoly."

Fred turned in his chair toward Jimbo. "What were you doing, exactly?"

Jimbo, still smiling, answered, "Supplying arms mainly, but also advising. What about you?"

Maria leaned forward, fascinated by the exchange.

Fred cleared his throat. "Well, we were there mainly to guard the railroad and the American property that had been sent over. We were also supposed to help the Czechoslovakians evacuate, but by the time we got there, they didn't need our help anymore. The other foreign forces wanted to actively pursue the Bolsheviks, but General Graves would have none of it. He commented that it wasn't our duty to interfere in the civil war, but that didn't stop anyone from attacking us. Never really knew who the enemy was, but the damn Cossacks were the worst. God, that was a miserable time."

Henry asked. "Why were you rescuing Czechs?"

Jimbo and Fred tried to answer at the same time, but Fred gestured for Jimbo to speak. "Well, the truth of it was that we needed more troops on the Western front, and there were forty thousand Czechs there that could have been used to bolster the front lines in Europe. The guarding of American property was really just a side note. Also, for the U.S. anyway, they didn't want the Japanese invading and taking advantage of the situation. On top of all that, we tried to hold off the Cossacks during all the chaos. That's the official story, anyway . . ."

Esther poked her head into the room. "Time for supper."

As they sat down at the large oak table, Esther passed the freshly made bread. Steam was rising off as Maria tried to take a piece. "Ouch! Oh, I love fresh bread! It's like heaven."

Esther passed her a small churn. Maria looked into the jar. "And homemade butter! You're spoiling us!"

Esther laughed. "It's just nice to have some company! And such good company, I might add."

Fred raised his glass to Jimbo. "True, true!"

Henry took a scoop of mashed potatoes and a scoop of the casserole. "Mmm . . . what's the casserole?"

Fred finished chewing. "It's salmon. Caught it myself."

Jimbo agreed. "It's really good!"

Fred pointed to his wife. "Well, you can thank my lovely bride of twenty years. She is the master cook who takes my killings and turns them into real meals." He turned to Jimbo and Henry. "So, where are you guys heading? Mongolia, did you say?"

Jimbo nodded. "Yeah, we will be providing supplies in the area."

Fred opened his mouth as if to ask for more details, but then he caught the expression on Jimbo's face. "Oh. I see."

Fred and Esther invited them to stay the night. Jimbo slept in the guest room, while Henry and Maria lay on the floor in front of the fire.

Henry lay on his back while the fire lightly crackled. "You

know, we have a pretty good life . . . are you happy living it with me?"

Maria touched his chest while shades of gold light danced around the room. "I love you, and I wouldn't trade our life for anything in the world." She kissed him intensely, and he rolled on his side to face her. His hands slid down her back and into her panties. They heard the floor creak and someone coughed, and she whispered, "Henry, we shouldn't, not in their house. They are so kind to let us stay here."

Henry mock-pouted at her, then nodded. "Yeah, you're right. But I do want you! Badly."

Maria smiled. "Me, too. Me, too. Maybe when we reach Midway. Now, let's go to sleep. It's a long flight tomorrow."

Chapter 6

Midway Island

In the morning, they thanked the couple for their hospitality, and soon they were flying south towards Midway. Henry looked back at Maria. "Have our fix yet?"

Maria looked at her note pad. "Yes, take a heading of 212 degrees. I can't locate the stations from Hawaii or the Pan Am beacon at Midway yet."

Henry adjusted the throttles, trying to dampen out their vibration. "Well, I wouldn't think so at this range."

He looked over at Jimbo. "Want to try your hand at the stick?"

Jimbo sat up straight. "Ah . . . sure. What do I do?"

Henry pointed to the compass. "Okay, we want to keep a heading of 212 degrees. See if you can do it."

Henry let go of his stick and watched. "Whoa, you have to compensate for the crosswind . . . now you are at 225, so turn the other way—whoa! No! Sloooow . . . take it easy, and wait a second for the controls to respond. This is a big bird. She takes a second to respond to your movements."

Jimbo was gripping the wheel tightly with both hands. "Okay . . ."

Henry pointed to his hands. "Loosen your grip—relax. There is nothing up here for us to run into, so don't worry."

Jimbo took in a deep breath. "Okay, okay . . ."

It was six hours later when Maria tapped Henry's shoulder from her post at the navigator's station "I got it! The beacon is at 215 degrees."

Henry glanced back at her. "Great! Then come back up front with me."

Maria hung up her headset, reached over, and pulled the blanket over Jimbo in his bunk, and hopped into the copilot's seat. "How we doing?"

"Pretty good. I think I need to get up, stretch, and maybe go the lavatory."

Maria smiled. "Okay, I'll take over. Oh, open up that basket Fred and Esther gave us and see what we have to eat."

Henry scanned around for the basket. "Good idea!"

As he opened it, he heard Jimbo ask blearily, "Time to eat?"

Henry looked up to see Jimbo sitting up in the bunk. "Yep. Looks like we have salmon casserole, some of that bread, a few hardboiled eggs, some crackers, and strawberries."

Maria yelled back, "Ooh—I'll take some strawberries!"

Henry doled out the food and jumped back into the pilot's seat. He smiled at Maria and gazed out over the ocean. It was a clear, sunny day, with a deep blue ocean below. Henry grabbed his sunglasses to get a better look at the ocean conditions. He could see occasional small whitecaps as he surveyed forward, but it looked pretty calm. "Wow. What a gorgeous day."

Maria, already wearing her green-lensed Anti Glares, looked out and down at the sea. "Yeah. Be a nice day for sailing . . . Hey! A ship."

Henry leaned forward, trying to see. "Oh, looks like a whaler."

She asked. "How can you tell?"

He looked over to see Maria staring at him with a curious smile. He pointed down at the ship. "The whale strapped to the side is a good clue", and winked at her with a smile of his own.

Maria reached over and shook Henry, still in the pilot's seat, awake from his nap. "Henry. We should be getting close."

Henry sat up straight and rubbed his eyes under his sunglasses. "Okay, how long have we been in the air?"

She glanced down at her watch. "Ten hours and forty-five minutes."

Henry quickly looked at his chart. "And we have had a bit of a tail wind, so . . . yeah, we should be. What's the beacon heading?"

Maria turned back to see Jimbo sleeping again. "I'll check. Just a second." She got out of her seat and moved back to the navigator's station. "We are still on course, 216 degrees. It's a strong signal. Let me triangulate using Hawaii." A few minutes later she sat back in her seat. "Well, looks like we are about a hundred eighty-five miles out, as best I can tell."

Henry did a quick calculation on his pad. "One hundred eighty-five miles, at ten thousand feet . . . Okay, we should be able to see it in about twenty minutes."

Maria examined Henry and tilted her sunglasses down. "Well, what should we do for twenty minutes?"

Henry caught the hint and gazed back to see his uncle

still sleeping. He reached up, unsnapped the curtain, and pulled it across.

Maria unbuckled and leaned over the controls, while Henry ran his hand around her neck and slowly released her hair from its pins. As she kissed him, Henry leaned into her. Her hands started at his neck and ran down to his khaki button-down shirt. She undid the first two buttons and felt the hair on his chest.

An air pocket made the plane jolt for a second, and they both glanced down at the controls while maintaining their kiss. They refocused, and Henry's hand slid from her neck to her silk white shirt. He gracefully unbuttoned the first button and ran his hand down inside to feel her soft, milky-white breasts. Another air pocket made them bounce, and Henry's face lit up, but with the sound of Jimbo's cough, they both retreated to their seats. Henry put a manual in his lap while buttoning his shirt back up.

Jimbo opened the curtain. "Hey. Whatcha got the curtain closed for? We almost there?"

Maria, a bit flustered, replied, "Uh, yeah. Less than an hour. Didn't want to disturb you . . . sunlight and all."

Jimbo rubbed his eyes. "Great. I'm going to see if I can find some more food. You kids want something?"

Henry shook his head. "No, thanks. We're fine."

As Jimbo turned to go to the back of the plane, Maria and Henry's eyes met and they tried not to laugh. Henry pointed at her shirt and cleared his throat. She looked down and buttoned back up. As she did, then began pinning her hair back up, she glanced back at him. "I love you."

Henry was watching her straighten out her shirt. "Me, too."

A few minutes later, Maria pointed. "There! Dead ahead."

Henry looked up to see a coral ring in the distance with two brown and green islands. "Yep! That's it! Good thing, too," he added quietly. He pointed at the fuel gauge. "Getting a bit low."

Maria nodded. "Uncle, strap in. We are going to land."

Jimbo returned to the navigator's station, looking forward as he buckled in. "So, that's it, huh?"

Henry nodded. "Yep. We are going to try and land on that one. Sand Island."

As they got closer, Maria pointed again. "Hey. There's the Pan Am dock, and those must be their buildings."

Henry flew over the island and they banked hard to survey the situation. "Well, looks like we can land on that road there. Doesn't seem like they have an official runway."

As they flew over, Maria pointed out her window, "Looks like we've been noticed. People are coming out of the buildings."

They came around once and Henry lined up with the dirt road. "Okay. Hold on, this is going to be a bit rough." He began putting out the flaps in preparation to descend, before he adjusted the throttle in an attempt to get a good glide slope. Henry heard Maria pull her straps tight as he watched the coral zoom by below. He glanced over at her. "Can you keep an eye—"

BAM!

Both Henry and Maria jumped in their seats, yelling, "Shit!" at the same time.

"Henry! What the hell was that?!"

Henry immediately leaned over to peer out Maria's window, as blood and feathers slid up his. "Bird!" He throttled up as his heart began to race, but then pulled it back again.

Maria screeched in a cracking voice, "Henry, there isn't enough room now! Go around!"

Henry growled, "Damn!" and throttled back up.

When they had reached a thousand feet, Henry ordered, "Switch seats! I can't see crap out this side."

After quickly swapping sides, Henry brought the plane back around to try again. He set up his glide slope again and eased her down, hoping he wouldn't hit another bird.

Dust swirled up as they touched down, and Henry's notepad slid onto the floor from the vibration. At the same moment, Maria tried to peer out to check how Henry was doing, but with no luck.

Maria finally let out the breath she had been holding as they came to a stop. She then turned to Henry, who was like a rock, noticing his muscular hand had a death grip on the throttles.

She continued to watch Henry as he taxied over to the buildings and shut down the engines. He was shaking a bit as he went down the checklist, so she put her hand on his. "It's okay. You did good!" Henry closed his eyes, took a deep breath, and let it out. Then he turned and stared at Maria for a moment before smiling.

From outside, they could hear voices and Maria pointed out her window. "A greeting party!"

As they opened the door, people clapped. "We thought you were a goner there for a minute!"

A tall thin man in the crowd came up. "Welcome to Midway. Where you folks coming from?"

Henry shook the man's hand distractedly, but didn't stop as he walked around to the front of the plane. The thin man pointed to the cockpit. "Yep. Damn Gooney birds, always flying into planes here! Especially this time of year."

Henry squinted up at the window, but couldn't see very much. "Do you have a ladder I could use?"

"Sure." The thin man signaled another young man, who took off running.

Henry finally looked at the man. "Oh, I'm sorry. I'm Henry, this is Maria, and the older gentleman is Jimbo. We're coming from the States via Alaska Territory, and heading to Mongolia."

The thin man nodded. "The name's Jim."

The boy Jim had sent for the ladder finally reappeared, and Henry climbed up to inspect the damage. Jim handed him up a mop, and Henry began wiping the nose and the windshield.

Maria watched from below, shading her sunglasses-covered eyes from the bright sun. "How does it look?"

He reached with the mop and pushed some of the bloody mess off the side. A few of the men below jumped backward to avoid being hit. "Well, it looks like it just dented the metal in front of the windshield. Didn't crack the window or anything, so that's good. Have to wash it down before I can really get a good look."

Jim bellowed out, "Get some buckets of water," and men scurried off.

Maria gestured to stop him. "Oh, we don't mean to be any inconvenience!"

Jim laughed. "Hell, those boys haven't had anything to do for weeks. This is an exciting day for them!"

Maria pointed to the buildings. "Are you guys all with Pan Am? Setting things up for the flying boat service?"

Jim responded, "Well, most of us are. Some work for

Commercial Pacific Cable, and there are a few Navy and Marines guys around. We're expecting a flight in October and hoping to have regular service after that, if this mess with Japan doesn't interfere."

That caught Maria's attention. "What mess? Do you think the Japanese would attack here?"

Jim thought for a second. "Well, I don't know about that, but they might interfere with our operations in China."

Henry came back down the ladder with the bloody mop. "I think it's just a dent. Should be fine."

Just then, the men that Jim had sent to get water returned with buckets full. Henry nodded to one of them, grabbed a bucket, climbed back up, and threw it against the windshield. "Hand back up the mop, will ya?" He then wiped it clean, and with another bucket, rinsed it again. The fuselage sparkled in the bright sunlight. "Okay. That should do. I can reach the rest and do a final cleaning from the side windows in the cockpit."

He climbed back down. "You guys have a mess hall or something around here? I'm starving."

Jim chuckled. "Well, actually, we have Gooneyville Lodge almost built. We've been using the kitchen. Got pretty good chow!"

Jimbo spoke up, "Sounds good to me!" and walked over to Jim. "Who do we talk to about fuel?"

Jim thought. "Well, this is Pan Am's fuel. We aren't supposed to sell it to anyone else."

Jimbo asked. "Well, what say the price we were willing to pay was twice what it cost?"

Jim grinned. "Then I would say 'I'm sure something can be arranged.'"

Chapter 7

Guam

In the afternoon of the day they left Wake Island, Maria was staring out over the deep blue ocean. "Hey. There's another island. How are we going to know which one is Guam?"

Henry followed her finger to where she was pointing. "Too small. Guam is the largest island around. When we get there, we'll make a pass and make sure it's the right one. Definitely wouldn't want to land on any of these, since they're Japanese."

Jimbo looked back at the cargo. "Yeah. Let's not do that."

Henry glanced at his watch. "Well, we should be able to see it soon, assuming your last position measurement was correct." Then he watched Maria for a reaction, and grinned as she gave him the evil eye.

A few minutes later Henry nodded in the eleven o'clock direction. "That looks like her."

Maria leaned forward. "Yeah, a lot bigger, and where my measurements say it should be!" She turned and gave him a wolfish look, to which his only response was another acknowledging grin.

As they approached from the north, Jimbo was leaning into the cockpit for a better view. "Well, it seems pretty flat on this end."

Henry nodded. "Yeah, but I don't know if there is any place we can use to land. I am going to take us down the west coast and see if we can't find Pan Am's base."

As they crossed over the northwest tip, they could see a barrier reef that seemed to surround the entire island. Soon, they were overlooking several points with high cliffs. Maria pointed ahead. "There. That harbor they're building. I bet that's it."

Henry responded, "Yeah, I think you're right." He proceeded to bank the plane slightly west and they flew towards the long jutting bars of dirt and sand that were obviously man-made. Henry came in low and banked again so they could get a good view. "That must be the village of Sumay . . . yeah, there's the clipper dock. And take a gander over there. That huge flat area. What is that?"

Maria looked at the maps as they flew a few hundred feet over the village and Pan Am's hangar. "Well, according to this map, that's the old naval station, but I think it's abandoned now."

Henry pulled up over the ocean, and they came around for another pass. As he flew in from the west, they could see the Pan Am's hotel, numerous thatched-roof houses, and a Spanish-style church. After that, there was a patch of deep green palm trees, and then a cleared area of land with what appeared to be housing and a big complex at one end. As they flew along the ground, Maria was watching out the side window at the terrain. "Yes, Henry, I think this will do."

Henry pulled up as trees approached on the far side. "Great; Jimbo, get strapped in, and we'll see if we can't land this thing." He banked the plane again, and headed south for a couple of minutes. He then pitched around as he approached the southern mountains and aligned with the grassy area. "Full flaps. Everyone ready?"

Both Maria and Jimbo responded in the affirmative and Henry started his approach. They crossed over palm trees at the south end of the clearing and Henry pulled the throttle. As the plane dropped, he pulled back on the yoke to a near stall, and gently touched down in the grass. The plane shook and shuddered as the landing gear dug in a bit and absorbed the impacts of the rough terrain. Maria was pushed against her restraints as Henry not only used the brakes, but also changed the pitch of the props to slow them as quickly as he could.

Jimbo startled in his seat as one of the bands on the cargo banged loudly under the strain. It seemed like a long landing, but in reality, it had only lasted for a few seconds. As Henry began his shutdown procedures, two men in pith helmets approached. Maria was watching them as they approached. "Um . . . I think they are upset."

The men moved around the back of the plane as Henry shut the engines down. Jimbo opened the door. "Afternoon gentle—"

"Who are you? And by whose authority did you land?!"

Jimbo put up his hands. "I'm sorry, is this some kind of restricted field?"

"Yes! This is the Guam Marine Barracks!"

Just then, Maria stepped out of the door. "Sorry, gentlemen, I just couldn't find any other place to land."

Both men, a little stunned by a beautiful female aviator, choked a bit. In a quieter voice, the taller one said, "Well, what's your business here?"

She walked up to them while removing her aviator helmet and gloves, which she had only just put on before getting out of the plane. She shook her head and let her hair loose. "We just need some food and fuel, and we'll be gone in the morning."

Henry, hearing the change in their demeanor when Maria

walked out, decided to stay in the plane.

The short one nudged the tall marine, who responded, "Well, I will have to check on that . . ."

Maria, with flirting eyes asked, "Well, in the meantime, where can a girl get a drink around here?"

The shorter one pointed towards the town. "The Pan Am hotel is really nice."

The taller one gave his companion a look and then focused back on Maria. "Right. We will go see about the permission." Both of them then walked off in the direction of the officer's quarters.

When they were out of sight, Henry stepped out. "Nice job!"

Maria turned to him quickly, letting her long hair swing around. In a tantalizing voice, she asked, "Do you really think so, big boy?"

Jimbo cleared his throat. "Um . . . I'll go see the officers about permission and get fuel arranged."

As Jimbo walked away, both Maria and Henry started laughing so hard they had a difficult time standing.

Once they caught their breath, Henry sealed up the plane. "Let's go have that drink."

They walked through the palm trees and down a row of thatched houses they had seen from the air. The locals watched curiously as they walked by, and Maria waved at a few of the kids. Some waved back, but most ran back to their parents.

They finally came upon a building that said "Pan American Airways" above the door. In front were a mixture of the local Chamorro islanders, Marines, and foreigners. One of the foreigners, an older fellow with a thick black mustache, spoke up. "You two in that plane that nearly took off the roof?"

Maria smiled, but Henry maintained his composure.

The man stuck out his hand. "Name's Braddock. That was bloody brilliant! Woke us right up!"

Henry shook his hand. "I'm Henry, and this is Maria. We're coming in from the—"

Maria interrupted. "How did you guess it was us?"

Other people started to gather around. Braddock pointed. "This lot, seen them every day for ever, but you two are new! Coincidence?"

Maria thought for a second. "Right . . . hey . . . well then, what do they have to drink around here?"

Braddock pointed to the bar with a cigar in his hand. "We've got everything you need." He put the cigar in his mouth and used his hands to direct the way. "What's your poison?"

A crowd began to form around them as they made their way up to the bar, but Henry was able to squeeze his way up to the bar's edge. "One beer and a . . . ginger ale if you have it, please."

The bartender responded "Where you from?" This made the crowd press in further with curiosity on their faces. Henry looked around at everyone and sat on a stool that suddenly opened up. The bartender handed him his beer and he replied, "Well, a little bit of everywhere . . ."

Maria and Henry entertained everyone with their tales of adventure, until, eventually, Henry happened to glance over and see Jimbo standing at the door with his empty pipe in his mouth.

Henry pushed through the crowd. "Uncle Jimbo!"

The older man saw him coming, smiled, and raised his pipe. "Well, Henry, seems like you guys got the locals eating out of the palm of your hand."

Henry laughed. "Yeah. Just telling tall tales. Care for a drink? Oh, wait. What's happening with the plane?"

Jimbo took a step out the door and pointed with his pipe to a fuel truck that was driving by.

Henry shook his head. "And the Marines?"

Jimbo nodded. "No problem. That's taken care of. Yes, to the drink. Don't suppose they have any Forty-Three here."

Henry put his arm around his uncle as they turned to walk back into the bar. "How the hell do you get these things done?"

As the sun set, Jimbo went to his room to pass out, while Henry grabbed Maria's hand and took her down to the beach. They cuddled on the sand with a half a bottle of wine, and watched the sun distort as it slipped into the sea. As the orange light faded, Henry scanned around the sky. "It's nearly a full moon tonight. Want to go to the east side of the island and watch it rise?" He took a drink from the bottle, before she slapped him on the stomach, causing him to choke on his sip.

"I thought you didn't drink dear."

He wiped his face "Well, this is romance. It's different."

She chuckled and gazed up at the sky. "But that's gotta be five miles. How are we going to get over there?"

Henry pointed back towards the bar. "I saw a couple of bicycles we could borrow."

She whispered, "You mean, just take them?"

Henry got up, quickly wiped sand off his behind, and grabbed her hand. "Sure! Come on!"

They ran down the beach and back up to the hotel. As they

stumbled around the corner into the light, a drunk man spotted them and raised a beer in salute. "Even-ninn' . . . you twos."

As he walked by, Maria giggled, only a little more sober than he was, and pulled Henry to keep going. They walked as upright as they could and tried to act normal as they crossed in front of the hotel. Struggling to hold their laughter, they headed to the far corner where the bicycles were. Henry turned to see if anyone was watching; then he whispered, "Let's go!"

Maria grabbed the bike with the basket on it and quietly set the wine bottle in it. As she started to push it, a bump made the bell ding. She stopped and looked around, but no one noticed. Maria hopped on the bicycle and tried to ride, but couldn't help but laugh. She began weaving all over the road and bumped into Henry, who tried to hold her up without losing his own balance.

Eventually, they stabilized and rode off down the road together.

Once they were clear of the town, they both let out their laughter and Maria yelled joyfully into the darkness.

It took a half-hour to reach the eastern shore of the island. As they made their way down to the beach, the horizon grew bright.

Maria found the perfect spot and loudly whispered, "Over here." She set the bottle in the sand, took off her shoes, and pulled Henry down as he got close. Henry lay on his back after planting his bare feet in the sand, and Maria laid her head on his stomach. They listened to the crashing of the waves and watched as the moon rose from the east. The big red orb was distorted, but as it rose it lightened to peach, then finally became a bright white ball that looked as large as a house.

"Henry, look how huge it is!"

Henry stuck his finger in front of the moon. "You know that's just an illusion. It's always the same size as the end of my pinky finger."

She smacked his stomach. "I'm trying to be romantic here!"

Maria's head bobbed on his stomach as Henry laughed. "I know. Come here." He pulled her up to him, peered into her partially moonlit face, and kissed her softly.

She ran her hand over his face and down his neck, and began to unbutton his shirt. "Henry . . . let's go skinny dipping."

Henry pulled his head back slightly and admired her. Her right eye was twinkling from the moonlight and its sparkle captivated him. "Sure!" He began quickly unbuttoning her shirt, while she tried to finish his. Henry reached around her back to undo her bra, but Maria kissed him with all her weight behind it. Henry, lost in the kiss, ran his hands down to her beige slacks. He rounded the curve of her and pulled her body in closer.

When they came up for air, Maria backed up to pull off Henry's pants. As she tugged them down, she fell forward onto Henry, who leaned forward to meet her. They both stood up together, kissing as they rose.

Henry ran his hands down her chest and bare stomach to the button that held her pants, but the wine had gone to his head just as badly as hers, and as Henry unbuttoned her, he lost his balance and stumbled. His pants, which were now around his ankles, prevented him from recovering. Maria, in a laughing yell, tried to slow his fall, but Henry landed on his back in the soft sand, and Maria fell square on top of him.

"Oopsie!" Henry looked up at her and they started giggling

like a pair of loons, laughing so hard they couldn't catch their breath.

Henry was still trying to recover when Maria reached down, giggling, "Let's get these pants off your ankles."

He grinned and took a deep breath before turning her. "And I'll take off this obstacle."

Maria turned back to face him and her bra slid down her arms into the sand. Her face was brightly lit by the rising moon, and her breasts and Henry's hand, which was coming up to meet them, all cast shadows on her soft belly. Henry ran his hand over her silky breast, stimulating her pert nipple and causing Maria to sigh in pleasure.

She pulled away from him with obvious reluctance, then stood up and let her pants drop. Henry growled at the sight, "Come here," as he jumped up and wrapped his hands around and dragged them down her back. They each lost their underpants to the other's wandering hands in the same instant.

Maria kissed him for a moment longer, but then turned and pulled Henry to his feet, leading him by the hand toward the ocean.

When she got to the water, Henry felt her fearlessness fade as she pulled him close. He enjoyed her clinging warmth as they both waded in together. "Are you scared?"

Maria shook her head. "Not as long as you're holding me."

They continued to move further out, and just as they were waist deep, a wave crashed over them and Maria let out a little scream. Henry squeezed her tight and held her close. Her chest pressed against his, and she wrapped her legs around his body and pulled herself even closer.

She stared up into his brightly lit face. "I love you."

He smiled and caressed her face with wet hands, feeling the calluses on his palms scrape gently across her cheeks. Maria closed her eyes, kissing his neck before working her way down to his chest. Henry gasped for breath at the sudden tug as she reached down to help him inside her. He let his feet sink into the sand to stabilize them; then, like the warm waves smacking their bodies, he and Maria allowed the passion to build and crash over them in waves that crested higher and higher.

When they finished, light-headed with drink and the strength of their pleasure, they let the tide push them to the beach and lay in the sand, gazing contentedly for a time at each other's glistening bodies.

As the moon continued to rise, the Milky Way began to fade, but it was still visible as Henry rolled on his back to feast his eyes on its wondrous depths. Maria cuddled up next to him and placed her hand on his chest, as she too stared out into the blackness of space. "What did you say earlier about our kids living out there?"

Henry looked over at her, amazed that she remembered. "Well, I was talking about our grandkids . . ." He pointed up. "I bet they will get to go out there, live on moon or the surface of Jupiter or fly in the clouds of Venus."

She squeezed him tightly. "Can you imagine? What a frontier that would be!"

As Henry and Maria rounded the corner to the Pan Am hotel, Henry whispered, "Stop!"

He could see a man with a white helmet and three other people standing where the bicycles had been. "Is that an MP?"

Maria started to giggle. "Uh-oh, guess we're in trouble."

Henry put his finger against his lips and pointed back the way they had come. "Let's leave the bicycles here and head down to the beach. We can come back up from there as though nothing is wrong."

Maria smiled and grabbed the now-empty wine bottle. "Brilliant."

Henry stopped. "Just a second. Let me throw in a five-spot." He took a couple steps back up the embankment, tucked a five-dollar bill into the basket, then they slid back down towards the beach.

A few minutes later, they appeared at the other side of the hotel. The MP looked up with suspicion, but Henry couldn't help but smile. The locals hadn't noticed him, so Henry pointed down the road, trying not to laugh again.

The MP looked in the direction he was pointing, aiming his flashlight, and spotted the obvious glint from metal and reflectors on the bikes' frames. He quickly glanced back, but Maria and Henry were already gone.

As Henry shut the door to their room, they both bent over laughing. Henry fell onto the bed, while Maria tried to wipe the sand off him. He pulled her on top of him. "Forget the sand . . . who cares! I love you!"

Chapter 8

Moving On

In the morning, a knock came at the door. Henry awoke with a slight headache; he tried to sit up, but his hand was stuck under a dresser. Bemused and sleepy, he stopped to take a look around the room. Maria was still asleep on the bed, but he was on the floor with half the sheet wrapped around his left leg. "Umm . . . just a minute!"

As he stumbled to his feet, Maria awoke and pulled the remaining covers over herself. Her voice cracked as she mumbled, "Morning . . . who is it?"

Henry found his pants and stumbled around as he tried to put them on. "I don't know." In a louder voice he asked, "Jimbo, is that you?"

Jimbo replied through the door, "Yes. We should probably get going."

Henry looked around for his pocket watch. "What time is it?"

"It's 7:30."

Henry fell onto the bed, frustrated at his left pant leg. "Okay, we'll be down in a few minutes."

Jimbo's voice, muffled by the door, sounded fondly exasperated. "Sure, I'll order us up some breakfast."

When Henry and Maria walked into the Pan Am cafe, twenty minutes later, Jimbo was sitting at a table next to a window chewing on his pipe, while he caressed a cup of coffee. He watched them as they approached. "You two look like hell. Where did you go last night?"

Henry pulled a chair out for Maria. "Thanks. I feel like it, too. We just went to the other side of the island."

Jimbo pulled his pipe from his mouth and pointed it east. "The other side of the island? Good God, how long did that take . . . and why?"

Henry leaned over after sitting down. "Well, we did appropriate some transportation."

Maria's face grew a huge grin. "Yeah, we couldn't miss the full moonrise!"

As Jimbo was considering the pair of them, the waitress set down two plates of pancakes and eggs in front of Maria and Henry.

Maria looked at it and up at the waitress. "Do you have any chocolate?" The waitress, with a confused look, shook her head. Maria tried again. "How about peanut butter?"

The waitress nodded. "Sure. Anything else?"

Jimbo shook his head with a slight grin of amusement.

Henry pulled out some charts that he had brought down from the room, as Maria scooped peanut butter onto her pancakes. He got up, pulled a nearby table over, and spread them out. "Well, I think we have a problem here."

Jimbo took his eyes off Maria's peanut buttered pancakes and squinted at Henry's chart. "What do you mean?"

Henry pointed to the tiny dot of Guam, and then to Mongolia. "We can't make the distance. It's just too far."

Jimbo pulled the pipe from his mouth and leaned forward.

"I thought we would have a three-thousand-mile range with the added fuel tanks."

Henry shook his head. "No. If we were flying completely empty, yes, but with the cargo, no. My preliminary thought was that we could get twenty-five hundred safely with what we are carrying, but during the flight from Naknek to Midway, which was 2,350 miles, we landed on fumes . . . and we had a tailwind then. There is just no way we can safely make it. We would most likely end up crashing or ditching in eastern China if we tried."

Jimbo sat back thinking. "Well, where can we go?"

Henry pointed to the Philippines. "We could make it to Manila, and that would be close enough for us to manage a final leg to Mongolia. Heck, it's practically America, right?"

Jimbo nodded slightly. "Yes; well, technically they are their own country now, but I suppose in reality you're right."

Maria swallowed. "Uncle. What are you worried about? The cargo being found?"

Jimbo sat forward again. "Yes. Well, this is a legal gray area. It's not really illegal, but we just don't want any complications. The Philippines should be all right, but we just can't land anywhere that the cargo, or we, would be considered illegal or hostile."

Henry nodded. "Well, yeah, that makes sense. Let's definitely not do that."

Maria, with her mouth full of pancake, interrupted with, "Well, unless we are getting paid a shitload of money."

Both Henry and Jimbo, surprised by her response, peered at her with raised eyebrows. She gave them back a huge smile, before returning to eating.

An hour later, they were back in the Marine barracks' field

with their plane. Henry was doing his external preflight check when two men walked up to Jimbo and one saluted. Jimbo saluted back, and they stepped off to talk.

Maria came up to Henry. "What's the lowdown on your uncle? Is he a general or something? How does he get everyone to salute and do things for him?"

Henry smiled as he checked the port flap assembly. "No, he is a colonel, I think. The man he's talking to is Colonel Randall. He's the CO of this place and, um," Henry stopped for a second, studied the men and went on, "that's acting-Sergeant James, I think." Henry went back to checking the wing pins, while Maria, with her hand on her chin, watched his uncle with curiosity.

A few minutes later, Maria glanced over to see Henry just standing there looking back and forth. She walked over to him. "What's up?"

Henry took a few steps back while looking at the horizon. "Well, I am a little concerned about those trees over there. We came in full flaps and I had to reverse the props, so I know it's tight, but I am a little worried."

Maria turned and considered the palm trees on the other end of the field. "Hmm. Do you think we need to dump some fuel or something?"

Henry looked the other way. "I think we can make it . . ." He put his hand into the air. "The wind is out of the south, so that will help. We will have to taxi over near the barracks to get the longest stretch."

Surprising both Henry and Maria, Jimbo spoke up from behind them. "What's the problem?"

Henry turned to see his uncle with the two officers. After

the introductions were made, Henry explained, "Just worried about the trees down there and the distance we have." He eyed the CO and then pointed to the barracks. "We will have to taxi close to the barracks and go from there. At least we have favorable winds."

Colonel Randall looked at the barracks and back toward the trees. "That looks a bit tight, but do what you have to." He turned and shook Jimbo's hand one final time. "Good luck! If you're back this way again, stop in for a drink."

Jimbo grinned. "Thank you for your hospitality!" Then he winked at Henry. "Well, let's see if we can't get out of here in one piece."

Ten minutes later, Henry yelled, "Clear prop!" and started the right engine. After he checked it, he started the left and began to taxi towards the barracks. As they got closer, men poured out to watch.

Henry swung the plane around and locked the tail-wheel. He set the flaps to 40 degrees and stared forward to the trees, then over at Maria. She smiled at him, buckled herself in, and gave him the thumbs up. Henry nodded and ran the engines to maximum power while holding the brakes. The plane shook and started to slip on the grass, so he let the brakes go. Henry and Maria were pushed back in their seats as they accelerated across the field. Henry glanced constantly back and forth between the airspeed indicator and the trees. Out of the corner of his eye, he saw Maria put her hands on the dash as the trees got closer. As the indicator hit "80", Henry began to rotate her.

Maria yelled, "HENRY!" as the left engine clipped the tips of a palm. A loud grinding sound came from the engine, but within seconds they were up in the sky over the ocean.

Henry, his grip starting to loosen, gave Maria a sidelong glance. "What?"

She stared back him with her eyes wide and her mouth open, as though she wanted to say something, and Henry just smiled.

As they climbed out, Henry pulled in the flaps and throttled back. His uncle cleared his throat and looked around from the navigator's seat. "Wow! That was really somethin'!"

Henry turned to him with big grin. "Yeah! Sure was!" He glanced over at Maria, who still hadn't said anything, then his gaze returned forward over the vast unending blue ocean. After a moment, he pointed to the south. "You know, just out there is the deepest place ever found . . . read about the Challenger expedition while we were stationed in Antartica"

Maria finally said in a loud voice, "Henry!"

He looked at her again, "What?" but she just gave him a bewildered look.

Jimbo strained to see ahead. "Looks just like more ocean to me."

Henry shook his head before he adjusted his headset and slouched into his seat, as nonchalant as could be . . . but he did take sideways glances at the left engine, just to make sure.

Chapter 9

The Phillipines

In the afternoon, Maria came forward with a sandwich and some fruit. She handed them to Henry, who nodded and thanked her.

"Henry, you getting tired?"

He took a bite of the sandwich. "Getting a little tired. Someone did keep me up all night last night!" and he winked at her.

Maria rolled her eyes with a smile and grabbed the yoke. "Why don't you take a nap and let me fly for a while?"

Henry nodded and unbuckled his harness. He put his hand on her shoulder as he got up, and smiled at her. As he was turning to head back, the harmonic drone of the engines skipped a beat. Henry immediately turned and sat back down, then it happened again. Maria, with an innocent, but fearful expression, asserted, "It wasn't me. I didn't do anything yet."

Henry glanced over the instruments as he buckled back in. "Everything appears fine; well, according to the instruments." He scanned out over the left wing as the gaps in sound came once more. Then he glanced back at Maria. "I think we have a misfiring cylinder," he said, grabbing the throttle knobs. "Let me try changing the RPMs." As Henry throttled up, the sound became more frequent and the cockpit began to vibrate, so he throttled down. "Okay, hmm . . . let me take her down under ten thousand feet.

Maybe it's the magnetos." A minute later, when he had brought them down to eight thousand, the roughness became less frequent.

Maria tapped the oil instruments, but they didn't move. "So what do you think it is?"

Henry eyed the oil pressure gauge she had been tapping on. "Oil pressure is a little low. Well, going to low altitude helped, so I would suspect an ignition leak . . . maybe a cracked distributor cap? But the drop in oil pressure would indicate something else."

Jimbo, who was listening in, asked "Will we make it?"

Henry turned back at him reassuringly. "Oh, yeah. Not a problem. Even if we lose that engine, we can still make it. Remember? That's why you picked this plane."

Jimbo nodded. "Oh, yes . . . good point."

An hour later, Henry was still in the cockpit and Maria at the navigator's station. She pointed ahead excitedly. "Land!"

Henry leaned forward, and through a few broken clouds, he saw it too. He smiled at her. "Good. Now we just have to find Manila."

She pointed forward. "Just maintain a heading of 275."

Five minutes later, Henry pointed out his left window. "I think that's it."

Jimbo peered out the window. "Yes, that's it on the water. The airport is south of the city."

Henry stretched his neck, scanning for an airfield. After a minute, he pointed. "There. That clearing with the four buildings."

Jimbo asked. "How do you know?"

Henry smiled. "'Cause the second building says 'Nichols Field' right on it!"

Jimbo looked harder. "Oh, so it does!"

Henry set the flaps as he came out over the ocean and turned south for his final approach. As he throttled down, the left engine started misfiring again and the plane began to shake. Henry glanced back at Jimbo to reassure him again. "It's okay. It will be fine." Jimbo quickly nodded back.

Henry kept one eye on the engine as he made his approach, but landed her without incident. Once down, he taxied over to the last hangar, which had several planes parked outside.

He shut down the engines with a sigh. "Well, here we are. Now let's see if we can't find out what the problem with engine is."

Nichols Field was a very quiet airport, at least at this time of the day. As Henry exited the plane, only one man came out to them, while another watched from a distance. The man was thin, with short salt and pepper hair and a mixed Caucasian-Filipino appearance to him. "Afternoon. You staying for a while?"

Henry noticed the oily rag in his pocket and shook his hand. "Well, we weren't planning on it, but," he pointed up to the left engine, "we have a drop in oil pressure and she is running rough."

The man was peering up at the engine when Maria, after hopping down out of the plane, walked over and stuck her hand out. "Hi. I'm Maria Elliot."

The man unglued his gaze from the engine to look at her. "Oh, I'm sorry, the name's Kidlat, but most just call me Kid."

Maria smiled at that. "Well, Kid, it's good to meet you. Seems like you might be a mechanic by the way you stare at that engine."

Kid laughed and took another gander at the engine. "Yes,

this is one of the new 1820s, right?"

Henry looked at him with surprise. "Right. Have you worked on these before?"

Kid shook his head, but pointed to Hangar Three. "The B3A—well it's technically a B5, over in that hangar—has the 1750s. Worked on them a lot."

Henry squinted and tried to see over to the other hangar. He could make out the vague outline of a large, twin-engine biplane inside.

Kid continued. "I'll take a peek at her, if you like. We'll have to tow her into the end hangar. You're lucky. I don't have much else going on today." He smiled and reached up to feel the prop.

Jimbo nodded. "Sure, let's get her fixed—"

Henry interrupted. "I think she's been running a bit rich too. We've been using more fuel than I expected."

Kid nodded as he considered. "Okay. We'll have a look. There is a nice hotel near the sea that you can stay at in the meantime."

Henry glanced at Maria and back. "That sounds good." He reached out his hand. "Oh, and the name's Henry. I think we will go get some food, maybe take a nap, and come back later."

Kid shook Henry's hand. "I'll get someone to take you there and get to work—"

Jimbo interrupted, "Do you know of a good restaurant? I really need to get a real meal."

Kid, having turned to walk back to the hangar, turned back towards Jimbo. "Sure. There is the new restaurant, called The Aristocrat. I have heard it's really good."

Jimbo smiled while pulling out his pipe. "Excellent. Thank you."

Kid paused a second, glancing at Jimbo as if checking he was really finished, and then walked off towards the hangar.

An hour later, the three of them were sitting at the restaurant eating. Maria spread chocolate sauce on her honey-cured chicken and pointed to Jimbo's plate. "How's the pork?"

Jimbo looked up while licking his finger. "Really good. How's your, um, chocolate-covered chicken?"

She nodded enthusiastically as she finished chewing a bite. "Mmm, fantastic!"

Jimbo's wrinkles showed as he grinned. "So, Henry, do you think we can leave soon?"

Henry cocked his head. "Why? The food is delicious, and it's—oh, wait. You mean, leave the country?"

Jimbo laughed. "Yes, I don't mean leave here; no, no, I like this place. I meant go to Mongolia."

Henry wiped his face with a white cloth napkin. "If they're able to fix it, we can leave tomorrow, but I don't even know exactly where we are going."

Jimbo took a bite of pork. "Yes, I will find out now. Let me make a phone call." He signaled a waiter. "Excuse me. Telephone?" The waiter pointed to a corner of the restaurant. Jimbo stood up, wiped his face and set the napkin in his chair. "Be back in a few minutes. Enjoy."

As Jimbo walked away, Maria spoke up. "He always laughs at the way I eat."

Henry was watching Jimbo walk away and thinking about the flight when Maria's comment registered. He turned to her slowly, reluctant to bring it up. "Well . . ." His head tipped to indicate her chocolate-covered chicken.

Her eyes turned to a glare. "'Well', what?"

Henry laughed, but then tried to hold it back, knowing he was on thin ice. "You are an odd duck, especially when it comes to eating."

She pointed the knife at him. "I am not!"

He backed up in his chair and underhandedly tickled her hip. "Yes, you are!"

Maria moved to stop him, but realized she was still holding the knife and instinctively stood up to avoid stabbing him. The restaurant became quiet. She glanced around at everyone, knife still in hand, and slowly sat back down.

Henry whispered. "Yes, you are."

Maria went back to eating, giving him a dirty look with each bite.

Henry, meanwhile, just tried not to smile.

Eventually Jimbo came back, his empty pipe in his mouth. "Okay. Everything is arranged. Here are the coordinates." He laid a scrap of paper in front of Henry.

Henry picked it up and studied the numbers. "Well, is this an airfield, or are we just landing some random place?"

Jimbo sat down and placed his napkin in his lap. "It's one of our bases in Mongolia. They will have food, fuel, and a place for us to stay."

Henry took a sip of coffee. "When did you tell them we would be arriving?"

Jimbo set his pipe down and picked up his glass of Forty-Three. "I just told them to expect us within the next week." He took a sip. "Oh, that's fine! There are definitely benefits to stopping in the Philippines."

Henry cocked his head a bit. "Are they just going to sit and wait for us?"

Jimbo nodded. "I pay them well enough. Most of them are nomadic anyway. They'll just set up their ghers and wait."

Henry nodded in acceptance, but Maria asked, "What's a gher?"

Jimbo glanced over at her. "The Russians call it a yurt. It's a big round tent, but the fabric lays over a latticed frame instead of just a couple of poles. They even have a chimney hole in the roof."

She replied with curiosity in her voice, while tipping her head in thought, "Oh, I see."

A couple of hours later, Henry and Maria had a taxi take them back to the airfield. After he paid the driver, they stepped out into the darkness and began to walk to the last hangar. Flashes of light from Hangar Three caught their attention. Henry watched with interest, seeing the B5 lit up inside and two men doing metalwork. Showers of hot sparks flew into the darkness as they worked.

He turned and began to walk towards the beautiful sight, but before he knew it, two men were standing next to him. "Sorry, sir, this area is off limits!"

Henry jumped. "Oh, sorry. It was just so beautiful I wanted to have a closer look."

Maria, who had walked off, turned at the exchange.

The men stood in front of Henry. "Sorry, you can't go beyond this point. What's your business here?"

Henry considered the young Americans, then pointed to the

last hangar. "I flew in earlier tonight. Engine trouble. Just checking in to see the progress."

The men glanced over at the hangar he was pointing at and then back at him without saying a word.

Maria finally came over and in a quiet voice, said, "Come on, Henry. They must have private cargo as well."

Henry took one last look past the guards at the large bi-winged beauty and then turned back towards his hangar. "Cheerio."

They walked around to the open side of the hangar, and there inside was their own beauty. The polished metal of the fuselage sparkled from the bright ceiling lights. Henry's gaze followed her line down to the left wing and saw that all the cowlings had been removed. A bare, nine-cylinder radial engine hung exposed from the wing, but one of the cylinders was missing.

A voice echoed across the hangar. "Hi, Henry! Maria!" Henry could see Kid sitting at a table with the missing cylinder head.

Maria waved and walked towards Kid, while Henry took a close look at the naked radial, as he ducked under the wing. "So, you found the problem?" he asked.

Kid stood up and walked over. He gave a nod and smile to Maria before answering. "Yeah. A couple of problems. You been flying at high altitude a lot?"

Henry locked eyes with Kid. "Yeah, a bit."

Kid reached up and pulled a piece of palm leaf out of the engine. "And low altitude?"

Maria nudged Henry with a mock-scowl. Henry, slightly annoyed, glanced at her and then back at Kid. "Ah . . . well, yeah.

A tree or two may have gotten in the way."

Kid smiled and shook his head slightly. "Well, I had to replace one of the magnetos and the plugs on cylinder seven. The cylinder ring was also leaking oil. I'll have to hone out the cylinder a bit to fit the spare ring I have. The oil was fouling up the spark plugs, but in addition, the magneto was shorting to the engine block."

Maria, with a slight grin, asked. "Those trees that 'got in the way' wouldn't have anything to do with this, would they?"

Henry put up his hands, and an "It's not my fault" expression appeared on his face. Kid laughed. "Nah! I just found those bits of palm tree in the cowling and the green stains on the prop. It didn't really do anything. The magneto problem could have been caused by altitude and icing, but the ring issue, I don't know. Maybe you just got a bad fit from the get-go."

Henry stared up at the engine. "How did you diagnose it so fast?"

Kid smiled and walked in front of the engine. "Well, the oil temp was rising without the cylinder head changing temperature, plus like I said, there was the oil fouling the plugs."

Maria peered inside the engine through the missing cylinder. "So, how long will this take to fix?"

Kid wiped his hand with his pocket rag. "Tomorrow afternoon, maybe."

Henry gaped at him with disbelief. "Really? Wow, you're good. Want to come work for us?"

Kid, at first taken aback by the question, shook his head. "No, sorry, I have a family here, and I have a three-year contract. But, thank you for the offer."

Henry smiled. "Nah, it's okay. Didn't think you would say yes anyway."

Maria asked Kid, "It's getting late; what time do you usually work till?"

Kid glanced at his watch. "It's okay. I like to work at night. My mind is clearer and there aren't so many distractions. I'll see if I can get this finished up before I go to bed, or at least get close."

Henry stuck out his hand. "Well, we'll let you get back to it. Thank you! Oh, and when you close down for the night, can you make sure the plane is secure? Don't want anyone messing with anything."

Kid nodded. "Sure. Sure. No problem at all!"

Maria pointed to the phone on the desk. "What's your number? And what time do you think we should come by tomorrow?"

Kid grabbed a small piece of paper and wrote the number on it. "Here you are. So, say about three o'clock?"

Henry nodded and caught Maria's eye. "You want to walk back to the hotel? It's a nice night out."

Maria cocked her head and shook it slightly. "Hmm . . . no. I am pretty tired, dear."

Henry glanced back at Kid. "Mind if we use the phone to call the cab back?"

Kid turned, grabbed a set of keys off a wall rack and pointed to a truck on the far side of the hangar. "Here. Just borrow the truck. You can bring it back tomorrow."

Maria clasped Kid's hand between hers. "Thank you, Kid. You've been so kind and helpful."

He touched his cap and nodded. "Oh, it's my pleasure."

Henry and Maria walked around the plane, but Henry stopped for a second to peek in on the cargo through the open door. He glanced at Maria and gave a slight nod. They then went around the tail, to the old black Model-AA truck against the far wall. It took a few seconds to start her, and blue and black smoke poured out the tailpipe. Henry put it into first and slowly released the clutch. The truck started with a lurch and almost stalled, but he hit the gas and they were off. Henry waved to Kid as they drove off into the darkness for their hotel.

Chapter 10

The Last Leg

Henry awoke to a gust of warm, salty breeze across his face. He opened his eyes, squinting a bit, to see Maria opening the window. The translucent curtains were blowing inwards and she was reaching up trying to pull them closed. Her shirt climbed her back, revealing her beautifully curved behind. Henry whistled.

Startled, Maria turned, grabbed a pillow off the chair, and threw it at him.

Henry instantly jumped up, grabbed her, and threw her playfully onto the bed. He kissed her as her head sank into a pillow. "Good morning, my beautiful bride! What a nice ass you have this morning!"

She gazed up into his dark brown eyes and then down. "Morning, Captain Standish . . . what a beautiful hard-on you have this morning!"

Henry smiled wide and replied. "Well, beauty is born of beauty."

She started to laugh, but he kissed her, and her laugh became a deep sigh of passion. They stared into each other's eyes as they made love. They could both feel the tender sweetness and contentment of being together that morning.

Afterward, they lay naked on the bed while the ocean

breeze blew across their sweat-slicked bodies. Maria rolled on her side, put her hand on Henry's chest, and kissed his cheek softly. "I love you."

Henry turned his head towards her. "I love you, too." He turned on his side and they kissed again. Then came a knock came at the door, and they both stopped to listen. "Morning, you two."

Maria pulled the covers over them and spoke up. "Morning, Uncle. We will be out in a little bit. Let's meet for breakfast at the coffee shop around the corner, okay?"

Jimbo replied, his voice muffled through the door. "Sure. Sure. I'll go grab a paper and see you over there."

Maria hopped out of bed. "Come on. Let's take a shower," she said, and ran into the bathroom, but peeked back around the door, "together. Maybe we can go again?" She winked and disappeared behind the door.

She heard the smile in Henry's voice as he jumped out of bed. "What do you think I am? Superman?"

She pulled him into the hot shower. "No, you're not *the* Superman, you're *my* superman."

Finally reaching the cafe, Henry opened the door, releasing a cacophony of cigarette smoke, burned sausage, and rice. Maria stepped in to find Jimbo sitting in a booth in the far corner, but Henry stopped before getting to the table and asked a waitress, "Bathroom?"

An empty plate with nothing but crumbs lay in front of Jimbo's open paper. Maria plopped down beside him as she watch Henry disappear around the far end of a long counter. "Morning, Uncle!"

Jimbo lowered the paper. He stared at her with a pained

expression while chewing on his pipe. "Morning, dear."

Maria's expression changed to worry. "What's wrong?" she whispered.

Jimbo closed the paper and set it down. "Oh, it's just—well, nothing . . ."

Maria put her hand on his arm. "Tell me."

Jimbo took in a breath, "You see that waitress at the end of the bar?" and he pointed with his pipe.

Maria's eyes followed his pipe. "Yes, the one with the green apron?"

Jimbo nodded.

Maria pushed for more. "Yes, she is beautiful. Is that what you mean?"

Jimbo shook his head. "No. Well, yes, she is, but . . . she looks like Zhanna." He paused. "Or maybe it's her movements . . . I don't know. She just reminds me of her. I used to see Zhanna everywhere, but now it's rare . . ." Jimbo looked up and blinked his eyes as a tear made its way onto his cheek "Dammit—it's been fifteen years, and it still—"

Maria tightened her grip on his arm. "It's okay to let it out. You shouldn't be ashamed."

Jimbo slammed his fist on the table and his coffee cup jumped. "Dammit! No!"

The cafe got quiet and everyone began to stare. Jimbo whispered. "I am a man. I won't let a moment of weakness get the best of me!"

Maria glanced up to see Henry, standing there with a wide-eyed expression. She gestured for him to sit and turned her attention back to Jimbo. "Do you want to go? Come on, let's get out of here."

Jimbo regained his composure. "No . . . no, I'm sorry. You two need your breakfast. I'll be fine." He feigned a smile and bit hard on his pipe.

Maria saw by his expression that she should stop. "Okay." She raised her hand for a waitress.

⅄⅄⅄

Thirty minutes later, Maria dipped her last piece of banana pancake into her hot chocolate. "So, what's the plan," she asked, leaning in to meet it as she pulled it, dripping, from the cup, "assuming the plane is ready today?"

Henry was leaning with his chin on his hands, just watching her eat. "Well, we should leave in the late afternoon, so we are in the air over China and Manchuria in the dark. Don't want to get shot at by the Chinese or the Japanese."

Maria paused her chewing, her expression sobering.

Henry continued. "We need to plan it so that we land in Mongolia at first light. We should do that after breakfast. I also want to check the weather."

Maria leaned into him and whispered, "Henry, I'm starting to get a little scared. This is it, isn't it?"

Henry nodded slowly, letting the realization sink in. "Yes." he said, and glanced at his uncle. "Playtime is over. It's time to earn our pay." At Maria's worried expression, he put his hands on hers. "It'll be fine. Just like the good old days flyin' booze."

At the comment, Maria pulled away from him abruptly.

Henry cocked his head slightly. "What's wrong? Those were good times . . . well, except for the part with Rocco's nephew."

Maria got up. "I'm going to the toilet. Get the check and let's get out of here."

Henry, puzzled at the reaction, thought for a second and flagged down the waitress.

They pulled up to the hangar an hour later. Henry drove around to the far side and parked Kidlat's truck where he had found it. When he killed the engine, he heard Kid yell, "Just a minute," from the other side of the plane. Henry walked around the front, and found that Kid had his head inside the cowling of the left engine. "It's okay, Kid, it's just us. Take your time! But it looks like you got her back together."

Kid yelled back. "Sorry, I almost got her back together. Just a minute."

Henry shared a grin with Maria as she came up beside him and put her hand on his arm.

Jimbo walked up behind them. "Impressive. Just have to see how she runs."

Kid had managed to extricate himself from the cowling. "She should run good!" He climbed down the ladder and stepped over to greet them. "I'll be done in a few minutes, just have to reconnect some cables."

Henry walked up under the engine, putting his hand against the shining metal. "How did you do all this yourself?"

Kid laughed. "I have two helpers, you know. I sent them to town to get some lunch."

Jimbo opened up the plane and stepped inside, inspecting their cargo. Henry and Maria joined him, and

Henry grabbed a chart as he sat on one of the bunks. "We

should leave about three hours before sunset. That will put us over China just after dark."

Maria sat at the navigator's station and tried to turn the light on, but nothing happened. Henry grinned. "Batteries are unplugged."

Maria nodded. "Oh, yeah."

She flipped through her radio frequency book while holding it up to the window. "We are going past Shanghai and Peking, right?"

Henry checked his chart. "Yes. Pretty much right over them."

Maria ran her finger down the book page. "Hmm . . . all these stations are fairly low wattage. Okay, so we have XGOA on 660 kilocycles. It's 7500 watts, but it's out of Nanking; 580 kilocycles for Shanghai, and 950 for XGOP out of Peking." She reached up to tune the radio, but then stopped, muttering, "No battery."

Maria set the book down and leaned back, glancing over at Henry who was still studying the charts, when the light at her station suddenly came on. She sat up and looked out the window to see Kid giving the thumbs-up, and stood over Henry to return the gesture. Henry looked up at her with a questioning look on his face, just as Kid appeared at the door. "Okay, you have power. Just don't start the engine!"

"Thanks!" Maria said, and sat back at the navigator's station. She tuned the radio, searching for a local station, and found the BBC. " . . . and Jesse Owens's win of the gold medal last week in Berlin has been an apparent upset. A spokesman for the US team said that he would—" Maria changed the station again until she found Clark Randall's big band orchestra.

"Oh, 'Icky Morgan'!" She stood up, and put her hand out to Henry. "Dance?"

Henry looked up from his chart, gave a big grin, and grabbed her hand. As the plane started to rock, Jimbo backed up towards the rear to give them dance room.

Kid popped his head in. "What is going on in—oh!" He smiled up at Jimbo, who glanced back at him while pulling his pipe out of his vest. Jimbo raised his eyebrows, bit down on his pipe, and leaned against the bulkhead. An expression of contentment came over his face as he stood watching the lovebirds "serenade" each other: "*When Icky Morgan plays the organ, look out!*"

After a few more songs, Kid again appeared at the door, calling, "It's ready!"

Maria and Henry stopped and caught Kid and Jimbo watching them. They both smiled, before Maria reached over and switched off the radio and Henry hopped into the cockpit. "Let me know when you are ready to start!"

Jimbo cleared his throat. "I suppose that means I should sit down, huh?" he quipped, and made his way up to the navigator's station.

Kid cleared everything out of the way and walked out in front of the plane. He signaled to start the right engine. Henry put his finger up to the windshield and yelled out his side window, "Just a sec—checklist!"

Kid nodded, and waited. A minute later Henry shouted, "Clear prop!" The right engine whined for an instant, then started, and black smoke filled the hangar. Kid gave the thumbs-up and pointed to the left engine.

Henry primed it and began cranking. The starter whined as he whispered to himself. "One blade, two blades, three, four, five, six, seven, eight, nine, ten, ele—" A piston caught, and then a second and a third, and then all nine. More black smoke poured into the hangar, but cleared as the engine got up to speed. Henry looked forward to see Kid smiling and giving two thumbs up.

Kid made a gesture to throttle up. Henry pushed hard on the brake pedals and began to throttle up the engines, watching Kid closely as the RPMs increased. The plane began to shake; the hangar echoed and amplified the tremendous roar of the engines. It made Maria laugh as she felt the power in her chest. Finally, Kid gave the kill signal, and Henry slowly throttled down to idle, not wanting to thermally shock the engines. After he shut them down, he climbed out of plane. "Wow. They sound great!"

Kid nodded. "Yeah! You should be good to go!"

Jimbo stepped out next. "Impressive. How much do I owe you?"

Kid put up his finger and ran over to his office. Jimbo followed, pulling out a handful of cash.

Henry walked around the engine, inspecting it. He took in a deep breath of the smell of exhaust, oil, and 100-octane fuel. A smile grew on his face. He glanced back down to see Maria watching him with contentment. "What?"

She briefly chuckled with apparent satisfaction. "You. Your love of beautiful machines."

Henry put his hand up and caressed the bottom of the wing as he walked towards Maria. When the trailing edge of the wing ended, his hand transitioned down to her glowing face. "And my love of you."

He kissed her softly on the lips, and she closed her eyes as he felt a shiver go through her body. She raised her arms to embrace him, but then Jimbo came out of the office. "Let's get this show on the road!"

Henry turned to Jimbo. "Right. To Mongolia!" He spun on one heel and headed back towards the plane's open door. When he had reached the door, he looked back to see Maria still standing there, with her eyes closed and melancholy look on her face. He cocked his head for a second, trying to figure out what she was thinking, but then just blurted, "Come on, dear! We have places to be. Worlds to explore!"

She took in a deep breath and turned towards him. Finally opening her eyes, she smiled and nodded, then burst into a run. She reached Henry, grabbed him around his waist, and used her momentum to pivot around his body and into the aircraft. "Well, come on, then! Let's go!"

Henry, a bit shocked at her sudden change in mood, nodded and climbed in. As he turned to close the door, Kid walked out. Henry put his hand up in a wave. "Thanks Kid, for all the help! I am sure we will see you again!"

Kid saluted him. "Have a safe journey!"

Henry nodded and closed the door. He patted his uncle on the shoulder as he walked by towards the cockpit. "Strap in. Here we go."

After his preflight, Henry opened the small side window, smiled at Kid, who was standing just beyond the wing, and announced. "Clear prop!" As the whine of the starter turned to the grumble of engine start, Henry felt Maria's hand. He could feel the power of engine in his seat as he stared down at his right hand, where it held onto the throttle. Maria's left hand was resting on his. He followed her arm up to her face to find the same expression of satisfaction he had seen on her under the wing. They stared into each other's eyes until Jimbo piped up. "You going to start the other engine?"

Henry snapped out of it, turning back to check the controls and then out of the window to make sure the left prop was clear. He started it, glanced quickly at Maria, and released the brakes. He eased forward on the throttle, and the plane rolled forward out of the hangar. Henry glimpsed back to see Kid's overalls flapping in the recurrent waves of prop wash.

Henry turned the plane and headed out to the runway. His gaze went beyond the hangar to the B5, sitting in Hangar Three. "You're right. I do love a beautiful machine!"

Maria started to lean forward to see past him, but she was pushed back in her seat as Henry ran the throttles to full. A minute later they were up over the harbor and climbing through light, wispy clouds into a pale blue sky.

"Henry, it's such a beautiful day. Should be a good flight."

Henry nodded as he adjusted the throttles and banked north. He leaned forward and glimpsed the sky. "Yeah. Let's just hope it stays this way." He then reached down to adjust the trim wheel. "Okay. We're set." His shoulders dropped and he leaned back into his seat, relaxed. He glanced over at Maria and down at the chart. "This should put us over southeast China just after dark."

Four hours later, Henry was getting his first glimpse of

the coastline. He looked over to see Maria asleep with her chin almost touching her chest, so he reached over and lightly stroked her shoulder. "Maria."

Maria woke with a start, and her headset fell off as she jerked her head up. She clumsily tried to catch the headset, but was unable to coordinate her hands properly and it fell to the floor. She instinctively leaned forward to try to pick it up, but her restraints stopped her. At that, she looked over at Henry. Through her bleary, sleep-fogged vision, she could see Henry smiling back at her.

He put his hand on her shoulder. "Sorry to wake you. You should go back and lie on a bunk, but I also wanted to tell you that we are about to cross into China." He pointed out the cockpit window.

Maria rubbed her eyes and leaned forward to see. She could make out city lights and the coastline, which barely contrasted with the ocean. After a minute, she unbuckled her restraints and leaned over to pick up the headset. "Okay, I think I will go lie down for a bit." She stood up, put her hand on Henry's shoulder and kissed the side of his head. "Let me know if you need me . . . or if anything exciting happens."

Henry tried to kiss her back, but she was already moving towards the rear, so he pinched her butt instead. "I will. Sleep well."

Maria stopped and turned her head to see him grinning at her. She must have seen his playful, loving protection in the way he was looking at her, because she turned around, grabbed his face, and gave him a real kiss . . . one that lasted until they felt the plane begin to dive.

Henry quickly pulled back on the yoke. "Oops."

Maria turned and let her hand drag up his chest "Well, I better go get some sleep before I make us crash."

⤙⤙⤙

Hours later, Henry jumped as he felt Maria's hand on his shoulder. He glanced up at her. "Did you sleep well?"

She nodded and sat in the copilot's seat. As she buckled in, she noticed something bright out of the corner of her eye. She peeked out her window to see the moon rising. "Whoa . . . beautiful."

Henry regarded her and the moon beyond her head. "Yes, it is, but I am a little worried about it lighting us up. It will make us easier to see."

Maria stared at the moon. "Oh, yeah. I hadn't thought of that." She scanned forward and out Henry's window. "Where are we?"

Henry glanced at his watch. "We should be approaching Manchuria." He pointed back to the navigator's station. "Why don't you check to get an exact fix?"

Maria unbuckled. "Okay." As she stood up, a bright light caught her attention and she pointed past Henry's head. "What's that?"

Henry followed her finger out his window while leaning forward. "Oh, that's just Jupiter."

Maria thought for a second while she looked at it. "Oh. It's just so bright! Okay, let me see where we are."

A minute later she spoke. "Well, it looks like we are north of Peking."

Henry glanced back at her. "I did see a lot of city lights not too long ago. How are we on course?"

Maria put her finger up and wrote some numbers down

on a pad. "Change five degrees to port. So, take a heading of 350 degrees."

Maria shut the radio off and got up to walk back to the copilot's seat. As she did, she glanced out the window. She then pointed directly ahead. "Henry, are those fireworks?"

Henry squinted. "I don't know. Hand me the binoculars."

She reached back and pulled the binoculars out of their fur-lined leather case. "Here you go."

Henry held the binoculars by the far ends, trying to stabilize them. "No . . . no—it looks like a battle! See those intermittent lines? I think they're tracer fire."

Henry handed Maria the binoculars and she took a look. "Who do you think it is?"

Jimbo's sudden voice shocked both of them into turning around. "They're probably anti-Japanese forces fighting the Japanese. Where are we?"

Maria recovered and responded, "North of Peking . . ." She pointed to the map. "Here, near Guyuan."

Jimbo angled one of the cockpit lights and studied the map. "Yeah, definitely. The Chinese had pushed the Japanese out of Guyuan and Duolun last month. I would guess that the Japs are trying to take it back."

Henry reached for the throttles and began to increase power. "Put your masks on. I am going to get us some altitude."

Maria looked at him with her eyes wide. "Why? Do you think they will shoot at us?"

Henry used his head to point out the window. "Well, they are already shooting into the sky. Best if we just try to get above all that, out of range, just in case."

Jimbo nodded in agreement, saying, "Good idea," before he turned and buckled into the navigator's station.

Flashes of light from explosions far below danced around the cockpit. It became deathly quiet except for the vibration of the engines. Everyone stared at the mesmerizing lights and billowing smoke below as they slowly grew closer.

Maria glanced over at Henry to gauge his reaction to the battle far below, when he suddenly pushed himself backward in his seat. Out of the corner of her eye, Maria saw the light from the city fires blink out for a second and Henry yelled, "Shit!" Before she could react to his expletive, she was slammed back into her seat as he yanked back on the yoke. Henry whipped his head to look out his left window as he maxed out the throttles. She followed his gaze to see two sets of blue flames, receding fast.

The city abruptly disappeared from the front windows, replaced with stars, as Henry continued to pull back into a steep climb. Maria's head was hard against the seat. She strained to yell over the roar of the engines. Her voice, muffled by the oxygen mask, finally released. "What was that?!"

Henry snapped a glance at her and then returned forward. She could see that he was trying to push words out. "A plane!"

As Henry began to calm, his grip loosened on the yoke and the city appeared once again. He finally looked over at her as they leveled off. "Whoa, that was close." He reached up with his left hand and wiped his brow. "I assume that was a twin-engine bomber?" He looked back at Jimbo for an answer.

Jimbo shrugged. "I didn't actually see anything. I guess it could have been."

Henry, with slight frustration on his face, turned his attention back to flying. "Okay. We are at 18,000 feet. We should be safe from random ground-fire, now."

Maria put her hand on Henry's throttle hand and could feel him shaking. Henry glanced at her, giving her a nervous smile. She looked down at her chart and turned a small reading light on. After studying it for a minute, she pointed forward. "Well, our destination should be about ninety minutes that way."

Henry tapped on the fuel gauge. He breathed a sigh of relief and relaxed a little as he adjusted his mask. "Well, we have plenty of fuel, so no problem there. All we have to do now is find this place."

Jimbo spoke up. "When they hear your engines, they will light up the runway with red lights. That's how we usually do it for night missions."

Henry glanced back at him and pulled a headphone off his right ear. "Usually do it?"

Jimbo grinned and spoke loudly through his mask. "Yes, we do have another plane, but it's small. We have been using it for a while now, but it's just not enough to do the job."

"Why didn't you tell us this before?"

Jimbo shrugged. "You never asked."

Henry frowned, and reminded him, "If we weren't so desperate, we probably would have wanted more details in the beginning." He glanced over at Maria, seeing a smirk visible on her face around her oxygen mask, and then back at Jimbo. "So, what kind of plane is it? Who flies it?"

Jimbo rubbed his mask. "It's an old O-2 biplane; a chap from Australia named Nick flies her. We use it mainly for emergency supply runs. They pay well and we can get by with the limited cargo room." Jimbo reached out and touched the walls of his DC-3. "We need this baby for moving real cargo."

Henry nodded with acceptance.

Maria curiously asked. "How does this whole operation work exactly? I mean, do we—"

Henry interrupted. "Never mind twenty questions; now would be a good time for those details."

Jimbo grunted in agreement while nodding heavily. "Well, we have a couple of landing strips in Outer Mongolia that we use for our main bases. We also have a strip west of Harbin that we use as a forward base. Furthermore, we have small delivery strips throughout Manchuria where we drop or pick up supplies."

Henry tilted his head. "All for one biplane?"

Jimbo chuckled and adjusted his mask. "No, no. We truck supplies in and out of these places as well. We used to use the railroads, with the appropriate bribes where needed, but security on the railroad has become too tight with the Japanese 'protecting' it. And with the KMT cutting off all rail service from the south, it's just not viable anymore." He cleared his throat. "Lately, though, our trucks have been getting intercepted . . . and we have lost some people. I think the time may come when trucking isn't going to be viable either, so that's where you two come in." He feigned a smile.

Maria, with a brooding face, glanced sidelong at Henry. Henry put his hand on her leg to soothe her. When they hit an air pocket, he suddenly looked forward, remembering that he was flying.

Jimbo continued. "We mostly supply the anti-Japanese

forces, but we also supply the Japanese, mostly with illicit stuff, and do supply runs of opportunity. Although, lately, we have been reducing our supply runs to the Japs."

Henry sensed something in his muffled voice. "Why?"

"Well, some of the stories we have heard about atrocities are pretty bad. The money has been good, but I do have a conscience, too. Unfortunately, we can't stop supplying them altogether, or they would wipe us out. Right now we are playing a balancing act. We have spies in their ranks that let us know about any suspicions, or when we need to change a rendezvous—of course, we have to pay them well . . ." He stopped and thought for a second. "I suspect that we might have a spy in our ranks as well," he added slowly. "Too many shipments have been intercepted lately for it to just be coincidence, but the Japanese high command must not know about us, or we'd be gone already." He looked Maria and Henry dead in the eye, one after the other. "So, be careful who you tell things to."

When Maria reached for Henry's hand and squeezed tightly, Jimbo's expression softened, responding to the fear that his warning had caused. "I'm sorry. I didn't mean to scare you. Don't worry about it. You will have an armed detail with you at all times, and we are safe in Mongolia."

Henry glanced back at Jimbo with a dark protective stare. Jimbo nodded ever so slightly in response and then, trying to change the subject, pointed out the window. "Hey, it's starting to get light on the horizon."

Chapter 11

Mongolia

Fifteen minutes after crossing the Mongolian border, Maria spotted the red markers. "Henry! Over there!"

Henry looked out her window to see a brightening sky and two rows of red lights on the dark ground. "I see it." He banked the plane to set up a baseline before turning on final approach. The ground began to brighten, and a grassy strip surrounded by rolling hills appeared out of the darkness. As Henry touched down on the rough surface, the sun peeked above the horizon. Shadowy figures appeared alongside the runway, and a few appeared to be running with the plane.

When the plane had come to a full stop, Henry throttled up and turned the plane around to taxi back. The landing lights lit up the group of people who had just been shadowy figures before. Some were waving and jumping up and down, obviously excited to see them. There were two large white tents off to the side of the runway, and people were coming out of them. As Henry approached the crowd, several kids ran up beside the plane waving furiously. "Whoa . . . look at all these kids!"

Maria, excitedly sat up in her seat. "Yeah, they're so cute— but Henry, they're too close!"

Henry immediately cut the engines and as the props slowed, people ran up to the back door.

Jimbo started laughing. He quickly unbuckled himself and

headed towards the back. "Hold on, hold on! I'm coming!"

Maria and Henry both turned to watch as Jimbo opened the door.

Kids and adults were clamoring together, all saying some version of "Welcome back, Mr. Mata!" The kids went on, asking, "Did you bring us anything? Did you, Mr. Mata?"

Jimbo laughed and leaned back. "Of course I did!"

Maria eyed Henry. "He's Santa Claus!" Henry smiled big and chuckled, but kept watching in fascination.

Hershey bars and Cracker Jack boxes appeared as if from nowhere, and Jimbo handed them to each child individually. He leaned out of the door and said something to each child as he gave it to them and often ruffled their hair in affection.

Once the kids had been satisfied, the adults came forward and started talking to him. Henry and Maria could see Jimbo pointing to the boxes of weapons, but couldn't make out what was being said. They glanced at each other and simultaneously unbuckled themselves. As they approached the back of the plane, Jimbo jumped down out of door to the awaiting children. When Maria and Henry appeared at the door, Jimbo pointed up and introduced them.

"Everyone, these are our pilots, Maria and Henry. Henry, Maria, this is Bayasaa, Khaidu, Temujin, Inalchuk; Temujin's wife, Bolormaa—"

Henry interrupted. "Hey, everyone! I am sure I will learn all your names soon, but honestly, I won't be able to remember much after flying so long."

Maria nudged him, whispering, "Well, that was rude."

Henry twisted his mouth and glanced sidelong at her,

before whispering back. "Sorry, I'm so tired and there are so many of them."

Jimbo extended his arms and helped Maria down out of the plane. The curious adults and children gathered around her, asking questions in Mongolian, while Bayasaa tried to translate.

Henry stood at the door and watched with contentment. He took in a deep breath of the fresh, crisp morning air, and watched as the fog from his exhale rose into the sky. The sun was now up and the green grass beyond the camp seemed to go on forever. It rolled over small hills to the horizon, where larger hills or mountains took over.

The sound of Maria laughing brought him back. He grabbed the block of stairs from inside the cabin and set them outside the door before he took a step down. The bright light of the sun shining off of the wing caused him to glance out at its orange brilliance and then up at the clear blue sky.

He felt the touch of Jimbo's hand. "Henry, the men want to see some of the cargo. Do you mind?"

Henry shook his head, "Sure, no problem," but then realized Jimbo was just asking him to move off the stairs. "Oh. Sorry, just looking at the scenery." He pointed to the horizon.

With that, Jimbo stopped and glanced around. "Yes, you are right. This place is beautiful. I should take more time to take it in." The moment only lasted a second before the locals started pushing him again. He glanced up at Henry and shrugged. "Maybe later."

As they started unloading the crates from the plane, Jimbo stepped out, pointed at Maria and Henry, and yelled something in Mongolian to a woman behind them. Henry and Maria both looked up at Jimbo, trying to understand what he had said; then the woman, with long, braided black hair down her back, and deep brown eyes just a bit darker than her complexion, came up from behind them and touched Maria on the arm. Maria turned to see the woman motioning them towards the tents. They both nodded and followed the woman to the nearest gher. It was a large white round tent, about twenty feet across, with furs and skins hanging off the sides as if to dry.

The woman opened the low door and put her hand forward, palm up, guiding them in. Henry and Maria ducked down and stepped in. The floor was covered in an intricately woven straw mat that stretched from one side of the tent to the other. There were beds around the edges, and various rugs and blankets hanging from the walls. The woman stepped in behind them and pointed to a small rug on the floor, which was covered with food. Some of it appeared to be fried pieces of bread and other items looked like dried meat. The woman bundled her fingers and put them up to her mouth in an eating motion.

Henry smiled and nodded, then he and Maria both walked over to the mat and bent down. The woman motioned for them to sit and then pointed to two beds. She put her hands next to her face in a sleeping gesture and smiled.

Maria thanked her in English, but the woman responded as though she understood, and made a gesture that seemed to indicate that it wasn't any big deal and that she didn't need to be thanked. Finally, she turned and walked out, closing the small door behind her.

Henry sat on the floor and watched Maria as she wiped the mat next to him before joining him. She picked up a fried bread piece and sniffed it. She nodded and took a bite. "Mm . . . pretty good!" She took the half-bitten piece that was left and forced it into Henry's mouth. "Good, isn't it?"

Henry nodded and responded, his voice muffled by the food, "Mm-hmm."

After trying a little of everything, Maria climbed into one of the beds. Henry helped her get undressed, and covered her as she lay down. He kissed her forehead and she smiled with her eyes closed, too tired to reopen them.

Henry got undressed, folded his clothes, and put them on the end of the bed. He lay down and pulled a large animal pelt over himself. He stared at the black and white fur of the skin and wondered what kind of animal it had come from, but before he could finish the thought he was asleep.

Chapter 12

Settling In

A few hours later, Henry awoke to the sound of a V-engine and shouting. He sat up in the bed and listened, glancing at Maria as she awoke, and then grabbed his pants. He was still buttoning his trousers while he exited the gher. As he stood upright, a black biplane taxied by.

He felt pressure on his back from Maria as she came out of the tent behind him. "Is that the other plane you two were talking about earlier?"

Henry rubbed his eyes and looked closely at it. "Yep. That's an O-2, all right." It was a large biplane, with rather large wheels, including the tail wheel. It had two seats, both enclosed by glass canopies, and a large cargo door on the side.

The plane pulled off the other side of the grass strip and cut the engine, before people ran across to it.

Henry watched for a second and then began walking over. As he got to the plane, a tall, thin man climbed down from the rear seat. He was wearing a brimmed hat with one side tacked up and had goggles around his neck. A brown, lambskin jacket hung heavily on him, with a name tag too faded to read. When he glanced over and saw Henry approaching, he pushed through the crowd that had come to meet him. His hand came out with enthusiasm. "G'day! The name's Nick. You must be Henry."

Henry, a bit shocked at the man's outgoing nature,

nevertheless smiled and shook his hand with confidence. "Yep, that's me. And this is my wife, Maria."

Nick tilted his hat. "Good to meet you, ma'am!"

Henry studied the plane. "Where you coming from?"

Nick turned and looked at the plane with Henry. "Well, we had to run some medical supplies and ammo to a place outside Guyuan. The Japs have been trying to take it back for the last few days, and we have been flying in supplies almost continuously."

Henry saw a hole and cracks in the windshield. He put his finger through what seemed like a bullet hole. "Run into trouble?"

Nick saw Henry's finger in the hole. "Yeah. A bit." He motioned down the side of the plane. Maria's eyes got big and she grabbed Henry's arm as it became apparent that the plane was riddled with bullet holes. Nick opened his coat. "But those weren't the close ones." He pointed to a hole in his jacket and pulled out his billfold. "Right through my bloody wallet!" He pulled a few notes out. "Good thing is that the bills should still spend." He held up an American five-dollar bill with a hole through Lincoln's head.

There were a few seconds of silence when the plane suddenly rocked, and Henry's attention changed to a Chinese man getting out of the front seat. The man was about five-foot six, nearly bald, with a green cap on. He wore thick brown wool pants and a button-down beige shirt. A trench coat covered the rest of his body. Nick followed his gaze. He then stepped towards the man. "Henry, Maria, this is Zhu Ai Ze. He's Mr. Mata's right-hand man. He's our best liaison with the anti-Japanese forces."

Henry shook his hand, saying, "Good to meet you," then tried his take at some Chinese. "*Ni hao.*"

Mr. Zhu had a hard-looking, round face, which stayed expressionless for a long moment before finally letting out the smallest of smiles. "*Ni hao.*"

Before Henry could say anything further, Jimbo interrupted. "A.Z.! Welcome back. I need to talk to you about some of the runs." Jimbo acknowledged Henry with a smile before he and Mr. Zhu walked off.

Henry watched them walk off. "Nick. How does it work exactly? I mean, how do you know where to fly and when?"

Nick pointed to what appeared to be a tree. "That's our antenna, on the other side of the medical tent. The radio equipment is in a bunker below. Most of the time we communicate in code via the radio, but we also get word by couriers. We have a network of people all over Manchuria, China, and the Soviet Union." His voice became quiet. "We even have a few on the Japanese side."

Henry was staring at the tree antenna. "Can we take a look?"

Nick nodded. "Sure, come on."

As they walked across the airstrip, Henry glanced over to the see the DC-3 covered in camouflage. He stopped for a second. "Oh, I hadn't even noticed."

Nick followed his gaze and nodded. "Oh, yeah. We cover everything up that would be suspicious, just in case." He continued walking. "You never know who might fly over."

Maria peered up at the sky, but continued walking.

When they came up to a small green mound, Nick pointed down. "Here we are." He bent down as though to open a hatch, when it flew open from the inside. A Chinese man, with his hand still gripping the inside of the hatch, peered up. When he saw Nick, he backed down the ladder. Nick smiled and motioned for Henry and Maria to enter.

When Henry had reached the bottom of the ladder he stopped and looked around in awe. There were a half-dozen men sitting with headsets, mics, and code keys. The code keys were clicking away, and the air was filled with multiple conversations, taking place in multiple languages all around him. A single light bulb hung from the ceiling in the middle of the room. It lit up rising smoke from several cigarettes. Behind the radio sets, the rough walls were lit with the soft glow of radio tubes, and a large glowing clock sat at the other end of the room. The room smelled of men, hot electronics, and cigarettes.

"Henry!"

Henry glanced up to see Maria still on the ladder. "Oh, sorry." He moved out of the way and helped her down.

Nick stepped off the ladder behind her and pointed to the two men on the right. "This is Zhou Qiang and this is Zhang Wei Guo, but we just call him Patriot or Pat for short. They talk to our agents in the field and process all the incoming requests." He turned to the left. "These two blokes are Zhong Cheng and Jiang Ya. They relay our drop-off times and confirm meet points." Then he pointed to the other side of the room, to a woman at a typewriter. Papers and boxes were stacked all around her and she faced away from them. She wore a dark green cap, and her hair was in a single pony tail that ran the length of her back. "And that is Zheng Zi Ling. She manages all the scheduling. She knows where everyone is and where they are going to be. This show wouldn't run without her."

Henry rubbed the sides of his mouth. "Wow, this is really

impressive."

Nick pointed behind him. "This is the final schedule." A chalkboard with names, dates, and cargo manifests, written in both Chinese and English, took up the whole wall.

Maria scanned down the list of places, shaking her head. "I didn't expect it to be so . . . organized."

A hand and cloth reached past Henry's face, and began to erase a cell of data. Henry turned to see the girl from the typewriter only inches away. He stared at her soft face, young but experienced brown eyes, small lips, a nose that was bit longer in the center than the sides, a freckle off to right side of her chin . . . She noticed him staring and returned the gaze with a smile, but never stopped changing the board. Maria noticed, too, and smacked him. Henry, surprised, turned his head to Maria with an innocent grin.

Maria gave him the evil eye and then the woman was gone again, back to her station.

Henry dragged his mind back to the subject at hand and pointed back at the blackboard. "So, when do we go?"

Nick looked over the board. He pointed down at the bottom. "Most of these are truck deliveries, but that one at the bottom, I think that's you."

Maria bent down to see. "It says Harbin."

Nick nodded. "Yeah. I know some of the guns you brought are going there, but I don't know what else."

Henry looked up the ladder. "We should go ask Uncle Jimbo," but when he glanced back down, he felt a bit dizzy. "Well, actually, I am still really tired." He grinned at Maria. "Maybe we should go back and lie down. I am sure they will wake us when they need us."

Maria reluctantly agreed, "Okay."

Nick patted Henry on the back. "Great plan, mate. I think I will do the same. I was out all night." Nick waved at the radio operators, with only one returning the wave. He then climbed back up the ladder, with Henry and Maria following.

⋏⋏⋏

The next morning, Henry awoke to the sound of the O-2 doing its run-up. Upon sitting up, he found most of the beds were empty. He looked past the end of his feet to Maria's bed, only to see her lying on her stomach staring back at him. He smiled. "Good morning, love. How—" He paused as the O-2 took off. He could feel the vibration in his bed from the engine, and watched Maria as she plugged her ears and smiled. As the plane took off, the sound faded and Henry continued. "So . . . how did you sleep?"

She glanced around the tent while replying. "Slept good! Well, until that."

Henry put his feet over the edge of the bed and down onto the straw mat. He wiggled his toes on the mat, feeling the smooth lines, before grabbing his pants and sliding them on. As he stood up to buckle his belt, a woman came in from outside, carrying a bucket of what looked like dried cow chips. She smiled and nodded at Henry, who glanced over at Maria with a shrug of confusion, but she just shrugged back. They both watched the woman put the chips into a small stove in the center of the room, before she blew into it. Her face lit up warmly from the flames inside, as her breath fed the fire.

The few others still in the tent were now getting dressed as well, but instead of walking out, they began to sit on the floor. Another woman then came inside with a bowl and set it on the stove. Henry looked into it, curious, but the woman shooed him away and signaled for him to sit. Maria slipped her pants on and sat down next to him. They watched as the two women prepared food and then handed them each a bowl.

Henry was drinking boiled goat's milk, when Jimbo peeked into the tent. "Oh, good. You two are awake."

Henry looked up from his bowl, "Yeah." then raised it. "You want some?"

Jimbo stepped into the tent. "No, thanks, I ate a few hours ago. I have a run for you today. The plane is loaded and ready to go when you are."

Maria took a big bite of meat and stood up.

Jimbo waved her back down. "No. No. Take your time. Eat."

Henry inquired. "What are we taking? And are we flying to Harbin? That's what it said on the chalkboard."

Jimbo nodded. "Yes. You will be taking some of the Thompsons, cigarettes, medicines, bandages, and . . . well, let's say, more recreational medicines." He sat down behind Henry and Maria and whispered. "The Thompsons will be going on one truck to the Chinese, and most of the rest will be going to the Japanese on a second truck. When you land, the first truck will be waiting. Get it loaded as fast as you can. The second truck will be there a few hours later. *Don't* talk to the second group about the other truck. They don't know about it, and they don't need to know about it."

Henry nodded slowly.

Jimbo continued. "I will be sending two guys with you to help you unload. They can do all the work on the second truck, but

I need you to help them with the first. We want to load it as fast as possible and get that truck out of there. We want that shipment tied to us for as little time as possible."

Maria put her arm around Henry's.

Henry was thinking about what Jimbo had said, when Jimbo got up and walked to the door. "You two enjoy your lunch, I will tell you the rest in a bit." He made a half-wave and ducked out of the tent.

Maria's grip tightened and Henry looked at her. He could see the concern in her face. "Don't worry. It will be fine. After all, would he risk his new plane on the first trip?"

Maria gave him a smirk and said sarcastically, "Well, that fills me with confidence."

Henry smiled, kissed her on the forehead, and whispered. "I would never let anything happen to you."

Chapter 13

The First Run

An hour later, Henry and Maria were on the plane making sure the cargo was secure and loaded correctly. Jimbo appeared at the back of the plane and pointed to the crates in the rear. "Those with yellow marks on them are for the first truck. The red marks are for the Japanese."

Henry looked up and down all the crates. "Okay."

Jimbo turned to the door and waved two men in. Henry recognized them, but couldn't remember their names until Jimbo introduced them again. "This is Bayasaa and Temujin. They will be going with you today. They only know a little English, but they are strong and know how to use firearms. Bayasaa is one of my local bodyguards, so he will take good care of you."

Jimbo reached out of the door and pulled in two Browning automatic rifles. "Here's a couple of BARs, and I put some Thompsons up front just in case you need them. Ammo boxes are up front too."

Maria looked up front and then back. "Do you really think we will need these?"

Jimbo halfheartedly shook his head. "Nah. They're just a precaution."

Maria glanced at Henry, who was smiling back at her. She took a deep breath and walked up to the cockpit. "Well, we might as well get this show on the road." She continued in a whisper,

"Why should we keep Death waiting?"

Henry started to turn towards the cockpit, but stopped. "Uncle. What about payment?"

Jimbo cocked his head. "Don't worry, you will get paid."

Henry's head moved back in confusion. "No. No, not us. Payment for the shipment. How much, and how do we get the payment?"

Jimbo's face showed slight embarrassment. "Oh, sorry. Yeah, don't worry about that. They get us the money in advance, most of the time, through other channels."

Henry thought about it with skepticism, and shrugged. "Okay."

Henry shook the hands of Bayasaa and Temujin and showed them where to sit. As he sat down and started his in-cockpit preflight, an older woman came up and handed them food wrapped in an animal-skin bag. Maria thanked her, and she quickly turned and exited the plane.

Maria started to peek in the bag, but Bayasaa motioned that he wanted to take it, so she handed it back. He carefully placed it under his chair. Maria asked, "Mmm . . . good?" while making eating gestures.

Bayasaa smiled at her gestures. "Yes, it's a-very good. Lamb, yak, a-fried snack."

Maria nodded largely. "Your English is good!"

Bayasaa waved his hand and shook his head in disagreement.

Jimbo set the stairs inside the plane and shut the door, then backed away from the plane and gave Henry the thumbs-up.

People gathered along the sides of the runway as Henry

throttled up and released the brakes. Huge clouds of dust filled the air as the windblown spectators waved enthusiastically. Within seconds, they were in the air and Henry set course for Harbin. It was three hours before Bayasaa pointed out the window. "It is there."

Henry looked over to see a nondescript grass strip with trees all around. A curved body of water bordered the northern half of the runway. "That? Are you sure? How can you tell?"

Bayasaa nodded. "Yes. I sure. The way the lake curve and the covered square building at the end."

Henry looked closer. "Oh . . . yeah. I didn't even notice the building. Good camouflage." He smiled at Bayasaa and turned for his final approach. As he touched down, a glint of light shone from the trees; Henry glanced over to see a truck parked near the building under a large tree. "Bayasaa, is that the truck?"

Bayasaa peered forward through the cockpit windows. "Yes. I believe so."

Henry responded, "Okay," and taxied over to it. As the plane approached, two men got out and walked over to them. Once Henry shut down the engines, Bayasaa and Temujin opened the rear door. Henry got up and began making his way back; they were already beginning to unload the crates. Henry pointed to the truck, which was twenty feet away. "Why don't you back the truck up right here and we can load faster?"

The driver held his ear. "*Ting bu dong.*"

Bayasaa then translated what Henry had said, and the driver nodded. He ran to the truck and backed it up to the door.

The six of them made quick work of the job, and the driver signed a sheet Bayasaa had brought. Then he and his assistant hopped into the truck, waved, and drove off.

Henry waved and wiped his brow. "Well, that wasn't too bad." He glanced around at the airstrip and at the "hidden" building. "Well, I guess we are going to be here for a few hours. Maria, want to take a gander?"

Maria, standing in the door, nodded and jumped down to join him. "Sure."

As they began to walk off, Bayasaa put up his hand. "Wait. I go you."

Henry turned. "Okay."

As Bayasaa caught up to them, he pointed back to Temujin. "He would watch plane."

As the three of them approached the building, it became apparent that it was a concrete bunker covered in vines. There were no windows, and it was very overgrown. Henry walked up to it and touched the concrete through the foliage. "What is this building?"

Bayasaa pointed around the end towards the trees. "This way."

As they rounded the end of the building, which was below the overhanging trees, they could see a steel garage door, with a smaller side door next to it. Bayasaa pulled out a large key and unlocked the side door, which creaked loudly as he opened it. He waved for them to follow him in. "Come."

The place smelled of oil, with a slight hint of mildew. Bayasaa put up his hand. "Wait just minute." He walked into the darkness, and after a few bangs and clangs, he spoke up, "Ah—here!" Light suddenly filled the darkness as he unlatched the garage door and began opening it. Beams of light shone through the disturbed dust to reveal two large covered objects.

Henry stepped down to get a closer look. "Are these cars?" He lifted the front of one of the tarps to reveal a black hood, surrounded by polished metal.

Bayasaa smiled and pointed to the car. "1934 Dodge Deluxe."

Henry glanced up at him. "Really?!" He pulled back more of the tarp and glanced over at Maria, asking rhetorically, "How did he get this here?"

Maria nodded and then shrugged. "Your uncle is getting to be pretty impressive."

Henry replied, "Yeah. You ain't kidding." He then pointed to the other car. "What is that one?"

Bayasaa looked over at the other tarp. "Oh. That just truck."

Henry, still curious, recovered the Dodge and walked over to the other tarp. He pulled it back to reveal a Ford AA truck with a canvas-covered rear end. "Yep. It's a truck, all right."

Bayasaa spoke up. "I forgot. Be right back." He then walked out the garage door and disappeared around the corner.

Henry glanced at Maria before he focused back on the truck. He felt the polished metal and the shiny black paint along the hood, until he noticed a small dent and a hole. He looked closer. "It's a bullet hole."

Maria walked up. "Really?" She looked at Henry's finger in the hole. "Henry, have you noticed the amount of bullet holes in things around here?"

Henry nodded stoically.

Maria grabbed his arm. "It's making me think we got in

over our heads on this one."

Henry turned to her. "It will be okay. Let's at least try it. Look, if we find it's too bad, we can just bail and go home, okay?"

Doubt started to form on Maria's face when the noise of Bayasaa's return interrupted their conversation. They both looked to see Bayasaa carrying the two BAR's and two Thompsons Jimbo had given them, with pouches of ammo over his shoulder.

Henry watched him enter, before leaning the guns against the wall and pulling the tarp off the car. "What are those for?"

Bayasaa pointed to the car and then the truck. "For safety. Just in case." He pulled the tarp to the back of the car and opened the rear door. "You can help, please?"

Henry nodded and worked his way over to the opposite door. "Sure. What do you need?"

Bayasaa grabbed the front of the lower part of the seat. "Lift seat."

Henry helped, while Maria watched with intense curiosity. Dust puffed into the air as the seat popped, then they lifted the seat bottom, revealing a rusty 1895 Colt Browning machine gun with ammunition. Bayasaa quickly picked it up and set it against the wall, then replaced it with a BAR. He dumped a few boxes of ammunition and clips next to it as he removed the old rounds with his other hand. "Okay. All good."

Henry looked up at him. "Upgrading?"

Bayasaa nodded with a smile. He pointed to the Colt. "Old."

Henry smiled and nodded; then, with his back turned so the other man couldn't see him, he shared a look of disbelief with

Maria, his eyes wide.

Bayasaa started to put the seat back down. "Careful." Henry quickly turned back to help him snap the seat into place. Bayasaa stood up straight and shut the door. He motioned to pull the tarp back over and Henry obliged.

Over the next ten minutes, they did the same for the truck. Once they had put the tarp back on, Henry asked. "So, what are the Thompsons for?"

Bayasaa looked over at the submachine guns, still sitting against the wall. "Just for us. Be safe."

Henry glanced at Maria, who didn't say anything, and then he walked over and picked up one of the Thompsons. "Okay. Now what?"

Bayasaa reached up to close the garage door. "We wait for truck. But we eat now."

Maria ducked outside before Bayasaa closed the garage door, and the cars again disappeared into the darkness. Bayasaa grabbed the other Thompson and the Colt while following them out the door, locking it behind him. He motioned toward the plane and they walked over to it.

Henry looked around at the area. "It's so quiet. Pretty deserted around here."

Bayasaa nodded. "Yes. Is good place." He then yelled something ahead to Temujin in Mongolian.

As they walked up to the rear door, Temujin appeared with the skin of food and handed it down to Bayasaa, who set it on the ground next to the tail wheel. He then sat down in the grass, leaning his back against the plane's silvery exterior, and pointed to the food. "Eat."

Maria smiled and sat down cross-legged in the shade of the fuselage. She glanced up at Henry, who was still looking around. "Come on, Henry. Let's eat. Look, they have those fried things."

He looked down at her and the fried dough, before setting the Thompson on the ground. He landed on his rear with a grunt. "Yeah. What else do we got?"

An hour later, Maria was lying with her head on Henry's stomach, taking a nap in the sun. Temujin was lying under the wing sleeping, while Bayasaa stood guard with his Thompson strapped across his front.

Maria sat up at the sound of an approaching truck. Temujin jumped to his feet and grabbed his Thompson, while Henry scrambled to stand up. Henry saw the dark shape of the truck move through the woods. "Is that them?"

Bayasaa watched for a second until the truck emerged from the woods. "Yes. I think it them."

A brownish-green, six-wheeled truck pulled up to the plane. The engine rattled to a stop and Henry heard Bayasaa cock his Thompson, so he did the same. Two men in the truck then opened their doors and started to get out, but slowed their movements when they saw the guns. Both of them were thin, with lighter complexions and had five o'clock shadows. They were in dirty civilian clothing, but the driver wore a Japanese military style hat, although it was a bit worn.

One of the men stared at Henry. "We get supply."

Henry nodded in response and used his head to point to the plane. The man then approached Henry and handed him a paper, but Bayasaa stepped over and took it. "Okay. Good. These the men."

Henry watched Bayasaa become much more relaxed, so he followed suit. Bayasaa motioned for the men to follow him and spoke to them in Chinese. Temujin joined them and began to help transfer the remaining crates to the truck.

Henry glanced at Maria and let out a sigh of relief. Maria looked back at him, obviously still tense. She didn't say anything and continued to watch the process intensely.

After fifteen minutes of loading, the two men got back into their truck. The truck cranked over a couple of times before starting and Henry heard the grinding gears being engaged. The man in the passenger seat waved at them, and they drove back the way they came.

Henry watched everyone, gauging their reactions. Bayasaa pulled out the clip and cleared the chamber of his Thompson, and Maria collapsed to the ground. In response, Henry cleared his gun and put his hand on Maria's shoulder. She looked up at him. "That was a bit tense, wasn't it?"

Henry nodded and replied, "A bit," before he took his hand off her shoulder and held it out to help her up. "Come on. Let's head back."

She glanced up and took his hand, blowing out a shaky breath. Bayasaa and Temujin noticed her standing up, and began to load their supplies back into the plane.

When they returned that evening, the camp held a large bonfire in their honor. The flames grew higher as everyone added more crates and miscellaneous wood to the fire; Henry got up with his hand in front of his face and moved back a couple of feet before sitting back down. "Jeez—that's a bit hot!"

Maria came up from behind and sat down next to him.

"Yeah, but it's great, isn't it?" She stared up, watching the smoke rise towards the Milky Way overhead, and slowly put her arm around him. "Wish we had some marshmallows."

Noise and commotion came from behind them, and they both turned to see a huge side of ox meat, being carried by two men on a heavy spit. The men set the ox over the fire and settled the spit onto two stands on either side of the fire. Henry felt a heavy hand on his shoulder and looked up.

Jimbo smiled and pulled the empty pipe from his mouth. "We are going to eat well tonight! Good job on your first run."

Henry motioned for him to sit, but Jimbo waved him off. "Well, it was actually easy," he began, until Maria nudged him slightly. He glanced at her with slight annoyance, but continued. "Well, a bit tense, but easy. What's our next mission?"

"In a few days, you will take a shipment to Kalgan."

Henry stared at the fire, watching them prepare the meat. "What's in Kalgan?"

Jimbo cleared his throat. "Mao's forces."

Henry glanced up at him. "You mentioned him before. Who is he?" Maria looked up at Jimbo, also wanting to hear the answer.

Jimbo put his pipe back in his mouth, took in a deep breath and finally sat down. "Well, he's leading Communist forces against the KMT and he is fighting the Japanese, which is all right, I guess . . . I mean China is in chaos, so who are we to say who will win?"

Henry tilted his head. "But?"

Jimbo stared at Henry as he took in another deep breath. "I have heard that he is being supported by Stalin. Now, that worries me."

Maria asked. "Why? Because he is part of the enemy you fought in Russia?"

Jimbo feigned a smile. "No, that's not the real problem. Since he has come to power, he has murdered or sent to the gulag millions of people. He's been executing anyone he sees as a threat, even loyal members of the military." Jimbo's expression changed to concern. "He is scary, ruthless, and if he is involved with the Communist Party here, we need to be careful."

Maria looked at Henry and then Jimbo. "Well, then who are the good guys here?"

Jimbo forced a laugh. "Good guys? I don't think there are any—"

Nick's voice interrupted from the darkness. "Us! We're the good guys!"

Jimbo looked down, bit his lip, and shook his head with a smile. "Here—it's just who is the lesser evil."

Maria asked as Nick appeared, "What about the anti-Japanese forces?"

Jimbo nodded. "Well, yeah. I would consider them the most good. After all, they are just defending their homes, but they are not a well-organized force like the other players."

Nick sat down with a plate of food. "You guys need to lighten up." He pointed to the ox cooking. "This is a party, mates."

Jimbo nodded heavily. "You're right," he smiled at Maria and Henry, "you two have some fun. Enjoy!" With that, he stood up and walked off into the dark.

Henry turned to Nick. "So, where did you go this morning?"

Nick pulled some jerky from his pocket and ripped a piece off with his teeth. "Enough with the work talk." He handed them the plate. "Here, some snacks." He reached behind him and a bottle of beer appeared. "Have some amber."

Henry laughed. "Okay."

A few hours later, the fire was barely lit, but the coals were still aglow. A nearly empty bottle of vodka was being passed around as each person told a story or sang a song. Someone passed the bottle to Maria, who was lying with Henry under a fur blanket. She looked around. "Again?!" Everyone was laughing, pointing and urging her on.

She sat up, took a swig, recovered, and put her hands up. "Okay, okay . . . I got one." She thought for a second and began. "Once there was a prince and princess. They sailed off to distant land in search of treasure, but they didn't do it out of greed. Only for the survival of them, and their kin, for they owed tribute to the dragon in their land. This evil dragon had promised not to destroy their village, if they supplied him with a monthly stipend of gold." Maria crossed her legs, and continued. "One day, when the village's gold supplies had dwindled to nearly nothing, the villagers, thinking they were surely doomed, began to fight, squabbling and complaining about all that had been denied them. Suddenly, a stranger appeared out of the west. This stranger sat tall on his white steed, while smoking a smokeless pipe."

Maria looked at Jimbo, and in response, he put his pipe in his mouth and smiled. Once Bayasaa's translation had caught up, everyone else suddenly turned to Jimbo as well. Maria raised her right hand. "So, this tall stranger claimed he had a solution to all their problems, and the only thing he would need was for the prince and princess to be willing to sail with him to a distant land and assist him. The villagers cheered and gladly 'gave' the princely pair away to the stranger.

"At first, the princely pair willingly helped the stranger, since his mission seemed honorable, but then they found about the hidden treasure he was seeking. They tried to bargain with the stranger to share the wealth with them, but he refused, and in the ensuing argument the local people became aware of this treasure. Soon, the couple and the stranger found themselves on the run back to their boat, with hordes of once-feuding tribes chasing them. As they reached the boat, the stranger was struck down, but with his dying breath he told them where the treasure was hidden. They quickly left the stranger lying on the sands of the foreign beach, and sailed off to seek the hidden treasure. Once they had found it, they decided to return home."

"Thinking they would be the new king and queen of the land, and be worshiped by all for saving them, they sailed across the sea in high spirits." Maria paused, staring into the night, and her face fell. "They finally returned home to find the village burned to the ground and everyone dead. In a rage, the prince ran to the dragon with the treasure in hand. He yelled, 'Why?!'

"The dragon stood tall, and in a large deep voice, grumbled, 'They missed a payment of my tribute!'

"The prince showed him the treasure. 'But we were going to get what we owed you, and more! You knew this!'

"The dragon sneered, 'I only knew that you ran away!'

"The prince fell to his knees. 'But we brought you all that you could ever want.'

"The dragon smiled and showed his sharp, sharp teeth.

'Yes, you have!' he said. The dragon then promptly crushed the prince, and gloated over his newfound treasure.

"The end."

It was quiet around the fire, and everyone was looking at each other to see how they should react.

Nick thought for a second. "Well . . . that was interesting."

Henry grimaced. "Yeah . . . so what happened to the princess?"

Maria put her finger against her mouth and looked up at the sky. "Oh, her . . ." Then her face brightened into a mischievous grin. "Well, she slayed the dragon, and lived happily ever after, of course!"

Henry rolled his eyes. "Oh, boy . . ."

Everyone paused before erupting into talking, and the bottle was passed on.

Chapter 14

Normalcy in a Foreign Land

Maria awoke to the sun peeking in through the partially opened tent door. The sounds of goats and women's laughter outside forced her to get up and investigate. Henry rolled over and began to snore as she was getting dressed. She let out a slight sigh and pushed open the tent door to a bright crisp morning. One of three women, who were rounding up goats, looked over and smiled before motioning for Maria to come over. She handed a rope to Maria and pointed to all the goats. "We need tie all goat for milking."

Maria pulled back slightly. "You speak English?"

The woman nodded. "Yes, I need to in order to do schedule coordination for everyone. My name is Zheng Zi Ling. She pointed to the other women. "This Bolormaa and this Miiga."

Maria smiled and waved at them. They shyly waved back and giggled a bit before walking off to collect more goats. Maria knelt down on one leg, while extending her hand "I'm Maria. So lovely to meet you."

Zi Ling shook her hand. "We tie goat heads to milk them."

Maria, a bit puzzled, watched her tie the first few goats together in alternating directions so they were facing each other, every other one being on the same side. Zi Ling motioned to her that they would be milking all the goats in a line, once they were all together, and Maria nodded in understanding.

When they had gathered all the goats together, Zi Ling showed her how to milk the goats on their side, while Bolormaa and Miiga milked the goats on the opposite side. Maria gently pulled on the teats, but the other woman shook her head. "No, harder, like this."

As they went down the line of goats, Maria started to get the hang of it, until Zi Ling asked her, "Do you have children?"

Maria stopped milking and stared at her for a second before shaking her head slightly. "No . . . I want them, but my husband worries too . . . well, no, it's really my fault."

Zi Ling's face changed to concern and she put her hand on Maria's shoulder.

Maria's defenses softened slightly. "We were dealing with bad people and I got scared . . . they won't ever leave us alone because of what I did." She looked the other woman in the eye as tears started to swell. "I used to blame Henry, but it's not his fault . . ." Maria saw the empathetic feelings on Zi Ling's face, but knew she didn't understand. "I'm sorry. We should get back to milking . . ." She smiled, and added, "Bolormaa and Miiga are going to beat us."

Zheng Zi Ling nodded while squeezing her shoulder compassionately.

Maria squeezed another bit of goat's milk into the bucket when, from behind, she heard, "Maria?"

She wiped her face and turned before putting forth a large smile. "Hey, sleepyhead! Come milk some goats with me!"

Henry stumbled out and held his head. "How can you be so bright and cheery after all that vodka last night?"

Maria set down the milking bowl and ran over to Henry. "Bad hangover, huh? My poor dear. You know you can't handle your booze. Come on . . . help me milk a goat or two. It will help you forget about it."

Henry pulled one hand away from his head and looked at her with one eye as if to say his lovely wife was crazy.

She grabbed his arm and pulled him over to the row of goats. She pointed. "See, they tie them all together to make it easier to milk them. You can just move down the row like an assembly line." Henry groaned as she pulled him along, while the other women laughed at the spectacle.

The next day, Henry, now feeling much better, found himself on horseback, along with Maria. The locals were trying their best to teach them how to round up the herds of goats and yaks, but after a few hours, they seemed to give up on the couple, laughing. They rode off with the herd, and left Maria and Henry alone on their horses.

With nothing else to do that day, Henry pointed to a nearby hill, "How about over there?" and they both rode off towards it. When they got to the crest, he and Maria looked out over the vast, rolling grasslands that extended in every direction.

Henry stared at the horizon in amazement until Maria got his attention. "Henry. Over here."

Henry looked down the hill to see her, now on foot, at the start of a small ravine full of bushes. He turned his horse and rode down the slope before dismounting beside her. "Yes?"

She stepped up and kissed him, sliding both hands, into his hair. She was still holding her horse's reins, and they tickled the side of his face as she pressed closer still.

Henry's face lit up. "Well, why didn't you say so?" He walked a few steps and tied his horse to a thick bush, before heavily embracing and kissing her. She responded eagerly, with one of her hands going down his back while, out of the corner of his eye, he watched the other flail about in the empty air, trying to find a place to tie her horse.

Under the weight of his sudden passion, Maria fell back onto a soft patch of moss, her right arm still hanging onto the reins. As Henry kissed her and ran his hands down her body, she released the reins; the horse, finally free of her grasp, tossed his head up and ran away, leaving a dust cloud behind him. Maria watched the horse with one eye as she kept kissing Henry, but the worry faded quickly under the passionate onslaught.

She unbuttoned his shirt hurriedly, and when she got to the last button yanked it off his right shoulder. Henry, smiling, pulled away long enough to roll to his side; Maria yanked the shirt the rest of the way off and threw it into the air, where it caught on the bush above, then ran both her hands up his chest as he held himself above her. He was still trying to kiss her as she let her hands continue past his head, his undershirt in tow.

Meanwhile, Henry had been slowly undoing her khaki shirt, one button at a time. The final button was giving him trouble and it forced him to glance down. Maria grabbed his face and pulled it back to hers. Then she dragged her hands down his chest, making him hiss, and unbuttoned his pants.

With one swift movement she removed his remaining clothes, save his socks, then undid her own pants and forced Henry to roll over while he was still trying to get the same button undone.

After wiggling out of her pants, she reached up, her hands going over Henry's, and undid the button in an instant. Relief became apparent on Henry's face and he again concentrated on giving her pleasure.

The green moss under them was soft and a bit cold, with the smell of fresh-cut parsley and wet soil. Henry could see the goose bumps on Maria's skin, but she didn't seem to mind the chill, and in fact, it seemed to add to her excitement. As she led Henry into her, she let out a loud moan and an unladylike aggression poured forth. Henry was a bit shocked at her sudden onrush of passion, but did his best to keep up. She rode on top of him, with her hair brushing through the bush above. After only a few moments, the slight chill they felt gave way to heat; sweat beaded across Maria's belly and his forehead, and steam began to rise from their bodies. As Maria reached her peak, her toes to wiggle furiously in the soft moss. Henry felt her squeeze him tightly and then she collapsed onto his sweat-slicked chest, sliding off onto the moss.

They lay on the moss, breathing heavily, when the low thunder of approaching horses caught their attention. They glanced at each other and then, in a bit of a panic, began the scramble for their clothes. Henry grabbed his pants and slid them on, while Maria donned her shirt. She reached for her pants and he for his shirt on the bush, but before he could free it, Bayasaa and another rider were pulling up in front of them. Their horses snorted and blew plumes of steam, panting from the gallop up the hill. Bayasaa spotted them, half-dressed and Henry trying to untangle his shirt from the bush, and smiled before signaling the other rider to retreat. As he turned to ride away, Bayasaa shouted back, "Jimbo want to see you . . . when you finished!" He waved his hand in the air while kicking the sides of his horse. Both horses galloped off, back towards camp.

Henry and Maria stood there, half-naked and disheveled, and watched them disappear over the next hill, before glancing at each other and laughing. Henry, finally getting his shirt free, pecked her on the lips and walked over to his horse before stopping to take a look around. "I wonder where your horse got off to?"

Maria, with one leg in her pants, stopped and scanned the horizon. "Oh, no—I don't know!"

Henry hopped up into the saddle to see better. "There! At bottom of the ravine." He pointed over the top of the bushes. Maria tried to see, but couldn't. Henry glanced down at her. "Grab your stuff and hop on. I will take you down."

She buttoned her pants, brushed off her behind, and wiggled her shoes back on. Henry slid forward in the saddle and put his hand down to help her up. Maria took his hand, swung up onto the horse, and squeezed into the saddle behind him. The horse stumbled forward with the extra weight and Maria's hands instantly grabbed for the saddle horn. Henry pulled back on the reins and the horse regained its footing. Henry turned to look over his shoulder at her. "You okay?"

Maria smiled. "Yeah."

They proceeded down the hill until they came up next to Maria's horse. Maria eased off of Henry's horse and gently approached hers. It had been eating the lush grass of the valley floor, but its head came up when she approached. The horse watched her with one eye, and Maria could tell that it was deciding whether it should run or not. She reached out and petted the side of his neck. In a low voice, "Good horse." The horse relaxed a bit and she slowly took the reins. Once she was sure it was calm, she put her foot in the stirrup and climbed up. She adjusted herself in the saddle and gave Henry the thumbs-up, then they both made their way to the other side of the hill and back to camp.

As they rode into camp, Bayasaa appeared and directed them to one of the tents. Two women came up and took the horses as they dismounted. Bayasaa opened the tent door as they approached. When he made eye contact with Henry, he couldn't hold back a knowing smile. Henry, embarrassed, proud, and happy, responded with a restrained smile and a slight nod.

Once inside the door, Henry glanced up to see Jimbo, Jimbo's right hand man, Zhu Ai Ze, Nick, and the schedule coordinator, Zheng Zi Ling, all sitting around a low table. They looked up, and Jimbo waved for them to come over. "Have a seat, you two. I hope you had fun out riding today." Henry, blushing slightly, turned back at Bayasaa to see his expression, but he was already gone. Jimbo continued. "We have a run tomorrow."

Zi Ling pushed a red, tasseled cushion out from under the table, and Maria sat down with a nod of thanks. Nick saw the gesture and began to search around for another pillow. Henry spoke, "Don't worry, Nick, I got one." He pulled another one from under the table, which had been out of Nick's view, and sat down. "So, Uncle, what's the scoop?"

Jimbo pointed at the map on the table. "We have a big one for tomorrow. Mao's forces are in need of weapons, medical supplies, and a whole list of other things." Jimbo eyed Henry and Maria. "They are loading your plane as we speak."

Henry studied the map closer. "Where?"

Jimbo began to point, but Ai Ze was faster. "We are going

here. Kalgan."

Henry followed Ai Ze's finger to a point on the map, glanced at Jimbo and back over at Ai Ze. "We?"

Ai Ze started to answer, but Jimbo interrupted. "Yes. A.Z. will be going with you. He is our best liaison and they trust him, plus we really don't want any kind of language misunderstandings."

Henry nodded. "Okay. Sounds good to me." He brought his hand up and extended it across the table.

Ai Ze stared at his hand for a second and then brought his own hand out to complete the shake.

Henry slowly nodded. "It's good to meet you . . . Ai-i Zue."

Ai Ze responded, "You may just call me A.Z. I think it's easier."

Henry looked him in the eye and nodded. "All right. A.Z. it is." He glanced over at Nick. "You coming, too?"

Nick jerked his head, not expecting a question. "Ah, no, mate. I've got my own run tomorrow. Up to the Soviet border."

Maria leaned over the table. "Where is this Kalgan?"

A.Z. pointed to it. "Here. Northwest of Peking, about a hundred kilometers."

Maria paused for a second while she converted to miles in her head. "I see. Is there anything we need to know?"

Jimbo pointed toward some paperwork on the table. "Zi Ling has the details there." Zi Ling handed them several sheets of paper all clipped together. Jimbo continued. "Maps, times, inventory, and alternates."

Maria took the papers while Henry tried to watch over her shoulder. She was starting to flip through them, when Henry nudged her. She ignored him, but he did it again. She nudged back. "Let me look at them. I'll give them to you in a sec!" Then Henry leaned and whispered into her ear. Maria stopped suddenly, looking down to see a gaping hole in her shirt where she had misbuttoned. The papers were covering it, but she froze, unsure whether to act like nothing was wrong, or try to fix it. Then the door of the tent suddenly opened and Bolormaa came in with a tray of tea. While everyone was stirring at the interruption, she turned and quickly re-buttoned her shirt.

When she turned back towards the table, only Zi Ling was watching her. The other woman glanced away for a second, but then smiled at her. Maria returned the smile and motioned towards her own shirt and made a face, trying to convey "I'm an idiot" without words. Zi Ling started to laugh, but instantly turned serious as Jimbo sat back down.

Jimbo took a sip from his tea. "You will be flying to an airfield we have near Kalgan, and the Communist forces should meet you there to retrieve the supplies. The landing strip is a ways out of town, so you should be safe, but once you have unloaded, get out."

Ai Ze put his hand up and took over. "Prince Demchugdongrub, the local leader, is head of a proxy army for the Japanese in the Kalgan area. You want to avoid them. That's why we will be landing out here." He pushed a local map to the center of the table and pointed to a line between forest symbols. "Mao's forces and Demchugdongrub's forces have been engaging each other in small skirmishes, but it's only a matter of time before the scale of the conflict increases." He pulled out another map. "This is northern Shaanxi. We believe the majority of Mao's forces are here. After the Long March, they've needed time to regroup, but our intelligence is pointing to an offensive soon."

Maria asked "What long march?"

Ai Ze, taken a bit off guard, answered. "It is *The* Long March. The communist forces retreated all the way from Southeast China to up here." He pointed to Shaanxi on the map. "They were being decimated by the KMT offensive at the time."

Jimbo interrupted. "We think this is why they are asking for more supplies and weapons." He picked up his empty pipe and slowly put it in his mouth. "It's all good for us, though." He smiled with the pipe clamped between his teeth.

Chapter 15

Kalgan

The next morning, Henry and Maria were in the cockpit finishing up their pre-flight, when Ai Ze came up behind them. "Okay. Everything is on and secure."

Henry glanced back at him. "You can take the navigator's position." Ai Ze nodded and buckled himself in, then handed a paper up to Henry. "Here is a better map of the area. Drew it last night. Just watch for those indicated reference points."

Henry studied the map and pointed to a few symbols. "These mountains?"

The other man stretched forward with his finger. "We will land in the far east end of this canyon. See where all the rivers come together, north of Kalgan? Just follow the valley out east, where the mountain range from the north sticks out the most. It's there." Henry nodded and he continued, pointing to the bottom of the map, "Here is Kalgan. We want to avoid this area."

Henry looked back at him again. "Okay. I think we can find that. Do you have their radio frequency?"

Ai Ze nodded and pulled a paper out of his unbuttoned shirt pocket. "It's 560 kilocycles. They change it all the time, but that is it for today."

Henry put up his hand. "No, just put it on the clip there in front of the radio. We will need it later."

Henry heard the clang of metal from the back of the plane

and turned to see. "What are they doing back there?"

Henry saw Maria glance up as Ai Ze pointed to the back of the plane. "They're installing the .30 machine gun."

Henry looked at him, then at Maria with raised eyebrows. "Where? The baggage door?"

Ai Ze thought for a second. "Yes, the small door, at the back."

Henry watched, seeing two men come through the rear storage door. One of them gave the thumbs-up and they exited the plane. Then Bayasaa stepped back in with a Tommy gun and a bag of food, before grabbing the stairs they handed up to him and closing the door.

Maria gave Henry a look of disbelief and then leaned around to look back at Ai Ze. "Are we really going to need that?"

Ai Ze shrugged. "I hope not!"

Henry yelled out the window. "Clear prop!" and started cranking the right engine. Maria turned forward again, watched the prop turn until it started, then stared at Henry. Her eyes were big and she motioned with her head towards the back. Henry just shrugged in response.

As Henry started cranking the second engine, Nick's plane flew by in a blur and climbed into the clouded sky. Henry had his hand on the throttles, adjusting them as the engines warmed up. He watched Nick's plane turn north and become a dot, before it finally disappeared.

Bayasaa rushed forward and buckled in. Once both engines stabilized, Henry checked out the window to make sure everything was clear. One of the men across the runway gave the thumbs-up and pointed down the strip, so he throttled up and turned in the direction Nick had come from. He taxied to the end, swung the plane around then glanced back at the cargo and his passengers. "Everyone ready?"

Ai Ze and Bayasaa nodded, and Maria said, "Aye! Let's go!"

Henry returned his gaze forward to see a crowd gathering on the side of the runway. He throttled up, and the DC-3 accelerated down the grass strip. Henry could feel the extra weight of the cargo and kept the plane on the ground as long as he could before rotating into the sky. They circled around to the north and west, gaining altitude until they finally turned south. It took a few minutes for them to climb into the sky between puffy white nimbus clouds. The sky between the clouds was deep blue and the sun was shining in brilliantly from the left side of their plane. Henry reached down, found his sunglasses and put them on, just as Maria did the same.

He smiled at Maria. "Beautiful day." He pointed to the larger nimbus clouds. "We just have to keep an eye on this weather."

She nodded and stared out at the clouds gliding by.

After a few hours, as they were approaching the Kalgan area, Henry motioned to Maria. "You want to get on the radio and see if you can locate our party?"

She nodded and unbuckled before she hung her headset and stood up. "Excuse me, A.Z., I'm going to need the station for a bit."

As he moved to one of the bunks, she tuned the radio directional to 560 kilocycles, before adjusting the antenna. "It's a weak signal, but I got it. Henry, turn six degrees to port."

The plane tilted ever so slightly as he complied. "Uh-oh.

How's that?"

She glanced up with an expression of puzzlement. "Just fine. Why the 'uh-oh'?"

Henry pointed forward. "Cumulonimbus clouds ahead. Big storm."

Maria unbuckled and came forward to her seat. "Can we go around them?"

Henry looked at her and thought for a second. "Did you get our position?"

Maria buckled her belts. "Yeah, we should be about forty miles out."

Henry looked forward at the huge clouds. "Well, I would guess that those are about thirty to forty miles away. If they aren't right over where we need to go, they are just north of it."

Maria looked at Henry and then back at Ai Ze. "Should we abort?"

Henry looked at her to answer, but seeing that she was looking at Ai Ze, he turned too, waiting for the other man's answer.

Ai Ze pointed forward past Henry and Maria. "They are desperate for this shipment, and they are paying us extra to get it quickly."

Henry glanced forward at the storm and back again. "We may have to fly around to the south to get there, if we are even able to get there . . . but that would mean flying over Kalgan."

Ai Ze nodded, rubbed his hand over his mouth, then responded, "Yes. I think we should risk it."

Henry angled his head. "Okay."

As the clouds got larger, Henry began to turn west. He flew

in a large circle around the storm head until he was on the south side of it. Other, smaller storms were scattered in all directions, but some were close. The plane shuddered as they suddenly flew through wind shear. He felt the tinge of fear on the back of his neck and the tickle in his stomach of weightlessness. He sat up in his seat and gripped the yoke with a little more force. He navigated his way in between two storm clouds and began reducing the throttles, trying to reduce their altitude to get below the clouds.

Maria watched Henry and saw the way he was holding the throttles and yoke. Sensing the fear in him, a chill went through her, but she didn't say anything.

As they descended, the mountains seemed to rise to meet them, becoming more three-dimensional instead of just a landmark on the faraway earth. Turbulence continued to shake the plane; Maria pulled her left armrest forward, trying to make herself feel more secure. Suddenly the cockpit flashed bright white, and a clap of thunder made everyone jump. Maria took in a sudden breath and looked back at their passengers. She could see that Bayasaa was losing it, but Ai Ze seemed calm. She called back to Bayasaa. "Don't worry. It's just a little weather. No big deal." Bayasaa gave a quick nod back as he gripped the arm rests on his chair.

Henry pointed forward. "There is the town, and I can see a gap in the mountains." He quickly glanced back at Ai Ze. "Is that the gap that leads to the canyon we need?"

Ai Ze unbuckled and made his way forward, using his strength to hold on. "Yes, that is it."

Maria looked at the valley between the mountains. The edge of the storm hung over the valley. "Henry. Can we make it through there?"

Henry nodded. "Yeah, sure. Plenty of room."

She glanced at his face, not sure if he actually believed what he was saying.

Henry continued to descend and turned north into the canyon. She knew that he was trying to fly between the mountains, but also follow visual flight rules by staying below the clouds.

Ai Ze looked out the window straight down to spot the town of Kalgan, only a few thousand feet below. "Well, they have to know a plane is up here. Hopefully, they just think we're Japanese."

Maria stared nervously out the side window as the canyon walls got closer. They hit a sudden downdraft, causing Bayasaa let out a yelp, while Ai Ze nearly fell before hitting a bulkhead. Maria put her hands against the side of her chair and the dash, trying to feel more secure. She looked over at Henry, but he didn't look back. He was apparently concentrating so hard on flying, the rest of the world had disappeared. After a few seconds, he suddenly said, "There!", and began banking the plane to the east.

When Maria sat up in her seat, she could see the cross valley below out the side window. "Oh, the turning point."

The sudden pounding of rain on the windshield made her jump. She jerked her head around to gaze forward, but couldn't see anything but gray. Henry whispered, "Shit," and turned the wipers on. He pulled back on the throttle and started to descend again, while watching the altimeter.

Maria pushed down hard on her seat handles. "Henry."

As the altimeter continued to wind down, she screeched in near-panic, "Henry!"

They suddenly cleared the bottom of the cloud, and Henry pointed ahead to the airfield as though there had been no question of their safety. "There we are." Maria looked at him and then forward, before loosening her grip on the handles.

Ahead, there were red flares and red-colored smoke indicating the field.

There was a mountain behind the strip and it was covered in clouds, so they only had one shot. Henry put down full flaps, lined up with the strip, and came in low and slow over the trees in the valley. After a suspenseful moment or two, they finally touched down safely on the wet grass strip.

As the plane coasted to a stop, Maria and the others could see people and trucks off to the north side of the strip. When Henry shut down the engines, one of the trucks and several people came over. The crackle of thunder could still be heard, but it was getting more distant. Bayasaa opened the back door and put up his hand to wave to their customers. One soldier waved back, but his comrades looked at him strangely for doing it.

They backed the truck up to the stairs, and two soldiers in green uniforms got out. Ai Ze stepped out of the plane and began talking with them. After a minute or so, they began off-loading crates into the truck, as Maria and Henry finished their post-flight checklist.

When they also stepped out, there was a light, cold drizzle falling on them, but the sun was starting to shine through in parts of the valley. Henry stretched his legs as he gazed across the valley to watch the storm they had just flown through.

As they unloaded the last of the crates, one of the soldiers raised his rifle at Henry and began yelling in Chinese. Henry, shocked, looked at Ai Ze for translation. Ai Ze listened to the soldier while putting his hands up in a calming manner. "He is asking, 'Why are we dealing with these foreign devils? We should kill them. They are the enemy.'"

Henry began to raise his hands and took a step backwards, when suddenly from behind him he heard the loud clang of metal and the cocking of a gun. The soldier's face turned from anger to fear, before he took a step back. The soldier glanced at his comrades, who were standing motionless. Henry turned his head towards the plane to see Bayasaa aiming the 1917 Browning .30 out of the now-open cargo door. Henry couldn't help but smile at Bayasaa, but then turned back to watch the soldier's reaction.

Just then another man then stepped out of the truck, walked up to the belligerent soldier, swiped the hat off his head, and hit him with it. He yelled, grabbed the rifle from the soldier's hands, and pointed back to a group of others who were waiting in the distance. The soldier, looking a bit embarrassed and more than a bit mad, stomped off.

The man, obviously in charge, said something to Ai Ze and got back in the truck.

Ai Ze translated to Henry. "He apologized for the unprofessional behavior."

Henry nodded slightly and looked back at Bayasaa, who was still manning the .30. "Well, I think we should probably go now."

They glanced at each other and then the remaining soldiers. Maria shrugged and they loaded back up, but Bayasaa never budged from his position.

Henry took a last look up and down the valley. The storm

was clearing, and patches of blue were showing through the clouds. He looked down the grass strip at the mountain to the east. "That's too close, we will have to take off back to the west." He gave one last glance at the soldiers as he boarded, gave a salute, and closed the door.

Henry started toward the front of the plane, stopped and looked back. "Bayasaa. You just going to stay back there?"

Bayasaa yelled back. "Just till we go. I enjoying look on their face."

Henry smiled, nodded, and made his way to the cockpit. The second he started the right engine, the soldiers finally cleared out. He then started the left engine and brought the plane about. He looked down the runway at the two trucks and men. "Let's wake 'em up, shall we?" He looked over at Maria.

She looked at him, glanced at the end of the runway and back at him. "Henry?"

A mischievous smile appeared on Henry's face as he ran the throttles up. The roar of the engines filled the canyon. "Hold on, Bayasaa!"

Henry released the brakes and the DC-3 quickly accelerated down the strip, but he purposely kept it on the ground. At the last second, he rotated, just clearing the trucks and trees. Some of the soldiers hit the deck in fear.

"That'll keep 'em on their toes!" Henry let out a loud howling laugh as he pulled back on the yoke.

Maria looked behind them, seeing the men starting to recover, and then looked at Henry. "First the landing and now this! What the hell has gotten into you today?!"

Bayasaa appeared behind them and sat in the jump seat.

"We need chair back there. I slide all over place. There no way I could used gun."

Henry quickly glanced back at him and the back of the aircraft, but turned back to navigate out of the canyon.

When they had returned to base, Henry walked up to Bayasaa and handed him his watch. "This is for you. Thanks for the quick thinking and covering our asses back there."

Bayasaa looked at him with puzzlement and then started to smile. He graciously took the watch, but then put his finger up. "Just minute." He turned and ran off to his gher. A minute later, he came back with something wrapped in a cloth and handed it to Henry.

Henry looked at it curiously as he began to unwrap it. "What is it?" A rock with beautiful sparkling green nodules and a black, partially-melted crust appeared. Henry took his finger and ran it along the rough surface. "Wow. It's beautiful! Where did you get it?"

Bayasaa pointed up. "It like you. Came from sky."

Henry smiled as he admired the rock. He put his hand out and shook Bayasaa's.

Maria saw them shaking hands and came over to investigate. "What are you two up—" She stopped when she saw the rock. "What is it? It's beautiful!"

Henry gently handed it to her. "I was just thanking Bayasaa for covering our asses back there, and we exchanged gifts."

Green sparkles of reflected and refracted sunlight danced across her face as she rotated the rock to admire its unusual beauty.

Henry pointed to the rock and then the sky. "He says it

came from the sky."

Bayasaa smiled. "Yes, like you."

Maria looked at Henry. "You mean like from outer space?"

Henry thought. "I suppose so."

Maria turned to Bayasaa. "Thank you. We will treasure it."

Bayasaa nodded and held out the Turkish pocket watch Henry had given him. "I treasure too."

Chapter 16

Summer's End and Winter's Beginning

Summer turned to fall and finally winter, and the rolling hills of Mongolia turned from endless green to endless white as the temperatures plummeted. With the two planes, Jimbo's camp of smugglers had made almost continuous runs for those months without major incident. Everyone in the camp grew wealthy from the good business, and an unbreakable bond of camaraderie formed among them. The camp expanded, as well. Forward observation posts were established in every direction from camp, and radios installed. The supply runs became efficient and regular.

On a late November day, Jimbo came into the main gher for lunch. It was warm in the tent, and he began to remove his snow-covered fur coat and hat. "Whew. Getting a bit chilly out there!"

Henry, sitting on a mat in front of a small table while only wearing a button-down shirt, raised his glass. "But it's perfectly warm in here!"

Jimbo sniffled and laid his coat near the door. "Yes, it is! What's for lunch?"

Temujin's wife, Bolormaa, said something in Mongolian to Jimbo and Maria added, "Yak soup."

Jimbo replied sarcastically, "Mmm . . . haven't had that in a while."

Bolormaa handed him a bowl and some fried dough. He sat

down, dipped the dough in the bowl, and took a bite. He turned to Henry, but before he could say anything, a man appeared at the door with an expression of urgency on his face, and said something in Mongolian to Jimbo.

Jimbo cocked his head. "Pepelyayev?!" The man nodded back. Jimbo stood up with a start and headed for the door, letting his bit of food drop to the floor. He grabbed his hat and coat and ducked out before even putting them on.

Maria looked over at Henry, but her husband was deep in thought. "What is it, Henry?"

Henry frowned at her. "Pepelyayev. Wasn't that the Russian general he worked for before?"

Maria thought. "It does sound familiar . . . let's go find out."

Henry grinned and they both got up, got their winter coats, and headed out.

The wind was blowing snow sideways, so thick that they could barely see, but they quickly made their way to the underground radio bunker. They stepped off the bottom of the ladder and looked over to see Jimbo with a headset on, while talking on one of the radios. The man who had come to get him sat next to him, adjusting the set. Jimbo was speaking a mixture of Russian and English, but the words were gibberish.

Maria nudged Henry. "Can you understand anything he is saying?"

Henry shook his head. "I know the individual words, but the sentences don't make sense." He looked over at her. "Must be code."

Maria nodded in agreement and looked back at Jimbo.

Jimbo glanced up at the two lovebirds as they came down the ladder, but could only nod a greeting as he continued his conversation. After a few minutes, he took off his headset, hung it on the radio, and got up, with a big grin on his face that he couldn't contain. He patted the radio operator on the back and walked over to Henry and Maria. "Let's go to your gher." He looked around. "Where is A.Z.?"

Zheng Zi Ling looked up from her main control desk and pointed up the ladder. "Dinner."

Jimbo nodded his thanks as he climbed out of the radio bunker. As he emerged from the hatch, the wind took his fur hat off and it disappeared into the white. "Son of a bitch!" he exclaimed, but before he even had a chance to go after it, A.Z. appeared in front of him, with the hat in hand. Jimbo took a step back in surprise and almost knocked Henry back down the ladder.

"Whoa! Sorry, Henry! Ah, and thanks. A.Z." He put his hand on his chest and then pulled the hat on tight. "A.Z., come with us to their gher. We have a high-priority mission, and we must keep it secret."

The four of them walked over to Henry and Maria's gher; when Jimbo stepped into the tent, there were two woman sitting next to the fire, sewing and talking. He looked at A.Z., and A.Z. spoke to them politely in Mandarin. The women nodded, put their winter coats on, and disappeared out the tent door.

Henry and Maria took off their coats and set them on their beds before taking seats next to the fire. Maria put her hands out in an effort to warm them. "So, what's going on, Uncle? The general back?"

Jimbo paused while taking his coat off. "How did you—?

Oh, in the tent." He set the coat down. "Yes." He looked over at A.Z. and pointed to the ground next to the fire. "Sit."

Jimbo's face flickered yellow and orange from the light of the fire, as A.Z. nodded and sat down opposite Henry and Maria. He smiled. "Well, good news. My longtime friend, General Anatoly Pepelyayev, has indeed been released from prison, and he wants to make a deal."

Henry cocked his head a bit. "What kind of deal?"

Jimbo decided to sit down. "Well, he says he still has an army loyal to him, but he needs weapons."

Maria leaned forward. "Is he going to try to take back Russia again?"

Jimbo took in a deep breath. "Well, something like that."

Maria, with concern on her face, pleaded, "But, surely, there isn't any way he could win? The Reds won years ago. Can't you convince him to give it up?" She looked at Henry. "It's suicide."

Jimbo nodded. "I know. I know, but I know Anatoly. There is no way I am going to convince him to give up on his country and his loyal men. The best I can do is support him. Plus, if he can shake up Stalin's government, all the better for everyone."

Henry scratched his head, while Maria looked up at him. He glanced over at her for a second and then spoke. "So, assuming we go through with this, what's the deal?"

Jimbo sat up straight. "Well, he's back in his old flat in Harbin, and he wants us to meet him there the day after tomorrow at 11AM."

Henry rubbed his chin. "With the weapons?"

Jimbo waved his hand. "No, no. To set up a drop place in the near future and make the down payment on the shipment.

For what he needs, it's going to take us a bit of time to get all the weapons together."

Maria spoke up. "So, if he has been in jail all this time, how is he going to pay for all this?"

Jimbo looked at her. "Ah, don't worry about that. It will be taken care of. I know where he is getting the funds, and he has plenty."

Maria looked at him suspiciously.

Jimbo waved his hand. "Don't worry. The only thing we need to be concerned with is the meeting. Since it's going to be in Harbin, we will have to fly to our local strip there and take the car in." Jimbo cleared his throat. "A.Z., coordinate with Bayasaa and the others and get things set up, but don't tell them too many details about the general."

A.Z. nodded, and Jimbo continued. "We will go in armed, but not be blatant about it. Let's just try to drive in inconspicuously, make the meet, and get out. A.Z., I will get you locations and plans. Keep them secure." He looked at Henry. "As for you two, just make sure the plane is in good shape and ready to go."

Henry nodded. "We have been keeping the heating generators running continuously to keep the engines warm. We haven't had any problems, but I'll go and make sure that everything is in tip-top shape."

Jimbo nodded. "Good. Okay. Well, I am going to go coordinate everything with Zi Ling, since she is the only one who really knows what's going on around here." He smiled, got up and grabbed his coat.

He felt the touch of Maria's hand on his shoulder and turned, with his coat half on. She spoke quietly. "Uncle. What's really going on here?"

Jimbo put his hand on hers. "Nothing. It will be fine. Just helping an old friend. Everything will be great. Don't worry." He finished putting on his coat and hat and stepped out the door.

Two days later, they were starting to load the DC-3 for the meeting in Harbin. After pulling the white camouflage tarp off of the plane, Henry walked around for his inspection. The buzz of the generators heating the engines, and the voices of the people loading the plane, filled the air. It was a clear, cold morning, but the sparkle of frost in the air could be seen. As Henry inspected the left aileron pins, Bayasaa came up from behind. "Good morning, Henry."

Henry turned, while his right hand still held up the aileron. "Morning, Bayasaa! You coming along today?"

Bayasaa nodded. "Yes, I operate the radio at airfield, you go town. Temujin and Khaidu escort you for guards."

Just then Temujin stepped up. "Hello, Henry. Yes, I guard."

Henry turned to him and smiled. Temujin was a short, but strong man. He had medium black hair that was always in a mess, but it wasn't visible under his fur hat. Henry patted his thick shoulder. "Thank you. I am glad to have you watching my back!"

Temujin's wife, Bolormaa, appeared behind him; she handed Temujin his lunch, adjusted a button on his coat, and then tried to straighten his hair under his hat. Temujin, looking a bit embarrassed, kissed her and tried to push her away. He said something in Mongolian, and Bolormaa smiled, waved at Henry, and ran off back to the gher.

As Henry finished inspecting the aileron and moved to

the inner wing, Maria joined the gathering crowd. "Hi, Bayasaa, Temujin. You two coming along with us today?"

Temujin looked at Bayasaa as he usually did, waiting for a translation, but Bayasaa just nodded. "Yes, a lot of us going."

Maria smiled. "Wonderful. Should be a fun trip with everyone."

Henry poked his head out from underneath the wing, looking at her with a facetious expression while Bayasaa replied, "Yes. I think it will."

When Bayasaa turned, Maria stuck her tongue out at Henry. He just laughed and continued his inspection.

Once the inspection was complete, Henry pulled the power cords. "We can shut down the generators now." He waved for everyone to board. "Let's get this show on the road before the engines get too cold."

Jimbo and Ai Ze were the last to board, and Bayasaa closed the rear hatch. Next, Bayasaa closed the rear door leading to the .30, then moved his way up to the front and sat at the navigator's station. Henry and Maria were going through the pre-flight checklist when Bayasaa spoke up. "The new seat seem really good."

Henry glanced back trying to figure out what he was talking about. "What seat?"

Bayasaa pointed to the back of the plane. "Machine gun seat."

Henry and Maria looked back. "Oh, that seat." Henry raised his eyebrows at Maria, smiled and gave a thumbs up before returning to his check list. After a minute or so, Henry opened his window, shouted, "Clear prop!" and started cranking the right engine. It took longer than normal, but she started and black smoke poured into the otherwise crystal clear air.

Maria, who was looking around the runway, asked, "Where is Nick today? I don't see his plane."

Henry gave her a pondering glance, before starting the left engine. "Don't know."

Jimbo spoke up from behind them. "He went up north to get Russian weapons. We might seem him today when he lands in Harbin to refuel."

Maria twisted in her seat to look back at Jimbo. "Really? Wow, this really is like a big family outing." She smiled appreciatively and Jimbo gave her the thumbs-up.

Henry glanced back again. "Everyone strapped in? We didn't forget anything, did we?"

Jimbo responded, "We are all good. Let's go!"

Henry put his headset on, looking over at Maria, who was putting hers on as well, and gave her a fond smile. "Ready, dear?"

She winked. "As always."

Henry checked to make sure the runway was clear, then throttled up. Black smoke and snow flew out across the camp. The snow and ice crunched under the weight of the aircraft's tires as Henry pulled out onto the strip.

The importance of today's event became obvious as everyone came out to wave, since the locals had become used to the comings and goings of the aircraft on a daily basis and generally ignored them. As Henry maxed out the throttles, the spectators were forced to cover their eyes and faces as the prop-wash generated an artificial blizzard behind them.

Within a few seconds, they were airborne and heading east. The brightness of the sun in the deep blue sky forced Henry to grab for his sunglasses. "Okay. We should be there in three hours or so."

Maria hugged herself and gave a fake shiver before adjusting the internal heaters to max. Henry grinned and adjusted the throttles to a matching harmony.

Three and a half hours later, they were all in the now snow-covered bunker at the Harbin strip. Bayasaa had started the generator and gotten radios online, while Jimbo fiddled with the car. After several attempts, he finally got it started and pulled it out of the garage. It had large winter tires on it, and with its weight, it drove smoothly through the shallow snow. Jimbo parked next to the plane and stepped out of the car while letting it warm up.

"All right. Temujin, you're driving. A.Z. and Khaidu, up front. All us foreigners will 'hide' in the back. Everyone got a Thompson?" Jimbo stepped over to the plane and came back with leather slings. "Here. Put these on so you can conceal them. Strap them to your back."

Maria reached over for one, stared at it, and looked at Henry. Henry signaled for her to take off her coat, and she leaned in close and whispered, "Henry. This is making me nervous."

Henry helped her fit the sling across her back. "Don't worry. It's just a precaution. We are only going to meet one guy." He pointed to everyone in the party. "Hell, we have enough firepower here to take on a small army. We'll be fine."

Maria nodded, but the worry didn't subside. Despite her husband's reassuring words, she could feel his nervousness, even though he tried to deny it to comfort her.

Jimbo opened the left rear door of the car. "All right. It's almost ten o'clock. Let's get going."

The six of them got into the car, but it took them a minute to get adjusted with the new metal across their backs. Jimbo put his hand on Temujin's shoulder, and Temujin shifted the car into gear.

Maria waved out the back window to Bayasaa as they drove off down the snow covered road. She watched until a clump of snow fell off a tree as they drove by, obscuring her view, then turned forward, grabbed Henry's hand, and watched out the side window.

The many lakes that Maria had admired on their summer runs in this region were all now frozen and covered in snow. The landscape was a beautiful unending scene of sparkly white, dark browns, and greens, with the occasional line of smoke rising from shacks that were otherwise hidden in the winter landscape.

As they approached town, Jimbo had everyone in the back seat cover their faces and keep low. They came upon an empty guard shack, but kept driving. As they approached the center of town, there was a bit of confusion in the front seat until Jimbo leaned forward and told Temujin, "Go left here. Two blocks, then left."

Temujin nodded, and when they made the final left, Jimbo leaned forward again. "There. Park back behind that building in the alley." He put his hand on Temujin's shoulder. "Stay here and keep the car running."

Chapter 17

Harbin

Jimbo looked out all the windows, and Henry followed his gaze. There were a few locals wandering by, but no one seemed the slightest bit interested in them. "Okay. Let's go." He opened the door and let Henry and Maria out.

Ai Ze stepped out of the front. "I'll stay here and guard the car and Temujin."

Jimbo confirmed his idea with a nod. "Okay. Then, Khaidu, you're with us." He pointed around the building. "This way."

As they walked toward the meet point, snow started to fall. The snow deadened the sounds around them, and all was quiet, save a few voices in the distance and the crunch of the snow under their feet.

They rounded the front of the building onto a narrow street, and Henry looked through the big glass window into a small grocery store. A woman in a thick white and green coat was busy behind the counter.

As they passed the entrance to the grocery, Jimbo stopped. "Okay. I think it's these stairs coming up."

Jimbo signaled to move forward, but before anyone took a step, Maria grabbed Henry and pulled him back. Henry looked to see her staring across the street with a look of absolute fear on her face. He followed her gaze to see three men, all Caucasians, sitting in a restaurant across the street. "What? What is it, Maria?"

She pointed and pulled Henry through the grocery store door. "Feds. G-men!" Puzzlement appeared on Henry's face. Maria yanked him harder. "Trust me!". Henry's expression changed to concern as he looked her in the eye.

Jimbo and Khaidu, hearing the fear and confusion, stopped and backed up to go into the store with them. Jimbo, with annoyance and puzzlement on his face, demanded, "What the hell is going on?"

Henry waved his hand in front of Jimbo while trying to hear Maria.

Maria, spoke with choked up fear in her voice. "Across the street. Those are G-men. What could they—"

The shop woman interrupted with a greeting and walked over to them. Everyone looked at the shopkeeper, having forgotten they were in a store. Jimbo put his hand up, but she kept talking, so he signaled Khaidu to take care of it. Khaidu smiled and started speaking to her in Mandarin while pointing to some meat hanging in the window, and drew her away.

Jimbo turned back to Maria. "What were you sayi—"

Sudden shouts from above stopped Jimbo mid sentence. A second voice yelled back, and Jimbo cocked his head as though he was listening to the ceiling.

Henry saw the expression on his face. "What?"

Jimbo put his finger up and turned his ear towards the ceiling. "It's Anatoly!" The sudden sound of something slamming of hard against the floor upstairs made them all jump, and Jimbo pulled out his .45. "Khaidu. Come with me."

Jimbo, seeing Maria looking around in apparent confusion; pointed to her and Henry. "You two stay here."

The front door dinged as they exited back out onto the street. Jimbo turned left and took a step in front of the stairs before coming face to face with one of the agents who had been across the street. Both men were equally startled and stood there in front of the stairs in temporary shock, with their .45s in hand and snow falling between them. Jimbo was looking at the agent's face when he saw a flash, and then nothing but red.

Jimbo felt Khaidu's arms wrap around him and yank him back, before they fell to the ground. He suddenly realized that he was hearing machine-gun fire, and his heart rate spiked as he scrambled backwards. He couldn't get enough traction to stand up and slid backwards to the grocery store door. Khaidu opened the door and they both fell back into the store. Maria made a small yelp, but didn't scream. That didn't stop the shopkeeper, whose shrieks filled the crowded space.

Jimbo was flailing around, unsuccessfully trying get up and wipe his eyes. Henry held him down and used his coat to wipe the blood from Jimbo's face. He finally began to calm down a bit once he could see again. Jimbo felt himself for holes and put his hand against his mouth. "My god . . . what the hell just happened?"

More loud sounds and screaming came from upstairs. Khaidu pointed upstairs. "They try to shoot you from upstairs."

Jimbo stood up and slowly made his way to the door. He peeked out the door to see the G-man dead in the street, his blood splattered across the white snow. He then looked across the street to see the caucasians pushing tables up onto their sides. Several waitresses and customers ran out of the restaurant.

Jimbo heard more shouting from upstairs and then his old friend, Anatoly's voice, crying out in pain.

Henry came up behind him. "What is going on?!"

Jimbo turned, pushed him out of the way, and yanked his own coat off. He pulled his Thompson from behind his back and cocked it, then walked to the back of the store with deadly purpose. The shopkeeper had stopped screaming and was now hiding behind the counter, but she let out a yelp as Jimbo walked by her. Jimbo turned and shushed her. He turned, stepped into a closet that was tucked under the stairs, and listened for a second. He emptied a clip into the ceiling, and the impact of a body falling down the stairs shook the steps over Jimbo's head.

Within seconds, gunfire erupted from upstairs and from across the street. Everyone in the store instinctively fell to the floor. Henry glared at Jimbo. "What the hell are we into, here?!"

Jimbo was looking around the store. "The men upstairs are probably Stalin's men. They want what Anatoly has. Damn. They probably followed him here hoping he would retrieve it, so that they could get it . . . no wonder they let him loose."

Henry, shaking his head with confusion, blurted. "Uncle! What the hell are you talking about?"

Jimbo looked at him, but he was deep in thought. His mouthed moved as though he was finally going to speak, when the front window of the store exploded. Everyone's instant reflex was to cover their heads again as the glass shattered.

Henry was the first to raise his head and he turned to Maria, putting his hand on her. "Maria! Are you okay?"

Bits of glass tumbled out of her hair as she raised her head, and more fell as she nodded. "Yes. I'm okay." She looked at him with fear on her face and loudly whispered, "Henry, what is happening here?"

Henry shook his head, scattering more glass and dust. "I don't know, but we need to get the hell out!" He took off his coat, shook it, and grabbed his Thompson, then helped her do the same. When he turned to look for Jimbo, he found him and Khaidu peeking out the front door. Henry got to his feet, but stayed bent over and started making his way over to the door. The shooting stopped, and it got quiet; Henry stopped at the change and listened. He could hear vehicles, and something else: a deep, rumbling sound.

Jimbo, still watching out the front door, turned back to Henry and Maria. "Japs!"

The sound of gunfire started up again, but it sounded different. Henry came up to the door and he could see flashes of light from shooting across the street. All the windows had been blown out, but the G-men were no longer shooting at the Russians.

Jimbo waved for Henry to come forward. "Everyone is shooting at the Japs. Come on! This is our chance to get Anatoly."

Jimbo and Khaidu stepped out into the street, but stayed close to the building. When Jimbo reached the stairs, he took a very fast glance up, saying, "No one there. Let's go," but before he could get into the stairwell, three Japanese soldiers came around the front of the building. The first one saw Jimbo and raised his rifle to fire, but Jimbo was faster and emptied half his clip into the three of them. Jimbo dropped to his knee as he shot, and watched for a second to make sure there were no more. He looked up the street and, exclaimed, "Holy shit!" then called back to everyone, "They have a tank! Let's go, now!" He raced up the stairs with Khaidu; Henry and Maria following close behind them.

As Jimbo climbed the stairs, one of the Russians crossed the hall from left to right, half bent over. Jimbo froze, but the Russian hadn't seen him. Jimbo turned and signaled the others with his finger over his mouth, then began to climb the stairs slowly. When he reached the top of the stairs, he looked to the right and saw three Russians, one with a heavy machine gun, firing out the window. Return fire was raking the ceiling and walls. Jimbo looked to the left to see Anatoly looking back at him.

His old friend was tied to a chair, his face covered in blood, but his eyes got big and a smile appeared as he recognized Jimbo. Jimbo smiled back and put his finger over his lips. Anatoly nodded.

Jimbo looked at Khaidu and pointed to the three Russians firing out the window. Khaidu nodded and took a position covering them, while Jimbo went to free Anatoly; Henry followed him, and Maria covered the stairs.

As Henry and his uncle were untying Anatoly, the room across the hall exploded from what could only be a tank shell hit. There were screams that cut short abruptly, and the inner wall collapsed into the stairwell. Jimbo watched Henry, with his Thompson at the ready, step back into the hall before immediately falling to the floor, saying "shit." Jimbo stepped towards the door and peeked around the door frame to see the room that had been there was simply gone; he could plainly see the smoking tank and troops below. Maria's muffled voice could be heard from under the debris and Henry glanced up at him before setting his gun down to lift part of the wall covering the stairwell. "I'll get her."

Maria was underneath, and grunting sounds could be heard from her pushing up. As Henry lifted the debris off her, she looked up at him, shaking. "I'm fine. You?"

Henry felt himself. "Yeah, fine . . . wait, Khaidu!" He lifted another part of the wall, but the movement attracted rifle fire from the Japanese and he dropped the wall.

Maria yelped, "Henry!" and pointed at the stairs and side wall.

Henry looked to see blood flowing and realized that Kaidu was beyond rescuing. "Shit, Jimbo, we need to—" He turned to see Jimbo gone. Henry scurried across the floor on his stomach and stuck his head around the corner to see Anatoly kicking in part of a wall and then ripping a board out of the floor. He curiously watched Jimbo reached in the hole and pulled out a small tin. Henry saw his face light up as he opened the tin, then yelled at him, "Let's get out of here!"

Jimbo shut the tin and put it in his pocket. Both Jimbo and Anatoly looked over at Henry and nodded in agreement. Since Henry's movement of the wall, the amount of fire was increasing. Bullets were hitting the ceiling and the walls and were preventing Jimbo from getting into the stairwell. Jimbo looked down to see two Russian grenades and a submachine gun lying next to the chair where he had shot through the floor. He grabbed the two grenades and looked at Henry. "I will throw these at the Japs while you make a break for it. Everyone, get back to the car!"

Jimbo watched Henry glance at Maria and back at him. He nodded. "Ready!"

Jimbo looked around, searching. "Where's Khaidu?" Henry shook his head and Jimbo immediately understood. "Okay. Let's go!"

Jimbo pulled the pin; the top of the grenade popped off, and he threw it out the side of the ruined building. "Go!"

Jimbo watched as Henry and Maria made a dash down

the stairs, slipping on all the debris. There was an explosion and screaming, before Jimbo threw the second grenade and raced down the stairs behind them, with Anatoly.

Henry peeked around the corner to see several troops trying to inch their way toward the stairs, but they were still under fire from across the street. The tank fired into their building again and the entire upper floor of the building disintegrated. Maria and Henry covered their heads and ducked in the door frame as part of the roof came crashing down into the street, debris raining down around them.

Once the crashing stopped, Henry wiped his face and looked out into the street. Seeing that the smashed roof had provided them with cover, Henry waved. "Come on!" They all ran out to the right, past the now half-destroyed store. Jimbo covered their back as they made their way around the building. Henry glanced over his shoulder to see the tank moving into the center of the street, crushing the roof and opening fire into the restaurant with the G-men inside.

As they ran down the alley to the car, Anatoly slipped on the snow and fell on his back. Jimbo quickly helped him back up before running to the car. Henry opened the rear door and pushed Maria in; Anatoly was next, but before Jimbo got in, he looked around. "Where the hell is A.Z.?"

Henry pointed. "There!"

Ai Ze was running down the alley, shooting behind him. Henry jumped in the front seat and Jimbo with him, slamming the door. Ai Ze leapt into the back seat, accidentally hitting Anatoly with the butt of his Thompson. Anatoly cried out in pain, but Jimbo only yelled, "Go! Floor it!"

Dirt and snow flew from the rear tires as the big car struggled for traction. A bullet shattered Jimbo's window before they cleared the alleyway. As they skidded onto the main street in front of the store, the tank fired at them. A huge cloud of smoke and snow blew out in front of the tank but the shell overshot, impacting a hardware store across the street. Debris flew out from the explosion, and shrapnel raked the front of the car.

Before they made their next turn, two Japanese staff cars came flying through the smoke in pursuit. They had imperial flags mounted on the hoods and men hanging out the sides, firing rifles. Maria spoke in a loud monotone voice. "Shit."

Henry turned back to see the cars. "We've got company!" He turned to Temujin. "Go, go. Faster!" and Jimbo repeated it in Mongolian. Temujin's face showed a blend of fear and hard concentration as he tried to control the sliding beast of a car. They made it onto the main road heading out of town, but Henry could see the two Japanese cars were in hot pursuit. A bullet hit the back window and then another hit the fender.

In the back seat, Anatoly grabbed the Thompson from Jimbo, who handed it back, and opened fire out the back window. As the window shattered and fell away in pieces, the lead car swerved, trying to avoid the fire. Maria turned, got on her knees, and began firing too. With the Japanese staff cars whipping side to side on the icy road, their gunmen were almost useless.

Anatoly, Maria, and now Ai Ze were all firing, while taking turns reloading. Maria yelled forward. "Were almost out of clips! Besides scaring them, we don't seem to be stopping them!"

Henry handed her back two more clips. "That's all I got."

Jimbo turned. "The BAR! Under the seat!"

Maria looked down at the seat, remembering that they had installed it there months ago. "Yes!" She hit Anatoly and yelled at Ai Ze. "Off the seat! We need to get the BAR." She slid onto the floor.

It took a second for the other two to register what she was saying, then they both slid onto the floor. The three of them lifted the seat, but with no one firing at the Japanese, their pursuers were able to get better shots. A high-powered round went through the now upright seat cover, between Maria and Anatoly, and struck the dash in the front. Henry ducked. "Holy shit!"

Maria grabbed the huge rifle and started dumping clips out onto the floor. Anatoly and Ai Ze did the same. They began putting the seat back down when Maria screamed, and she fell back onto the floor.

Anatoly bent down to get her and Henry, hearing her scream, squirmed over the top of the front seat. He tried to pull her up. "Maria!"

Henry heard the crack of another round go past his head and shatter the front windshield. He glanced forward while still trying to help Maria, and saw that the windshield was covered in blood with Temujin slumped across the seat. No one was driving, and the car was already drifting toward the side of the road.

Trying not to panic, he let Maria go. "Uncle! Anatoly! Somebody take her!" He spun in his seat and jerked the wheel back to the right, but the car started to slide and stall. Frantically, he slammed Temujin's body against the door and with his left foot, hit the gas. It took him a few seconds to get the car under control and going in a straight line.

"Dammit. I can't shift. His legs are in the way of the clutch."

He looked in the rearview mirror just as a round went through it, and shards of glass hit him in the face. "Ah! Goddammit!" He struggled to wipe his face on his sleeve without losing control of the car. "Maria?!"

Maria's voice was like heaven to his ears. "Henry! I'm fine. Just a graze!" Henry turned back to see her grab the BAR from Anatoly. Anger was pulsating from her face. "Give me that damn thing!"

Maria slammed a magazine into the BAR, cocked, and aimed out the back window, then let the first twenty rounds of automatic fire rip into the first car. Its radiator blew and the hood flew up into the air, slamming against the windshield. The car swerved off the road and crashed into the ditch before rolling onto its side and sliding back into the road. The second car swerved to miss the first one, but clipped it, ripping their rear bumper off.

Maria screamed. "YEAH! Take that! Give me another clip!"

Anatoly, wide eyed, handed her another one.

Henry yelled back. "There is a curve ahead! If I slow, I may stall her!"

Jimbo reached behind Henry. "I'll try to pull Temujin from behind you. Can you take his place?"

Henry nodded nervously and leaned forward. His legs were split over the stick, with his left foot on the gas. Jimbo began to slide Temujin's body across the seat behind his back.

Maria opened fire on the second car. A few rounds hit the left side, shattering their front windshield. Their right door fell off, and two men spilled out onto the road. "Clip!"

Anatoly handed her another.

Henry sat straight up. "Too late!" He hit the brakes, trying to slow for the icy curve, but the car began to slide sideways and he was forced to let go. He hit the gas again, trying to straighten out, but still couldn't reach the clutch to shift and the car stalled. "Oh, shit."

Henry continued to try to steer straight, but the car was slowing rapidly, and Jimbo was still attempting to get Temujin's body out of the way. "A.Z.! Help me." Ai Ze immediately leaned forward over the seat and began pulling the body.

A bullet hit the rear fender, and the left rear tire exploded. The extra drag pulled the car to the left and Henry yanked the wheel to the right to compensate.

The remaining staff car was only thirty feet behind them when Maria opened up with another twenty-round magazine. The front of the car ceased to exist as the front axle broke. The front right wheel went flying off the road and the car fell onto the axle parts, which dug into the ground and flipped the car in a plume of steam, smoke, dirt, and snow.

Jimbo and Ai Ze finally managed to get the body out of the driver's seat, but by that time, the car had come to a complete stop in the middle of the road.

Henry looked in his only remaining mirror, which was mounted on the spare tire, only to see what was left of the car that had been chasing them, and the smoke rising from it. He turned in disbelief to look for himself. It became very quiet except for the tinging of the engine as it started to cool. "We have a flat."

Jimbo, breathing heavily, replied, "Forget it. We don't have far to go. We don't want to wait around for any more of them, or their air force."

Henry nodded and slid fully into the driver's seat. He cranked the car over until it started again. The sudden firing of the BAR made him jump, and he turned to see Maria finishing off the staff car.

Maria turned after firing, shaky and looking a bit insane. "They won't be bothering us anymore."

As Henry released the clutch, the car groaned, jerked, and slowly gained speed. Henry had to constantly play with the gas pedal to keep traction and keep them going in a straight line, but after about ten minutes flat tire thumping, they made it back to the airstrip.

As they drove up, they could see Nick refueling his plane from barrels on the truck. Henry just let the car stall out, and pushed down the emergency brake. He took a deep breath and laid his head on the steering wheel. The excitement of the chase was wearing off, and now he only felt exhausted.

Jimbo got out of the passenger side and stumbled to the front fender. Maria opened her door, but let out a yelp of pain. Henry, suddenly remembering that she had been shot, jumped out of the car and helped her out of the back seat. "Are you all right? Where are you hit?"

Maria smiled at his concern. "Henry, it's not a big deal. Just a scratch."

Henry began feeling her body and searching up and down, until he finally saw a bloodstained tear in her pants. He reached for the waistband, yanking them partway down, and she yelped in surprise. "Henry! It's okay!"

Henry looked at her injury as Ai Ze stepped out of the car. Then Maria finally pushed Henry away. "It's fine. Stop messing with it."

Henry looked at her face for signs of pain or shock, trying to determine if she was really all right. When he was satisfied, he sat down on the running board. Anatoly climbed out past him, grunting in discomfort, and tried to stand in a completely uncoordinated way. Henry leaned out of his way and wiped his brow. "Whew . . ." He took deep breath, but halfway through he froze, and suddenly stood up. "How did you know they were G-men?"

Maria looked at him. Her eyes wandered and her mouth moved as though she was trying to speak, but nothing was said. Henry cocked his head and suspicion came over his face. "How did you recognize those guys? How did you know?"

Maria took a step back. "I—Henry . . . it was . . ." She put her hand up to touch his face, but now Henry was thinking of possibilities and he began to get angry. "*How did you know?!*"

From across the runway, Nick and Bayasaa yelled and came running. Nick stopped when he saw the carnage, but Bayasaa ran to Jimbo. Jimbo had walked around the left side of the car to stare at Henry and Maria, a puzzled expression on his face. Bayasaa looked at Ai Ze leaning on the front left fender and, with hand shaking, handed Jimbo a telegram.

Maria began to cry. "I'm sorry. There wasn't a choice."

Henry took her by the shoulders. "Wasn't a choice? What have you done?!" His jaw dropped at the sudden realization. "It was you! You were the rat! *You* told the Feds about us . . . and you got Rocco's nephew killed." He pushed her away. "All these years and you never told me!"

Maria tried to touch Henry again, but he pushed her away

a second time. "This hell we have been through, working our asses off, risking everything to pay back Rocco, all that was because of you?!"

Jimbo was growing very concerned and took a step towards Maria, but when he started to read the telegram, his focus suddenly turned to Ai Ze. Jimbo's eyes narrowed; Ai Ze started to stand up and Bayasaa backed away with fear taking over his face. Ai Ze suddenly reached for his Thompson, but Jimbo was faster with his .45. A single shot to the head ended Ai Ze, but he had already reached the trigger, and the Thompson sprayed bullets into the wheel well. As the front tire went flat, the car and Ai Ze both slumped.

Henry and Maria both jolted at the sound and spun around in shock and horror. Henry watched Ai Ze slide down the fender and fall onto the running board. "Uncle?"

Jimbo reached down and ripped open Ai Ze's coat. He felt the pockets and pulled out a large envelope full of cash. "Traitor's Jap bribe!" He put it into his own pocket, then turned his still smoking .45 at Maria. "Just how many traitors do we have, here?"

Henry looked at the gun in disbelief and then at Maria, who was crying and putting her hands up. "No! No! Henry, you have to understand. I am sorry. I did it for us. It was the only way! They were going to lock us up!"

Henry stepped in front of the .45 "Uncle! Put the damn gun down. I will handle this."

Jimbo, his eyes still narrow and suspicious, shifted his focus from Maria to Henry. After studying Henry's face for a few seconds, he finally pointed the gun at the ground and manually released the hammer. "What a goddamn mess," he muttered as he put it back in his holster. He looked at his now destroyed car, riddled with holes and splashed with blood. "Goddamn mess!"

He looked over at Anatoly, who was still leaning against the car, almost expressionless. "Let's get the hell out of here. Bayasaa, Anatoly, help me with Temujin's body. We will take him home." He pointed at Ai Ze's body. "As for this scum, we'll just leave him here for the wolves."

Henry turned back to Maria. "I can't believe after all these years, that you never told me. You betrayed me, lied to me all this time!"

She tried to hug him, but he backed up. "Henry . . . Henry, I got caught. They said they were going to throw the two of us in jail forever if we didn't help them. I did it for us!"

Henry pointed his finger and scolded her. "Why did you never tell me? Why? How?! How could you lie to me all these years?!" He waved his hand in anger and walked away towards the planes.

Maria took a few steps after him with her hands out. "Henry, please! I'm sorry—I tried to tell you so many times . . . I'm so sorry . . . ." She collapsed to the ground and fell against the rear fender of the car. She sat in the snow, weeping and whispering to herself. "I'm sorry, I'm sorry."

As Henry walked past the totally stunned Nick, he asked, "Where are you flying to?"

Nick stared at him, wide-eyed, and Henry pointed to his plane. "Where are you going?" he repeated.

Nick glanced back at his plane. "Kalgan."

Henry nodded. "I'm taking her. You take this lot home with the '3." He looked back at Maria, who was huddled, still crying, in the snow, and sighed. "And take care of her for me."

Nick, with horror on his face, just nodded in agreement.

A few minutes later, the O-2's engine roared and Henry took off into the sky. Nick was helping Maria limp across the runway, when they stopped to watch Henry take off. Maria screamed into the air, *"Henry! I'm sorry!!"* She turned and cried on Nick's shoulder while whimpering, "Don't go. I never wanted to hurt you . . . I love you, Henry, you are all that I love."

Nick, looking bewildered, patted her on the head. "It will be okay. I think he just needs to blow off some steam. What happened back there?"

Maria looked up at him with tears streaming down her face. In a garbled voice, she tried to explain. "I got caught years ago for smuggling booze. They were going to lock us up. I had to tell them." She shook her head. "I didn't know how to tell Henry!"

Nick, still confused asked, "What about Ai Ze?"

Maria paused her crying and glanced over at the smoking car. "I don't know. He left for a while. I guess he was getting paid by the Japs, so he was a traitor?" She looked back up at the sky. "Where is Henry going? I have to go . . ."

Jimbo yelled from across the field. "Let's go! We don't have much time before more Japs show up!"

Nick pulled her with him to the DC3 and got her on board before making his way to the cockpit and starting the engines. Snow whirled in the DC3's artificial snow storm as they taxied and finally took off. As they began to climb, Bayasaa pointed out the right-side window. "Japanese!"

Jimbo leaned over to see a convoy of trucks and tanks on the road to the airstrip. "Damn! So much for that place." He shook his head and leaned back in his seat. "Goddamn mess."

Chapter 18

Down Into Darkness

Henry flew south, gaining altitude over the winter landscape. He could see his breath in the cockpit, but he was so preoccupied that he didn't even think of the cold. He banged his fist on the dash and tried to kick something not vital. "Dammit!" His head fell back and he yelled at the top of his lungs. "*WHY?* What the hell were you thinking?! Maria! I can't believe—of all the son of a bitch things—Argh! Goddammit!" He banged his fist around the aircraft until the left side window latch gave way.

The sudden rush of freezing air brought him back to his senses. He looked at the banging window, barely able to keep his eyes open in the frigid wind. The emotional battle inside his head caused him to hesitate, but he finally reached up and latched it again. It held for a second, but reopened; Henry looked at the latch closely, and saw that he had broken the tip off when he'd hit it. "Damn . . . idiot." The cold was starting to get to him; he turned the heat on full in the little cockpit, then looked around to find something to secure the window. He eventually found a bit of cloth on the floor and jammed it into the latch, and after fiddling with it for a bit, it finally held. Henry relaxed a bit as he rubbed his forehead and closed his eyes, thinking of all that had just happened.

After a few hours, he found the airstrip at Kalgan and brought the little craft in for a smooth landing. As he shut down the engine, several troops came over. They knocked on the side of the plane, and Henry got out to help them unload.

A young woman with two braids flowing from under her dark green hat and a single-shot rifle slung across her back helped him off-load several crates. After stacking a third crate, she looked up at him and gave a small smile. The gesture made him snap out of the funk he was in. He suddenly felt like he was back in reality and he looked around at his surroundings. It was getting dark, and the valley was beginning to disappear into the blackness.

The woman said "*Wie.*" and Henry looked to see she wanted help with the next crate. As he reached for the crate, lights suddenly appeared at the other end of the strip. Both Henry and the girl turned to look as machine-gun fire erupted. There was sudden yelling, and men grabbed for their rifles. The woman ducked behind the crates and pulled the rifle off her back.

Henry ducked with her. "What?" Then, trying his best at Chinese, "*Shi ma?*"

The woman glanced at him. "Kuomintang! Kuomintang!" She pointed at him, then the plane, and made "take off" gestures. Henry nodded and patted her on the back.

As soon as Henry started the engine, the noise drew fire. He throttled up as he heard bullets penetrating the plane's skin. He looked in front of him to see the shadow of the mountain against sky, and knew that he had to take off towards the enemy. As he came about, he could see the flashes of the rifles from the girl and the men that had been helping him unload. Some of the lights started to go out as the fire fight intensified, and Henry pushed the throttle to maximum, with full flaps down. He watched the needle on the speed indicator move, praying that he could just get enough speed to get off the ground.

As he approached the end of the runway, he was finally able to rotate into the sky, but as he did, two bullets hit the windshield. Then more hit the upper and lower wings. He saw sparks fly off the engine cowling and then flames emerged. In a panic, he looked for the fire suppression system—if there was one on this plane, he wasn't familiar enough with it—as the flames grew.

Henry looked down at the ground, which was nothing but blackness. His heart started to pound, then part of the engine exploded and the prop locked. The sudden stopping of the propeller transferred the rotation momentum to the body of the plane, and it inverted.

Henry's blood pressure skyrocketed for the second time that day. He looked at the artificial horizon indicator, showing that he was nearly upside down, he immediately tried to flip the plane back using the ailerons. He had just begun to level off the craft when Henry was slammed against his belt, the sound of ripping sheet metal filled his ears, and the world went black.

Back in Mongolia, Nick finally landed the DC-3. As they rolled to a halt, people emerged from their ghers to welcome them back. Jimbo opened the back door with sadness and concern on his face. As the crowd gathered around, Jimbo put his hands up and told them in Mongolian "Please back up . . . back up a bit, please."

He and Bayasaa gently brought Temujin's cloth-covered body out of the plane. Blood had stained the white cloth, and everyone became quiet. The gathered crowd watched everyone get off the plane, and someone asked, "Henry?"

That made Maria cover her face and start crying again, but

Jimbo shook his head. "No, I am afraid it's . . . Temujin."

Temujin's wife, Bolormaa, ran up to the body and tried to pull the cloth off, but Bayasaa stopped her and hugged her. She screamed, and Bayasaa tried to hold her up, but she fell to the ground. From behind Bayasaa, all the women came and surrounded Bolormaa to help.

Then Maria collapsed to the ground, too, and a few of the women, including Zheng Zi Ling, went to help her as well. Confusion erupted in the crowd as everyone tried talking at once.

Jimbo tried to explain, "Bolormaa, all of you . . . I am truly, deeply sorry . . . we must—", but it was too much. He put his hand over his eyes and let it slide down to his mouth, then began to walk to the big gher, weakly signaling for everyone to follow.

Nick, still overwhelmed, just stood at the rear door of the airplane and watched.

⚘⚘⚘

Later that night, Henry awoke in total darkness. He was hanging on his left side by his seat belt, and his head was throbbing. He began feeling around for a flashlight, but the sounds of gunshots and yelling in the distance made him reconsider. He tried looking up to his right, and through the partially smashed windshield, he could see stars. He rubbed his eyes and let them adjust. He could see the tops of trees, but couldn't see anything below.

Feeling around carefully, Henry was shocked to feel the bark of a tree where the left side of the plane should have been. He tried to move, but felt his waist was tightly locked by the crushed fuselage. He squirmed to get loose, but metal began to clang as the plane moved. He heard more yelling and stopped dead, his heart pounding. Henry sat in the dark and just listened for a long time.

He heard sporadic gunfire and yelling, but it didn't seem to be getting any closer.

It felt like he did nothing but sit and listen for hours. His fear of falling to his death or making too much noise made him stay put, trying not to make the plane wreckage start rattling again as he shivered from the cold.

Eventually, the trees began to light up as the nearly-full moon rose over the mountain behind him. A few minutes later, he could clearly see that he was indeed stuck in a tree. The left wings of the biplane were completely gone, and the right lower wing was missing, but the upper wing was supporting what was left of the plane, which was wedged into the fork of a large tree.

Henry looked down at all the branches below; it didn't seem like too bad a climb down. He unbuckled himself and tried again to free his waist, but the aluminum was bent in around him. He looked around to find something to pry the metal away from him. A piece of strut from the left wing was sticking in through the window; Henry tried to rip it off, but it was still attached to cabling from the wing.

He pulled the dangling cables in along with the strut and then tried to use it to pry, but finally had to resort to hammering at the aluminum instead. He banged it five times as hard as he could, and made a considerable dent.

He stopped and listened, but didn't hear anything besides his own breath, frosting in the chill air. He then wiggled his way loose and fell forward onto the dash. The plane rocked and made horrible clanging sounds. Henry's heart began to pound again; someone had to have heard that much noise.

Carefully but quickly, Henry climbed out onto the large

branch on the left side of the plane, then turned back to find a weapon. He felt around and found his Thompson, but it only had one clip. He remembered that he had given his extras to Maria. The thought of Maria made him stop and feelings of anger, worry, and love surfaced into a tangled, disabling mixture of emotion. Henry collapsed onto the branch, unable to move—but when a piece of bark broke loose from under his foot, he lost his grip. He grabbed for anything and caught a dangling strut of the plane, causing the plane to clang and creek. The sudden return of fear brought him back to reality and he regained focus.

Henry leaned out over his tree limb and looked down again. With the moon rising even higher, it was easier to see, but, he thought, it would be easier for others to see him as well. His leg was badly bruised and caused him considerable pain, but knowing that his survival was at stake, he was able to ignore it and eventually made his way down the tree. Several times, he became entangled in wing cabling and had to work his way free. Finally, near the bottom, he put the Thompson over his back and jumped the remaining six feet.

He landed hard and let out a groan, which he tried to stifle. He let himself fall to the ground and lay there listening for a few moments. He could hear voices and rustling sounds getting closer, so he got to his feet and walked as fast as he could, away from the voices. His bruised right leg began hurting him more and he started to limp, but fear kept him going.

Henry looked up at the stars through the tree canopy and could see that he was heading west, more or less. Recalling the map in his mind's eye, he remembered where the two valleys crossed and made for that landmark. He could escape to the north, once he reached it.

Chapter 19

The Rescues

Maria sat in her gher, wrapped in fur, next to the fire, talking quietly to herself. "Henry . . . you know I would never hurt you. I did it for us." She rocked back and forth, hitting her fist on the floor as she wrestled with her thoughts. "I should have told you . . . but I couldn't find a way. You were so adamant with that Rocco that we didn't do anything. You would have been so mad if I told you we did—just like you are now." She put her hands over her face and sobbed. She choked on her words as she whispered. "I am sorry, so sorry . . . please come back . . ."

Days had gone by, and there was no sign of Henry. Maria had become more and more withdrawn and she refused to eat. On the third day, Bayasaa came in the tent to check on her. He handed her a hot plate of food, but she put her hand up in refusal. He took a piece of the steaming meat and tried to hand it to her. "You have to eat!"

She just turned her face away. "I'm not hungry."

Bayasaa slowly sat down next to her, and set the plate aside. "Maria, can't let starve self. I sure Henry okay."

She glanced at him and mixed emotions ran across her face. "Then where the hell is he?"

Pain swept across Bayasaa's face, but he said nothing. He just sat next to her, motionless. Eventually, Maria reached her hand over to him. "Thank you for trying to help."

He slowly nodded. His face showed sincerity and she took some comfort from it. She tilted her head slightly. "Bayasaa."

"Yes?"

She looked him in the eye. "Can we go look for Henry?"

Bayasaa's head backed up an inch. "I would help, but where we look?"

She thought for a second and then stood up. "Come with me."

She put her coat and hat on and headed out the door. Bayasaa pushed the food aside and followed.

She led him to the radio bunker and climbed in with a purpose. When she got to the bottom of the ladder, she started barking orders. "Where is my husband? When did we last hear from him? Has anyone heard from him?" Everyone stared at her, but most didn't understand. Bayasaa interrupted and tried to translate. When he finished, Zi Ling gave orders and walked over to Maria.

She spoke "We found Mao's forces received shipment, but they attacked by the KMT. There is report of plane going down, but we did not hear anything about his capture."

Maria started breathing heavily and leaned against the ladder. Bayasaa stepped over to stabilize her, but she grabbed him instead. "We have to go find him! I can't live without him!"

Bayasaa looked at her with empathy on his face, but didn't move.

She grabbed his shoulders and pulled him in. "Let's get a truck, some cash, go to Kalgan and find him!"

Bayasaa looked over at Zi Ling, who was watching with concern. Maria pulled on him harder, making him turn to look at her, face to face. He said in a yielding voice. "Okay."

She released him. She said, "Good. Let's go!" before turning and making her way up the ladder. Bayasaa, a bit stunned, looked at Zi Ling. She shrugged, so Bayasaa followed Maria up the ladder.

Maria was standing at the top of the ladder, looking around, trying to figure out which way to go. When Bayasaa got to the top, he put up his finger, said, "Moment," and ran off to one of the ghers.

Maria spotted a truck on the other side of camp and ran over to it. She jumped in it, but the keys were missing. She beat the steering wheel and climbed back out again, frustrated at not knowing what to do. Then Jimbo appeared with Bayasaa, and they both came running to her. Jimbo reached over and pulled her coat together. "Careful or you'll freeze out here! What are you trying to do?!"

Maria stepped toward him. "Trying to get my husband back! And nothing you do or say is going to stop me!"

Jimbo took a step back at the aggressive response. He looked at Bayasaa. Bayasaa responded. "We must do boss.", but Jimbo just stood there.

Maria, with her frustration growing, started beating her fist against his chest. "Do something! Goddammit! I can't just sit around here and not know! I have to do something!"

Jimbo put his arms around her, trying to calm her and stop her from continuing to beat him. "Okay. Okay. We are!"

"We are what?"

He released her and stepped back. "We are looking for him. Using all our contacts and networks. What else do you want us to do?"

"You could have told me this a couple of days ago, for starters!"

"Why? What good would it have done to tell you we don't know anything? You're already near to killing yourself with worry, not eating, not sleeping. I wanted to leave you in peace!"

"I've had it with peace." She pointed to the truck behind her. "Let's take a truck, go to Kalgan and find him!"

Jimbo responded, "That's crazy! It's dangerous and your chance of finding him is—"

Maria started pounding on him again. "Goddammit! Are you listening to me?! I am going to find him and neither you, the damn Japs, or any other goddamn army is going to stop me! Do you hear me?!"

Jimbo rubbed his mustache, and gave in with a reluctant sigh. "Okay. I will send a few men with you, but you stay hidden, okay? A white woman is going to stick out like a sore thumb."

Maria began to calm down. "Okay."

Jimbo looked at Bayasaa. "Grab two more men and take her to Kalgan, but be careful! Take the back roads and avoid everyone. Take weapons with you."

With the truck fully loaded with extra fuel, food and a small arsenal of weapons, they set out at first light, driving south over the snowy landscape. Jimbo had at least managed to convince Maria that trying to find Henry in the dark, in a war-zone, would be foolhardy at best. The ground was frozen and made it fairly easy going for the truck. They drove for hours, with Bayasaa hiding with Maria in the back. The bumping and shifting of the truck kept knocking Maria off the bench, so she just sat on the floor, together with Bayasaa.

He watched her, with empathy on his face, until she finally looked up at him. "Stop looking at me like that!"

Bayasaa looked at the floor. "Sorry, I worried about you."

Maria took a deep breath. "I know. I am sorry, too, for being so harsh."

Bayasaa put up his hand. "No. No. I understand completely."

A few more hours went by, and the ride became a little more bearable as they switched from cross-country driving to dirt roads. Bayasaa pounded on the cab and the truck stopped. He yelled something in Mongolian and turned to Maria. "Pee."

Maria nodded and they both got out of the back of the truck. The road was lightly forested and Maria walked off to a nearby bush for privacy.

When she came back, everyone was stretching and walking around. She walked up to Bayasaa. "How much longer?"

Bayasaa turned to the driver and asked. Then he turned back to Maria. "Maybe five more hour. Depends if we have to change roads."

Maria nodded. "Okay. Then let's go."

Bayasaa nodded and signaled for the driver to continue. He and Maria climbed into the back and secured the tailgate as the driver started the truck.

Another two hours passed and Bayasaa, getting hungry, pulled out some jerky and took a bite. He handed Maria a piece and smiled when she ate it. Maria acknowledged his kindness by putting her hand on his, but she suddenly whipped it away, trying to steady herself as the truck came to an abrupt halt. Maria and Bayasaa both flew against the cab with a loud bang. Maria was holding her head as they peeked through the front, and saw a car blocking the road. Sudden fear made her heart rate shoot up and she grabbed Bayasaa's arm.

Two Japanese soldiers approached the truck. Bayasaa grabbed for his Thompson and moved to the back of the truck, while Maria instinctively followed. While the Japanese yelled at the driver and passenger, Bayasaa peeked out the back and jumped down. When he hit the ground, he rolled and shot the yelling soldier on the left, then he rolled right, and before the second man could aim his rifle, shot him with three rounds.

Bayasaa stood up and called, "Maria, let's go!" He started to lift her over the tailgate, when a shot rang out from behind. Bayasaa's face turned to both pain and apology as he slipped down, falling to the ground. Maria looked up to see a Japanese soldier aiming a smoking rifle at her. She froze with fear starring wide-eyed at the soldier. Sudden shots from up front made her jump and the soldier ran up to her and pushed aside the tarp, aiming his rifle inside the truck. When he saw no one else, he undid the rear gate and pulled her out. She fell hard on top of Bayasaa's bloody body.

The soldier yelled at Maria, and kicked her to get up. She grabbed at Bayasaa, not wanting to let him go, as the soldier finally yanked her off his body. She screamed. "No! Bayasaa, Get up!" The soldier threw her against the truck and switched to a pistol before pushing her around the side of the vehicle. A dead soldier lay on the ground alongside her Mongolian driver. With sudden heavy thoughts of guilt, she bent over to touch the driver. "What have I done? I didn't mean for—"

Maria felt an abrupt pain burst across the back of her head, and everything went black.

Maria awoke to a blurry vision of the bottom of a car seat. Her head pounded as she was bounced around by the rough road. She flinched when her head hit the seat bottom, unable to catch herself due to her restrained hands and feet. She wanted to scream, but held it back when she heard the soldiers talking. Thoughts of Henry, and those she had just gotten killed, raced through her mind. Guilt and despair flowed over her at the realization that this was probably the end. She whispered to herself. "It's all because of me, everything, all of it."

Two days later, Jimbo was pacing between ghers rubbing his mustache furiously, with mixed feelings of betrayal, guilt, and helplessness. The realization that he had lost his top, most trusted . . . and most loved people, with nothing he could do about it, was tearing him apart inside. He was desperate to find a solution, but nothing was of any use. There had been no information from any contacts and his now-decapitated operation was in serious jeopardy. He turned to pace on the bare ground he had created, when Inalchuk, Jimbo's best English translator and radio operator, startled him. She stood at attention with her black ponytail over her left shoulder. "Sir. Ops report a contact to the south."

Jimbo's face turned from helplessness to serious concern. "Who? Who is it? Japs?"

Inalchuk shook her head. "Don't know."

Jimbo dashed for the radio bunker, slipping on the ice and snow as he did. He quickly slid down the ladder. "What do we have?"

Zi Ling said, "Motorcycle. One man with white flag."

Jimbo looked puzzled. "Who the hell could that be? He

turned to Inalchuk. "Get armed men ready around camp, but don't shoot unless I say!"

Inalchuk nodded and climbed back up the ladder.

Jimbo pulled out his pipe and chewed on it. "Hmm."

A few minutes later, Jimbo and a few men were lying on the ground with machine-guns aimed south. They started to hear the sound of the motorcycle, and Jimbo peered into the distance through his binoculars. As described, all he saw was a motorcycle with a sidecar and a large white flag with writing on it.

Jimbo strained to read the flapping flag. "H . . . E . . . N . . ." He scrambled to his feet. "It's Henry!" he shouted. "Don't shoot! It's Henry!"

Everyone stood up and began to relax. The motorcycle came flying through the snow until it approached Jimbo and his men. At the last second, the motorcycle, with the blue star Chinese Nationalist symbol on the side, skidded to a sideways stop and Henry removed his goggles and hat. "Hey guys! What's up?"

Jimbo, with shock on his face, ran to him and gave him a huge hug. "Oh my god! How? What happened?!" Everyone excitedly gathered around Henry, and he was soon the center of a large group hug.

He pushed back, grinning. "Whoa, whoa! Calm down! I'm okay! What a nightmare! I got shot down into a tree. The KMT showed up and . . ." He trailed off, looking around in sudden apprehension. "Where is Maria?"

The crowd became silent.

Henry felt a chill run down his spine. "What happened?"

Jimbo's eyes began to shift. "Henry . . . let's go back to the gher. Get you some food."

Henry stepped off the motorcycle with anger in his voice. "Jimbo! What the hell happened to my wife?"

Jimbo pointed south. "I couldn't stop her. She went out to find you with Bayasaa."

Henry grabbed Jimbo. "What?!"

Jimbo looked him in the eye. "I sent armed men with them. They took a truck to go find you in Kalgan. We'd heard you were shot down. There is no way I could have stopped her without physically tying her up!"

Henry thought for a second and released Jimbo. "Goddammit. She is so damn stubborn! I have to go get her. Anything could happen to her! When did she leave?"

Jimbo rubbed his mustache. "Two days ago, but it's just as dangerous for you to go as it was for her. I can't let you go—"

Henry interrupted. "Dammit! It's my fault! I have to go. I shouldn't have left her in the first place. But I was so goddamn mad!"

Jimbo tried to put his arm on Henry, but Henry pushed it off. "No time for the sentimental crap! We have to find her!"

Jimbo nodded.

Henry thought. "How the hell are we going to find her though?"

Jimbo pointed to the radio bunker. "A white woman in these parts won't go unnoticed for long, especially if she's been captured. We already reached out to our local contacts, but no one has heard anything yet."

Henry looked at him. "Captured? Oh, god."

Jimbo started to walk to the bunker. "Come on, Henry. Come with me to the radio bunker and we'll keep trying. At least we'll be doing something."

Henry, clearly distraught, followed.

Snow whipped across the runway as Henry, followed by the entourage of people, walked toward the bunker. He tried to climb down the ladder, but many of the locals were smiling and putting their hands on him in their excitement to see him again. When he descended two rungs, he looked up at everyone. "Thank you all for the warm welcome! I am glad to be back, but we have to find Maria."

The expressions on the people changed from smiles to worry when he mentioned Maria's name, even though he knew many didn't understand his English.

Jimbo was already directing radio traffic, so Henry walked over, but Jimbo just pointed to a seat. Henry sat and watched, hoping that some bit of information could be found. Guilt flowed over him in waves, forcing him to get up and pace. After half an hour, Henry was making a visible trail in the dirt floor and the radio operators kept glancing over at him, while they tried desperately to find any new information.

Another thirty minutes went by and Henry interrupted Jimbo, "Anything yet?"

Jimbo turned and took hold of him by the shoulder. "Look, my boy, maybe this was a bad idea. Not looking for her, but having you down here while we do. You're driving yourself crazy, and no one can concentrate. I think you should go topside and get some food, and some rest. You will be the first to hear if we find something."

Henry started to protest, but then just closed his eyes and

gave in. "Okay. Okay. I'll be in the main gher." He walked to the ladder and pointed back at Jimbo. "If you hear anything!"

Jimbo nodded. "Yes, of course."

Henry was exhausted and he knew he needed food. When he entered the gher, Miiga, anticipating his need, immediately brought him food. He sat, closed his eyes and took a bite of the grilled meat. It tasted amazing, and his hunger spiked. He'd had no idea how hungry he was until that first bite. His eyes opened wide and he began to eat at a furious pace, and Miiga kept the food coming until he was finally full.

After that, exhaustion set in from the past several days' ordeal, and he lay down. It felt as though he had barely closed his eyes, however, when the door opened and Jimbo looked in at him.

Henry sat up with a jolt. "You have something?"

Jimbo nodded. "We found her."

Henry ran to the door and to the radio bunker. As they climbed down the ladder, he asked in a loud cracking voice, "What do you have?"

Jimbo pointed across the room, which was even more crowded now; Nick and Anatoly had joined them while Henry slept. "Zi Ling has her location on the map."

Henry quickly made his way over to her. "How do we know?"

She pointed on the map. "One of our Japanese informants says white woman is being held here—small airfield in Chifeng."

Jimbo interrupted. "He says that she will be transferred to intelligence for interrogation tomorrow afternoon."

Henry looked at the map. The airfield was about halfway between Harbin and Kalgan. "We need to go get her!"

Jimbo looked at Henry and carefully chose his words, not wanting to infuriate him. "We could try to work out plans of attack on the airfield, but we just don't have enough men, plus they would wipe us out once they got their aircraft up."

Henry thought for a minute before looking up from the map. "Then we need to eliminate the aircraft. Do you have a more detailed map of this airfield?"

Zi Ling turned and quickly went through a file cabinet, before pulling out a hand-drawn map of the airfield.

Henry studied the drawing intently. "How many aircraft and men are here? Any tanks?"

Jimbo put up his hands while looking around. "We don't really know. I suspect it's just a small wing of fighters, a few bombers, and some recon aircraft. There are probably fifty to a hundred men stationed there. I doubt they would have tanks. Mostly machine guns, mortars, antiaircraft guns, maybe some artillery."

Henry pointed to the valley next to the runway. "Okay. If we attack just before dawn—"

Jimbo stood up straight at the boldness of the statement. "Attack?! I just told you—"

Henry pointed to the map. "Listen! The small valley next to the runway would provide excellent cover for an attack, but, like you said, we will need air cover and that's where the '3 comes in."

Jimbo looked around to see everyone watching Henry with keen interest. "How are we going to give cover with a cargo plane?"

Henry glanced up. "You still have those M-2 .50's?"
Jimbo nodded.
Henry straightened up and looked at everyone. "Good! We

will mount them under the wings." He pointed to the drawing. "Strafe the hell out of these aircraft and any vehicles on the runway. Then I will just orbit, with Bayasaa . . ." He paused at the mistake, then continued, " . . . one of you, on the .30. They can blast any Jap movement they see. Once we have created total chaos, your men will open fire from across the runway, while we send a small team in to retrieve Maria, Bayasaa, and the others.."

Jimbo made motions to protest, but then began to think. He rubbed his mustache, like he always did when he thought intensely. "Hmm . . . That might actually work. *If* we take them by surprise, of course."

Henry pointed to the buildings on the drawings. "Can your contact tell us what building she is in?"

Jimbo angled his head. "I doubt he could inquire about that without suspicion, but I'll ask him."

Henry looked around. "Who can help me mount the .50s on the wing?"

Nick and Anatoly, who had been standing in the corner listening, raised their hands.

Henry grinned at them. "Good. We will need a couple more guys. Let's get to work. Jimbo, you get trucks and weapons together and form an assault group. And see if we can find somewhere nearby to land to pick everyone up. Don't want to win the battle only to be surrounded by Japanese forces after."

Jimbo cleared his throat, and asked "Which of us is in the military here, my boy?" He was holding his pipe in the air with a sardonic expression on his face, and Henry realized that he'd been trying to catch their attention for some time now.

Henry paused, only a little sheepish. "Do you, uh, have

anything to add?"

Jimbo chewed on his pipe for a second, then said, "Nah. You're doing just fine. I'm still not used to incorporating planes into my strategy."

"Glad to hear it." Henry turned and scrambled up the ladder. "Come on, let's go! We don't have much time."

Jimbo snapped back into action, started giving orders and people began to scramble in all directions.

A fever pitch of activity, driven by purpose, took over the whole camp. As the sun set, Henry, Anatoly, and Nick were attaching the second .50 under the inside of the left wing. Sparks flew and lit up the snow as they cut a hole in the fuselage for the belt feed.

After threading the homemade belt feeds into the hole, Henry stood up and stretched his back. To the west, the sunset was deep red, with bands of orange clouds hovering higher in the sky. Overhead, some of the brighter stars were already out, and Henry watched his breath dissipate into the sky as it rose. He whispered, "Don't worry, dear, we're coming."

Nick pointed to the cockpit. "We should test these guns and put a sight in the cockpit to aim with."

Henry looked down to see him standing right in front of him. "Right. Let's do it."

After another hour, they had a rudimentary sight and electric triggers in the cockpit. Henry and ten men helped to turn the plane around so it was facing away from camp; they then lifted the rear onto some barrels to make it level. They set up targets and loaded the guns. Henry sat in the cockpit, yelling out the window. "Okay, I will fire a few tracer rounds and you and Anatoly adjust the guns. Ready?"

Everyone backed up from the plane and covered their ears. Henry pushed the triggers and the right gun fired a burst, but it was high and to the left. He looked out the window at the left gun. "Did it not fire?"

Nick shook his head. "Safety it, and let me look."

Henry heard Jimbo yell up. "Henry! The assault force is ready. I am going to send them out soon. That should give you about eight hours to finish."

Henry looked at him with a satisfied smile. "Thank you, Uncle."

A minute later, Nick appeared under the cockpit. "All right. Try it now—well, once I'm clear."

Henry replied, "Will do." He looked around, called, "Clear guns!" and pulled the triggers. The plane rumbled as two lines of tracer fire flew into the darkness. "Yeah! That's better!"

Nick came back over to the plane with Anatoly, and Henry pointed to the targets. "The right gun is still a bit low, but the left one is pretty close."

Nick threw Henry a mock salute. "Right, boss. We'll get it."

As they were adjusting the guns, a convoy of trucks formed on the airstrip. The first truck had a Russian heavy machine-gun mounted on it. About thirty men and women began loading themselves, weapons, food, fuel, and ammunition onto the trucks.

Henry climbed out of the plane, signaling to Nick and Anatoly. "Be right back."

He met Jimbo as he walked up to the first truck. "Hey."

Jimbo stopped in front of Henry and turned to point at

the trucks. "Here's your assault force. They will head out in a few minutes and run hard to get to the outskirts of the airfield before dawn." He turned back to Henry. "I told them not to stop. I told them to open fire on resistance, but, no matter what, not to stop."

Henry nodded his head in deep appreciation. He then walked past Jimbo and started to shake the hands of everyone in the convoy. It turned into quite an emotional affair. Henry suddenly felt a strong brotherly bond with all his comrades that he had not felt before, even despite living with them all this time.

Jimbo followed Henry as they came up to the rear vehicle. "We put radios in this truck. They will be on 580 kilocycles and will let you know when they are in position, or if things change."

Henry nodded. "Good."

A car pulled up behind the last truck and Zi Ling stepped out. Henry looked at her. "Are you going too?"

The young woman looked at him with slight confusion on her face. "Maria is my friend."

Jimbo nodded. "We need everyone that's able. This car will be the rescue force. They will come at the runway from the other side and attempt a rescue while you and," he pointed to the trucks, "they keep the Japs occupied."

Four heavily armed men and Zi Ling readied the car. Henry stepped over to them. "Thank you so much for helping."

Zi Ling turned to him, smiled and shook his hand. "We are in this together!"

Henry nodded and smiled.

From across the strip, Nick called, "Hey, mate. We're ready to try again."

Henry glanced over at Nick, then turned and paused,

watching the final loading of the trucks. His heavy heart was being lifted by the family nature of the effort, yet he was full of guilt for making them risk their lives for him and Maria. He sighed and walked to the plane.

As Henry sat in the cockpit, he heard the trucks start up. He wiped the side window glass and watched the convoy slowly drive off into the darkness. He felt a tinge of fear come over him that hadn't been there before.

Nick yelled up, "Hey, you going to test them?"

Henry looked down at Nick. "Oh, right—the guns." He fired another burst and tracers from both guns nailed the targets. He put his thumb out the window. "That'll do it!"

Not long afterward, Henry, Nick, Anatoly, and Jimbo were sitting in the back of the DC-3. Henry leaned against the fuselage. "Well, I think we are as ready as we can be. Just have to wait a few more hours."

Jimbo nodded. "Wow. Amazing"

Nick looked at him. "What?"

Jimbo returned the look. "How fast we put this operation together." He turned to Henry. "I suppose I shouldn't be too surprised; even though almost nobody here is a soldier, we're a well-oiled machine when it comes to the shipments, but . . . You know, you're a natural leader."

Henry sat up and looked at him with surprise. "Well, let's just see how this works first." He coughed. "We should get some sleep; and Anatoly, you want to man the .30 while Nick flies with me?"

Anatoly nodded. "*Da. Harasho*—sure."

"Jimbo, that leaves you for the radio."

Jimbo looked at Henry. "Oh, no. I am not going, my boy. I need to stay here and keep control via the radio bunker. Control of this operation and all the others we still have going on. I will get a couple of guys for you, but we still have to maintain some personnel here."

Henry nodded in understanding and stood up. "Gentlemen, I am going to get a little shuteye, if I can. See you in a few hours."

At 5:30 AM, everyone was back on the plane. Inalchuk sat at the navigator's station, and Nick took the copilot's seat. Henry looked back to see Anatoly getting the .30 ready. A fifth man was standing, not knowing what to do. Henry pointed to the .50 belt feeds. "Make sure to keep these loaded and prevent any jams." The man looked at Inalchuk, who translated smoothly. Henry watched the interaction, shook his head at the realization of how untrained and untried everyone was, and sat in the pilot's seat. "Okay. Everyone ready?"

He looked around the plane to see everyone giving him the thumbs-up except the new guy, but when he saw everyone else doing it, he mimicked them uncertainly.

Henry asked Inalchuk, "What's his name?"

Inalchuk replied, "Jack."

Henry did a double take. "Jack? That's it?"

Inalchuk nodded. "Yes. Just Jack."

Henry put his hand back. "Jack!"

Jack shook it. "Henry."

Henry smiled, turned, and put his headset on before he reached down and quickly wrote in his flight log:

"*December 5th, 1936: Rescue Maria.*"

Henry looked out onto the airstrip. "Clear prop!"

A few minutes later, they were airborne. The moon was in the east of a crystal clear sky, with stars twinkling in all directions. Henry could easily see the terrain, but he worried that they might be easily spotted themselves. The plane shook and rattled as they encountered light turbulence.

Ninety minutes went by and everyone's nerves began to rise. Inalchuk sat at the radio, monitoring 580 kilocycles, while Henry looked hard out the window to find the airfield. Nick was the first to speak up. "There. I see some lights."

Henry looked to where he was pointing. "Well, maybe that's it."

Inalchuk, her voice raised, said, "Got them. They say they are in position."

Henry looked back, with his eyes wide. "Tell them we are close. Wait for our attack first!"

Henry turned the plane towards the light. He called back, "Anatoly. Get ready!"

Cold air suddenly filled the cockpit as Anatoly opened the small luggage door and cocked the .30. "Ready!"

As they approached the lights, two large, extremely bright search lights came to life and began scanning the skies for them. "That's it! It has to be! Here we go!"

Henry increased throttle and began diving at the lights. One of the lights found him and the brightness practically blinded him. He aimed the sight at the light and opened fire. Tracers flew from the wings and into the brightness. A few seconds went by and the light disappeared and a fireball erupted into the sky. "Whoa! Hit something!"

With the searchlight out, Henry could clearly see the runway, with its planes, tower, buildings, and vehicles. He opened up again, and strafed down the parked aircraft. The planes, full of fuel, exploded into fireballs that lit the entire area. Henry, realizing he was getting a bit low, pulled up and strafed the tower, before flying by at wing's length going 200 miles per hour. He heard the sounds of bullets hitting the fuselage and pulled up to climb back into the sky.

After thirty seconds, he banked around to the left for another run, and heard Anatoly firing the .30 as they came around. As he lined up with the runway again, he could see a fighter pulling out and starting to accelerate down the runway towards them. "Shit!" He let the .50s rip again and banked the flying beast back and forth until the tracers made contact with the accelerating plane. It burst into flames and collapsed onto the runway, but Henry kept firing, trying to hit everything he could before buzzing by again. More ground fire hit the right side of the plane, and he heard one of the windows crack. "Inalchuk. Tell them to attack!"

Inalchuk began yelling on the radio.

Henry banked to the left and started to orbit the field, while Anatoly let the .30 rip. Henry watched out his side window as the airfield turned into a blazing inferno. He could see Anatoly's tracers taking out men and equipment along with streams of fire from across the runway.

Maria was tied to a chair in the corner of a small concrete room. Her clothes were half ripped off, and she was shivering from the cold. The soldiers hadn't raped her yet, but they had had their fun. She was trying to be strong, but her situation and all the guilt

she felt for what she had done was overwhelming her. Her head was down, chin lying on her chest, and tears were slowly running down her face. When she heard the alarm and sudden explosions, her heart jumped and she looked up, trying to see.

The pitch black room was suddenly lit up in shimmering, bright, glowing yellow, as fireballs billowed into the sky outside—and then she heard it, the DC-3. She knew that sound anywhere, and when it sailed by at full throttle with guns firing, Maria tried to jump up for joy, but she, and the chair, just fell on their side. She tried to get back up, struggling against the weight of the chair, but bullets began ricocheting everywhere, so she changed to squirm against her restraints. Tracer rounds flew past the small windows and people were shouting and screaming.

A stray bullet flew through the small window and hit the back wall. Maria froze in response, and lay there listening as her heart pounded in her chest. She heard the Japanese planes starting their engines, and began to worry about Henry, but then she heard the DC-3 again and more explosions. The other engine noises suddenly ceased with the explosions, and her excitement began building when she heard Henry buzz the airfield once again. "Henry!"

Japanese voices were yelling outside, and then Maria heard the sounds of the Tommy guns. A few seconds later, someone was trying to get into her room. She tried pushing her chair around to see. Flashes of gunfire lit up the room and the door slammed open. Through the smoke appeared Zheng Zi Ling's glowing face. She bent over Maria, with her ponytail hanging over her Thompson. Maria looked up at her. "Oh my god! Help me. I can't believe you're—Henry? Is Henry okay? Is that him—"

Zi Ling put her finger to her lips. "Shh!"

Maria nodded while the other woman untied her. Another man guarded the door until they slipped out to the east, the way they had come.

⋏ ⋏ ⋏

Japanese resistance faded as the overwhelming intensity of the surprise attack devastated the airfield.

Henry continued to orbit for fifteen minutes, but soon they found that there was nothing to shoot at. Then the news came. Inalchuk yelled in excitement. "They have her! They have her!"

Henry almost fainted as relief came over him. "Great! Let's meet at the rendezvous and pick everyone up."

Henry circled the airfield one more time, as Inalchuk acknowledged and radioed the orders. As the sky became bright, he could see the carnage on the runway. Dead soldiers and burning equipment were everywhere. He could also see his comrades running west, away from the runway, and then he spotted the car from the night before. "Maria!" He pointed. "That's Maria!" He excitedly turned the plane and buzzed the car.

Below him, he could see that Maria tried waving while hanging out the window, her mouth shaping the word "Henry!!", but Zi Ling pulled her back in.

Henry then turned and landed on a road a few miles north. Once they were down, he turned the plane around and made it ready for takeoff. He kept the engines running and waited, practically twitching with anticipation.

He saw a truck coming down the road, but it wasn't one of theirs. "Everyone! Guns!" They all looked forward and then scrambled to the back and out the side door. The truck, upon seeing the plane in the road, stopped. Then, from behind, and at full speed, came the car carrying Maria. Snow and dust flew into the air behind them as they went around the stopped truck. The tension in Henry's chest eased with relief, but he continued to watch the truck with suspicion. When he heard Maria's voice, he looked out to his left. He pressed his face against the window before opening it up.

She stepped to get closer, but the spinning prop made her back up. Henry excitedly pointed to the back door and Maria ran as fast as she could to it. She then climbed in and made her way to Henry.

"Henry!" Tears were rolling down her face. "Henry." She kissed him over and over. "I love you. I am so sorry!"

The others got in and came to the front to wait for the trucks. Minutes went by, and Maria started to calm down, but Henry began to get nervous. "Where the hell are they?" Then, from around the truck that was still sitting in the road, came the three vehicles from their convoy. The front one was full of bullet holes and the front fender had been torn off. As they pulled up next to the plane, everyone unloaded what they could, helped the wounded, and they all loaded into the DC-3 as fast and they could. Anatoly was the one to shout, "Everyone's here! Let's go!"

Henry nodded in acknowledgment, but the truck was blocking the road. "Maria, go and get some rest; Nick, take copilot." He suddenly turned and grabbed Maria's arm. "Where is Bayasaa?" She shook her head and began tearing up, but before Henry could say anything, Nick interrupted. "We should go! What are we going to do about the damn truck?"

Henry released Maria and spoke gently. "I'm sorry, go get strapped in . . ." He turned and stared at the truck for a second, before glancing back at Nick. "Well, I guess we have to send them a message."

The .50 gun sight was high over the truck, so Henry let a few rounds rip. Everyone became quiet and looked forward to see what was happening. The truck ground its gears and immediately began backing up. It quickly turned around, and dirt and snow flew from the tires as it sped away. Henry smiled, a little viciously. "There . . . I think that was persuasive enough."

He hit the throttles and they accelerated down the road. The truck swerved below as they took off over it. Henry pulled back on the yoke and they headed north. The sun was shining brightly as it rose, and it lit up the black clouds of smoke in the distance. Henry looked at them and said cheerfully, "I think the Japs are going to be pissed."

Nick turned to look at the smoke and nodded in agreement. "Yeah. We might be in trouble."

Chapter 20
The End of Beautiful Plans

When they landed back at base, Jimbo came out to meet the plane. Everyone began unloading and Jimbo counted as they disembarked. There were several wounded and they were taken to be cared for, but after the final person from the assault group had left the plane, Jimbo had only counted twenty-four. Then Maria appeared, covered in a blanket, and a smile grew on Jimbo's face. He was relieved and happy to see her.

Behind her was Henry, and when he exited, Maria hugged him and wouldn't let go. Henry hugged her back, kissing her repeatedly on the forehead. He pulled Maria along over to Jimbo and reached out as if to shake his uncle's hand. Jimbo reached his hand out in turn, but Henry just pulled him in close. "Thank you, Uncle! Thank you for letting me get my wife." Tears rolled down Henry's face as he finally released his emotions, but he did his best to wipe them and cover it up.

Jimbo just smiled in response, then turned to the others. "Welcome back Nick, Inalchuk, Anatoly," he spoke up so everyone could hear, "all of you. Today is a remarkable day, but I know all of you are exhausted. Everyone, get some sleep and we will have a debriefing at 1600, in the main gher."

Jimbo couldn't hide his pride, and his face beamed as he ran around helping everyone get situated, until, after about thirty minutes, the camp became quiet again. Jimbo brought out a chair and sat in the cold morning air, looking at the plane. He could see bullet holes scattered along her fuselage and lines of blood from the wounded along her side. He sat chewing on his empty pipe as while clouds of hot breath rose into the air like pipe smoke.

Someone yelled from the hatch of the radio bunker. "Sir. Ops has a contact to the south."

Jimbo turned in his chair, his pipe in his mouth, still lost in thought. When the comment registered, he immediately stood up and hustled to the radio bunker. "What do we have?"

One of the radio operators put his finger up, then pulled his headset to the side. "Single truck. They say one of ours."

Jimbo tilted his head while thinking. "One of our trucks? But how could they make it back so fast? And I thought everyone got out by plane."

The operator only shrugged.

Jimbo started to climb the ladder again. "Let's go on alert. Everyone cover the south, but again, don't fire unless I give the order!"

Jimbo watched the truck approach through his binoculars. It was lumbering slowly across the snow while weaving back and forth. As the truck got within a hundred meters Jimbo yelled, "Hold your fire." He only saw one man and was trying to make out who it was, but the truck suddenly stalled and the driver fell over. Jimbo let down the binoculars and then looked through them one more time. He turned to the two men next to him. "Let's go find out who it is. The rest of you, cover us."

As they approached the truck, Jimbo and the other two had their Thompsons raised. Jimbo covered the driver's door as the man to his left opened it.

Bayasaa fell out onto the ground, trailing blood.

Jimbo dropped his weapon and ran to help. "My god! Bayasaa!" He turned Bayasaa on his back and yelled. "Get help!"

The two men ran off, yelling for the doctor.

Henry awoke to the sounds of shouting and sudden commotion outside. He looked at Maria, who was lying with him; one of her eyes opened and she met his gaze.

"What is it, Henry?" She let out a cry of pain as she tried to rotate.

Henry put his hand on her to stop her from moving. "Take it easy, hon. I don't know what's going on, but I will go see. You stay here and rest."

Half conscious, she nodded and Henry scooted out of bed, trying his best not to move her.

Once outside, Henry saw someone being brought across the runway on a stretcher, with an I.V. held over their head. Then he saw Jimbo escorting the stretcher, and ran to see. "Who is it?"

Jimbo looked up at Henry with joy on his face. "It's Bayasaa!"

Henry, shocked, looked down to see that it was indeed Bayasaa. His face was covered in blood and dirt, but it was definitely him. "Will he make it?"

Jimbo shook his head. "I don't know. He was shot through the back and they are going to try doing surgery now."

"What about the other two men?"

Jimbo shook his head. "We found one dead in the passenger seat, but the driver is missing."

Henry put his hand over his mouth and spoke under his

breath. "Dammit. I shouldn't have taken Nick's plane." He turned and started to walk away. "None of this would have—"

Jimbo put his hand on his shoulder. "Henry. Don't beat yourself up. You didn't know any of this would happen! The things we went through that day in Harbin . . . no one is prepared to handle that kind of emotional trauma, not even you." Jimbo stepped in front of Henry. "Listen to me. You are an honorable man, and you risked your life to save others. I mean, look at the rescue you performed this morning. I would never have thought such a thing was possible! But you did it for love. You did it for the love of Maria." Henry finally looked Jimbo in the eye and Jimbo continued, "That woman loves you more than anything on this Earth and everyone knows it."

Henry's eyes were tearing up, but he didn't want Jimbo to see, so he pushed him aside.

Jimbo responded, "Don't worry my boy. You think I don't cry?" He chuckled a bit and put his hand back on Henry's shoulder. "I try to fight it like you, but love gets the best of us. Sometimes it's too powerful to stop."

Henry wiped his eyes and looked at him, but Jimbo pointed to his gher. "Go be with Maria. I'll let you know how Bayasaa's doing. All right?" Henry nodded, grateful, and walked back to his gher. When he got to the door, he took a last look at Jimbo, who smiled back.

Henry tried to get back into bed with Maria without waking her, but she asked with her eyes closed. "What was it?"

Henry thought for a second. "Get some sleep and I will tell you later."

Maria's eyes opened. "What? Tell me. What was it?"

Henry cleared his throat. "It's Bayasaa."

Maria instantly sat up and Henry could clearly see the pain on her face, both mental and physical. "Bayasaa! Is he okay?"

She turned to get out of bed, but Henry pulled her back. "He was shot, but they are working on him now. There is nothing we can do. Jimbo will let us know."

Maria tried to pull away, but Henry held her. "I have to see him. I watched him get shot right in front of me. I thought he was dead. I have to see him—"

Henry held her tight. "Maria! You are injured. You were a prisoner just a few hours ago. There isn't anything you can do for him, but I need you to rest. I am worried about you . . . I love you."

Maria looked at the sincerity on his face and relaxed slightly. "Henry, I can't explain the feeling when I heard you fly over. I dreamed you would come, but I never thought you actually would. I thought I was going to die . . . after getting so many others killed and, and betraying you. And I felt like I deserved it."

Henry put his hand over her mouth. "Don't say that! You did what you did with the Feds out of love for us. Out of love for me! I understand that now."

Maria began crying, and she hugged Henry tight. Henry returned the hug as a lump formed in his throat. He tried to hold back and be strong, but the quivering in his stomach muscles gave it away, and Maria began to cry harder in response.

⚜ ⚜ ⚜

At 1600, Jimbo opened the tent door. "Everyone up for debriefing."

Maria awoke, not knowing when she had fallen asleep, and

looked at his outline contrasted with the brightness of outside. In a gravelly voice, she asked "Bayasaa?"

Jimbo stepped in, walked over to her and Henry, and bent down. "They think he will make it."

Maria covered her mouth. "Can we see him first?"

Jimbo nodded. "Sure."

Henry smiled at Jimbo in appreciation and they started to get up. Jimbo made his way back to the door. "I'll see you outside."

Henry and Maria, who was feeling every one of her bruises and wounds, made their way to the medical tent at Jimbo's direction; she leaned on Henry as they went. Once inside, Maria gasped at seeing Bayasaa. She limped to him as fast as she could go. Henry came up behind her and gave her a chair to sit in. Maria touched Bayasaa's now-clean face.

"Bayasaa . . . can you hear me?" She looked at Henry and back to Bayasaa. "Thank you for trying to protect me . . . I thought you were," she started crying, "I thought you were gone . . . I am so glad you're not." She turned to Henry, who was bent over, and hugged him.

After a few minutes, Jimbo cleared his throat. "We should go. He should be fine. He just needs time to recover."

Henry lifted Maria and helped her to the door. Jimbo continued, "Apparently the bullet nicked his liver, but went clean through otherwise. He just lost lots of blood and has a couple of cracked ribs."

Maria looked up at him. "Probably when I fell on him."

Henry looked at her. "Fell on him?"

She nodded. "Yes. The soldier pulled me out of the truck and I fell on Bayasaa."

Henry smiled. "Don't worry about that. I am sure he will forgive you."

Maria stared at him with guilt on her face, but Henry tapped her cheek. "Stop that guilt stuff. It's not your fault and he will be okay! When he wakes up, he will be very happy to see you. You just wait!"

A tentative smile appeared on Maria's face.

Jimbo pointed to the main gher. "Come on, we have a meeting to attend."

The gher was really noisy and everyone was talking excitedly, but it began to quiet when Jimbo stepped in. Jimbo stood up in front of everyone and he put his hands up to quiet them further. He spoke while Inalchuk translated. "Today was the most amazing day that I have seen in my entire life! I feel as though we are one giant family supporting and caring for each other. Risking our lives to save each other. Today, we attacked the Japanese military to rescue one of our own . . ." Jimbo raised his voice, and finished, "and we whipped them!" Cheers erupted from everyone and Jimbo was unable to get them to calm down for several minutes.

Jimbo finally had to yell. "Quiet please ,,, please! We have a lot to discuss."

The crowd finally calmed down, and Jimbo began to speak again. "First, I know we lost seven people this morning. What happened? Did we lose them in the airport battle?"

A man stood up and began speaking in Mongolian. Inalchuk translated. "He says they ran into a Japanese road block during the night. He says they just kept driving and shooting and made it through, but they lost four." Inalchuk paused while listening. The man got excited and punched the air. Inalchuk looked at Jimbo.

"He says they rammed the car that tried to stop them and shot them all."

Jimbo looked at him. "Is that all he said?"

Inalchuk pursed her lips. "Well, there was a lot of profanity in it."

Jimbo smiled. "And the other three?"

The same man spoke up. "They were hit in the crossfire at the airport."

Jimbo nodded. "Now, as some of you may know, Bayasaa made it back. He was shot in the back by a Jap soldier, and he somehow drove all the way back. He is recovering and should be okay." The crowd roared in excited discussion.

Jimbo cleared his throat while waiting for the noise to die down. He spoke loudly. "We will have a memorial service for everyone we lost tomorrow morning at 0900." It became quiet again and Jimbo paused for a bit. "Does anyone have anything to add?"

Maria raised her hand and Jimbo signaled for her to come up. She limped to the front and the room became dead silent. She tried to speak, but her throat became tight. "I—I want to thank all of you. All of you risked your life to save me . . . and some of our friends gave their lives." She paused, having trouble speaking. "I now look on what I have done by not listening to you," her eyes moved to Jimbo, "and going off on a hopeless crusade to find my husband. I thought I was only risking myself, but now I realize I was risking all of you." She coughed, and stumbled and everyone stepped forward to catch her, but she recovered and stood up slowly. With tears running down her face, she said. "I don't know how to thank all of you. You have sacrificed so much for me. I . . . I don't know what else to say. I love all of you."

She began to walk back to her seat, but the crowd erupted in support. They clapped, surrounded her and tried to show their love.

Henry got up and made his way through the mob. He lifted Maria in his arms and turned to everyone. They again became quiet. "And from me. I can't thank you enough for returning my love to me! I couldn't live without her." He turned and carried her out of the tent in near silence. The group erupted again as Henry carried Maria off to their gher.

Henry set Maria on the bed, pulled her boots off, and put a fur blanket over her. Maria put her hand on his leg just as Jimbo walked into the tent. Maria partially sat up and Jimbo looked her in the eye. "Wow. You really got them stirred up. I think they would do anything for you."

Maria puzzled, questioned him. "Me? Why? I endangered them! They sacrificed for me, not the other way around."

Jimbo nodded. "Yes, but you show your love for them. You've spent the last year telling stories, milking goats, sharing in their lives. You show they matter and that they are good people, and they love you for it! You have given them more to fight for than just money."

Maria stared off, apparently in thought, as she lay back down.

Henry looked seriously at Jimbo. "So, what was in the tin?"

Jimbo blinked at him, visibly caught off guard by the question. "What tin?"

Henry, with a dubious expression on his face, asked again.

"*What was in the tin.* The one Anatoly gave you?"

Jimbo, perturbed, thought for a second and then grabbed a chair. He looked around the gher and sat down. Quietly, he whispered, "Diamonds."

Maria sat up again. "Diamonds?"

Henry eyed Maria for stealing his question. "From where?"

Jimbo looked down and the ground and pulled his pipe out. "Well, during the Russian Civil War, the US was funding the Whites, and it was done with diamonds. Easy to transport and hard to trace. Anatoly ended up with a stockpile of them when Kolchak was killed." He looked at Henry and Maria, who were fixated on him.

Maria sat up. "Go on."

Jimbo put the pipe in his mouth. "Well, you remember when I told you that Anatoly got sick and had to go to Harbin?"

They nodded.

"Well, he took those diamonds with him, and after his recovery, he came to me with some of them to pay for weapons for his re-invasion, I'm sorry, liberation, of Russia. I knew he had more and that he had hidden them in Harbin, but I had no idea where."

Henry face grew suspicious. "So wait. When you found out he was being released, you wanted those diamonds, didn't you? That's what all of this is really about?"

Jimbo leaned back in his chair while chewing hard on his pipe. "Well, there is a fortune in diamonds in that tin and I figured this would be the last job we would ever have to do."

Maria spoke up in a scolding voice. "So, you are just going

to let Anatoly march off to his death while you get rich?"

Jimbo pulled the pipe and sat forward. "No! That's not it at all! I have begged him to forget about his damn fool, idealistic crusade. I've begged him to just come to some tropical isle with me and retire with good drinks and hot women . . . but he believes in his country and I can't dissuade him from his ideals. I've tried! He is more than happy to give me the diamonds, if I will supply his loyal men with arms, so that is what I will do." Jimbo went on, mumbling, "I know he'd go anyway; without weapons, they don't stand a chance . . . not that they really do even with them." Jimbo grunted in frustration.

Henry rubbed the stubble under his nose. "Hmm. So what the hell happened in Harbin? How did it end up in a full blown war, with us in the middle?"

Jimbo pursed his lips. "Well, I figured the reason the Soviets let him go in the first place was because they found out about the diamonds. That's why I assumed the Russians were Stalin's men. They followed him to get the diamonds, and we just happened to crash their party."

Henry raised his eyebrow. "And the Japs?" He then looked at Maria. "The Feds? What the hell were they doing there?"

Jimbo, anxious, stood up and started pacing. "Well, the Japs . . . that was AZ. Traitorous bastard! Apparently, he had been selling our trade routes to the highest bidder for months, but he did it at random to not raise suspicions. Then he must have found out about Anatoly and the diamonds, and figured it was worth a pretty penny to tell the Japs." He stopped and looked at them. "Do you remember when we were getting in the car and he was nowhere to be found? He was getting paid. That bastard!" Jimbo stood there for a few seconds letting his anger subside. "As for the Feds, I can only assume that they were there to get the diamonds back. After all, they do technically belong to the US government." He looked at Maria and slowly sat down. "So, how the hell did you know they were G-men?"

Maria's face became red and she started fidgeting. Henry spoke for her. "Remember when we told you that we got pinched, runnin' booze for Rocco, and his nephew got killed? The whole reason we owe Rocco so much damn money?"

Jimbo nodded.

Henry started to speak, but Maria slapped his stomach. Henry let out a gush of air and looked at her in surprise as she cut him off. "Let me tell my own damn story!"

Maria continued. "A few weeks before that, the G-Men picked me up while I was out shopping. They had been watching me and Henry for quite some time. They said they had enough on us to put us away forever if I didn't cooperate. So . . . to save us, I told them I would. They arranged to arrest us in Wisconsin, as to not look suspicious. They told me to stay in the cockpit and to keep Henry there, and that they would let us go if they got Rocco or his nephew."

Henry looked at her in disbelief. "Is that why you were all over me in the cockpit that night?"

She nodded with shame showing on her face. She then took a deep breath. "Well, to make a long story short, one of the agents—Hicks . . . Agent Hicks . . . yes, that was his name. He was the one who interrogated me, and he was the one I saw in Harbin. I will never forget that face!"

Jimbo was chewing heavily on his pipe. "What the hell is the chance that the same guy was in Harbin as busted you? Hmm. But it's a good thing!" He pulled out his pipe and rubbed his eyebrow with his right hand. "If you hadn't stopped us, we would have been hamburger walking up those stairs."

Jimbo leaned back in his chair and looked at the ceiling. "My god, what a week!" He then leaned forward again. "Henry, you were shot down by the Kuomintang, right?"

Henry nodded. "Yes. That's what the girl said."

Jimbo tilted his head and Maria looked over at him simultaneously, asking, "Girl?"

Henry let out a smile at the implication. "The girl helping me unload the plane. She yelled 'Kuomintang!' and began shooting, but then she turned and told me to take off, which I tried to do."

Jimbo thought for a second. "KMT, this far north. Hmm . . . that's troublesome."

Henry shifted position on the bed. "Why?"

Jimbo scratched his hear. "Well, if the KMT are up here, they are probably trying to wipe out the Communists. They are Chiang Kai-shek's main concern."

Henry leaned on his fist. "What about the Japs?"

Jimbo rubbed his mustache while he thought. "Well, Chiang Kai-shek has made a deal with them; my guess is that he won't fight them directly, if he doesn't have to, not unless some of the Western powers give support. In any case, if the Communists are wiped out, the Japanese will continue to roll west and eventually south, maybe unchallenged—except by local factions, but they wouldn't stand a chance." Jimbo scratched his head. "Well, maybe the Russians . . . nah, scratch that. I think they have too much to worry about in the west."

Maria spoke up. "Do you think we will have to leave soon?"

Jimbo cleared his throat again. "I am thinking we are going to have to leave anyway. After what we did to the Japanese in Harbin and at the airfield, they will be out for blood. Plus, there is no telling what AZ told them!" Jimbo thought for a second and muttered, "Although, I would have thought they would have moved on us already, if they knew where we were."

Henry stood up, walked to the edge of the tent and back. "Can we move somewhere safer?"

Jimbo shook his head. "I am afraid not. I am really starting to think we need to make Anatoly's run our final run and then get out of Dodge. From what I am seeing in Europe and here, I think we may be in for another Great War all over again."

The door opened and Anatoly appeared. "My run?"

Jimbo smiled. "Spying on us, hmm? Come on in, Anatoly." He stood up. "With all the shoot outs, I haven't been able to formally introduce you. This is my nephew, Henry Elliot, and his wife, Maria."

Henry stood up and shook his hand. "General."

Anatoly laughed, and with a Russian accent replied. "No, no. This was a long time ago. Just call me Anatoly." He grabbed another chair and sat down. "So what is this about my run?"

Henry spoke first. "Well, Jimbo thinks we have hurt the Japanese a bit too much lately for them not to come after us."

Anatoly looked at Jimbo. "So, you mean you will have to evacuate?"

Jimbo nodded. "Yes, I am afraid so. It will only be a matter of time before they find us . . . even if AZ didn't give them our position." He wiped his face from top to bottom with both hands. "We should start packing up and dismantling everything tomorrow."

Maria leaned forward. "What about all these people? We can just fly home, but where will they go?"

Jimbo smiled knowingly at Maria and then pointed up at the gher. "It's okay. Most of them are nomads anyway. They can tear down these tents and move surprisingly fast."

Maria turned to Anatoly. "Jimbo told us what you're planning to do. Why don't you just come with us? You can have a good life! I think you have fought enough for your country."

Jimbo's eyes rolled; however, Anatoly stood up in anger, but after standing for several seconds, he cooled, and sat back down. He pursed his lips and looked at her.

She shrank back on the bed. "I'm sorry. I didn't mean—"

Anatoly interrupted. "I understand your intentions and caring for my safety, but I cannot let those whose destroyed my country stand, especially with this Stalin. He is a power-hungry maniac, and will bring Russia to ruin through suffering on an enormous scale! It is my duty, my *honor* to try to do something to help my fellow countrymen. Who knows? Maybe my assault will stir others to rise up with us."

Maria leaned forward "But you—"

"Maria!" whispered Henry sharply, putting his hand out to stop her. Aloud, he said, "Well, we are happy to do what we can to help you and —"

Jimbo interrupted. "Quite right. We have about half the arms you need. The other half, we will, ironically, have to go to the Soviet Union to get."

Anatoly eyebrows went up.

Jimbo nodded. "We have someone who has been supplying us with arms for more than a year now. Of course, he thinks they are going to anti-Japanese forces, not to fight his own government . . . but we just won't tell him that bit."

Anatoly wryly smiled. "Yes, quite ironic. Is he a Bolshevik?"

Jimbo's looked up at the ceiling in thought. "I am not sure. I don't usually ask those kinds of questions of my suppliers."

Anatoly nodded. "When can you be ready?"

Jimbo stood up and smiled. "In a hurry to die, as always, huh, Anatoly?" He slapped him on the back. "Well, let's get the camp packed up and everyone on their way. After finishing up all the loose ends, hmm . . . maybe next week?"

Anatoly stood up, smiled, and shook Jimbo's hand. "I will inform my comrades and get things rolling." He turned towards the door. "Mind if I use your radios?"

Jimbo patted him on the back. "No, not at all. Let's go see what we can do." Jimbo turned and waved at Henry and Maria before leaving the tent with Anatoly.

Maria relaxed and lay back down. "Well that was informative." She looked up at Henry. "How did we get mixed up in all this?"

Henry smiled at her while caressing her hair. "Well, a while back someone snitched to the Feds, and there was this cat named Rocco . . ."

She reached up and hit him. "Hey! That's not funny."

Henry laughed and tried to kiss her forehead but she pushed his head back, so he reached down to her sides and began tickling her.

She started to laugh and groan and the same time. "Henry. Stop."
She squirmed and tried to fight back. "Ow . . . ouch . . . Henry."

Henry finally stopped and Maria, after a slight protest, let him kiss her on the forehead. He whispered ,"I love you."

Her eyes looked up at him. "How can you?"

Henry, shocked, took a step back before kneeling down to her level. "We all know what you have done, and what you've done to try to make amends." He looked at the ground while wiping his hand over his upper lip. He looked her in the eyes. "We have to get past this. We all forgive you, and we understand."

He tried to caress her hair, but Maria jerked her head away and looked the other direction. She whispered, "You say nice things, but how can anyone really forgive me?"

Henry forced a hug on her until she finally stopped resisting and whimpered in sadness.

Chapter 21

The Rising and Setting of the Sun

A few days later, everyone was busy tearing things down and making preparations to leave. Three of the ghers had been taken down and put on the truck that Bayasaa had driven back.

Jimbo was supervising the removal of some of the radio equipment from the bunker, to be loaded onto a second truck. He pointed and directed, but he mostly stood in the snow sipping his steaming tea when Henry came up and pointed to the trucks.

"Looks like they won't have enough room with only two trucks."

Jimbo swallowed his sip of tea. "It shouldn't be too much trouble. Before I bought all the trucks, they just used pack animals, which they still have." He pointed to some Bactrian camels in the distance.

Henry looked over at the snow-covered, double-humped camels, who were searching for grass under the snow. "Oh. I see. How far do you think they will move?"

Jimbo thought for a second. "Not sure, but I told them to go as far as they could to avoid the Japs."

Maria came over, wearing a traditional Mongolian outer coat and fur hat. "Morning. How is it going?"

Henry smiled, "Just talking about camels and the moving—", Jimbo interrupted when a nurse signaled for him to come to the medical tent, "Excuse me." Jimbo turned and started walking towards the tent.

"What is it?" Maria asked.

Jimbo increased his pace. "Bayasaa—he's awake."

Maria's face lit up and she ran to the tent, passing Jimbo. Henry, still standing there, saw her run and tried to catch up.

When Henry entered the tent, he saw Maria starting to kneel next to Bayasaa, while her hand reached for his swollen face. Bayasaa's eyes barely opened as she touched him. Henry stood next to Maria as she whispered quietly. "Bayasaa, are you okay? Thank you for trying to protect us." She sniffled and her eyes began to water. "I am sorry for making you go with me and—"

Bayasaa opened his eyes fully and made a shushing noise while trying to lift his right arm, but the pain stopped him. He whispered in a painful and scratching voice. "It not your fault . . . Is my honor to protect you . . . I wanted to—"

His face turned to pure pain, and the nurse stepped in speaking in Mongolian. She pointed to Maria and then at Bayasaa himself, then put a finger in front of her mouth.

Bayasaa let out the faintest of smiles and nodded. Maria looked at the nurse, but the expression on Maria's face did not change from guilt and worry.

Jimbo stepped forward. "Maria, we should let him rest."

Tears rolled down Maria's face as she turned to Jimbo and nodded. She then stood up and kissed Bayasaa on the forehead. "If there is anything you need, you just let us—"

A man at the door suddenly yelled in Mongolian, and everyone looked over. Even Bayasaa tried to look, but the pain stopped him. Jimbo said one word, "Shit," and started heading for the door.

Henry followed him. "What? Shit what?"

Jimbo bent down and stepped through the door, glancing back. "Japs!"

Henry stopped and glanced back at Maria, who was looking back at him. She whispered to Bayasaa and got up to follow Henry. "Japs? Are they coming?!"

Henry shrugged and waved for her to follow, and they both dashed out after Jimbo. He was already yelling orders and pointing to the trucks and the plane.

Henry came up next to him, but had to wait for fear of interrupting an apparent emergency.

Men and women grabbed branches and brooms and started smoothing out the snow, while others scrambled for weapons and adjusted the camouflage nets on the tents and vehicles.

Henry finally asked, "What is happening?"

Jimbo yelled out a few more instructions and then glanced over at Henry. "Jap patrol plane." He turned and pointed north. "One of our northern outposts just spotted him heading west."

Henry tried to listen. "I don't hear any engine noise."

Jimbo lifted his binoculars, which someone had brought him, and he scanned the sky to the north. "Well, he is pretty far out."

Henry nodded. "Let just hope he stays far out."

A few minutes went by. The runway and surrounding area began looking like pristine snow, with a few large lumps remaining. Several heavy machine guns were set up and waited anxiously for the intrusive plane. One man spoke to Jimbo and pointed west, then Jimbo began scanning the western sky. "Well, apparently he turned south, and he's out about five miles."

Everyone started looking as hard as they could to the west. Someone shushed everyone and it became quiet, except for the wind and the sudden cocking of one of the heavy machine guns. The quiet was then interrupted by the engine noise of the Japanese plane before it faded again. Henry cocked his head and listened; the sound came and went as it reflected off the hills and density layers in the atmosphere.

Minutes passed and no one made a sound. They listened to the wind and the coming and going of the engine sound. Henry could sense the tension of everyone around him, even though they said nothing. A man whispered to Jimbo and Jimbo turned his binoculars to the southwest. "Well, he has turned back to the East, but now he is eight miles southwest of us." He took a deep breath and let out a sigh of relief. "If he keeps that heading, we are in the clear."

After another ten minutes, Jimbo announced in a loud voice, "All clear! He's heading south again."

One of his men translated for him, and everyone relaxed. They started putting away the brooms and branches and packed up the machine guns. It only took them a few minutes to go back to what they had been doing, with no trace of the tension that had existed for the last half hour save the now trackless and pristine snow.

Jimbo called a meeting in the radio bunker. He sat down at the far table, while Zheng Zi Ling stood to the side. Jimbo was looking through communiques and maps while he waited for everyone to settle down.

Maria made her way over to Zi Ling and put her hand on her forearm. The other woman looked at her and smiled, and Maria squeezed her arm. "Thank you so much for rescuing me. You don't know how wonderful it was to see your face that night. I thought I was dead for sure, and I would be if it wasn't for your bravery and courage."

Zi Ling shook her head. "No. No. We are like family. It was my honor, and I know you would have done it for me."

Maria's eyes blinked quickly as she tried not to cry again. "Yes, but I wanted to let you know how much I appreciate you."

Zi Ling put her right hand on Maria's and gave her a comforting smile.

Jimbo looked up at everyone to speak, but when he saw the interaction of Zi Ling and Maria, he paused, and gave a smile before he started. "Well, after the incident this morning, we need to hurry up the pace for evacuation." As Inalchuk translated, Jimbo held up a list and caught Zi Ling's eye. "We need to organize all the radio traffic we need to get done, let everyone know we are shutting down, and then get all this equipment loaded. We will use a portable radio in one of the trucks after that." He looked around at everyone. "Once we have all the radio gear loaded, we will take down the ghers and begin moving out." He looked at Henry, Maria, and Anatoly. "As for us, we will leave on the DC-3 for our final run. After that, Henry, Maria, and I will return to the US via Alaska." He looked at Nick. "What about you? Do you want to go with us, or find your own way back to Australia?"

Nick smiled. "Actually, I thought I would stay with everyone and move out with the ghers. I'll take my chances and see what happens."

Jimbo nodded. "Sounds good. As far as the money goes, I will make sure everyone gets paid what they are owed by tomorrow."

Maria raised her hand. "We should have a going-away party." She held out a hand, taking in Zi Ling and the others. "You have really become my family, and I am going to miss all of you so very much."

As her sentence was translated, everyone began nodding and giving back good sentiments, but soon the whole meeting turned into chaos as hugging and handshaking took over.

Jimbo spoke up, "Quiet down please", with no effect. He then stood on the chair. "Please! Everyone quiet down! We will have time for this later!" He looked at Maria. "I agree with Maria, and we will have a going-away party tomorrow evening, once this gear is packed up!"

On hearing that, the group quieted down and gave Jimbo their attention once again.

Jimbo stepped down from the chair. "Thank you." He then sat down and pulled out a file with Russian wording all over it. He looked up at Anatoly. "Well, since we are cutting this evacuation short, we won't have time to wait for a truck to deliver the weapons from our man in the Soviet Union."

Anatoly nodded and Jimbo continued, "We are going to have to fly in and get the shipment. Henry, you consult with Nick on the particulars, as he is the one who usually makes this run." Henry nodded and smiled at Nick.

Jimbo glanced back at Anatoly. "We are going to have to hide you in the plane somewhere . . . maybe back with the machine gun. They see you, or get a hint that these arms are being used against them, and the jig is up."

Anatoly cocked his head. "Jig?"

Jimbo smiled. "This party will be over." He then made a slicing of his throat gesture.

Anatoly nodded with sudden understanding and smiled. "*Da, da*, I will stay hidden."

Jimbo smiled grimly. "Good." He looked at the radio operators and pointed to the radio schedule on the desk. "Okay. Let's see if we can get this done today and finish packing this stuff."

Inalchuk raised her hand. "What should we do with the bunker after we have emptied it?"

Jimbo thought for a second while looking around at the bunker. "Well, if there is any equipment we have to leave behind, we need to destroy it, but the bunker . . . well, we'll just leave it. Maybe someone can use it for shelter or for food storage in the future. Just don't leave any personal traces."

Jimbo put his hand up. "See you all tomorrow at the farewell party. That's all. Let's get to it."

The whole room erupted in movement and conversation. The feeling of the base's finality was in the air and serious tear down began in earnest.

⚐ ⚐ ⚐

The next morning, Henry awoke to the sound of howling winds. He slowly got dressed and went to the door to peek out. It took a second for his squinting eyes to adjust to the bright outside world. Snow was blowing sideways across the airstrip, and vortices of snow whipped around the tent. A subzero wind suddenly pressed the door in and he pushed hard to keep it from opening further.

From behind him, Maria complained, "Whoa! Shut the

door! That is seriously cold!"

He turned while pushing and latching the door shut. "Yeah. Nasty out there! We're definitely not flying anywhere today! . . . but neither are the Jap patrols."

Maria hid under her fur blankets. "Good. Now come over here and keep me warm!"

A shiver ran up Henry's back and slight quivering could be heard in his voice. "No problem. You don't have to twist my arm!"

He made his way over to Maria, kicked his boots back off, and snuggled under the covers with her. They passed the next few hours together in peace and quiet, until the door opened and any warmth that had been in the tent was suddenly gone. Jimbo spoke. "Henry, one of the generators froze and the other one will too, unless we insulate it better!"

Henry's head appeared from under the fur blanket and his breath rose into the air as he spoke. "What about the batteries?"

Jimbo shook his head. "I would assume they're fine for the moment, but not if we lose the second generator."

Henry slid out from under the fur, still fully clothed from the morning, donned his boots, and followed Jimbo out the door, making sure it was tightly sealed behind him. He had to suddenly grab at his hat before the wind could take it away. With the blast of the cold air, he became fully alert. He looked around, seeing shadows moving in the blowing snow, then followed Jimbo towards a group of shadows near where the plane was supposed to be. He could feel the crunch of the snow below his feet, and as they got close, Henry was finally able to see the outline of the plane. There were three men trying to break the frozen generator free from the snow. Henry tried to ask them about it, but he couldn't hear their voices over the sound of the camouflage tarp slapping the end of the wing.

One of them looked up at him and Jimbo and pointed to the generator, and then to the remaining ghers. Jimbo nodded and nudged Henry, while pointing towards the other generator. He waved for Henry to follow, and made his way under the plane as snow pelted his face. Inalchuk was already there working on it. It had a box around it, but she was tying to put more stuff around the outside to keep the heat in.

Jimbo pointed to the plane and yelled, "Check the batteries."

Henry gave him a thumbs-up and walked around the rear of the plane to the door. The handle was frozen, and he had to hit it with his fist twice to break the ice free. Then he was force to yank several times until the ice broke free of the seals and the door swung open. The wind caught the door, and Henry had to quickly duck to keep from being hit by it. It slammed against the plane as Henry cried out. "Jesus!"

He slowly stood up erect again, and once he was sure the door was stable, he hopped inside and went to check the battery in the lower left forward baggage compartment. He pulled off his glove and felt it. Since it felt warm, he decided to go forward to check the voltage and it appeared fully charged, but the voltage on the second battery was reading low. He made his way to the rear luggage area to check on it, but when he grabbed the rear door handle, his hand partially froze to it and he instantly jerked it free. He looked down to see a thin layer of skin still on the door handle, while whispering to himself, "Dumb." The battery was by the baggage door next to the .30. Frost coated the outside of it, but after what happened with the door handle, he didn't test it with his hand. He thought for a second, then grabbed the heating and charging cables from the other battery, pulled them back, and swapped them. There was a crackle when he connected the leads, confirming its low charge. Henry was a bit startled by how the battery acted like a living hungry impatient thing pulling such a large spark.

Henry headed back to the rear exterior door, but his heart jumped when he unexpectedly found himself face to face with Jimbo. "Jeez! Scared me."

Jimbo chuckled and asked loudly, "So, how are they?"

Henry pointed towards the first battery. "The front battery is fine, but the rear battery was low and it could have frozen—well, it might have already, so I swapped cables. The front battery should be fine for a while, as long as it doesn't lose any charge . . . and assuming the temperature out there doesn't drop below minus 80." He smiled and continued. "I disconnected it from the plane to prevent anything from draining it."

Jimbo just nodded. "Sounds good! They took the frozen generator into the main gher to warm it up, and we've insulated the other one as best we could."

Henry scratched his head under his hat and looked around the inside of the plane. "Well, I guess that's all we can do for the moment. Let's hope it's enough."

That afternoon, everyone was gathering in the main tent. Jimbo was one of the last people to come in, with the exception of perimeter security. He walked up to Henry and Maria, who were having a drink with Nick. "Well, looks like we are just about done packing. Only three tents to go and getting the wounded ready."

Maria looked up at him. "How is Bayasaa doing?"

Jimbo pulled over a crate and sat down. "He's doing better. The nurse said he was trying to sit up and talk, but she has to keep him relaxed. They worry about his wounds reopening."

Maria sighed. "I will have to go see him in a bit. Do you think he can eat regular food?"

Jimbo smiled. "I don't see why not. It's not like they shot him in the stomach."

Maria didn't return the smile and Henry tried to lighten the mood by changing the subject. "Uncle. Want a beer?"

Jimbo gave a big nod. "Yes! I need one."

Nick handed him a bottle and pointed toward the central fire. "Isn't that the generator for the plane?"

Henry snickered. "Yeah. Apparently it ran out of fuel and froze solid, so they needed to thaw it out."

Nick pointed at the door. "What about the plane?"

Henry looked over at Nick. "Well, the other generator is still running and keeping the batteries good. We'll get this one back out there in a few hours. Hopefully, it still runs."

Inalchuk's voice got his attention and when she turned, she saw a large group in front of them. Inalchuk raised a glass. "It has been a wonderful journey with all of you. All of us will miss you so greatly." She looked at Jimbo. "Thank you for supporting us and all our families. We have grown rich financially, but most importantly, rich in our hearts."

Maria, Henry, Nick, and Jimbo all stood up and toasted back. Jimbo then spoke. "This has been one of the best experiences of my life, and all of you have been so wonderful to me and to each other. I think we have grown to become a large family; it hurts my heart to have it end, but all good things must come to an end, eventually. Who knows, maybe we'll be back after things calm down, but until then, I wish all of you the best of luck, and be safe."

They toasted, and then Zi Ling stepped forward. "I have never felt so at home and needed as I have with all of you." She looked around at everyone, and Maria put her hand out to her. She continued, "I feel like I could and would do anything for any of you, and you would do the—"

"Japs!" The shout came from a man standing in the doorway, with a fur hat covering his forehead and fur coat dropping snow onto the floor. Silence fell as everyone turned to look, and Jimbo immediately made his way through the crowd.

A large commotion ensued, and people scrambled for their winter gear before pouring out of the tent.

Henry, Maria, and Nick looked at each other. "I reckon we should probably grab our own gear too, yeah?" said Nick with a sly grin.

As Henry pushed the door of the tent, he found himself face to face with Jimbo, who had been trying to come back in. They both backed up to let the other past, and then Henry just pushed through.

"What the hell is going on? Another Jap plane?" He looked up. "In this weather?!"

Jimbo backed up a couple of steps to let them all out. "No! The Japs are inside the perimeter to the east!" He pointed with a stiff finger. "They got past the OPs, because they couldn't see them through the snowstorm." Henry tried to speak but Jimbo just spoke louder. "I need you to get that plane started. We are leaving, and so is everyone else." He spun on his heel to talk to four men that had come up behind him with two heavy machine guns in hand. He spoke to them briefly, urgently, and pointed to the east again, and the four ran off into the snow. He turned back to Henry. "They are going to try to slow them down and give us some time. Now, get to it!"

Henry saluted in respect, grabbed Maria, and headed for the plane. He glanced back. "Nick. Come help!" Nick, looking a little confused, nodded and followed. His beer still in hand, he took a sip and threw it into the snow.

Henry tried to do the fastest pre-flight he could, but he was forced to slow down to knock ice and snow off the pitot tube. Nick helped him while Maria went inside to go through the internal checklist. After a minute, Maria yelled out the window, "Everything is dead! No power!"

Henry looked up at her. "Oh, shit. The battery! I disconnected it!"

Maria looked back. "What! Where is it?"

Henry started to move, but stopped. "Hey! Try using the emergency battery. It should be good. I'll get the main hooked back up."

She nodded. "Okay!"

Henry looked at Nick and handed him the list. "Take over. And no shortcuts. I don't want to die today!"

Nick nodded as Henry shuffled his way through the snow to the back door. As he stepped up, machine-gun fire filled the air. He stopped and listened. "Holy shit, that's close!"

Henry quickly stepped inside and opened the battery compartment. He tried to reconnect the battery, but his gloves were too bulky.

Maria yelled again. "We have power! The other battery is good. 90% charge."

Henry pulled his glove off and quickly tapped the battery to see if his hand would freeze to it. "Great! I am reconnecting the main battery now." His hand didn't stick, so he grabbed the cable and reattached it. As he tightened the cable, Maria yelled in pain.

Henry looked forward. "What? What happened?"

Her face appeared as she looked back. "My hand froze to the control panel, and it's bleeding."

He yelled back. "Are you okay?"

She yelled again, but Henry couldn't hear her over further eruptions of gunfire. Henry, struggling not to panic, closed the battery compartment and made his way to the front. "You okay?"

Maria raised her right hand. The thumb and forefinger were bleeding and wet from her sucking on them. "Yeah, I think it will be fine, but it hurts like a son of a bitch."

Bright streaks caught their attention, and they both looked out the window to see tracers flying through the sky. They looked at each other, wide-eyed, and scrambled through the rest of checklist.

Nick yelled up from the back. "Okay. Outside is good!"

Henry glanced back. "Great! Thanks! Now get your ass out of here!"

He nodded and waved. "Good luck, you two!"

Henry looked out the window and watched Nick run to the two trucks that were just pulling out. His glance then centered on the engine. "Crap!"

Maria looked at him. "What now?"

Henry pointed to the engine. "The temperature! We have

to thin the oil." He reached up to the overhead electrical panel and engaged the oil dilution solenoids.

He caught Maria's eye. "Can you look to make sure Nick disconnected the heater element in the right engine?"

She opened her window and looked back at the engine. "I don't see—wait. Yes, it's coiled up on the ground behind us."

Henry was looking at the left engine. "Good, looks like he got this one too." He glanced back at her. "Ready?"

Before she could respond, they felt an explosion and saw a fireball in the distance. She enthusiastically said, "Yes! Let's get the hell out of here!"

Henry yelled, "Clear prop," and began cranking the right engine. The starter whined and the prop began to turn. Nine turns came and went and Maria looked at him with worry, but on the twelfth rotation, the engine began to pop as cylinders fired off. It took a few more rounds, but soon all nine cylinders were firing.

Henry, a bit relieved "Okay. That's one." He looked to his left. "Now for the cold one."

Anatoly suddenly called from the back, "Hey! I'm here, and as soon as Jimbo is on board, he says to go!"

Henry looked back at him. "Okay—assuming we can get the other engine started." He turned back to his left, again called, "Clear prop!" and began cranking the left engine.

As he was watching the engine turn over, he glanced up to see that the vehicles and most of the people were gone. He counted fifteen turns, and still nothing.

Henry heard the rear door being slammed shut and Jimbo shouted from the back, "Let's go!"

Henry and Maria yelled at the same time, "*We're trying!*"

Henry continued to crank the engine over, but he suddenly remembered the rear battery cables. He yelled back "Jimbo, the rear battery charging cables. Throw them out the cargo door! We don't want to drag a generator behind us."

Jimbo yelled back. "Right. On it!" He and Anatoly headed back, just as Henry heard the first piston catch. A few seconds later, two more caught. "Oh, come on, baby . . . start, start, start . . ." The engine suddenly roared to life, and black smoke poured out behind it. Maria cheered.

Henry looked around the airstrip as best as he could. Two of the ghers were barely visible through the snow. "Here we go!"

He began throttling up the engines until he finally heard the plane break free of the crust of ice around the wheels, and start rolling through the snow. Anatoly and Jimbo felt the movement and quickly came forward past all the arms crates to buckle themselves in.

Henry twisted in his seat to peer back at them. "Did you get it?"

Jimbo nodded. "Yep. It's gone."

Henry turned into the wind, which there was a lot of, and slowly brought the throttle to maximum, but before he even let go of the brakes, the plane began sliding forward on the snow. With the flaps down and the wind speed so high, they were airborne in seconds. As they headed out to the east, Maria pointed out her side. "Look."

Henry raised his head and leaned forward to see several burning vehicles. "Boy. I think we owe those four machine gunners our lives."

Maria eyed him and nodded in agreement. She then stared

back at Jimbo. "Okay. Now what do we do?"

Jimbo looked at Anatoly. "We should go to the airstrip in Russia, where we were going to pick up the shipment tomorrow. We will just have to wait, and you will have to stay hidden."

Anatoly nodded. "I remember."

Henry turned north and gained altitude, but visibility was terrible. "I just hope we can see Russia when we get there!"

Maria turned back to talk to Jimbo. "Do you think everyone made it out before the Japs got to the camp?"

Jimbo nodded. "I believe so. I made sure that everyone evacuated before I got on the plane, except for the few I sent to slow them down. They did a damn good job, but I doubt they will make it . . . but in this weather, who knows?" He looked at Maria's face and knew her next question. "Yes, Bayasaa is okay. They put him in the passenger side of one of the trucks before rolling out."

Maria smiled in relief.

Henry noticed the time on the dash clock. "Crap," he muttered, and increased the throttle to maximum.

Maria looked forward in response to the increase in thrust. "What's going on?"

Henry pointed to the clock. "It's going to be dark before we get there unless we go faster, and since they aren't expecting us until tomorrow, the strip won't be lit."

Jimbo, overhearing part of the conversation, asked. "What's the problem?"

Maria turned to him. "We are running out of daylight and we won't be able to see where to land."

Jimbo glanced at Anatoly and back at Maria. "Um, yeah, that would be a problem."

Henry yelled back. "I have maxed out our speed and we should be able to make it."

Anatoly spoke up, with a philosophical look on his face. "Living is a good choice, I think."

Chapter 22

Familiar Faces

As Henry leveled off, Maria unbuckled herself and held up her wounded hand. "I am going to go back and clean up my hand."

"Okay. Jimbo, can you help her?"

Jimbo got up and helped her with the first aid kit as they wrapped her finger and thumb. As he finished up, she asked, "Do you think the Russians will be suspicious when we arrive with this plane?"

Jimbo sat back down in his jump seat. "Oh, nah. I already told them that we have a bigger plane for bigger shipments." He glanced at Anatoly. "We just have to keep Anatoly here hidden, like I said before, in case someone recognizes him." Anatoly smiled at the remark.

Maria examined her wrapped fingers. "Looks good. Thanks." She got up and went back to her seat in the cockpit. She scanned out the front window but couldn't see anything except gray and continuous white streaks of snow. "How are you doing?" she asked Henry.

He looked at the clock and gauges. "Well, everything seems fine except that I can't see anything." He turned to her and feigned a smile. "Can you get on the radio and get a fix on our position? Right now I am just using the compass, but I want to make sure." Maria moved to the navigator's station and operated the radio gear for about ten minutes before looking at Jimbo. She pulled her headphones to one side. "These are the right coordinates, right?"

Jimbo leaned forward, and she handed him a piece of paper that Nick had given her. He looked at the numbers. "It looks right. If this is what Nick gave you, then it's right."

She nodded. "Okay. Henry, turn twenty-one degrees to starboard."

Henry looked back at her. "Twenty-one degrees?!"

She nodded slowly and ended with a smile.

Henry turned back. "How the hell could I be so far off?" He whacked the compass in the center between the windshields, but it didn't change. "Okay, changing course twenty-one degrees starboard."

It was another hour before Jimbo came forward. "We almost there?"

Henry looked at the clock. "We should be getting close, and thank goodness, the weather is breaking up." He pointed forward.

Jimbo leaned forward and could see the white terrain below. "Oh. It's looking better."

Henry nodded. "Yeah, if we can spot any of the landmarks that Nick told us about, we should be able to find it now, assuming we are on the right course." He eyed Maria suspiciously and she returned the look by sticking her tongue out. Henry smiled, which made Jimbo glance at Maria, but she had already returned to looking at Nick's map.

Jimbo, with the feeling of having missed something, turned back to Henry. "How much daylight do we have left?"

Henry looked at the clock and then at the horizon. "Not much. Look, it's already getting dark to the east."

Jimbo bent down and looked out Maria's window, but Maria's hand blocked his view as she pointed out Henry's window. "There! That's the two lakes he has on the map—so Borzya should be dead ahead, and the airstrip should be on the west side of town, just over a twisty river."

Henry looked and saw the frozen lakes. He then looked at her and the map. "Twisty river?"

She looked at him impatiently and pointed to map. "Twisty. Like this," she said, and gestured with her finger, back and forth in a continuous "S" shape.

Henry laughed. "Sure . . . okay."

She then pointed out the front window. "Like that! See—it's twisty!"

Henry looked to see a frozen river with continuous bends in it. He immediately cut the throttle and started to descend. "How far is it from your 'twisty river'?"

Her eyes narrowed for a second while looking at him and she looked down at the map. "He says it's only two miles, and that it runs parallel with the river's general course."

Henry squinted and looked at the landscape, scanning for a long white strip that could be a runway.

After a few minutes, they descended to 1500 feet and flew low over the river. Henry finally saw the runway, just as they flew over it. He then turned east, came about and lined up for a landing. It was getting dark, but the white snow made the runway easy to see against the terrain.

As they landed, Maria pointed out her window. "There's a

vehicle coming."

Jimbo leaned and looked out his side window. He then looked at Anatoly. "Get in the back. Go!"

Anatoly nodded and unbuckled himself before making his way to the back where the .30 was mounted. He slipped into the hatch, closing the door behind him.

As the plane came to a stop, the vehicle pulled up next to them and two armed men got out. Henry looked back at Jimbo as he shut down the engines. "Looks like we have a greeting party."

Jimbo feigned a smile and made his way to the back door, then opened it. The two men, wearing long black fur coats and mink fur hats, were standing in front of the door with their guns half raised, but when one of them recognized Jimbo he smiled and used his hand to lower the other man's weapon. In boisterous Russian he spoke aloud. "Jimbo! Welcome! We weren't expecting you till tomorrow." He stepped back and spread out his hands while looking at the plane. "Moving up in the world! Such a big plane!"

Jimbo smiled, set out the stairs, and stepped down to greet them. "Yuri! Yes! Business is good! How are you?"

Yuri looked at his comrade. "We are well. As well as can be expected nowadays." Yuri waved his hand for Jimbo to come with them. "We have your weapons, but let's go have a drink first."

Just then Maria appeared at the door. Yuri stopped and looked up at her in surprise. "Wow! Who's the *goryachaya devushka*?" He looked at Jimbo. "Business *is* good!"

Jimbo laughed. "This is my *nephew's* wife, Maria." Switching to English, he went on, "Maria, come on down. They want us to go have a drink with them." He winked at her when he knew no one else could see.

Maria paused for a second and glanced forward at Henry. "Um, okay . . . but we . . . shouldn't leave the plane too long, because of the cold. It will be hard to restart the engines."

Jimbo smiled and translated. "She says she would love to have a quick drink with you, but we have to be back quick."

Yuri had an expression of disappointment, but Jimbo continued. "The engines. We can't let them sit in the cold too long, or we won't be able to restart them."

Yuri nodded and smiled again. "I see. Sure. We will go have a few quick drinks and bring you right back. I will send Dmitri here to get the cargo while we drink."

Dmitri's face showed immediate disappointment.

Yuri waved to Maria again. "Come on. Have a drink with us!"

Jimbo translated, but used his facial expression to show it wasn't a request.

"Sure!"

As Maria went to step out of the plane, she stopped and put up her hand towards the cockpit and shook her head. Jimbo saw the movement, and realized she was telling Henry to stay.

As Maria approached them, Yuri opened the truck door for her with a smile. She returned the gesture with a tentative "*spasibo*".

Yuri was clearly tickled with her attempt at Russian, and responded heartily. "*Pozhaluysta.*"

They all got in the truck and drove off into the darkness.

It wasn't long before the truck reached a small bar on the edge of town. There were a few vehicles parked in front of a log cabin-style building, but there wasn't any indication that it was in fact a bar. When they pulled up, Jimbo opened the door to let Yuri and Maria out, but before Jimbo shut the door, Maria caught a glimpse of Dmitri's disgruntled expression. Jimbo slammed the door as Dmitri ground the truck's gears and drove off.

Yuri put his hand forward and motioned for Maria to go inside. Maria quickly looked the place over; a single light bulb was swinging in the wind under the eaves, and the few windows she could see were covered. She opened the door, glancing nervously at Jimbo, and the wind blew a whirl of snow across the entrance. The sudden blast of cold air and snow made a few rough-looking patrons look up. They turned back to their drinks before realizing they had seen a woman at the door, and looked up again before the bar became silent. Two men moved aside and motioned for her to sit with them, but Yuri stepped in front of her before leading her to a corner table.

As they sat down, Yuri put up his hand to signal the barkeep; a few seconds later, three vodkas appeared, and sound returned to the bar. Maria looked down at the strong drink and smiled.

Yuri lifted his vodka and toasted in Russian. "To good business!" Jimbo and Maria lifted theirs in response. Jimbo took a sip, but Maria downed it in a single go. Yuri laughed. In English he said, "Good. *Da?*"

Maria nodded and put the shot glass down on the table with vigor. "*Da!*"

Yuri laughed harder, before Jimbo turned and discreetly handed him an envelope. Yuri nodded and they talked quietly in Russian.

Maria watched, but couldn't understand. She figured it

was all just business talk until the expression of shock came over Jimbo's face. She cocked her head. "What is it?"

Jimbo put up his finger and finished his sentence, then turned to her. "Apparently, Chiang Kai-Shek has been kidnapped in Xi'an."

"The leader of the Kuomintang?"

Jimbo nodded. "Exactly."

Maria scratched her cheek. "So what does that mean?"

Yuri tried to speak, but Jimbo stopped him and he answered Maria. "Yuri says that the Chinese Communists have him, but are being supported by Stalin. Not exactly sure what it means—"

Yuri interrupted; Jimbo talked to him for a minute or so, then continued, "Yuri thinks the Russians want to force a united China to fight Japan so that the Russians don't have to."

Maria looked at Yuri and back at Jimbo. "So does that mean there will be full-out war now?"

Jimbo shrugged. "Don't know . . . but it's probably good we got out when we did."

⊥⊥⊥

Anatoly was sitting on one of the bunks, chewing on a piece of beef jerky, when he heard the truck approaching. He and Henry shared a look, then he hurried to the back of the plane to hide again. When the truck pulled up, Henry opened the door and waved.

Three men got out of the truck and made their way to the rear. The lead man half-waved to Henry and pointed to himself, "Dmitri", before opening the tailgate. The truck was stacked with wooden crates, and the men began to off-load and carry them to the plane. As Dmitri helped put the first crate in the plane, he looked to see all the other crates that were already loaded. He pointed to the crates and said something in Russian.

Henry shrugged and pointed to his ear. "Sorry . . . I don't speak Russian."

Dmitri looked at him in response, shrugged himself, and went back to loading.

It took about ten minutes for them to load the cargo and secure it. As the two men finished tying down the crates, Dmitri pointed to the back and again asked something in Russian.

Henry didn't understand and became immediately concerned about Anatoly. He tried not to show it on his face while he came up with an idea to quickly to distract him. He looked around for the beef jerky to offer it, but Dmitri was already going through the back door.

Henry began to move towards the back of the plane, but Dmitri's two assistants were physically in the way. There was sudden shouting and the bang of metal. Henry, not being able to see what was happening, turned and grabbed a Tommy gun that was sitting behind his seat.

A few seconds later, Dmitri appeared with Anatoly behind him. It was obvious that Anatoly had a gun in Dmitri's back, and it sounded like they were arguing, but their voices were becoming quieter. The other two men stepped toward Dmitri to help, but Anatoly yelled at them in Russian. They then turned and spotted Henry, pointing his Tommy gun at them. Both of their faces turned to surprise and they raised their hands in surrender.

It took them a few minutes to tie the three Russians up. Dmitri asked in Russian, "Why are you doing this?"

Anatoly responded in kind as he bound Dmitri's hands

behind his back. "We need to clear this up with your boss. Then we will release you. Where is the bar that they took Jimbo and Maria to?"

Dmitri refused to tell him.

Anatoly rolled his eyes and sighed. "Look, you can tell me, and we can get this cleared up, or we can leave you tied up all night." Anatoly looked out the window. "Looks like it's going to get really cold out."

Dmitri glanced at Henry with his Thompson and back at the threatening face of Anatoly, and started talking.

Anatoly nodded in satisfaction and turned to Henry before saying in English. "He told me where they are."

Henry waved him forward and they went up front to the cockpit. "Now what do we do? Jimbo and Maria will be expecting the truck to come back and pick them up."

Anatoly rubbed his forehead. "Well, let's go pick them up."

Henry indicated the prisoners with a nod of his head. "We can't both go. Someone has to watch them."

Anatoly nodded. "Okay. I should be the one to go."

Henry bit his lip. "But, you're supposed to stay hidden."

Anatoly waived his hand at him, "No, I should go. I speak the language and know my people. You stay here and guard them."

Henry looked at the prisoners and back at Anatoly. "Okay, but you will have to hurry. I really am worried about the engines getting too cold. That wasn't just a ruse."

Anatoly checked their prisoners' restraints one last time, grabbed a Thompson, looked to see that Henry was guarding them, and waved as he stepped out the door. "Be back shortly."

A few minutes later, he pulled up to the bar, thought for a second about what to do, then just blew the horn.

When the horn blew for the second time, Yuri peeked out a crack in the window. He looked at Jimbo and motioned for him to get up. "What the hell is wrong with Dmitri?" He threw his hands up, put money on the table, and headed for the door. "He's probably just pissed because he didn't get to drink."

Jimbo and Maria grabbed their fur hats and followed him.

Yuri stomped out into the snow and swung the passenger door open. "What the hell is the matter with—"

Jimbo saw Yuri starting to raise his hands, looked at Maria, and ran to the truck. Over Yuri's shoulder, he saw Anatoly holding a Thompson. Jimbo pulled out his .45 and in English demanded, "What the hell is going on, Anatoly?"

Yuri half looked at Jimbo, but didn't move.

The light in the cab of the truck illuminated Anatoly's face, and Yuri leaned in to get a better look. Anatoly responded in Russian, "Hey! Hey! Don't move."

Yuri kept his hands up, but glanced at Jimbo. "Anatoly? Anatoly Pepelyayev?"

Anatoly's expression became one of surprise as he heard his name, and Maria just stood with her eyes wide, watching.

Jimbo stepped up and removed Yuri's pistol. "How did you know?"

Yuri cautiously glanced back and forth between the other two men. "I was there at the retreat across Lake Baikal." He looked at Anatoly. "I thought you had been executed."

Jimbo asked Yuri. "You said earlier that things are 'as well as can be expected nowadays'. What did you mean?"

Yuri got a little nervous and whispered, "I meant with Stalin in power. You can't make a ruble, at least not legally, without the government coming to take it, and if you complain about it, you just disappear."

Jimbo holstered his gun. He looked at Anatoly. "Put down the gun. We are on the same side." He looked at Yuri. "I suspected you felt this way, but we couldn't be sure, and we couldn't take any chances." Jimbo handed him back his pistol.

Yuri watched Anatoly lower the Thompson and accepted his pistol back. "I understand." He holstered the pistol. "No hard feelings, right?" He looked at Jimbo. "We can still do business?"

Jimbo smiled. "Sure. Sorry about this." He looked at Anatoly. "Anatoly was supposed to remain hidden, so we wouldn't have this problem. What the hell happened?"

Maria finally spoke up. "Jimbo! Could you please tell me what is going on?"

Jimbo turned to her, realizing that she hadn't understood anything that had happened. "Oh. It's okay." He put his arm on Yuri's shoulder. "He agrees with us on . . . certain political views."

Maria looked at the three of them. "So, how did Anatoly get here?"

Jimbo smiled. "I'm trying to figure that out."

Anatoly put the gun on the dashboard and in Russian said, "Let's go. Henry says the engines are getting cold."

Jimbo nodded and motioned for Yuri to get in.

As Anatoly put the truck in gear, Yuri asked, "What about my men?"

Anatoly looked at him. "They are fine. Just tied them up." He smiled.

Yuri shook his head. "Useless. You just can't get good help these days." He looked back at Anatoly and then at Jimbo. "So, what's the story here? I thought you were running arms to the Chinese?"

Jimbo shrugged. "Things change, and this is a special favor."

Yuri looked at Anatoly with confusion on his face. "How did you come to be here? Where have you been for all these years?" He cleared his throat. "You were a great leader, but I heard you got caught and executed."

Anatoly smiled, "Well, I almost was, but they just decided to put me in prison for the last ten years." He looked at Jimbo. "They just let me out."

Yuri turned to Jimbo. "What kind of scheme have you got going, here?"

Jimbo said nothing, but a large smile grew on his face as Anatoly stopped the truck in front of the plane.

"Your men are inside," said Anatoly. He leaned forward to look at Jimbo. "You should probably go in first."

Jimbo nodded and motioned for Maria to get out the passenger side.

Jimbo walked up and peeked inside the plane. Henry was behind a seat with his Thompson pointed at the door. Jimbo saw the three men tied up and chuckled to himself. "Henry, it's okay. Yuri is on our side and we are coming in to release everyone. You can put down the gun now."

Henry stood up. "Are you sure?"

Jimbo stepped into the plane with Yuri. "Yes."

The three men all started frantically talking at once and wriggling in their restraints. Jimbo watched as Yuri put up his hands and in Russian said, "It's all right. Just a misunderstanding. We are going to release you. Remain calm." He pointed to Jimbo and Henry. "We are on the same side, they were just being very cautious."

Jimbo pulled out his pocketknife and cut them free, one at a time. Dmitri stood up in anger and threw down the remainder of his ropes. Yuri grabbed him. "Calm down. We got paid, and I'll take you all for drinks afterward."

Dmitri glared at Yuri and banged the side of the fuselage, before he pointed at Henry. "Who the hell are you that you can treat me like this?" He lunged for Henry and Yuri did his best to hold him, but it took Jimbo stepping in to stop him.

Yuri yanked Dmitri close and spoke in his face. "It's over. We're done here. Is that clear?"

Dmitri turned and glared at Jimbo before finally nodding in response to Yuri. Yuri released Jimbo's grip and led Dmitri out of the plane.

Jimbo pointed to the front of the plane. "Henry. Go ahead and get her started. We will be leaving shortly."

Henry, still wide-eyed, nodded and proceeded to the front.

A few seconds later, Maria stepped up into the plane questioning, "What the hell was all that about?"

Jimbo glanced at her. "I'll tell you later."

Yuri, standing in the doorway, grabbed Maria's hand, and

kissed it while trying his skill at English. "You beauty. Thank you."

Maria smiled at him and nodded. "Thank you, and thank you for the drink. I, I have to go start the plane now." She turned and walked quickly to the front just as Henry yelled, "Clear prop!" and started the right engine.

Anatoly was the last on the plane, and Yuri turned to him. "Well, I am glad you are still around—and whatever you are up to, best of luck!"

Anatoly grinned. "Thank you." He pointed to the truck. "Give my regards to your men and my apologies."

Yuri nodded and turned to Jimbo. "Let me know if you need anything in the future. Good to see you in person."

Jimbo shook his hand. "Yes, Yuri. It was a pleasure to see you as well." He pointed out towards the truck. "Apologize to your men for me as well." He handed Yuri a wad of cash. "Show them a good time."

Yuri smiled and gladly accepted the money. "I will!" He then stepped down the stairs and handed them up to Jimbo. "*Do suidaniya!*"

⋏⋏⋏

Jimbo waved and pulled the door shut as Henry started the left engine. Then, as he turned to walk towards the front, Henry yelled back. "Hey! Where are we going?"

Henry looked back a few seconds later to find Jimbo and Anatoly right behind him. "Hello? So, where are we heading? Straight to," he pointed to Anatoly, "your coordinates?"

Anatoly nodded. "Yes, we can. They should already be there and we can radio them to light up the runway for us, if it's still dark when we arrive." Jimbo nodded in agreement.

"Okay then," said Henry, checking his instruments. "Plenty of fuel, and everything looks good. Should take us about eight to ten hours to get there."

He looked at Maria. "Ready?"

She nodded. "As always."

Henry smiled. "Everyone take their seats." Looking out the window to see Yuri and his crew driving off in the direction of the bar, he brought the plane around. In less than a minute, they were airborne, heading east through the clearing, star-filled sky, towards Kamchatka.

Chapter 23

The Final Delivery

Nine hours later, Henry reached over and woke up Maria. "Sorry, dear, we should almost be there, but with no moon, I can't see anything. Want to check our position and radio Anatoly's guys?"

He watched as she rubbed the sleep out of her eyes and performed a squirming stretch in her seat. She glanced over at him, a greenish instrument glow lighting a sleepy smile, before she nodded and headed back to the navigator's station. A few minutes later, she pulled off her headphones. "I can't get any stations to triangulate off of. Everything is too far away and I am just receiving atmospheric bounce. I will try radioing Anatoly's people now."

Henry looked back at her and nodded. "Okay. I am going to turn off all the interior lights and see if I can at least see land." He reached up and shut off all the instrument and internal lights. After a minute of adjusting his eyes, he leaned over and gazed out the window, but still couldn't see anything. "Steel yourself, this is going to be cold." He opened his side window and moved his head out of the draft while trying to open his eyes all the way. Using averted vision, he began to see the shape of land against the sea. Henry called, "I see land—let me try and draw its shape and see if we can't find where we are. Oh, and can you hand me up my sextant?"

Maria didn't respond and began talking on the radio. The

light from the radio dials was enough to reveal Anatoly, now sitting up on one of the bunks. She pulled her headset to one side. "Can you talk to them?"

He nodded and switched places with her. After a few moments, he turned to Maria. "They will light the runway in a few minutes. Is there anything else?"

Maria nodded. "Yes. Can you ask them to keep transmitting so we can home in on their signal?"

Anatoly nodded and began speaking into the microphone again. He tilted his head while he listened to the reply, and translated. "They say they are willing to leave it on for thirty minutes, but no longer. They say Reds have been spotted on the peninsula, and they are worried they will be found."

Maria nodded quickly and swapped seats again. She turned the antenna until she was receiving the strongest signal. "Henry, turn left thirteen degrees."

Henry brought up the instrument lights just enough to see the heading indicator. "Okay. Thirteen degrees port. Can you bring me my sextant?"

Maria replied. "Sure. Just a second." She hung up the headset and felt around under the desk for the wooden case, before carefully pulling out the brass instrument. She then made her way back to the cockpit and handed it to him. He put his hand up and groped the air until he felt it. "Okay. Got it."

He first measured the angle of Polaris with respect to the horizon, while checking the position of the Little Dipper to see if he needed to add or subtract half a degree, or something in the middle. "Fifty-two point five degrees north." He brought up the lights slightly. "Maria, can you write it down?"

Maria buttoned her coat tight as the open window began dropping the temperature of the entire cabin. "Sure," she replied, and before he could ask, she handed him rise/set time chart of the brightest stars. He closed the window and looked dead ahead to see what was rising. After a few minutes, he told Maria, "About one-fifty-eight east."

Maria reached down for the local charts that she had stowed next to her seat. "Is it okay if I turn on the map light?"

Henry glanced over. "Sure, go ahead. I saw the coastline and drew it. See if you can match it to the chart." He handed her the piece of paper that he had drawn on in the dark.

She turned on the light, and found the position on the map that he had measured using the stars. She then compared the coast line of the map to his drawing. "Well, I think we are here . . . or here . . . but in either case, it only puts us about fifty miles out and we are close to where we need to be."

Henry smiled and relaxed slightly. He glanced at the fuel gauges, which indicated that their tanks were about 1/8th full.

Maria yelled aft, "Anatoly, Jimbo, watch out the windows for our runway lights." She then got up and checked the radio bearing again. "Henry, adjust two degrees right."

For the next fifteen minutes, they all stared out the window, watching for any lights that could indicate the runway.

Henry began to see isolated lights, but nothing concentrated.

Maria suddenly reached up and tried adjusting the radio set. "Damn. They stopped transmitting."

Henry looked back, worry on his face, but Maria reassured him, "It was a very strong signal. It should be dead ahead and very close."

Henry turned off the internal lights again and scanned the horizon. A flashing light slightly south of dead ahead caught his attention. He reached over to grab his binoculars, but they weren't there. "Maria. Where are my binoculars?"

Maria jumped up and felt her way to the back of his seat. "I put them away; here they are."

Henry focused on the flashing light. "Well, someone's flashing a light and there appears to be a row of lights . . . that has to be it."

Maria climbed back into her seat. "Yes. I see it!"

As they flew over the string of lights, it became apparent that the flashing light was a pair of vehicle headlights, with a row of burning torches indicating the runway. Henry turned and lined up for landing. "Everyone strap in." He put down full flaps and slowed his airspeed. When he switched on his landing lights, the reflection against the white snow made him squint. Henry managed to touch down smoothly, with large billowing clouds of snow engulfing the plane.

When they had come to a complete stop, he turned and taxied back toward the vehicle. As he taxied, the torches and the car headlights were already being extinguished. Then, when he saw two men walking towards the plane with flashlights, he shut down the engines.

⚙ ⚙ ⚙

A knock came at the rear door and Anatoly opened it up. When Anatoly set out the stairs and stepped out, one of the men gasped. "General!" The two men suddenly saluted and Anatoly saluted back. "It is an honor to have you back with us, sir."

Anatoly glanced around. "Get more men to unload these weapons and start refueling the plane."

They saluted again, "Yes sir!" and ran off into the darkness.

Jimbo stepped up behind Anatoly. "Impressive. It's as though you were never gone."

Anatoly turned to him and smiled, but Jimbo maintained a serious face. "So, what is your plan? Build a force and then ship them to the mainland?"

Anatoly nodded somberly. "Something like that."

Maria came up from behind Jimbo. "What's going on? We at the right place?"

Jimbo turned and grinned at her. "Yep. They are off to get more men for unloading and to fuel the plane."

Anatoly motioned for Jimbo to follow and they both walked off into the darkness, following the two men. Jimbo yelled back, "Just stay with the plane."

As they walked off, Henry made his way over to Maria just as she took off her hat and began scratching her head. "A bit warmer here."

Henry took a deep breath, "Yeah. It is."

When they heard the sound of a truck, both of them peered through the dark to see a tanker. Henry nudged Maria. "Wow. We're moving up in the world. No oil drums and jerry cans. A real fuel truck!"

The truck pulled up and two men began the process of refueling the plane. Right behind it was a cargo truck, which pulled up to the rear door. Several men in white got out and walked around to the back of the truck. One of them eyed Henry and Maria and asked a question in Russian. Henry assumed they wanted to get the crates from the plane, so he stepped aside and waved them in. The man nodded before they stepped in and began to unload the crates.

As they pulled the first crate out, a car pulled up with Anatoly, Jimbo, and an officer. The men had loaded the first crate on the truck, but the officer had them pull it back off, then motioned to them to put all the crates on the ground.

Jimbo and Anatoly walked over to Henry and Maria. Jimbo was watching them unload the crate from the truck when he leaned over and whispered. "What is he doing?"

Anatoly responded with a whisper. "Most of his men have no weapons, and he wants to distribute the small arms immediately."

Hundreds of men could be heard walking down the airstrip before they appeared out of the darkness. The officer ordered the crates to be opened and he began handing out guns; they were mostly submachine guns, but there were a few rifles as well.

Jimbo watched as the men inspected their new weapons and he remarked quietly to Anatoly, "They seem to be happy with them."

Anatoly nodded. "Yes. Many of them have not had a real weapon of their own in years, or maybe never. Trained with fakes, or shared one to practice. This is a good day for them."

✈ ✈ ✈

The fuel truck finished refueling the plane just as it began to get light out. The men reeled up the hoses and drove off towards what seemed like barracks. With the new day's light, Henry could see crates stacked and opened all along the side of the plane. Men were polishing their new weapons and loading ammunition into magazines. There was a sense of joy in the air and the men were in high spirits. The head officer was smiling and thanking Jimbo and Anatoly. The officer then asked Anatoly, "How long before we take back Mother Russia?"

Anatoly smiled at the enthusiasm and pointed to the men. "We need to get the men trained with these weapons first, then we will go. I have arranged everything in Okhotsk when we are ready, including a ship."

Jimbo pulled out his pipe and began chewing on it as Anatoly explained the basic plan to the officer. Anatoly also instructed the officer to form squads around the types of weapons. He pulled out a heavy machine gun, but then stopped. He turned to Jimbo and pointed to the plane. "Do you need those .50 caliber M-2's?"

Jimbo turned and looked at the two heavy machine guns mounted on the wings. He laughed, "No. Not at all." He chewed on his pipe. "They ruin the plane's aesthetics anyway. Have your men take them."

Anatoly nodded and told the officer to have his men remove them. A few minutes later, they were unbolting the first one. Henry, hearing someone working on his plane, jumped down the stairs to investigate. Jimbo stepped in front of Henry. "It's okay. I told them they could have the .50s"

Henry glanced at the men. "Oh, okay. Was a bit worried someone was tearing apart my plane." Jimbo cocked his head and Henry supplemented his comment. "I mean, your plane."

Jimbo smiled, but before he could respond, a loud bang of metal sounded next to their head. Henry jumped at its loudness and looked to see what the workers had done, but they had stopped, too, and were looking back at him with surprise on their face. Then came the report of a rifle. There was a second ear-splitting bang of metal as Henry saw the spark off the plane, and he immediately ducked.

Within seconds, gunfire erupted. The sounds of ricochets and men screaming filled the air. Some of the men were already dead or dying on the ground before they even knew what was happening. The rest formed up behind crates and the truck, and they started firing back with their new weapons. Henry ran, half bent over, and jumped into the plane. Maria was taking cover on the floor of the plane, so Henry pulled her up. "Come on! We're getting out of here!"

Bullets smashed through the windows, and holes appeared in the aluminum skin, while Henry started the right engine as fast as he could. Maria followed him up and sat in her seat, but out the window she saw Jimbo and Anatoly ducking behind crates trying to return fire. She got up and returned to the back of the plane.

Henry turned. "Maria! Where are you going?!"

Maria screamed out the door as a bullet hit the frame. "Uncle!"

Jimbo and Anatoly turned to look at her in the door of the plane. Anatoly waved for Jimbo to go, and he opened fire again over the top of the crate. Jimbo ran towards the plane while waving his arms for Maria to get back in.

Troops, wearing white but with red collars, began advancing across the runway as Anatoly's men frantically tried using their new weapons against them.

Maria was forced to duck as more rounds hit the plane. When she looked back up, she couldn't find Jimbo. Then, she saw his pipe on the ground at the bottom of the stairs. She leaned forward and looked under the plane to see him face down in a patch of red snow.

"Uncle!" She immediately began climbing down the stairs while repeatedly screaming, "*Jimbo!*"

Yelling from Anatoly suddenly registered when a bullet forcefully tugged through the left arm of her jacket. She lost her balance and fell back into the plane. She felt her arm and the new hole in her jacket as she kicked her way across the floor sliding on her butt.

Maria heard Henry start the second engine. She suddenly scrambled to her feet and back to the cargo area before letting open the cargo door. With tears streaming down her face, she cocked the .30 caliber machine gun and opened fire. A hail of bullets and tracers raked the runway, and men fell like dominoes. The onslaught was so heavy that Stalin's men were forced to retreat and the shooting died down. Anatoly yelled out, and the troops began to reorganize and get into defensive positions, while Anatoly scrambled on his hands and knees to Jimbo.

Maria, who had stopped firing, leaned forward to see how Jimbo was, but she cried out in pain when she touched the red-hot, empty water jacket of the water-cooled machine gun. Anatoly, who had been trying to move Jimbo, heard her and ran to the door. "Henry, Maria—get out of here!"

Maria, holding her burned hand, appeared from around the corner. "Come with us!"

Anatoly shook his head. "My place is with my men. We have been set up and betrayed, and I won't let them die alone—go!"

Henry yelled back as more gunfire erupted. "Maria!"

Anatoly jumped down from the stairs and took cover, while Maria went back to the gun. She opened fire again until the ammo belt ran out.

Henry suddenly appeared at the back and grabbed her. "Come on! I need you up front!"

She turned sobbing helplessly and screaming gibberish. Henry yanked her away from the gun and then pushed her towards the front before he tried to close the side door. "Where is Jimbo?" He slammed the door, but it wouldn't seal. He went to try again and saw Anatoly holding Jimbo's blood-covered body in the snow behind the rear wheels of the truck. Henry stopped, staring in disbelief as Anatoly waved him off. More bullets passing through the fuselage made him try slamming the door again, but to no avail.

Henry shook his head to overcome the paralyzing effect of emotion, and ran back to the cockpit while pieces of metal, fabric and paper flew everywhere. The second his butt hit the seat, he rammed the throttles to max power, slamming him and Maria against their seats.

A huge storm of snow formed in their wake, providing cover for Anatoly's men as the plane accelerated down the airstrip. The downside of Anatoly's men being obscured was that, now, the plane drew all the fire. The front windshield cracked and bullets penetrated the left wing. As the plane began lifting into the air, the left engine started pouring out smoke. Henry watched the engine with growing concern, but had to cover his face when another round shattered his side window.

He glanced over at Maria, who was still trying to buckle herself in, but with her hand burned and shaking uncontrollably, she couldn't get the buckles together. He glanced at her again, but when he looked back, the engine was on fire. "Fire!" He frantically looked down for the fire suppression system. He tried lifting the door in the floor, but debris was blocking it. "Maria! Help!"

She bent over the side of her seat and cleared the top of the door, so Henry was able to open it. He looked out at the engine to see a piece of cowling suddenly rip away. With the door open, he set the selector to left engine and pulled the CO_2 release handle. He watched the engine as his heart pounded in his chest.

The flames began to die, but so did the engine. The plane started pulling left with the imbalance of power, and Henry had to quickly trim it out. With the loss of power, the propeller went partially into its "feather" position, but it didn't go all the way. Henry reached up and pushed the feather solenoid button with no effect. The propeller still wouldn't turn away from the wind, and continued to cause enormous drag.

Henry heard Maria's shaking voice, half-yelling over the wind noise. "Can you restart it?"

Henry, still trying to make the plane go straight and level, glanced out at the charred engine. "I don't think we should risk it." He then remembered to switch the vacuum pump selector valve to the good engine, but he was still fighting the controls.

Chapter 24

The Crash

Maria started shivering as her heart slowed, her tears dried, and she began to calm. She looked around the interior of the plane, and saw holes everywhere. Wind was coming in through broken windows and bullet holes in the fuselage. She turned the heat to maximum, but it barely made a difference, so she got up and grabbed blankets off the sleeper bunks.

Henry was starting to get the hang of flying the plane with only one good engine and one partially-unfeathered engine. He glanced over at Maria, all wrapped up in blankets and suddenly felt the cold himself. A shiver made its way up his spine. "Can you get me some blankets too? I'm freezing . . . and see if you can plug up some of these holes."

Maria, who was as close to fetal position as she could be while sitting in the seat, nodded, got up, walked back, and pulled anything cloth down, to bring to the front. She handed some to Henry. "Here are the remaining blankets. This curtain, I am going to cut up and stuff in the holes."

As Henry tucked the blankets around him, the plane suddenly shuddered and a loud slamming noise came from the back. Wind filled the cockpit, while paper and debris swirled around. "What the hell was that?!"

Maria, holding on to her seat, looked back. "The rear door! It's open and it's slamming against the fuselage."

Henry glanced back, but couldn't see it from his seat. "Shit—well, I'll try and fix it in a minute. First we have to figure out where to go." He thought for a minute. "I think our only choice is Alaska. We talked about it before. We should be able to make Naknek," he looked out at the dead engine, "well, at least we could before we lost an engine."

Maria eyed him with worry on her face. "If we can't make it to Naknek, where can we make it to?"

Henry began turning the plane to the east. Up until then, he had just been trying to fly it, not worrying about direction. "Well, I think daylight is going to be our limiting factor." He glanced at the clock. "Crap!"

Maria sat up straight. "What now?"

Henry pointed to the clock, which had a bullet hole straight through the center of it.

Maria followed his finger. "Oh." She then looked out trying to see the sun, but it was too overcast to tell what time it was. "How long will that give us?"

Henry thought for a second. "Well, the sun has been up for about an hour, so maybe seven hours; and our maximum speed at the moment is about 120." He stared out at the disabled engine and the propeller that was turning in the wind. "If I could fully feather that prop, we could get some more speed, but right now, we are looking at a max range of 840 miles." He cocked his head. "Oh no, wait—we are heading east, so we are going to lose daylight." His eyes got big and he looked up at Maria. "Maybe five hours? So, 600 miles."

Maria scanned around for her charts and got up to go to the navigator's station. She stopped and called to Henry over the wind noise, "Can we just fly all night, since we are only using one engine?"

Henry glanced back. "Hmm . . . maybe, since we have a full . . ." He glanced at the fuel gauges and then jerked straight up and looked out at the left wing once again.

Maria came back up with a map of Alaska and the Aleutian islands. She glanced over to see him leaning close to the side window, trying to look out at the wing. "What is it?"

He glanced back and tapped on the left fuel gauge, then back out the window again.

"Henry, what is it?"

He looked at her, seeing the toll of events on her face. "Bullet holes in the left wing. We are losing fuel." He pointed to the gauge. "We have already lost twenty percent!" He immediately switched the fuel selector to left wing, trying to use what fuel he could from the wing, before it was gone.

Maria quickly opened up the map of the Aleutians. "Well, I guess the overnight flight plan is a 'no go'."

Henry looked at her and pointed to the map. "At this point, I just hope we can make it to anywhere."

The plane shuddered again as they hit turbulence and the rear door slammed against the fuselage. Henry unbuckled himself. "Take over. Keep her banked about five degrees into the good engine and she is controllable. A bit squirrelly, but you'll feel it out."

Maria had been holding down the map in her lap, but was forced to stuff it beside her seat to keep it from flying away. She felt the controls as Henry released them to her.

"Okay. You got it?"

She winced in pain as the plane oscillated back and forth a

bit before leveling out. "Yeah, my hands . . . I think I do."

Henry nodded and put his hand on her shoulder. "Be right back."

Henry was having trouble balancing as Maria kept trying to adapt to the plane's new characteristics.

As Henry approached the door, he could see it banging against the opening it was supposed to fit into. When they hit turbulence again, Henry, trying to use the ceiling to stabilize himself, ended up falling to the floor. He slid across the floor as the door opened wide. He yelled out at the sudden prospect of flying out the door, but then it slammed shut again and he caught a foothold before regaining control of himself. Breathing heavily, he glanced around for something to tie himself off with, while Maria was looking back and yelling to see if he was hurt. The plane started to heave back and forth, and Henry shouted in response, "I'm fine! Fly the damn plane!"

After a few seconds, the plane returned to a semi-controlled state and Henry again searched for something to tie himself with. There were cargo straps still hanging from the wall, so he took one off and tied one end around his waist, while leaving the other end attached to the wall. He sat on the floor for a second, watching the door while trying to catch his breath. The freezing cold air was slamming him in the face, but the new rush of fear and excitement had warmed him up. He grabbed another strap off the wall, detached it, and slid across the floor on his butt. When he reached the door he yelled forward, "Can you bank harder to the right? I am going to try to tie the door off."

He heard Maria's voice, but couldn't hear the details with the noise of the rushing wind. When he felt the plane tilt to the right, he watched the door, which seemed to be semi-stable, and threw the extra strap around a handle on it. The plane suddenly dropped, while he felt himself partially weightless and the door swung open again. The strap he had just thrown around the door handle began to pull him across the floor. His feet kicked at the floor and his instinct was to let go of the strap, but he glanced back just as his waist strap stopped him with a sudden jerk. Henry put his foot against the fuselage, next to the door, and pulled as hard as he could on the door. The door closed with a loud bang, but still didn't seal. Henry pulled the strap as tight as he could while pushing himself back across the floor to the far wall. The strap pulled hard against him, but he was eventually able to make it to the wall and secure it. Finally, he sat on the floor, exhausted, as the strap above him creaked and popped under the strain.

Maria hollered back again. "You okay?"

Henry responded with his hand in the air, "Yeah! Just give me a minute to recover!" He took a deep breath. "Make our heading east again!"

After a few minutes, Henry made his way back to the cockpit.

"You okay?" Maria looked at him and cocked her head with a wan smile and reddened eyes. "You look tired!"

Henry paused and his eyebrows raised, but didn't say anything as he slowly buckled himself in. His expression suddenly changed to concern and he jumped back up to help her buckle in. She smiled up at him in appreciation, and once he had her snapped in, he went back to his seat and began the process for himself.

Maria motioned with her head to the side pocket of her seat. "Can you take over so I can study the map?"

Henry took a hold of the yoke. "Okay. Got it."

Maria slowly released her yoke and watched Henry, who nodded at her. After a few seconds, she snatched the map and held it in her lap, grabbed a ruler from her pocket, and began to measure.

Henry watched her with intense worry, until she finally glanced up at him. He waited impatiently for her to tell him something. "Well?"

She glanced out the front window and back at him. "Well, we are in range of the most remote of the Aleutians, but there aren't any people, let alone airstrips."

Henry pulled his glove off, put his hand over his mouth and rubbed the stubble on his chin. "Well, that leaves us with three choices." He eyed Maria. "One, we try to land on Attu or the other empty island. Two, we fly as long as we can and ditch in the sea." On hearing that, Maria looked out her window at the iceberg filled ocean below. Henry continued. "That option is not too appealing, as we wouldn't last five minutes down there—"

Maria asked. "What's option three?"

Henry studied the horizon in front of them. "We fly into the night and try to land on an inhabited island in the dark, before we run out of fuel." He glanced down at the fuel gauge. "Shit. Only a third of the left tank is left!"

Henry turned to see the fear on her face. She stared down at the chart and measured again. She then looked up at the ceiling and he saw a tear run down her face. "Are you okay?"

She turned towards him while wiping her face. "No! We are about to die in some godforsaken frozen wasteland and never be found and—" She looked back down at her chart while putting her hand over her face. "Jimbo . . . he was in the snow—the blood was everywhere—" She sat up. "—and what about Anatoly? His men? Bayasaa?!" She screamed, "It's too much! I don't want to do it anymore!" and tried to stand up, but her belts held her down.

Henry yelled, "*Maria! Stop! Look at me!*"

She looked at him with despair on her face and tears dripping from her chin.

"It's going to be all right. We are still here. We can use the radio to call for help. We're not dead yet!" He glanced at the map that the wind had taken off her lap. "Okay. We are going to land on Attu. It's the safest for us, and we can use the radio to call for help. I am sure there are fishing vessels or some kind of ships that we can talk to. Now, what I need you to do is go around and stuff all these holes and broken windows with whatever you have to make it warmer in here." He leaned toward her. "Do you hear me?"

Maria made a slight nod, wiped her face and sniffled. Then she reached down with her wounded hands and clumsily undid her belt. She grabbed the curtain material she had brought up, took off her right glove, and placed it in front of Henry. "Can I have your pocket knife?" Henry glanced up at her, smiled reassuringly, and handed her his knife.

Maria walked back and sat on a bunk. She tried carefully to cut the curtain into long strips, but the bumping of the plane and the cold made it difficult. Her hand became stiff and she started to shiver as she cut jagged pieces out of the cloth. Her main goal, as she kept a close eye on her work, was simply not to cut herself.

After successfully cutting a couple dozen pieces, she folded the knife, got up, and began to search for holes to plug. They weren't hard to find. She twisted the material and stuffed it into the holes and it seemed to hold.

Henry glanced back to see how she was. "Dear, why don't you plug up the holes in the cockpit first?"

She glanced up at him, paused, and slowly nodded. Henry could see the toll that events were taking on her, and his heart sank. He wanted to comfort her and take away her burdens, but at the moment, there was nothing he could do, except offer her words of encouragement.

As she began plugging holes in the cockpit, Henry put his hand on her back. "Getting warmer already."

She turned and stared at him, clearly skeptical, but Henry, with his sunglasses on and hair fluttering in the cold wind, only returned a sincere smile. After a moment, Maria's shoulders dropped, and her expression softened. The smile she gave him in return wasn't much, but she went back to plugging holes with a little more enthusiasm.

An hour later, after cutting more strips of curtain, she had most of the small holes plugged. She stood over Henry with a large piece of curtain in her hand while holding on to the back of his seat, and eyed the hole where Henry's side window used to be. Henry looked at her and the window hole. "Yeah. It would be nice to plug that! My head hurts like a son of a bitch."

She glanced down at him and gave a slight smile, but the sudden sound of the right engine sputtering made her instantly turn the other direction.

Henry tensed up and pushed her to the side. "Crap! Out of fuel!"

He reached over the control pedestal and switched the right engine tank feed to the right tank, but the engine continued to cough. Henry tried frantically adjusting the controls to keep the engine going, but it stalled, and the prop came to a stop.

"Shit!" He pushed Maria towards her seat. "Sit down!" he ordered, and started priming the engine again as the plane began to drop.

Maria fell into her seat and put her good hand against the dash as she looked forward to the iceberg-filled sea. "Henry!"

Henry started cranking the engine again.

Maria, now with her hands against the right window, watched the prop turn under the starter's power. She whispered to herself desperately, "Come on, come on!"

Henry kept cranking as his grip on the yoke tightened. The cold wind from the broken side window continued to blow against his head and he shivered in anticipation of the freezing water below.

He watched forward and could see the white caps of the sea growing larger. Then he heard it: the pop of a cylinder firing, followed by another and then another. He looked at the engine to see the beautiful black smoke pouring out as it fired up. The plane rattled and shook as the engine came up to power.

Maria eyed Henry while holding her hand against her chest. "I thought you meant totally out of fuel." She looked out her window, down at the icebergs that were frighteningly close now, and then back at Henry. "That really scared me!"

Henry glanced at her with concern. "No, no; just the left tank is empty. The right is still almost full." He tilted his head slightly and wiped his brow. "Sorry to scare you." He then stared down at his shaking hands and admitted, "Damn—that scared me too."

The two of them sat back in their seats for a moment, just catching their breath, before Maria looked over and frowned at Henry's window.

Henry glanced over to see the sun peeking through some clouds. "The sun is really moving around the horizon quick." He looked over at Maria and back at the navigator's station. "See if you can triangulate our position, and if we are clear of Russia, start calling mayday."

Maria was holding a clump of curtain in her hand, ready to give it to Henry for his window, but she set it down. "Okay. I'll see if I can pick anything up."

She spent fifteen minutes on the radio before hearing Henry, with worry in his voice, ask, "Anything?"

Maria leaned to the side and looked up at Henry while pulling her headset partway off. "No. Nothing." She stared down at her chart. "If we have been flying east this whole time, we should be more than halfway there and out of Russian territorial waters." She glanced back up at Henry. "Want me to try sending a mayday now?"

Henry looked back and nodded solemnly. "Try the nautical bands at 500 kilocycles and 2182 kilocycles." Henry glanced at the clock, forgetting it was destroyed. "Damn." He turned back to her. "The first one is reserved for emergency traffic at fifteen after and forty-five after the hour, but we can't tell the time!"

Maria thought for a second. "I guess I'll just transmit continuously." She tuned the radio to 500Kcs and began broadcasting "Mayday. Mayday. Mayday. This is DC-3 November Charlie one-seven-three-three-zero. We are declaring an emergency. One engine out and low on fuel. We will attempt a landing at Attu . . . Mayday. Mayday. Mayday. This is DC-3 November Charlie one-seven-three . . ." . . ."

An hour later, she put down her headset. "I can't get anything! Something is wrong."

Henry looked back. "What do you mean? You mean you can't get any signal at all?"

She nodded. "Nothing! Just static. Maybe the receiver antenna is damaged." She glanced around at all the bullet holes. "Wouldn't surprise me."

Henry returned his gaze forward and then back at her. "What about the transmitter?"

She got up and moved to the cockpit. "It's transmitting. I can see the output amps and hear it on the auxiliary speaker, but if that antenna is damaged too, well," she looked at Henry, "we're dead ducks."

Henry watched out at seemingly-unending blue ocean and the occasional iceberg. "Let's just hope someone heard us, then." He looked back at her to find her chewing on a piece of yak jerky. "Where did you get that?"

She pointed behind her seat. "It was in this bag. I don't know whose it was, but I'm eating it."

Henry grinned slightly. "Any for me? I'm starving."

She felt in the bag and pulled out another piece. "Here."

Henry chewed it quickly and with enthusiasm. He looked at her while he continued gnawing. "When the hell was the last time we ate—Mongolia?"

Maria thought for a second. "Yeah, I think you're right." She looked back at him. "And we haven't slept, either."

Henry wiped his eyes. "No wonder I feel so damn tired!"

When he pulled his hand away from his eye, he noticed a white bump on the horizon. He wiped his eyes again and leaned forward. "Can you hand me the binoculars?"

"Here. What do you see?"

He glanced at her. "Take the yoke. It might just be a cloud, but it could be the island."

When Maria took over, he focused the binoculars, then pulled them away from his face, rubbing his eyes again. "Well . . . I think I see a peak." He took back the controls and started changing their heading towards the possible island.

He handed the binoculars to Maria. "Keep an eye on it. Do you see it?"

She nodded and pointed to the 11 o'clock position. "That one there?"

He nodded. "Yes."

As they approached, Maria suddenly put the binoculars down. "Yes! It is definitely an island!"

Henry looked at her with a smile. "Get back on the radio and keep calling for help."

She nodded and went back to the navigator's position.

As they drew near the island, the sun began sinking in the sky. Henry turned to Maria. "Help me look for a good landing spot."

She finished one last call for help and moved up front. Below were snow-covered peaks and fairly flat valleys. Jagged rocks could be seen protruding from the snow where the slopes were too steep, but there were also many small iced over lakes and scars from glaciers.

Henry pointed to one of the lakes. "The terrain isn't as bad as I expected. One of those lakes might be our best bet."

Maria, squinting suspiciously, pulled out the map of the Aleutians. After a minute of looking at the map and comparing the view, she pointed down. "That's not Attu!"

Henry looked at her with his eyebrows raised. "What?" He looked down at the map she was holding. "Then where the hell are we?"

She put up her finger, while she compared the map to the view. "I think it's this one." She held up the map and pointed. "Agattu."

Henry looked at the map and out the window. "Crap, I think you're right." He pointed back to the radio. "Get on the radio and broadcast our new location!" He then pointed to one of the larger lakes he could see on the south end of the island. "I am going to take a look at that lake for a landing spot and I can circle while you transmit." He pointed to the setting sun and added, "But we have to land before that goes down!"

She nodded and hurried back to the navigator's station once again.

Henry circled the lake several times while flying through patches of fog. "It looks pretty good. Mostly smooth, but a few rough patches. Better than most of the other terrain around here." He looked at the sun, which was now disappearing below the horizon. "Maria! Get up here and buckle in. We can't wait any longer. We have to land!"

Henry turned to line up with the lake along its longest axis. He looked over to see if Maria was ready, but she was still fiddling with her seat belt. "Shit, I forgot! Take over—I'll get it!" She grabbed the yoke and tried to keep the plane level while Henry buckled her in. He kept looking out the window nervously, while fumbling the buckles.

Maria looked down. "Concentrate on the belt first!"

He finally snapped the pieces together and jumped back into his seat; he buckled himself in and took back control of the plane, but by then they were already over the lake. "Damn. I'll have to go around again."

As he circled around again, the orange sky faded into blackness and the fog started to thicken. He could still see the white of the lake, but the detail was quickly disappearing. He lined up again, and not wanting to stall the plane by countering the force of only one engine, slowly engaged the flaps. As he approached, he added more flaps. He glanced at Maria. "Brace yourself. I love you."

The sentiment caught Maria's attention and she looked at him with wide, fearful eyes. Her right hand slid down to hold onto the seat.

Henry turned on the landing lights and lowered the landing gear. He watched until the indicators all came up green. "Well, at least something still works."

ↄↄↄ

Henry came in over the northern part of the lake and slowly eased back on the throttle while trying to keep the plane level and straight. As the plane approached the surface of the ice, he began having trouble perceiving his altitude or even seeing the ground through the fog. Even when he could see, the darkness, combined with the seemingly featureless ice, made his depth perception useless. He tried moving his head back and forth while moving his eyes in an attempt to get a sense of the distance.

Henry suddenly glanced up and saw the other end of the lake approaching fast, and knew he had to get it down immediately, or face going around and landing in complete darkness. He took a deep breath and let off the throttle more quickly. The sudden impact with the ice and the tremendous rumble made Maria cry out.

Upon touching down, Henry immediately cut the throttle and hit the brakes hard, but against the lake ice, they weren't having much effect. The plane began to slide to the right and Henry instinctively throttled the right engine up to compensate, but then they hit something solid; the sound of banging and ripping metal filled the cabin as the right landing gear collapsed. The right wing suddenly dug in, and the plane spun to a sudden, violent stop.

A minute later, Henry reached up, rubbing his sore neck, before looking over at Maria. She had one hand on the dash and the other on her forehead. Eventually, she looked over at Henry, her hands trembling. Henry unbuckled his belts and groaned as he got up. "Are you okay?"

She nodded, and a small amount of blood appeared from under her hand. Henry stepped around the center pedestal. "Let me look at your forehead." He pulled her hand away. "Whew, it's just a small cut. Did you hit your head on the dash?"

She shook her head and pointed to a switch that had fallen from the electrical control panel and was now hanging by its wires.

Henry used a piece of cloth to dab the blood away, but as the stress wore off, Henry began to shake and had to sit down. The remaining light of day faded quickly and it became pitch black in the cabin. Henry felt along the back of the seat for a flashlight. He turned it on and shone it at the instrument panel. "I didn't turn off any off the lights, or anything for that matter." He shone the flashlight towards the back of the cabin. "Must be the batteries or the electrical."

Maria glanced back and then looked at him, her eyes serious. "With no power, that means no radio."

Henry nodded and tried to get up, but felt weak. Maria put her hand on him. "Take a break, dear. We just crashed. At least give yourself a minute to recover."

Henry smiled, but it quickly faded. "Yes. All right." He shone his flashlight on the bag behind her seat. "Any more jerky?"

Maria felt around for the bag, and pulled it forward with some effort. "Yeah. And some of those fried dough things." She pulled one out and banged it on the chair's armrest. "A bit old, but it's food." She handed him a piece of jerky, while taking one for herself.

After resting for about ten minutes, Henry helped Maria get unbuckled and he made his way to the back of the cabin.

He opened the forward battery compartment to find the battery cracked and leaking. "Damn." He shone his light towards the back cargo area. "I'll check the backup battery."

While he was in the back, Maria grabbed a second flashlight and began looking through bags and boxes that were lying around the plane.

Henry yelled up from the back. "This one seems okay. Try switching to the backup battery."

She turned and sat in the navigator's seat, then reached up to the switch to the auxiliary battery. The radio came alive and the soft glow of the dials appeared. "It works!"

She grabbed the headphones, put them on and started transmitting the distress call again.

She kept it up for several hours, until the battery and her voice finally gave out. She put the headphones down with shivering hands and sat in the dark, until Henry looked in through the outside door. He was holding a can of aviation fuel and some branches. He shone his flashlight towards her and saw her shivering. "I am building a fire and making us a shelter. Are you okay?"

With her teeth chattering she rasped, "For the moment. I am so damn cold, and the radio is dead."

Henry nodded. "The cold probably isn't helping the battery any. Give me a minute . . ." He then disappeared. A few moments later, a warm glow appeared and illuminated the entire plane.

Maria's face lit up and she walked, shivering, to the other side of the plane to look out. A fire was going under the left wing; while Maria had worked the radio, Henry had been busy stacking branches, snow, and debris into a makeshift shelter. Maria jumped at the sudden sound of Henry's voice. "Come on, dear. It's ready."

Henry helped her down and had her sit on some of the cushions he had taken from the plane. There was also a mattress under the wing and some blankets.

She looked around. "Looks a bit cozy."

Henry smiled. "Yep. That's the idea."

Maria looked at all the tree debris that was smashed and splintered. "Where did you get all this wood?" She turned her flashlight on and looked around. "And how did you split . . ." She trailed off, seeing the tree trunk the plane had hit. She looked at Henry and started to laugh, a little hysterically. "You hit another tree? First the car and now this plane! What is with you?"

Henry pointed to it. "It's not my fault! How was I supposed to see that, landing in the foggy dark!?"

Maria only kept laughing until Henry joined in. "I guess it is a bit ironic."

He walked away from the fire, looking up at the stars and feeling the bitter cold. After a minute or so, he walked back. While still looking up at the sky, his good humor vanished, and he roared as he threw down the wood from his hands. "Ahhhh! What the hell are we supposed to do now?!"

Maria looked at his face, flashing orange and yellow against the black sky. "Well, someone had to have heard our mayday."

Henry took a deep breath of the crisp air and looked at her sitting in front of the fuselage. "Yeah. You're probably right. I just hope they all aren't looking for us on the wrong island."

That night, they slept huddled together under the wing shelter Henry had created. Every few hours, he had to add more wood and aviation fuel to the fire to keep them somewhat warm. The night seemed to last forever and whenever they heard a noise, they would suddenly sit up and look around with flashlights, hoping for a rescue, but none came.

Eventually, it became light again. Henry, exhausted, but knowing how little daylight they had, got up and surveyed the wreckage. Maria followed him around to the right side. "Wow. This side is pretty trashed. Where is the landing gear?" She looked back, following the grooves in the ice back to a large tree lying across the frozen lake. "Oh, there it is."

Henry looked to see the landing strut and wheel stuck between the tree trunk and a large branch that the plane had broken off. "Hmm."

They decided to walk to higher ground to see where they were. Maria looked back towards the plane. "I don't believe it!"

Henry looked around. "Believe what?"

She pointed around in a 180-degree arc. "There isn't one tree on this whole friggin' island, except the one you hit!"

Henry looked around trying to find another tree sticking out of the snow, but there wasn't one. "I . . . I—what the hell?" He gave her an innocent, dumbfounded look and she giggled in response.

She walked a few steps up the slope and turned. "Look, Henry. The ocean."

Henry stepped up onto a rock and looked out to see the ice covered sea to the south. He scanned the horizon searching for any ships, but saw nothing except ice, water, and low clouds.

The wind, which had just been a light breeze, suddenly blew Henry's hat off and he had to jump down from the rock to retrieve it. He put his fur hat back on tightly, but the wind only got stronger. After a few minutes, blinding snow was being whipped up and Henry yelled to Maria. "Let's get back to the plane!"

It took them quite a while to get back while fighting the headwinds. Once they reached the plane, Henry helped Maria get inside before he closed the door as best he could. "Whew. Damn, it's getting nasty out there. We'll have to stay in here for a while."

They sat in the cabin and rested for a few minutes before Maria noticed a bag under the bottom bunk. She knelt down and reached under to grab it. "It's Uncle Jimbo's." She pulled the bag close and hugged it, as tears welled up in her eyes.

Henry sat beside her and leaned in, wrapping his arms around her, but after a moment he was able to speak. "What's in it? I'm hungry."

Maria gave him a funny look, but didn't say anything. She opened the bag and started pulling things out. "Two clips of ammo, some paperwork . . . my god, his pocket watch!" She held it up. "We sure could have used this yesterday!"

Henry rolled his eyes. "What else is in there?"

She reached in and pulled out a small tin. "Hmm. What's this?"

Henry recognized it immediately. "That's the box he got from Anatoly, in Harbin!"

She looked at him as her eyes grew. "You mean . . ." She pulled the tight lid off and gasped. "Diamonds!"

Henry leaned forward for a better look before they both sat on the floor staring at them. Maria tore her eyes away long enough to look at Henry. "Well, at least we're going to die rich."

"Hmm, some comfort that is."

Henry suddenly put his hand on the bed as he felt the plane move. He listened. "The wind is getting strong!" He looked back down at the bag. "Anything else in it? Food?"

She felt around in the bag. "Just some lint."

Henry looked over at one of the Thompsons. "I wonder if there is anything to hunt on this island. If we stay here any longer, we are going to need food!"

Maria nodded. "Well, here's two more clips."

Henry stood up, collected two Thompsons, three full clips and one half clip of ammunition, then walked around the plane looking for more. He stopped and looked to the back of the plane. "Oh yeah, we have the .30 in the back—just in case we want to wipe out an entire herd of something." He winked at her, but went back to look at it in any case.

He reached down and picked up a loose belt of ammunition that Maria had pulled out in the heat of battle. He set up the ammo box that had been on its side and started to put the belt of ammunition back in it, when the green tipped bullets caught his attention. He thought for a second and pulled the belt back out, then called up front. "I have an idea!"

Maria hurried back. "What?"

He raised a green tipped round. "Tracers!"

Maria tilted her head. "Yeah, so?"

Henry pointed to all the boxes of ammo. "If we just make belts of tracers, we can use it as a signal. Send up 'SOS' into the sky!"

Maria's eyebrows raised and she grabbed a box. "Let's do it."

For the next hour, they sorted all the bullets and created three entire belts of pure tracer rounds. Once they finished, Henry looked outside to see it was already getting dark, but the wind wasn't letting up. "I think we are going to have to sleep inside tonight."

Maria hugged him. "Keep me warm."

He turned and kissed her. "I will do my best, dear."

She smiled at him. "So, how long before we can try to shoot the gun?"

Henry looked out the one of the side windows. "Well, I think it's dark enough now. Let's try it."

They moved back into the luggage area and Henry opened the cargo door, which clanged against the fuselage. "Hand me a belt."

She did and he loaded it and cocked the gun. He looked at her. "Ready?"

She nodded.

Henry fired one round, and a fiery dot flew into the sky. He fired a second, and then a third shortly after. Then he fired three with long pauses between, before firing another set of three with almost no pause.

Watching the tracers flying into the sky, Maria grabbed Henry tightly, and he smiled in matching excitement. He fired off one more succession before stopping. "All right. Let's wait an hour and we will do it again."

Maria pulled the pocket watch out of her pocket and wound it. "Okay. One hour." She looked forward. "Now, let's see if we can't find anything to eat in here."

They spent the next thirty minutes tearing apart the plane for anything to eat. Maria pulled off the middle bunk's mattress. "Bingo!"

Henry jumped up. "What did you find?"

She held up a Hershey bar and a bag of shelled peanuts.

Henry looked at the bunk. "Where the hell were those?"

She pointed to the front of the mattress. "Stuffed in the corner behind the mattress, with some napkins and other junk." She thought for a second. "That's where your uncle usually rested. Thank you, Uncle!"

She ripped open the chocolate bar, which had obviously been melted a few times, and broke it in half. "You pick."

Henry smiled at the childish fair-portion game. "This one."

Maria moaned at its deliciousness. "Damn. This chocolate

may be old and turning white, but when you're starving, everything tastes so damn good!"

Henry smiled and toasted her with his. "Cheers!"

She returned the gesture with hers already bitten half.

Chapter 25

The Whalers

After finishing the chocolate and all the peanuts in the bag, Maria looked at the watch. "Time to signal again. Can I try this time?"

Henry smiled and motioned for her to lead the way. A minute later, she was firing streaks of light into the pitch blackness.

Shortly after, Henry created a fortress of mattresses, blankets, and curtains in the center of the bunk area. At one point, he even went out into the wind to retrieve the mattress and supplies from outside.

They huddled together in the makeshift fort and slept when they could. Every so often, Maria would wake and use her flashlight to check the watch to see if it was time to fire off more rounds. Halfway through the night, they had already used up the first belt and had to load a second.

A few hours later, Maria heard a bang and awoke. She sat up, turned on her flashlight, and stared at the watch. "Henry. We missed an hour, no wait, it's been almost—" A loud bang and knocking made Maria jump out of her skin, and she accidentally hit Henry in the head with the flashlight.

Henry instantly sat up rubbing, his forehead. "What the hell did you do that for?" Then he heard the voices outside. They looked at each other and Henry scrambled to stand up, pushing cushions and blankets out in every direction. "Hello?! Hi! Just a second!"

He slipped and tripped his way to the door, yelling, "Just a second," over and over as he tried to untie the rope holding the door shut. When he finally got it, the door swung open and three men in heavy arctic gear were standing in front of him.

"Wow, you folks okay in there?"

Henry nodded, but he was so excited he could hardly speak. "Yeah—ah . . ." He pointed in toward Maria and all around.

The men, seeing his flustered excitement, stepped inside. One of them sat Henry down and the other two looked at Maria all wrapped in blankets and cushions. "You okay, ma'am?" When she nodded, he continued, "We are from the whaling ship, *Discretion*. We heard your distress call and came to investigate. My name is Lars and—"

She pointed up. "Did the bullets help?"

Lars smiled. "Yes. We were south of here, but heading to Attu when we saw them. You fired off another volley just as we came ashore. Are you two all right? Are there any more of you? What happened?"

She put up her hand. "Um, just us." She pointed to the bullet holes and the man's eyes got big.

"You were shot down?! By who?"

One of the other men in the back, yelled up. "Whoa, this is a hell of a signal flare gun!" He peeked around the corner, smiling.

Lars glanced back, brow furrowing in confusion, then looked back at Maria.

"The Russians," she said simply.

Lars cocked his head. "The Russians shot you down?"

She nodded. "Long story."

A large gust of wind shook the plane and howled through the door. Lars glanced at the other men and back at Maria. "Let's get you out of here." He bent over to help Maria up. "Are you hurt?"

She shook her head while taking his hand. "Just cuts and bruises. Nothing serious." The men wrapped her and Henry in thick fur coats that they had brought with them, and helped them out. Maria broke free for a second, grabbing the tin. Lars eyed the tin curiously and Maria smiled. "Sentimental value," she said lamely, sliding it into her front coat pocket.

"Did you have anything else you needed to pack up?"

"Thank you, but no," said Maria. "We're wearing pretty much all of it!"

The wind pelted them with ice and snow as they exited the ruined plane. Henry turned his face from the sting of ice and tried to follow the men. Lars turned to him and tightened up his hood. "Better?"

Henry nodded.

"Okay. Let's go."

Henry aimed his flashlight back and took a last look at the plane. Maria squeezed his arm. "A bit hard to leave her, huh?"

Henry nodded. "Yes; because we have left so much behind lately." He squeezed her back. "I am just thankful I still have you."

The team made their way through the snow and darkness to the shoreline. After about thirty minutes, they could hear men on the landing boat yelling to see if they were okay. Lars yelled back and it drew the beams of the boatmen's flashlights.

As they approached the boat, the sound of waves and

crunching ice became louder. Henry watched as Lars aimed his flashlight at the boat. It was a large, white, open-hulled boat with a mast sticking up through a tarp covering the middle. Two men sat at the back with a large outboard motor between them.

Another man in the front hopped down and the four of them, including Lars, started to put the boat back into the sea. Lars signaled to Henry with his flashlight. "Get in!"

Henry climbed in and turned to help Maria up, but she slipped on the wet side rail. Her arm reached for the rail but she couldn't get a grip. Henry grabbed her by her jacket as she fell backwards and the tin slid out of her front pocket onto her chest, coming to rest against her neck. Hanging by Henry's strength, she grabbed the tin tightly, while Henry fell against the bar and pulled her up. With his eyes wide, he whispered loudly, "Jeez . . . don't lose that!"

She nodded quickly and, after settling herself down onto a cross member inside the boat, pushed the tin snugly back into her pocket.

As the boat slid into the water, the four men jumped on board and pushed off with paddles. The two in the back lowered the outboard and started it up, quickly turned the boat around, and headed into the surf. Several waves crashed over the boat, and Henry felt the bitter cold sea spray hitting his face. In response, he put his hands over his cheeks, trying to protect them from the cold. When he glanced over at Maria, he could see her doing the same. When a wave hit, she would have to put down one of her hands to stabilize herself, but then she quickly put it back on her face.

Henry glanced around at Lars and the other men, only one of which had a hat on; they seemed not to notice the cold. "You guys been out here for a while?"

Lars looked down at him. "Yeah. This is our third trip this year. We've caught a big fin and a bowhead on this run."

Henry asked. "Are those big whales?"

Lars smiled. "Yeah, the bowhead was forty tons. Good thing is, that it's about all we can handle, so we will take you back to civilization shortly."

Lars scanned ahead and waved his flashlight back and forth. Then flashes of light lit up the dinghy and Henry turned to see its source. A large ship was now visible through a thin bank of fog.

Henry glanced up at Lars with a smile. "I'm gonna guess that's your ship."

Lars replied without looking down. "That she is."

Henry turned around on the plank to face the ship. His face was starting to get used to the cold, and he was able to put one of his arms around Maria. He felt her hand checking her pocket and he smiled at her before he continued talking to Lars. "So, where are you based out of? Where will you take the whales?"

Lars yelled out some orders, and the men on the motor turned the dinghy towards the back of the ship. He glanced down at Henry. "We will take them to Akutan. From there, you should be able to get home or wherever you want to go."

Maria turned and glanced up at him and around to the crew, whose faces were only lit intermittently by stray light from flashlights. "Thank you for rescuing us!"

Lars looked at her and smiled. "It's our pleasure, but we do expect stories in return!"

All the men nodded and spoke up at the same time, causing a bit of a ruckus.

Henry laughed. "Now, stories we've got!"

That night, they told their tale, slightly edited, to the crew, while eating their first hot meal in days. After an hour or so, they were given their own cabin and they slept hard, finally waking the next afternoon.

⋏⋏⋏

The drumming sounds of the engines filled Henry's ears as he made his way to the main deck. He emerged to a cloudy sky and a cold wind. A black line of smoke trailed the ship from a single tall smokestack above. The smell of saltwater filled the air, with intermittent whiffs of another strange odor, not quite like fish.

He heard the sounds of footsteps coming up the metal stairs behind him. "Morning dear. Sleep okay?"

She rubbed her eyes. "Yeah, better than I have in a while."

Henry kissed her forehead. "Let's have a look around."

She nodded and they made their way forward along the rusting metal railings. Henry stared out at the sea with its small white caps and bits of ice churning in the waves.

At the front of the ship was a huge whaling harpoon gun on a raised platform. Henry raised his hand to point it out when Lars suddenly appeared. "Good afternoon!"

Maria smiled back. "Good morning."

Lars nodded up at the harpoon. "You two want a tour?"

Henry nodded. "That would be great. I haven't ever—"

Maria interrupted. "As long as we don't take too long. I'm hungry."

Lars chuckled and put his hand forward. "Okay. The quick tour it is."

He led them around to the front of the boat. "This is the

harpoon gun. It's our main tool for catching the whales." He pointed to the front of the harpoon. "This is the explosive tip, and these barbs in the back are held by these wires, which break after hitting the whale. It opens up inside and because of the line that runs through this groove, we can reel the whale in once it succumbs."

Maria gazed at the deck gun and the white-capped sea in front of it, and cringed.

Lars slapped the gun. "Johnny is our gunner and he's pretty good," he said, then turned and began walking down the port side of the boat, "and he gets paid a hell of lot more than any of us for doing it!"

As Maria began walking to follow, she spotted the tail of a whale tied to the side of the boat. She stepped back and Henry caught her. She turned and looked at him. "They just drag it beside the boat?"

Henry glanced down at her and then at Lars, who had turned around to see them staring at the baleen whale hanging over the side. "Yeah, our ship isn't big enough to haul it on board, so we will take it back to port that way. The other whale was a bit smaller, so we have already begun processing him." Lars pointed forward.

Maria looked at the deck and saw men cutting an enormous carcass into pieces. The red sea of blood on the deck and the odd smell made her sick to her stomach. She suddenly sagged against the railing, and Henry grabbed her quickly.

Lars, upon seeing her reaction, motioned to the stairs below deck. "I'm sorry. We're used to it, of course, but seems like the sight is a bit much for you. Let me take you two back downstairs."

Henry nodded and led Maria while she held her stomach

with one hand and put the other over her mouth. Once they were downstairs, Lars pointed to the galley, but Henry shook his head. "Thank you, but unless you've got just broth or a seasickness cure in there, I think we should wait a bit to eat." He smiled at Lars and shook his hand. "Thank you so much for rescuing us, and I apologize for our reaction."

Lars laughed. "Oh, that's quite alright. Most people lose it the first time they come on board. It just takes some getting used to. For me, I love the sea, and I just remember that it's feeding my family and keeping a roof over their heads."

Henry glanced down at Lars's hand to see a gold ring. "Oh. I hadn't realized you had a family. Do they live in Alaska?"

Lars nodded. "Sure. They live up in Naknek. Hoping to see them soon after we—"

He stopped speaking as Henry's eyes got big, while Maria's hand fell from her mouth. "Naknek?" Henry asked. "Really? Can you take us there . . . when you go?" Henry glanced at Maria and back. "We were there awhile back, and we have friends."

Lars grew a big smile. "You've been to Naknek! Wow. Small world, eh?" He scratched his head under his knitted cap. "Well, sure. We're heading there anyway, as soon as we drop these whales and get paid."

A few days later, Henry awoke to a clanging against the hull. He sat up while rubbing his eyes. The meager sunlight was shining in through a small translucent curtain covering the brass porthole. Pushing it to the side and peering out, at first he saw nothing but waves and shoreline; then a fin eclipsed the sun as it went by. Henry pushed his face against the glass and could see workers, wading alongside the carcass as it slid up an incline.

The glass of the porthole quickly fogged up, so Henry pulled his head back and glanced over at Maria, who was still sleeping. Her black hair covered her face and she was snoring lightly. Henry grinned, bent over, pushed her hair back, and kissed her on the forehead. Maria moaned slightly and rolled over to face the cabin wall.

Henry quietly got dressed and made his way to the top deck. The sky was blue with traces of cirrus clouds high above. Industrial noise caught his attention, but before he had a chance to look, a touch on his shoulder stole his attention; he turned back to see Lars handing him a cup of steaming coffee. "Gorgeous morning, isn't it?"

Henry accepted the cup and nodded.

Lars continued while pointing up at the sky. "Don't get many days like this around here. Mostly cloudy and foggy all winter." He slapped Henry on the back and pointed ashore. "Plus, it's payday!"

Henry, trying not to spill his coffee from the sudden slap, looked in the direction he was pointing. He stopped mid-sip at the view. Three large whales were in various stages of disassembly while the *Discretion's* whale was being pulled ashore by a giant winch. Steam was rising from the processing plant and men were scattered about, some even on top of the whales. As they used tools to cut, slice, and drag meat away from the whales, the sounds of metal tools, machines, chains, and men yelling filled the air. Henry's shoulders sank as he looked around. A yell from his left made Henry turn to see two other ships docked at the port. Their cargo already ashore, the ships were preparing to leave.

When Henry heard Maria's voice, he turned to stop her from seeing the carnage, but she was already staring at it. Henry stood in front of her, but she didn't look at him. A mixture of horror and disgust appeared on her face, but only a few seconds later, it disappeared and she glanced at Henry. "Morning dear." She glanced down at his coffee. "Oh, I could use some of that."

Lars, who was still standing nearby, turned toward her. "I'll get you a cup."

Henry interjected, "Here, have mine. I'm afraid I can't really stomach it at the moment."

Maria hesitantly took it from him. "It's okay," she said to Lars. "I'll just have his."

Lars cocked his head and studied both their faces. "Is it the view?" he asked Henry.

Henry nodded as Maria chugged the coffee. She turned back to Lars and handed him the now-empty cup. "On second thought, I think I will take one."

Lars had a mixture of concern and amusement on his face as he nodded and headed below deck with the cup in hand.

Maria looked at the sky and around the whaling station. "Want to go for a walk on shore?"

Henry shook his head. "No, I think I've seen enough. I'm going to go below, see if I can't find a book to read until my appetite returns."

Maria put her arm around him and smiled. "Okay."

Henry turned as he started down the stairs. "What about you?"

Maria stretched and took a deep breath. "I'm starving. Think I will go find some breakfast and walk around a bit."

Henry smiled, nodded and went below. There was just no fathoming that woman, but he wouldn't have it any other way.

Late in the afternoon, the crew of the *Discretion* finished putting their whales ashore and cleaning the deck. After getting paid and stowing new supplies, the men were in a joyous mood, and beer was passed around liberally. Henry, recovered from the day's sights, had a voracious appetite and ate plenty, laughing and celebrating with the crew, before they set sail for Naknek.

Chapter 26

Return to Naknek

enry and Maria were up on deck, watching as they docked in Naknek. The sun had already set, and the stars shone brightly through the broken clouds that moved quickly across the sky. A cold, fresh breeze swept across the deck, and they could hear the sounds and see the lights of the town on shore.

Both of them felt a longing need to be with someone who was at least partially connected with the experience they had gone through over the last six months. Maria put her arm around Henry and stared up at him. "It feels like we are in a dream or something. Doesn't it?"

Henry thought, and then he nodded. "Yes. Very strange, but I'm with you and that is what matters most." He kissed her forehead, but she tilted her head up and kissed him back.

They watched as the crew worked to dock and secure the boat. When it came time to leave, Henry and Maria were met by the crew at the bottom of the ramp. Henry shook all of their hands and Maria handed out hugs. Henry finally spoke up in a loud voice. "I don't know how to thank you all for rescuing us. We would have died out there without you, and you have our sincerest gratitude. We live far away in Iowa, but if there is anything you ever need, just let us know. The captain here has our information." Henry hugged him with a slap on the back and shook his hand heartily.

The captain, feeling something in his hand, glanced down.

He looked closely at it as it sparkled off the dock lights.

Henry leaned in and whispered in his ear. "A little something for your trouble."

Lars' smile grew big, though he eyed Maria and Henry with a bit of suspicion. He laughed and asked rhetorically. "What were you two really doing in Russia anyway?"

Henry winked and reached for Maria's hand. "Well, we better be off. Old folks like to go to bed early, so we don't want to wake them."

Maria waved back at them as they walked up the wooden pier with a few of the crew, who then said their final goodbyes and walked off in separate directions, apparently heading to their own homes.

Maria and Henry walked down the snow-covered, wide lane towards the airstrip, until they found the familiar white fence they had seen months earlier. They stopped at the gate and Maria smiled up at him while squeezing his hand. Henry opened the small gate and closed it behind them, but before they could knock, Fred opened the front door.

"Hello?" he asked, but then turned on the porch light. "Oh! Oh, my! Hello!" He pushed open the screen door. "Come in. Come in! Get out of the cold!"

Esther called from the kitchen. "Who is it, dear?"

Fred turned his head and said loudly, "The three—" He glanced back at Maria and Henry, noticing Jimbo's absence. "It's Henry and Maria. The couple that visited us last summer."

With the sounds of pans and utensils being set down, Esther suddenly appeared at the door while Henry and Maria stepped inside. The fire was going in the fireplace, and the smell of fresh-baked bread filled the house. Henry took a large whiff. "Wow. Nothing smells as good as your house!"

Fred laughed as he took their coats. "Yep. My Esther keeps me well-fed. I am sure you two are tired and hungry."

Esther kissed and hugged Maria. "Come, you two. I will make you something."

Esther led them to the kitchen, while Fred hung up their winter clothes. She urged them to sit, while she put a pan on the stove and threw another piece of wood in. A minute later, Fred walked in. Esther waved him away from her and he sat down at the table.

"So, what brings you to Naknek again?" He cocked his head. "I didn't hear your plane come in."

Henry glanced at Maria and back to Fred, before picking up a fork and rubbing the handle between his thumb and forefinger. "We came by ship this time."

Fred leaned back in his chair. "You have a ship, too?"

Henry smiled. "No. No, we were on a whaling ship. We crash-landed at the end of the Aleutians."

Esther turned around and Fred's face turned to concern. "What happened?" He looked at the two of them. "Jimbo?"

Maria's eyes began to tear up and Henry put his hand on hers. "Uncle Jimbo was killed in Russia."

Fred put his hand over his mouth; Esther dropped the spoon she was holding, then walked to the table and sat next to her husband. Maria started crying and Esther got up again and tried to comfort her. Fred watched for a second and looked back at Henry. "What happened?"

Henry squeezed Maria's hand. "It's such a long story,

but basically, we were forced to evacuate Mongolia and we were making one last run into Russia."

Fred sat up straight. "For General Pepelyayev?"

Henry stared at him with surprise, and he continued, "Jimbo told me before that he was going to help out the general."

Henry nodded. "Ah. Yes, you're right. We were taking one last shipment for him and his men, but we were ambushed. Jimbo was killed in the crossfire, and the plane got shot to hell before we could get out. We were trying to make it here, but the plane was too badly damaged and we were forced down on Agattu, where we were rescued by Captain Lars."

Esther looked up. "Captain Lars? Lars Albinsson?"

Maria nodded while wiping her eyes.

Esther continued. "I know his mother, she is—" Fred put his hand on hers, and she glanced at him before putting her head down.

Fred turned back to Henry. "I am sorry for your loss. I only knew him for a short time, but I feel it as well. He seemed like a great man to me." He cleared his throat. "What do you plan to do now?"

Henry sat back in his chair and stared up at the ceiling, thinking, then glanced over at Maria. "Go home, I guess."

Maria looked at him with tears still in her eyes. "Yes, home—" she put her free hand on his and sat up straight. "—in our plane."

Henry cocked his head and raised his right eyebrow. "In our plane?"

She nodded. "Yes. That plane saved us so many times . . . and your uncle gave it to us. I'll be damned if I am going to let it rot on some deserted, barren island."

Henry scratched his head, surprised by the sentimentality. "How are we going to get it back to Iowa?"

Maria tilted her head with a smirk. "Why we'll fly it!" When she saw Henry's questioning expression, she added, "Get Kid or someone up here to fix her up, and we will fly home! We have plenty of money now."

Henry leaned back in his chair and took a deep breath. Fred gave a slight shrug and smiled back, as Henry released his held breath. "Okay, then . . . Kid knows this plane better than anybody, even if he is in the Philippines. You're right; tomorrow, I will send him a telegram, with an offer he can't refuse."

That night, Henry and Maria slept in front of the fire, like they had done months earlier, but so many things were different. Maria stared into Henry's eyes as the yellow flicker from the fire lit his face. He was watching her in return with serious, intense love in his heart. There was no sense of playfulness, as there had been before.

He leaned on his right arm and used his left hand to slowly caress her warm face. "I don't know what I would do without you," he said, "or what I would have done without you. When I think of almost losing you—"

She put her hand on his lips. "I feel the same. I went crazy when you disappeared on that Kalgan run."

Henry rolled over top of her, putting both hands around her head and kissing her hard. She took a breath and moaned as her hands ran around his bare middle back, before pulling him in tight.

Pulling back to take a breath, Henry's eyes sank from her face down to the red buttoned floral pajamas that she had borrowed from Esther. He began kissing down her neck and unbuttoning as he went. After the third button was opened, he paused to admire the beautiful shape of her breasts as they glowed in the flickering firelight, before he reached up to cup them, making them appear fuller than before.

Maria sighed heavily and arched her back, before a cough came from the darkness. Both of them froze, listening for further sounds, but after a few seconds of only hearing the fire crackle, they gave in to their desires.

Maria grabbed the bricks from the edge of the fireplace and fought hard not to cry out as she climaxed under the aggressive motion of Henry's body. Henry kept up the tender assault until she reached her peak once more, then he followed her into ecstasy and collapsed upon her glistening body. Their toes wiggled contentedly against one another, before the combined sweat of their bodies made him start to slide off to one side. He grabbed her and pulled her over on her side with him, still breathing heavily.

As the heat from their bodies subsided, the chill in the air became more noticeable again, and Henry pulled the fur blanket back over them. Maria rolled to her other side and pulled his arm over her. "Hold me tight."

He squeezed and pulled her toward his chest. "I love you."

She squeezed his arm. "I love you . . . more than you could ever know."

Maria's mind began to wander and she thought of everything they had been through. The joys, the ups and downs, and the loss. She started to cry and Henry pulled her in even tighter, while kissing the side of her neck. "It's okay. It will be okay. We're together and here to support each other, through thick and thin."

Maria nodded slightly before rolling over to look at him, feeling the tickle of tears run down her cheeks. "I can't believe Jimbo is gone. All that he was . . . he was bigger than life. I understood losing some of the fighters, but Jimbo, he was—well, it just seems wrong to have him just die in the snow for *nothing* like that. He brought so many worlds together, affected so many lives . . . how can he be gone?" She hugged Henry hard and let out all she had been holding back for days. The lump in her throat gave way to whimpers, then escalating crying until it became wails of sorrow. Henry pulled her close, trying to comfort her and muffle the sound.

From the darkness, a door creaked and Fred spoke. "Are you two okay?"

Henry looked in his direction, with tears now running down his face. "Yes, Fred. Sorry for waking you. We have been through a lot and haven't had time for it to really catch up."

Fred nodded. "That's all right. I completely understand. You don't worry about us. Get it all out and do what you have to do. We will be in the next room if you need anything."

Henry nodded while Maria peeked up from the curve of his neck. "Thank you very much."

Fred nodded again, turned, and disappeared back into the darkness.

Maria and Henry comforted each other until they finally slept.

↟↟↟

Henry opened his eyes to sunshine coming through the

eight paned glass window. He watched the sun distort through the old glass as he rubbed the dried tears on his face, and Maria brushed the hair out of her face. She partially opened her eyes, turned her head, and looked up at him. He used his thumb to rub clean her cheeks and she gave him a faint smile.

The sound of dishes clanking in the kitchen brought them around, and they got dressed under the large fur blanket before going to the kitchen. Maria walked into the kitchen to see Esther cleaning dishes. "Good morning."

Esther turned with a large smile. "Good morning, you two. Are you all right this morning?"

Maria nodded as she pulled a chair away from the table. "Yes. Thank you. I am sorry for disturbing you last night."

Esther brought over bread and a glass jar of jam, which shimmered in the morning sun shining on the table as she set it down. "Please, don't worry about that. You have been through so much." She chuckled. "We can sleep any time. We've done it every day for the last seventy years. A few hours aren't going to matter."

Maria smiled and leaned her head on her right hand, while watching Esther. "Thank you."

A sparkle from the jar of jam caught her attention and she stared at it as she listened to Henry speak "Where's Fred this morning?"

Esther pointed out the window with a butter knife in her hand. "He went down to the docks to ask about a salvage team."

Henry sat down at the end of the table, blocking the sun with his head. Maria glanced over at him with the interruption of her daydream, and Henry continued. "Salvage team? For what—

us?"

Esther lit a fire in the stove while she replied. "Yes. Sure. He said he knows there is a salvage team around. They raised a ship near here last year."

Henry tilted his head thoughtfully. "Really?" He pondered a moment longer as he glanced back at Maria. "Where can I send a telegram?"

Esther cracked eggs on the pan as she replied, "There is a telegraph office down by the cannery."

Henry started to get up. "Great. I'll go over and send a—"

Maria and Esther both interrupted at the same time. "Eat some breakfast first!" They looked at each other with impish grins on their faces, and Henry slowly sat back down.

An hour later, Henry sent a telegram to Kid. : *"We need you. Crashed landed DC3. Need new engine, right landing strut. Will make worthwhile. Order engine, parts needed to Naknek, Alaska. Henry Elliot."*

Later that day, a telegram courier came by the house with the response. *"I will need $2000 up front plus all expenses. Send billing information for parts. Take next ship out. Kid."*

A few months later, Kid had arrived and a salvage team had been assembled, along with a new Wright R-1820 engine and various parts. Worrying about the lake melting and losing the plane into the water, they rushed to set out by mid-March.

When they arrived at Agattu, and after waiting impatiently for several days for good weather, the salvage ship purposely ran itself aground. After breaking through some ice, they lowered a ramp for their blue-gray Caterpillar bulldozer to drive ashore.

Everyone went ashore, and Henry, leading the pack, walked over the frozen ground to the crash site, while Maria, Kid, and the salvage team followed. When they came over a rise just before the lake, they saw the plane right where they had left her, covered with snow. Henry glanced at Maria with a large smile on his face, and they both ran down onto the frozen lake.

Henry slipped a few times, but got right back up, so excited to see the plane that had done so much for them. When Henry reached the nose of the plane, he put his hand on it, dusting off some of the snow, before bending over to catch his breath. Maria soon caught up and they both stood in front of their plane, breathing the cold foggy air, while smiling at each other. When they had caught their breath, they made their way around the back of the left wing and began to move snow off the back door.

Kid started uncovering the left engine, which wasn't covered by much snow because of its height and angle. The bullet holes and charring were apparent. "Well, you did a nice job trashing this engine."

Henry, uncovering the bottom of the door, looked up to see him smiling. "Can you fix it?"

Kid stood up on the wing and pointed to his chest. "Isn't that why you called me?" He winked and went back to pushing snow off the wing.

The salvage team made it down the hill, and studied the wreck and the lake.

Henry and Maria finally cleared the rear door, which was still slightly ajar, and both of them pulled on it until it swung open with the cracking of accumulated ice, then climbed into its freezing interior.

A light dusting of snow was on everything, with a bit of ice coming in through some of the holes. Henry made his way to the cockpit and sat in the pilot's seat after dusting it off. "Wow. Seems like we just left her." He glanced back at Maria, who was coming forward to sit on her side. He blew the dusting of snow off the instruments. "Doesn't look too bad."

Maria sat and smiled at him while she ran her glove over the throttles and instrument panel. "Feels so strange to be back. So many feelings . . ."

Henry jumped when Kid knocked on the side of the plane. Henry removed the curtain pieces that Maria had stuffed into the window months ago and peeked out. "Hey."

Kid pointed to the engine. "I think you are right. It will be easier and better to just replace that engine. It's a real mess."

Henry nodded. "What about the other one?"

Kid smiled. "Well, I think we have to dig it out first."

Part of the salvage team began clearing snow from the plane, while a few went back to get equipment and the bulldozer.

After several hours, most of the plane was uncovered and Kid had found the landing strut that had ripped off.

When the team had finished clearing the right engine, Kid got inside the cowling and looked it over. Henry walked around the front with Maria following. "What do you think?"

Kid peered out from the engine. "Well, this one seems good." He pointed to the propeller. "You destroyed the prop and air intake, but it shouldn't take too much to fix this one."

Alec, the salvage team leader, came up behind them. "We checked the ice." He stomped the lake with his boot. "I think it should be thick enough for the 'dozer. The men are bringing it up now."

Henry pointed to the pieces of the strut sticking out of the wing into the ice. "How are we going to tow it back like this?"

Alec studied the protruding metal and torn pieces of aluminum for a second, then shrugged. "No problem. We have skis that we will attach to it." He pointed back in the direction they had come from. "I think we can get her off the ice tonight, if all goes well. We will save the move down to shore for tomorrow."

Henry nodded and smiled, then glanced at Maria and winked.

The excitement built as they finished uncovering the plane and the bulldozer was brought up. The sun was getting low in the sky by time they got it cleared and a cable hooked from the bulldozer to the plane.

Alec ordered everyone out of the way as the tractor revved up. Dark black smoke poured from the vertical exhaust pipe as the driver let the clutch out. The plane creaked, and the sound of cracking ice came from everywhere. Maria jumped when she felt the ice on the lake shudder and pop. She began to back up toward the shore. "Henry?"

Henry glanced at her, then at the plane and bulldozer nervously. There was a loud crack and splinters of ice flew forward, but the plane began to move. Cheers erupted and Henry, almost jumping up and down, turned and hugged Maria.

They watched as the bulldozer slowly began to pull the plane across the lake. Deep popping and cracking sounds came from the ice, and with each pop, Henry felt Maria's squeeze tighten on his arm. Henry was only breathing intermittently at the points where he could feel the ice move. It seemed as though it was surely going to give way, but they finally made it to the far side of the lake, and the plane was dragged ashore. By then the sun was setting, and Alec called a halt to operations. "Chow time! Secure everything, and then everyone back to the ship."

Henry kept watching over his shoulder at their plane as they made their way over the hill, until it finally disappeared.

Dinner in the galley was loud, boisterous, and in high spirits. That night, Henry had a hard time sleeping and found Maria to be in the same state. "What is it about that plane? I know it's only a plane, but it feels like a dear friend, with whom we have been through so much." He pulled his eyes away from the cabin ceiling to focus on Maria.

She nodded and smiled. "Yes. It's like coming back and rescuing someone we have lost . . ." She rolled onto her side. "And we have lost so many. I can't tell you how good it feels to get some part back—it's a witness to what we experienced. Something nobody else will understand."

Henry gave a serious smile. "I am so glad you made us come back for her. I now feel the same."

Maria smiled and kissed him.

⚜ ⚜ ⚜

The next morning, the ship's PA system announced morning chow. Henry jumped up, glanced out at the rising sun, and excitedly reached for his pants. A few minutes later, Henry and Maria were in the galley eating eggs, fried venison jerky, and toast. The excitement that had been in the air the day before was still present, as though everyone had just lain in their bunks waiting for Christmas morning.

Soon, the entire crew was back at the bulldozer. The day

was mostly spent clearing shrubbery and large rocks that were sticking out of the snow, as the bulldozer slowly pulled the plane across the frozen terrain. Fog rolled in intermittently and slowed operations down.

When they had reached the final slope down to the shore, drag ropes were attached and the men pulled back on the plane as the bulldozer slowly pulled her down the slope. By the time they reached the shore, the sun was already setting and heavy clouds were moving in. Captain Alec, with one eye on the sky, ordered all the lights to be switched on so the work could be completed that night. The shoreline was lit up like daylight and the ship's crane was brought around. Large wide straps were fastened under the fuselage and under the inside of the wings.

After a few hours of making sure the rigging was secure and balanced, the plane was lifted off the shore and onto the ship. As the plane was let down, Kid pointed to the inside of the right wing. "What was attached there? It tore part of the wing away."

Henry stepped up beside him to see at what he was pointing at. He smiled. "Oh. That's where we had one of the .50s mounted."

Kid raised eyebrows at him. ".50s? . . . you mean you put machineguns on the wings? What the hell for?"

Maria put her arm on Kid's shoulder. "To rescue me."

Kid looked at her with surprise. "Okay, you have to tell me that story!"

Henry laughed. "Sure. We can tell you on the way back."

It took them a week to arrive back in Naknek. Kid had been working on the plane as best he could on the ship, but it still needed a lot of work. Since there wasn't a dock big enough to offload the plane, they again ran the ship aground, and offloaded the DC-3 with the crane as near to a road as they could get it. A tent was set up over the right wing, and Kid took a few days to replace the ripped off landing gear. While Kid was replacing the gear, the crew used the bulldozer to blaze a trail to the nearest road. When they had completed that, they widened the road where necessary.

After Kid had finished rebuilding the right-side landing gear, the bulldozer towed the plane to the airfield. A crowd gathered around, including Fred and Esther, to watch with excitement as the plane was moved slowly down the dirt road, past the town. Things went smoothly, and the plane was towed to the airfield in just under an hour. Once there, they put the plane in a hangar and Kid got to work replacing the left engine and the right propeller.

The next morning Henry came in through the side door of the hangar to see Kid and several others hoisting the propeller onto the right engine. Kid glanced over at Henry and waved. "Good morning, Henry! Give us a minute."

Henry waved his hand. "No. Take your time. I'm in no hurry."

Kid and another man stood on ladders on either side of the engine, while a third was on the ground. Henry watched as they lined up the propeller and pushed it onto the propeller shaft. They wiggled it back and forth until it finally slid into place.

Kid stepped down from the ladder, removed his gloves, and wiped his forehead. "Okay!" He turned to Henry and shook his hand. "Morning." He pointed to the engine. "Just about have this one done. I replaced the air intake and the lower cowling, but everything else seemed fine." He waved for Henry to follow him under the plane. "Fixed the fuselage where the gun had torn it, and patched up most of the bullet holes." He then pointed across the hangar. Henry looked to see the old burnt engine sitting in the corner with a new, partially opened crate next to it. Kid continued, "As you can see, we removed the old engine."

Henry studied the wing and then the crate. "So, is that the new engine?"

Kid nodded. "Yes, sir. It shouldn't take us too long to get it installed. Maybe tomorrow, if it goes well."

Henry walked over to the crate and peeked inside. "So how long before she is ready to fly?"

Kid rubbed his head while scanning the plane. "Two days. Maybe three?"

Henry patted him on the back. "Fantastic! Well, I came in to let you know that we cabled the money to your account, and we arranged transport back to the Philippines this weekend, assuming you want to go then."

Kid smiled big and shook his hand. "Yes. Thank you very much! It's too damn cold for me here!"

Henry walked towards the left wing. "No. Thank you, Kid. I don't know of anyone else who could have done this so fast," he said, feeling the underside of the wing where bullet holes had once been, "and so well."

One of the men signaled for Kid. The mechanic put his hand on Henry's shoulder as he walked by. "It's my pleasure. Well, I have to get back to work and get this prop on."

Henry nodded. "Alright. I will leave you to it. See you later. Let me know if there is anything you need."

Henry and Maria were eating lunch with Fred and Esther

two days later, when a knock came at the door. Fred leaned over and peeked out the window. "Looks like it's for you, Henry."

Henry leaned back in his chair to see Kid at the door. He jumped up and quickly made his way to the door. "Hey, Kid!" He made a welcoming gesture. "Come on in."

Kid, smiling, nodded. "Good news. The plane is ready to go."

Henry smiled and put his hand on Kid's shoulder. "Amazing! Come in and have something to eat." Henry turned to tell Maria the news, but she was already standing next to him, grinning from ear to ear. "Hi, Kid!"

She turned to Henry and started bouncing on her feet. "We can go home!"

Henry's excitement was showing as well. "Yes!" He pointed to the table. "But first let's finish lunch."

Henry pulled out a chair for Kid. "Please sit." He glanced at Fred. "If you don't mind?"

Fred waved his hand. "Not at all!" He smiled at Kid, "You are more than welcome in our house." Fred grabbed some mashed potatoes and passed them to him. "Here, try some of my wife's taters."

Kid pulled his chair in and took the bowl of potatoes. He smiled and nodded as he scooped some onto the plate that Esther set in front of him.

After a few bites and Esther helping to put more food on his plate, Kid turned to Henry. "So, when are you planning to go back home?"

Henry glanced at Maria and then back at Kid. "Well, tomorrow morning, if that's possible."

Kid nodded. "Sure. She's ready to go." He looked at Maria. "Not used to being away from home so long?"

Maria shook her head slightly after taking a bite of spiced venison. "It's not that. We spent almost two years away when we went to Antarctica." She set her fork down and put her hand on Henry's arm. "It's different this time. This time, we lost too much, too many people . . . we just want to return home to normalcy, whatever that might be." She grinned slightly and stared at Fred and Esther. "It's been wonderful to be here with you two, but we just have to return home." She paused and tried to swallow. "Home is like . . . well, it's a different world—a different reality. I want to wake up and be happy, and not on the verge of crying every day. I want some stability for once."

Henry turned in his chair and put his hand on hers.

She looked at him while holding back tears. "I want to know that someone isn't going to randomly be shooting at us and taking away people I love."

Henry hugged her and the table became silent.

Esther was the first to get up, blinking away tears as she took a deep breath. "I made pie." She walked over to the counter and back, and presented a strawberry rhubarb pie. She cut a slice and put it on a small plate. Maria watched with wet eyes as Esther brought the pie and a fork over to her. "Here, this should help cheer you." She smiled and lightly touched Maria's cheek.

Maria let out a gasp and a sniffle while smiling. "Thank you. You have been so wonderful to us. I don't know how we can ever thank you."

Fred responded, "The pleasure has been all ours." He glanced at Esther and back. "It gets a bit lonely up here, and it's been wonderful having such great and interesting company. You are welcome here anytime, and we aren't just saying that." Esther put her hand on Fred's shoulder and he clasped it. "We sincerely mean it."

Henry tilted his head and smiled. "Thank you so much. We really love you two. If you are ever in the States, you should give us a ring and come to stay with us. We would love to have you, and, just maybe, we could try to return some of the hospitality."

Esther handed him a big piece of the pie and smiled at Fred. "That's sounds wonderful. We might just do that."

Chapter 27

Home

The next morning, the plane was towed out of the hangar, and now it sat on the snow-covered runway. There was a clear, dark blue sky with wisps of bright yellow cirrus clouds above, glowing from the rising sun. Kid made final checks to the plane while Henry and Maria said their goodbyes to Esther and Fred. Maria hugged them both, shivering, then pointed to the plane. "I'm going to get inside. It's still too cold for me around here!"

Esther smiled. "Go ahead dear. Don't freeze." She leaned up against Fred. "Guess we're a bit used to it."

Henry spoke while his breath billowed up into the sky. "Thank you again for everything! We will send you a telegram when we make it home." He shook Fred's hand. "Well, I better go help Kid and get this thing going." He turned and stepped inside the plane, emerging a few seconds later with his pre-flight checklist, then went around to the left engine to see Kid. "How is everything?"

Kid, who was pulling on a cowling, glanced over at him. "It all looks good. Everything seems snug and well fit." He stared down the runway. "Guess the next thing is to get her into the air." He smiled.

Henry nodded. "Sounds good to me. Let me just run through the checklist and we'll be off."

Henry slowly made his way around the aircraft, double checking everything, especially areas that he knew had been damaged. When he had finished, he joined Maria in the cockpit and went through the internal list. "Well, everything seems to be good . . . like new."

Maria cleared her throat. "Well, except this." She pointed to a small hole next to her seat behind some padding. "Guess he missed that one."

Henry leaned forward to see a small bullet hole. "Well, we have to have some souvenir to take home with us. How else are we going to prove our wild stories?"

Maria smiled and nodded. "You know, we should write a book about this whole thing."

Henry nodded while he primed the right engine. "Well, let's get home first and make sure it has a happy ending."

Maria looked out at the right engine, smiling.

Henry slid his window back with some effort. "Clear prop!"

Kid backed away from the plane and Henry pushed the starter. The engine whined, caught once or twice, whined some more and finally came to life. Snow and black smoke flew away from the plane. Henry adjusted the throttle while he let the engine warm up.

Kid hopped in the back door and made his way to the cockpit. "Sounds good!"

Henry turned with surprise, and grinned. "Yeah. Ready for the left?"

Kid nodded.

Henry yelled out again and Fred and Esther backed even

further away. The left prop turned over five times and started easily, and Henry grinned at Kid. "Wow. Like eggs in coffee! Terrific."

Kid returned the smile. "Well, I better let you two get home!" He patted Henry on the shoulder. "I'll catch you two later. Have a good flight."

Maria turned and grabbed his hand. "Thank you for everything! We will miss seeing you. Tell your family we send our love, and send us a telegram when you get back home."

Kid nodded. "I will." He turned and exited the plane, shutting the door behind him. He walked over and stood with Fred and Esther, as Henry waved and ran up the engines. Flames exited with the exhaust as Henry throttled up to free the plane from the snow.

Everyone grabbed their hats as the prop-wash swept by them. Henry did a brief run-up to test the engines, waved out his window one last time, and then they were off down the runway.

Out of the cloud of snow the plane rose into the blue sky, with its wings glistening in the yellow morning sun.

Henry circled the field wagging his wings, before finally turning southeast and disappearing over the horizon.

They had lunch in Seattle, refueled, and telegrammed their neighbor to mow the field for them, before setting off again. They overnighted in Salt Lake City, and the next day they finally made it back to Iowa.

Maria let out a piercing cheer when she finally saw their farm from the air. "Woooo! There it is! Henry! It's home!"

Henry partially pulled his headset off at the loudness of her yell, but gave her a big smile. "Yep. We made it!"

Henry circled the house a couple of times. "Doesn't look

much different than how we left it."

Maria pointed down. "Well, we are going to have to clean up that yard. What a mess, but at least the neighbors did a good job mowing."

As Henry made his final approach, he could see some of the neighbors walking through the fields towards their airstrip. The plane touched down gently, and the gear took most of the roughness away. Once he had come to a stop, he pointed to the house and glanced over at Maria. "Where should we park this thing? It certainly ain't gonna fit in the old barn!"

Maria laughed. "Guess we can just park it behind the house for now."

Henry angled his head. "Okay. Sounds fine by me." He throttled up and taxied up to the back porch before shutting down the engines, then leaned back hard in his seat, put his arms up, stretched, and let out a yell. "It's great to be home!"

A knock came at the back door, and Maria excitedly got up and ran to the back. She opened the door to find the neighbors standing there. "Hi, Mr. Weaver! Kids!"

Mr. Weaver stepped back and scrutinized the plane from end to end. "It's a bit bigger than your last one!"

Maria laughed and set the stairs out, before climbing down. She took a deep breath of air. "It is so great to be home!" She smiled wide at Mr. Weaver. "Thank you so much for keeping after the place for us!"

Henry chimed in from the plane's door, "And for mowing the field."

Mr. Weaver waved his hand. "It was nothing."

Henry climbed down and shook his hand. "Well, we at least

owe you a fancy dinner and a night out. Where's your wife?"

Mr. Weaver pointed out towards the road. "Oh, she went to see her sister. She'll be back in a few days."

Maria stepped slightly in front of Henry. "When she gets back, we'll fly you two in our new plane to Chicago for a night on the town. Sound good?"

Mr. Weaver grinned. "I think Mae would like that—and I think I would too," he said, pointing to his house, "but for now, I know that you two don't have any food in the house, so why don't you come over for dinner?"

Maria glanced at Henry. "We would love to. I am starved, actually."

Mr. Weaver turned and led the way. "Well, come on, then."

⋏⋏⋏

It was dark when Maria and Henry made it back to their house. The boards creaked quietly under his weight as Henry climbed the front porch and felt for the doorknob. When he found it, he pulled, but instead of opening, the screen door fell on him. Henry jumped back, and the door fell to the side with a crash.

Maria jumped. "Are you okay? What happened?"

Henry used his foot to push the rest of the door out of the way as he grabbed for the main door. "I'm fine. The damn screen door just fell off!"

He tried to turn the knob. "Oh, yeah, locked. Did you get the key from the neigh—"

Maria handed him the key before he could finish his sentence. He smirked, though he knew she couldn't see it, and opened the door. The homely smell of cherry wood came over them and they paused at the entrance to take it in. Henry reached over and felt for the lamp before turning it on. "Home, sweet home."

Maria scanned around. "Home, sweet dust. My god. It's going to take me weeks to clean this."

Henry hugged her shoulders and smiled. "Don't worry. We're rich now. We can just order some people to clean it for us."

Maria smiled up at him. "No, no. I can do it, I just like complaining about it."

Henry said under his breath, "Ain't that the truth," and Maria smacked him in the stomach.

Maria walked towards the kitchen. "But, we do need to order some food. If you can get the freezer and the fridge up and running, I can order a side of beef and go grocery shopping."

Henry walked up to the kitchen threshold and leaned against the wall. "Okay. I will look at them tomorrow. In fact, I will look at everything tomorrow, but for now, let's just go to bed. I'm exhausted."

Maria looked around the kitchen and ran her hand down the counter before glancing at her dirty hand. "Jeez. Yeah, you're right. Now that you mention it, I am really tired too." She wiped her hands together, shut off the light, and followed Henry up to bed.

Henry walked into the bedroom and sat on the bed. A cloud of dust rose into the air and he innocently looked up at Maria. Maria shook her head. "Well, that won't do. Get off the bed. Let's change the sheets and everything."

She went to the closet and pulled sheets and a blanket off the bottom of the pile. "Here, these should be clean enough. Guess laundry will be a priority, too."

Half an hour later, they were finally lying in bed. Maria turned on her side and hugged Henry. "I can't believe we are back home, in our own bed." She listened to the crickets and frogs and smiled. "I love it here. I think it's my favorite place in the world."

Henry turned his head towards her. "Being beside you, is mine."

She kissed him. "I love you."

They lay in bed listening to the sounds of their farm until they finally succumbed to exhaustion.

⚓ ⚓ ⚓

The next morning, Henry awoke to the sound of metal doors slamming, and then the rumble of a truck driving away. He put on his pants and made his way downstairs into the kitchen. "Who was tha—Oh! I see."

Meat wrapped in wax paper was everywhere, along with other foods, and Maria was putting some into the fridge and some into the freezer. "They helped me with the appliances, before unloading. Nice guys."

Henry stared at all the food. "Wow. Guess we're going to eat good tonight." He picked up a block of cheese and carried it to the table. "When did you order this?"

Maria watched him with a smile. "This morning—four hours ago."

Henry cut a piece of cheese off the block with his pocket knife and stuffed it in his mouth. "Four hours ago? What time is it now?"

Maria pointed outside. "It's afternoon, dear." She then looked back at him cutting more off the cheese block. "That's not breakfast—or should I say lunch!" She grabbed the block from him, but he stuffed the piece he had cut into his mouth before she could grab it.

She put the block of cheese in the fridge and bent down to see the lower shelf. "Here, I made you a ham sandwich on rye." She pulled it out and handed it to him, along with a glass jar of milk.

He opened the sandwich. "Can I have some cheese on this?"

Maria cocked her head, "You've had plenty of cheese," she said, and shut the fridge.

Henry chugged some of the milk after taking a bite of the sandwich and looked around. "So much to do . . . where to start?"

Maria leaned to look through the living room. "Why don't you start with the screen door, which is lying on the porch?"

Henry nodded. "Okay. I'll do it as soon as I finish this." As he took a second bite, he glanced out the back window to see the nose of the DC-3. "Whoa. That's kind of weird." He got up, sandwich in hand, and stared out the window, admiring the shining plane.

That evening, after dinner, Henry came into the kitchen and hugged Maria from behind. "Wow. The kitchen looks great. Especially compared to this morning, but that's enough work. Come out and sit on the porch with me."

She turned to him and stared into his eyes. A soft smile appeared on her face and she set down the cloth in her hand. "That sounds wonderful."

As they went through the front door, Maria stopped and moved the screen door back and forth a few times. "Good job, honey. It doesn't even creak."

Henry smiled and pulled her to the front porch swing. She sat down feeling the wood. "The swing. You fixed it." She put her arm around him and kissed him as he started rocking the swing gently to and fro.

The shadows grew long until the sun finally set, leaving wisps of clouds in a fire-like sky. Maria shook with a chill. "I have to go get a coat, but I'll be right back." She stopped as she opened the door. "Hey, you want some hot chocolate?"

Henry nodded enthusiastically. "That would be perfect. Oh, and can you turn off the lights when you come back out?"

Maria returned a few minutes later with two steaming hot chocolates. She handed one to Henry, then reached her hand around the door frame and turned off the living room lamp. The Milky Way grew bright in the sky as their eyes adjusted. Henry cuddled up next to her and sipped the chocolate. "I have an idea. Why don't we lie a blanket on the grass and sleep out tonight. Come on, we haven't slept under the stars in a long time . . . since Mongolia, and it's so gorgeous out."

Maria thought for a minute. "Well, okay. Help me get the blankets and pillows out. Where should we set it up?"

Henry looked out at the dark yard, making out the shapes of the barn and the driveway. "Over next to the barn. It has the most unobstructed view."

Henry and Maria dragged armfuls of bedding across the yard and created a sleeping area. Henry lay down on the blankets, letting out a sigh of pleasure. "Just fantastic."

Maria was still walking around adjusting things, when Henry sat up. "Come on dear. Lie with me."

She threw a blanket on him. "I will in just a second. I am going to put some hot chocolate in a Thermos bottle and bring it out."

When she finally returned, Henry opened the blankets for her and she slid in. She cuddled with him as he pointed out things in the sky. "For those navigators that don't know . . . that bluish white one is Vega. This one is Deneb and that's Altair."

Maria, playing along, pointed south. "What's that yellowish one?"

Henry turned his head. "That's Arcturus; you can find it by taking the tail of the Big Dipper and—"

Maria interrupted him with a kiss. Henry, still pointing at the sky, gave in and put his arm around her. They cuddled close and soon they were both asleep.

⊁⊁⊁

Maria awoke sometime during the night to the sound of crunching gravel. She stared up at the sky and could see that the stars had moved considerably. Then she heard the crunching sound again and sat up. She watched in the darkness and saw movement. Feeling her heart suddenly start to pound in her chest, she turned slowly and put her hand over Henry's mouth, before nudging him. He woke with a start, but she tightened her hand over his lips to keep him silent.

He struggled slightly, but stopped when another crunching sound came from the darkness. Quietly, he sat up and looked over at the driveway. He pushed away Maria's shaking hand and whispered in her ear. "The Thompsons are still in the plane. Let's go around the side of the house and get them." She slowly nodded.

Henry put his hand on her and directed her towards a ditch

next to the corn field. They slowly crawled to the ditch and then made their way walking hunched over, to the backyard. Maria heard noises coming from inside the house as Henry opened the plane's rear door. At first there was just a slight click, but then came the sound of metal grinding. He stopped and Maria whispered, "They're in our house!" Henry nodded, pushed up on the door, and pulled it open quietly, before putting his finger in front of his lips and climbing into the plane. Maria waited impatiently at the door while Henry made his way forward and retrieved the guns.

Henry handed her a Thompson and motioned for her to follow him back to the ditch. They made their way back to the front yard, stopping every minute or so to listen. Henry whispered back, "They're still in the house. Let's go around the barn and into the trees out front. Then we'll catch 'em as they come out, whoever they are." Maria nervously nodded her head and they began moving again. It took a few minutes to get to the other side of the barn before they came to the driveway. Henry stopped. "Okay. Let's run across to that big tree . . . ready?"

Maria nodded and grabbed Henry's arm tightly. Henry glanced at her and then the tree. "Go!" They made a mad dash across the driveway, and a few seconds later were behind the tree. Henry took a breath, quietly cocked his submachine gun, and took aim at the front door. Maria, watching him, followed his lead.

Sweat ran down Maria's face as they waited for whoever it was to exit the house. The sudden sound of breaking glass and swearing made them both jump. Then the front door burst open and three men stepped out onto the porch. "Where are you two little rats?!"

Henry and Maria, shocked at the familiar voice, looked at

each other. "Rocco!"

Henry adjusted himself to take aim, but his elbow slipped on a rock, and it made a clunk sound.

Rocco yelled "Look, there they are!"

He and his men raised their pistols and began shooting without taking cover, apparently believing that Henry and Maria would be easy prey. Certainly they yelled in shock, as much as pain, when Henry and Maria returned fire. Muzzle flashes, screams, glass breaking, and relentless shooting, even as the gangsters collapsed, shattered the night's silence. Henry quickly grabbed another clip and unloaded it into the darkness before finally stopping.

He and Maria hid behind the tree for what seemed like an eternity. After not hearing a sound for quite a while, Henry put in a third clip and slowly made his way up to the house. The ground was becoming easier to see and he quickly glanced to see the eastern horizon brightening. He turned to Maria, murmured, "Cover me," and made his way up the last fifty feet to the porch before ducking down. He slowly lifted his head and he could see the outlines of the three men. He waved for Maria to come up to the other side of the porch. Then he motioned that he was going to take a look. Maria nodded, trembling.

The sun was beginning to shine as Henry slowly climbed up onto the porch. He called, "Maria! Cover me!" and jumped down from the railing, aiming his gun at the men. Maria appeared at the other end of the porch with her Thompson pointed at the motionless bodies. Her gun shook in her hands as she watched for the slightest movement. Henry cautiously reached down to check their pulses, before turning and collapsing onto the porch swing. "They're dead." Then he put his head down in his lap and began to tremble.

Maria made her way over to him, still aiming at the dead mobsters. She sat on the swing next to him and kicked Rocco's body with all her strength. "Damn greedy bastard!"

The yellow glow of the rising sun shone on them as they sat on the porch swing, both shaking heavily. Maria's Thompson fell to the floor and she began crying. Henry looked up in response, before sliding over and hugging her. "It's okay . . . we got them. We'll be fine. It's all right . . ." Henry continued to hug and caress her as she let go of all the emotions she had been holding back.

After about twenty minutes of sitting on the swing together, the sheriff pulled into the driveway. He stepped out of his car, staying behind his door, and glanced suspiciously at the house. Henry stood up and leaned his Thompson against the railing. The sheriff relaxed a bit and came around the car door. "Henry? Maria? What the hell is going on?! The neighbors called and said it sounded like a war over here."

Henry pointed down at the three dead men on the porch. The sheriff walked closer to take a look. "Oh, I see."

Henry explained, "They're gangsters from Chicago. They came to kill us," he went on, pointing at the Thompson, "but we took care of them."

The sheriff looked at the Thompsons. "Where the hell did you get those?"

Henry glanced over at Maria and back. "We just got back from China last night. We brought them back with us."

The sheriff studied the bodies and saw their pistols lying next to them. "No. You went into the gangster's car, pulled out a Tommy gun and got lucky. Of course, that means I will have to confiscate the 'one' machine gun you have."

Henry lifted the Thompson, pulled the clip out and cleared the chamber. "Of course. Here you go."

Henry pointed to the other Thompson. "Maria, maybe you should clean the porch up a bit."

She glanced down at her gun, nodded, and took the Thompson inside the house.

A few minutes later, Maria came back out of the house with lemonade. Still shaking, and with lemonade spilling over the sides, she handed a glass to the sheriff.

He grinned. "Thank you, ma'am."

Henry rubbed his chin. "You know, the one thing that really bothers me, is how the hell did they know where we lived, and that we were back?"

The sheriff took a sip. "Well, have you called anyone or talked to anyone since you got back?"

Henry shook his head and pointed to the neighbors. "Just the Weavers, but I don't think they would—wait." He looked at Maria. "The grocery company this morning. Did you call anyone else?"

She shook her head. "Nope. They were the only ones."

The sheriff scratched his head behind his brown brimmed hat. "What's the name of the place?"

Maria stared down at the ground and furrowed her brow as she tried to think of the name. "Fost . . . Forstine—no, Faustini's."

The sheriff lifted his hat. "The place over in Des Moines?"

Maria nodded. "Yeah. Do you know it?"

The sheriff nodded. "Sure do. They are one of the mob's legit businesses. Everyone knows it, but no one can prove it." He rubbed his face and wrote down something in a small book he pulled from his pocket. "Yeah, I bet that's how they knew."

Henry watched her expressions. "Did you use our real name?"

Maria, with an apologetic look on her face, responded in a rising voice, "I didn't think ordering groceries would be dangerous. Oh, I am so sorry. I didn't—"

Henry hugged her. "Don't worry about it. It's okay." He pulled back and looked at her face. "Look, we're safe. There aren't any more bad guys and we're free. It's fine now. You actually did us a favor, if you think about it!"

Maria smiled slightly as tears rolled down her face.

Soon the coroner arrived to take the bodies. He and the sheriff took photographs, wrote reports and collected the casings and guns. The sheriff told him what happened and no one asked Henry or Maria a single question, with the exception of, "Are you all right?"

As the coroner and his assistant finished loading up the bodies, a tow truck showed up and hooked up to Rocco's car, which had been parked a hundred feet down the dirt road. The Weavers had come over and tried to help out, but the shock of the sight of all the bodies kept them pretty quiet.

Eventually the coroner left, and the Weavers didn't stay long, not wanting their kids to see the horror, but they offered to help with anything that needed helping. The last person to go was the sheriff. Henry had sat back down on the porch swing and Maria was leaning on his shoulder. The sheriff approached the porch. "Well, I think that just about does it. Don't worry about a thing, and if you need any help, just call me. Okay?"

Maria lifted her head and wiped her eyes. "Thank you, sheriff. Thanks for everything."

The sheriff nodded before he turned, got into his car, and drove off.

Maria got up from the swing and put her hand out for Henry. "Let's go inside."

Henry nodded and stood up before walking to what was left of the front door. The screen door consisted of a single piece of wood with one hinge holding it on and some screening hanging off. "Dammit! I just fixed this damn door!"

Maria smiled at him and patted him on the chest. "It's okay dear. Let's just buy another one." Henry nodded and went to step through the door, but Maria held him back. "Wait, with this whole mob thing over, does this mean we can have a baby now?"

Henry, taken aback, laughed as he leaned against the door frame. "You know, I guess it does."

Maria looked up at him, and then pushed herself into the house. "Good, because I'm pregnant."

Historical Context

When one thinks of the 1930s, the Great Depression and the "dust bowls" of the Great Plains come to mind, but much of what happened in the '30s is often eclipsed by the nearness and sheer magnitude of World War II. The signs of war and the unstoppable momentum towards it built throughout the decade of 1930. The mass unemployment and desperation of people in Europe led to their willingness to follow dictators headlong into conflict, while in the West, the lingering backlash of WWI kept the United States and England from doing anything militarily to preempt the largest war in history.

In the year that this book takes place, 1936, the first conflicts that will eventually lead up to WWII are already breaking out. In Spain, a civil war between the Fascists and the Republicans has begun. Germany has broken the Treaty of Versailles, and a campaign of appeasement begins by the West that will not end until it is too late.

In China, the Japanese have invaded Manchuria, and are slowly taking more and more land from China. A treaty exists between the largest faction of China, the Kuomintang (KMT), and the Japanese. A demilitarized zone has been set up that both sides have agreed not to cross, but there are anti-Japanese forces native to Manchuria that don't abide by this treaty. These units consist of partisans, bandits, warlords, and regulars. They have been fighting the Japanese occupation since 1931, but now have been reduced to small guerrilla bands.

Generalissimo Chiang Kai-shek has cut off supplies to these forces, for fear of helping his greatest enemy, the Communists, and also because he wants to avoid direct conflict with Japan until he can convince one of the Western powers to intervene. Chiang has the forces to defend China against the Japanese, but is saving them to maintain his own power, to unite China, and to fight off the Communists instead.

Some of the Manchurian peoples have joined the Japanese along with some Mongolian proxy armies, while others fight the occupation. The Japanese forces were at first led by a rogue arm of the military, and the civilian government tried to stop this action. However, those who opposed the military were quickly assassinated or found themselves politically too weak to make a difference. Now, the military has almost total control over Japan, and its insatiable appetite for resources is only growing, forcing further expansion and further need for resources.

The United States, wanting a strong China in the Far East, is ostensibly supportive of China, but because of overall public sentiment against getting involved militarily, the U.S. finds its hands are tied.

In addition, Japan won German concessions in China upon signing of a WWI peace treaty. This was a treaty which President Woodrow Wilson felt obligated to sign, but the Chinese interpreted his doing so as an act of treachery, breaking the strong trust between the U.S. and China.

Japan wants China's resources, but has proceeded cautiously up to this point, measuring the response by the U.S. and the British. It also has the desire to convince the Chinese to simply accept Japanese rule and join an "Asian Co-prosperity Sphere", thus avoiding the need to occupy all of China.

The U.S. government sees the inevitability of war coming, but Roosevelt can't do anything overt about it. The U.S. is not ready for conflict with Japan and cannot ask for the funds to prepare, as this would be looked upon as betraying the will of the people. This, in effect, leads to American appeasement of Japan, until the attack on Pearl Harbor five years later.

There are Americans, however, who see the upcoming conflict and can determine that it is in the best interests of the U.S. to support China as much and as soon as possible, but the government, as a whole, is forced to ignore these requests. One such man is then-Colonel Joseph Stilwell, probably the most experienced U.S. officer in dealing with China. In this novel, another is Colonel James "Jimbo" Mata, but unlike Stilwell, Mata decides to take matters into his own hands, and make some money while doing it. Having lived and done business in Manchuria since the end of the Russian Civil War, Colonel Mata finds himself in the perfect position to supply the beleaguered anti-Japanese forces.

When Chiang Kai-shek cuts off supplies to Manchuria, Colonel Mata finds his services in more demand than ever, but he is unable to get his supply trucks through reliably, and all use of the railroad is hopeless, so he turns to the thought of airlifting supplies. He can easily afford a cargo plane, but finding good pilots that he can trust turns out to be the difficult part. When he finds that his best candidate is coming available, his nephew Henry Elliot, Mata quickly flies to the United States to make him an offer that he can't refuse.

Characters

Maria and Henry at the peak of their
rum-running career, circa 1929.

Henry Elliot: Born in 1903 in Cleveland, Ohio, Henry saw his first airplane at a barnstorming show in 1914 and fell in love with it.

With encouragement from his father, he took lessons and received his license in 1920. He worked as a crop duster for a short time, but after meeting his future wife, Maria, he knew he had to make more money in order to start a family. Shortly after Prohibition was enacted, he got a job flying illegal alcohol in from Canada. After Prohibition, he took various jobs, usually risky and high-paying, such as the Graham Land Antarctica Expedition.

Portrait of Maria Elliot in 1923.

Maria Elliot: Born in 1905, outside of Des Moines, Iowa, Maria grew up with three older brothers. She was regarded as a tomboy by most, as she loved to hunt with her father, ride motorcycles, and later, fell in love with airplanes. Maria would often hang out at the local airfield on weekends, watching the planes come and go, occasionally getting rides. She instantly fell for Henry when she met him at the airfield, while he was working as a crop duster. He taught her to fly, and when he switched to flying illegal alcohol, she became his copilot.

Jimbo Mata in 1926.

Jimbo Mata: Henry's mother's brother, he was born in 1876 in Erie, Pennsylvania. He joined the military in 1895 and rose to the rank of major, before being promoted to colonel and sent to Russia as an adviser to the Whites during the Russian Civil War. After the war, he used his many underworld connections to build a large international supply (smuggling) company.

Rocco: Mob boss in Chicago. Made his fortune smuggling alcohol during Prohibition.

Seamus: US body guard for Jimbo.

George: 2nd US bodyguard for Jimbo.

Fred and Esther: Retired couple living in Naknek, Alaska. Fred was involved in the Russian Civil War under U.S. General Graves.

Kidlat (Kid): Excellent aircraft mechanic from the Philippines. Worked for the US military on their planes in Manila and freelanced on the side repairing civilian cars and planes.

Bayasaa: A Mongolian worker for Jimbo. He speaks English, Chinese, and Mongolian.

Khaidu: A Mongolian who works for Jimbo.

Temujin: One of Jimbo's Mongolian workers. Short, but strong man. He has medium black hair that is always in a mess.

Inalchuk: A radio operator and translator. She is Jimbo's best English translator.

Zheng Zi Ling: Woman who organizes all of the drop-offs and pickups in Manchuria.

Zhou Qiang: Radio operator for incoming requests.

Zhang Wei Guo (Patriot or Pat): Radio operator for incoming requests.

Zhong Cheng: Radio operator for relaying drop-off times and meet up points.

Zhu Ai Ze: Jimbo's right hand man in Manchuria. He has been an adviser on the Chinese for Jimbo since 1930.

Nick: Aussie pilot who flies the O-2 for emergency supply runs.

Anatoly Pepelyayev in 1918.

General Anatoly Nikolayevich Pepelyayev: White General from the Russian Civil War. Jimbo worked with him as an adviser and in weapons supply.

Admiral Aleksandr Kolchak: White Russian Admiral commanding over General Anatoly Pepelyayev. He was recognized as the leader of the Whites. He was executed in February of 1920 by the

Bolsheviks.

Viktor Pepelyayev: Anatoly's older brother; Prime Minister in Kolchak's government, was also executed with Kolchak.

Moa Zedong: Became the leader of the communist forces when all the other Communist armies were decimated during the Long March.

Chiang Kai Shek: Leader of Nationalist China.

Prince Demchugdongrub: Leader of the Inner Mongolian Army and a puppet of the Japanese army. Would later go on to be the chairman of the Mongolian Autonomous Federation with its headquarters in Kalgan. In 1945, after the defeat of the Japanese, the Russian and Mongolian Red armies invaded and the Mongolian Autonomous Federation, also known as Mengjiang, ceased to exist.